Drag

Dragon Rock

Book 2 in the Norseman series

By

Griff Hosker

Dragon Rock

Published by Sword Books Ltd 2025

Copyright ©Griff Hosker 2025

The author has asserted their moral right under the Copyright, Designs and Patents Act, 1988, to be identified as the author of this work. All Rights reserved. No part of this publication may be reproduced, copied, stored in a retrieval system, or transmitted, in any form or by any means, without the prior written consent of the copyright holder, nor be otherwise circulated in any form of binding or cover other than that in which it is published and without a similar condition being imposed on the subsequent purchaser.

A CIP catalogue record for this title is available from the British Library.

No generative artificial intelligence (AI) was used in the writing of this work. The author expressly prohibits any entity from using this publication for purposes of training AI technologies to generate text, including without limitation technologies that are capable of generating works in the same style or genre as this publication. The author reserves all rights to license use of this work for generative AI training and development of machine learning language models.

Dragon Rock

About the Author

Griff Hosker was born in St Helens, Lancashire in 1950. A former teacher, an avid historian and a passionate writer, Griff has penned around 200 novels, which span over 2000 years of history and almost 20 million words, all meticulously researched. Walk with legendary kings, queens and generals across battlefields; picture kingdoms as they rise and fall and experience history as it comes alive.

Welcome to an adventure through time with Griff.

For more information, please head over to Griff's website and sign up for his mailing list. Griff loves to engage with his readers and welcomes you to get in touch.

www.griffhosker.com
X: @HoskerGriff
Facebook: Griff Hosker at Sword Books

Thank you for reading, we hope you enjoy the journey.

Contents

Dragon Rock i
Prologue 1
Chapter 1 6
Chapter 2 19
Chapter 3 32
Chapter 4 49
Chapter 5 65
Chapter 6 78
Chapter 7 92
Chapter 8 108
Chapter 9 124
Chapter 10 138
Chapter 11 151
Chapter 12 165
Chapter 13 180
Chapter 14 193
Chapter 15 207
Chapter 16 221
Chapter 17 234
Chapter 18 247
Epilogue 262
Glossary 266
Historical Background 268
Other books by Griff Hosker 272

Dragon Rock

The crew of *'Ægir'*

Leif Wolf Killer
Joseph the Healer
Oddr Gautisson
Asbjørn
Dagfinn
Brynjar
Galmr
Falco
Frode
Gudmand
Nils
Lars
Bjarni
Benni
Anders
Halvard Halvardsson
Siggi the Smiler
Einarr
Harland
Galmr
Leif the Silent
Fritjof
Gunvald
Erik Broken Nose
Angmar
Folki
Bjorn Larsson
Haraldr Long Nose
Eirik Red Hair

Dragon Rock

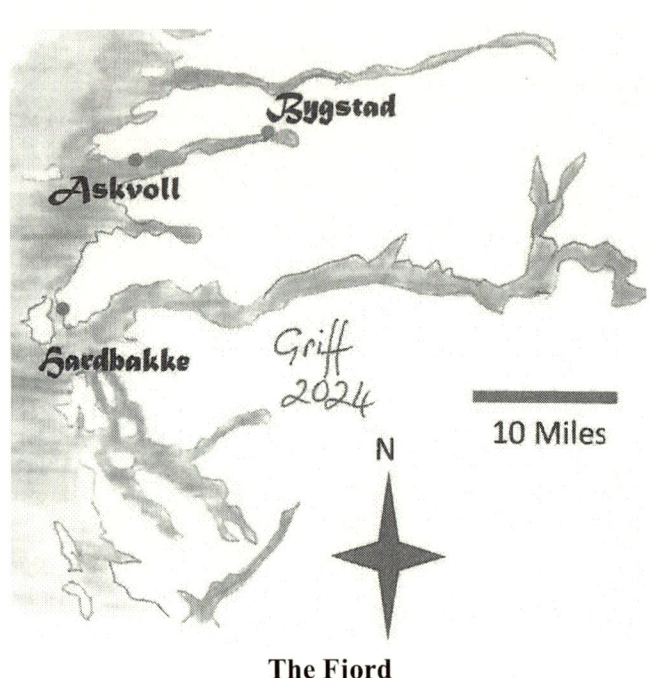

The Fjord

Prologue

Tahert, Rustamid Imāmate 805

Abd ar-Rahmān ibn Rustam picked the date from the platter held by the slave boy. He enjoyed these Safawi dates which were specifically grown for him. They were his favourite date and had a rich flavour. He chewed it thoughtfully as he viewed the advisors before him. That he had survived thirty years as Imām was no mean feat. His predecessors, Abu l-Hatim al-Malzuzi and Abul-Khattab Abdul-A'la ibn as-Samh had both died after a short time in power. He knew that as he was not of a local tribe, his family came from Persia, he had to tread a careful line. There were some advantages however, for he was seen as being as close to neutral a leader as possible. Added to that, he had guided the Rustamids well and he had enlarged their land by taking over the Emirate of Tiemcen to the west. He knew that he could not rest and simply enjoy his later years. He had to keep enlarging the land that they ruled or some younger man would take over and he would follow the fate of his predecessors. He had to ensure that his sons would inherit the Imāmate when he went to Allah.

He waved forward the young warriors who had come to him with an idea that would bring not only gold but increased land. "Tell me your idea again."

The elder of the two brothers, Abd al-Bakri, bowed and held a map before him, "The Umayyad Caliphate, as you well know, Imām, has now conquered all the Frankish lands that the Romans called Hispania. Al-Andalus is now theirs. My brother and I have ships and we would sail north to the lands controlled by the Frankish Emperor, the one they call Charles the Great. We believe that they are ripe for the plucking. From Genoa to Narbonne they have towns and villages with gold, food and slaves. It is a rich land and undefended. We would take our ships and raid them."

He studied the young men before him. They were ambitious men and they had a small fleet of ships. What did they really want of him? "And why do you need my permission to do so?

They are Christian and not protected. Just raid." He picked another date from the dish. He paused and said, "And your information is a little out of date for some of the Christians have reconquered the Asturias. It would be a foolish man who thought these Franks were defeated."

"We know that, Imām, but we have devout warriors who follow our banner and we are masters of the seas. We hunt them much as the lion hunts in the desert." Abd looked at his brother who nodded, "There is an old settlement not far from here. There is little left but a ruined fort and a small port. It was known in earlier times as Cartennae. My brother and I would like it as our home. We would be the rulers of it."

The old man had the date poised close to his mouth, "You seek power." He said it neutrally. He understood the need for power and he relaxed a little. He could now see what motivated them.

"All men seek power, Imām, if only to spread the word of Allah."

Abd ar-Rahmān ibn Rustam slipped the date into his mouth, savouring its rich sweetness. He wiped his fingers on the cloth held by the second slave and then waved the two slaves away. This was not for the ears of slaves who might gossip, "And how many ships do you have?"

"Three." He knew they had more but he understood the reason for the deception. They did not wish to seem to be a threat to him.

"Warriors?"

"Two hundred."

"That does not seem a number that should worry me. You could have just occupied the port and raided. Why come to me?" His eyes were like those of a hawk and they narrowed, "What made you seek permission?"

Abd licked his lips nervously. In battle he feared no man but this Imām terrified him, "We would increase the numbers of our men and our ships, Imām, but we are not a threat to you, I swear."

The old man smiled. He now believed the man. He also saw how he could use this for his personal benefit. He nodded, "I give you permission but there will be a price to pay. A tenth of whatever you take, gold, slaves, ships, all are mine. Do you understand?"

"Of course, Imām."

"And you will do it all in the name of the Rustamid Imāmate."

"That goes without saying."

The old man gave a wry smile and said, "It is my experience that things which go without saying need, most of all, to be spoken." The two men bowed. "One more thing, to ensure that all is done well my second son, Bahram, will go with you to make sure that my wishes are carried out."

The two brothers hid their disappointment well and smiled, "Of course, Imām." Abd al-Bakri was the elder and the stronger but his younger brother was the clever one. His eyes narrowed. He did not like the command.

They had no intention of crossing the Imām but they could do without the presence of the preening peacock that was his son. The Imām was getting old and once they had enough power and he was no longer the ruler…that was for the future. They had begun to ascend the steps to power.

As they headed for the courtyard where their horses awaited, the younger brother Mohammed said, "Why has he sent his son? We do not need him." Already the cleverer brother was working out how they could stop him from sailing with them.

As he climbed on the back of the black stallion, Abd smiled, "I think his father wishes him gone from the palace. He struts around the court wearing the armour that is painted to look like gold and he believes he is a great warrior. The rumour is that many others wish to kill him. The Imām is getting old and he wants as little trouble in Tahert as possible. If he is with us then he is protected. Do not worry, little brother, we will leave him in charge of the fort. He will not wish to tarnish his armour at sea. We have what we want. We are not pirates, we are the servants of Allah. We have the blessing of the Imām. Our men will fight all the harder for us knowing that heaven awaits them."

They headed for the coast and the three ships that were already in the harbour. While the fort had yet to be repaired, the port was already in perfect condition. They had two bigger galleys. They relied mainly on sail but they had oars that they could use. The third ship was not as big as the ones with oars but could carry more men. It also had three sails and with the right wind could fly. The rest of their fleet was made up of smaller ships that were little bigger than fishing boats but they were fast and they were lithe. They could find their prey and shadow them until the two larger consorts joined them. Their galleys would race out and attack, first, the ships that sailed the Blue Sea and, when they had taken enough ships and recruited more men, head north to Frankia and the riches that awaited them. Most importantly they were crewed by men they had recruited from every fishing village along the coast. The men were loyal and they were fierce. The brothers had ambitions and the men ready to help them achieve those ambitions.

Dragon Rock

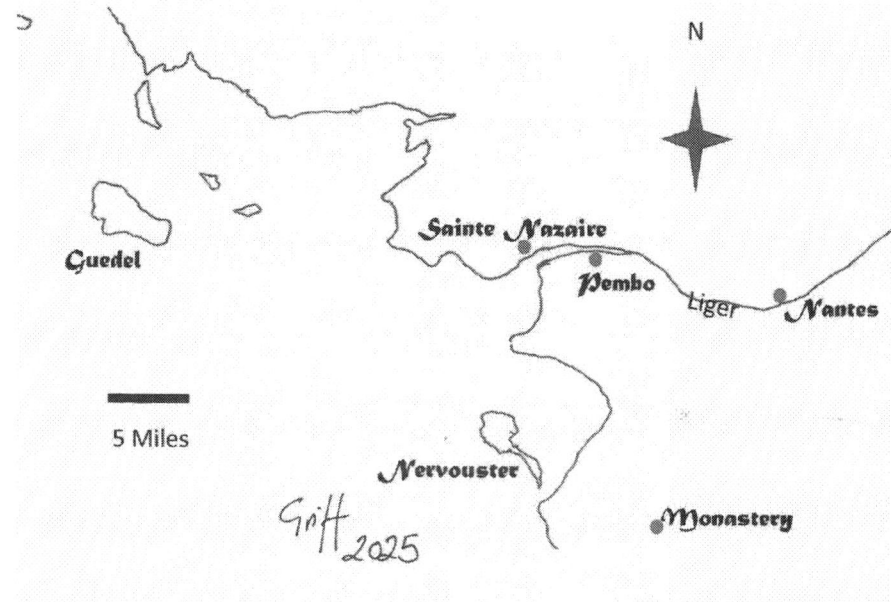

Chapter 1

Jarl Bjørn Haraldsson and his cousin Lord Arne were animated as the jarl told his cousin all that had happened since he had sent Mikkel and the trader back with the treasures we had taken on our raids in Frankia. Their faces and those of their hearthweru, reflected the excitement they felt at the prospect of more treasure now that we had three ships. I still felt empty, for any joy of the treasure had gone; taken by the death of my mentor, Gandalfr. He had died on our drekar and his loss was greater than any treasure we might take. He had begun to teach me and yet I had much still to learn. I was now the one who would steer our ship, *'Ægir'* and I was a man of importance but all I wanted was to go home and see my wife and mourn Gandalfr. The one good thing about the arrival of *'Nidhogg'*, Lord Arne's ship, was that Bjarni, who had come from our home, was able to tell me that my wife had given birth to a son and that Freya and Leif Leifsson were both healthy. The news eased my mind. The baby had been born a week after I had left and would now be almost three months old. When would I see him?

We had worked hard since returning to the island of Nervouster which was now our temporary home. Since the battle we had been busy making repairs to the ships which had been damaged in the fight with the Franks, but now the ships were ready and we were enjoying a warm sun, a hot fire and food and drink taken from the people of this land. We had made this small island our fortress. We had fought and defeated the Franks who lived to the north of us and destroyed many of their boats and ships. I knew that they would seek to oust us but I hoped that we would have left before they had enough men and vessels to harm us. We now had three ships and Lord Arne's was fully manned.

Oddr and Snorri sat with me. Snorri had been Gandalfr's brother and he was the helmsman on the jarl's ship, *'Byglja'*. Oddr Gautisson was the leader of the warriors from our home, Bygstad. Around us were some of the others from Bygstad who mourned Gandalfr. For my brother, Birger, this was his first raid and he had not really known what to expect. There were other young warriors who had been battle virgins. Now they had whetted their swords and as they had survived were eager for more glory. Dagfinn and Brynjar were my shield brothers and we took comfort from that fact. Asbjørn was Oddr's friend but we all had one thing in common, we mourned Gandalfr. His death had been a shock and came so suddenly that I had not had the chance to think about what to do. I had obeyed his last command and taken the helm. The others were fulsome in their praise of me for they said I had saved their ship and many lives. I had not thought about what I did but just reacted. I think that if I had thought about the enormity of my responsibility I might have frozen. Snorri had been quiet since his brother's death. Repairing the ships and advising me had taken his mind off the death but now that it was clear we would be leaving the place we buried Gandalfr, Snorri wanted to know more about his brother's demise.

Snorri said, quietly, "You say he had his hand on his sword when he died?"

I nodded, "One hand on the helm and one on the sword."

That made him nod, "Then he knew he was dying and he is now in Valhalla."

There was silence. I fingered my Hammer of Thor. We all wanted a warrior's death but I wanted to see my wife and son before I made that journey. We sat in silence as we reflected, each in our own way, on the navigator's end.

Birger smiled and changed the subject. He had not known Gandalfr as well as the rest of us. He said, "And I am now an uncle. Bjarni said your son had a fine set of lungs, Brother."

"And it is good that they are well but..." I shook my head, "I would return to my family. We have silver and treasure."

Oddr sighed. He led the men of Bygstad, "And you are the helmsman of *'Ægir'*. You were chosen and trained by Gandalfr. Until we all return home you are bound to the quest and the ship, Leif Wolf Killer. We can afford no distractions. Your wife and son are safe at home and there are many who will protect them. We need your mind to be on the task. Steering the drekar is a great responsibility. You have to fill Gandalfr's boots." He saw my look and put an arm around my shoulder, "I know you seek your wife and son. I have a wife, two sons and a daughter at home. I am keen to see them too but when we return as rich men it means we do not have to go to sea again quickly. We can enjoy a year at home and by then Gauti, my son, will be ready to come to sea as a ship's boy. Let us just concentrate on the task in hand and put thoughts of home to the back of our minds. A warrior does not need distractions." He nodded to the jarl and his cousin, Lord Arne, "They wish to raid. The Franks in this part of Frankia do not yet know of our people. This is an opportunity for us to raid and to take. The next time Norsemen come to raid they will be ready."

Brynjar said, "And what is that to be? The plan was to raid the Liger and perhaps Bordèu. Have we enough ships for that?"

Just then Joseph, the slave I had rescued from the Franks and who acted as a healer, came over with a platter of food from the fire. "I thought you would be hungry." His words were for all but the intent was for me to eat. I knew that Joseph wished to return to his home and that he saw me as his best chance to do so. He looked after me like a mother hen with a solitary chick.

I asked, "Joseph, you know the Franks. Is Bordèu a place we could take?"

While the others joined me and picked food from the platter every eye was on the man from the other side of the Blue Sea. They knew his value and trusted him. The Three Sisters had been truly spinning a fine web when they had sent him to me. He considered his words. As he had only learned our language since coming to live with my family it was a most foreign tongue for him and he always paused before speaking to any other than me. He wanted to choose his words carefully. "I have heard that the Franks who live there, they are Vasconians, have made a citadel. The Arabs from the south," the word Arab was not a Norse word but we had heard him use it before, "often raid this part of the world and they are as fierce as you. I think it might be hard."

Snorri tore the meat from the fowl's leg and asked, "The river that leads to Bordèu, is it wide?"

Joseph nodded, "I have heard that for much of its length it is as wide as a sea."

"Then we will be raiding for the jarl will know we can sail safely, and with the new men brought by Lord Arne we could take it."

Birger said, "And then go home?" I knew why he spoke that way. He assumed that the taking of Bordèu would be as easy as the raids here had seemed. He was keen to strut around Bygstad showing off all that he had taken on the raid. We had been successful and he wished to flaunt that success.

Oddr shook his head, "We are here until we have taken enough silver to satisfy Lord Arne. The jarl's cousin will not have sailed all the way down here to raid one town and then return north. No ice and snow for us, Birger. By the time we return you will be as hairy as a bear in autumn." He said it with a smile. Birger was young and his beard, whilst growing, was thin and wispy.

Dagfinn said, "Aye, Leif, and your son might well be walking."

"It is good that Mikkel went home. He was missing Borghildr. He said that he will watch over your family, Leif." Brynjar had changed more than any since we had first trained as warriors. His cousin Axel had been a bad influence. Once they had fled Bygstad, he had changed for the better.

"I will fetch wine, Master."

"Thank you, Joseph."

"I would prefer mead."

Snorri nodded and belched, "As would we all, Asbjørn, but the Franks prefer wine or cider. We drink what they have."

I said, "Joseph told me that the men who live south of here do not drink at all. It is against their religion."

I could see that I had shocked them all, even Snorri. "Not even beer?"

"Nothing."

"Then why raid them at all?" Brynjar was incredulous at the thought of men who did not drink having anything that was worth taking.

"Because they have spices, gold and jewels." My slave had given me so much information that I was considered a wise man despite my youth.

"How do you know, Brother?"

"Joseph told me. He said that spices are worth more than gold itself and yet weigh much less. They bring them from the far side of the world on the backs of animals who have a hump in which they store water. Those with money like kings and lords pay a fortune for them. They are supposed to make the food taste better." I saw the doubt on their faces for it sounded fantastic. I smiled, "Like you I was dubious but Joseph told me and you know that he is a truthful man."

Oddr nodded and wiped his hands on his breeks, "Then, so long as we have plenty of barrels of wine and beer, that seems a good place to raid."

Just then Haldir approached. He was one of the jarl's hearthweru. He was a good warrior and seemed to like me. He said, "Snorri, Leif, the jarl would speak to you."

We stood and wandered over. I was keenly aware that every eye was on us. The three crews, the deck watch apart, were ashore on the island. With fires and food, not to mention a sun that warmed, this was as close to an easy time as we would get. Men had discarded armour and some lay, half naked, enjoying the rays of the sun. We were more used to rowing in icy seas sprayed by salt water and enduring cold food and cold beds than having a hot sun beat down upon us. As raids went this one was almost perfection. We had spent more time on the island than we had raiding and thought of it as a home. The warriors would all be wondering what was the portent when two navigators headed for the two lords. Did it mean we were returning to the world of the warrior?

Lord Arne was the reason we had come south. He had traded in his knarr and discovered the treasures that the land of the Franks had to offer. He had co-led the first raid. He and his cousin had similar looks. It was said they looked like their grandfather.

"How are the ships?" As the navigators it was we who had the responsibility of ensuring that the ships were seaworthy.

Both drekars had been damaged in the flight from the Franks. *'Ægir'* had sprung strakes and we had had to beach her to seal the damage with trenails and pine tar. There was other damage but it was superficial. Arrows, spears and blades had left marks on her. She had been a new ship when we had left the fjord but now she looked more like a veteran.

Snorri answered for us both. He had helped to supervise the repairs, "Both are seaworthy, Jarl. The sails are undamaged and the hulls are sound." He spoke to the jarl even though Lord Arne liked to give the orders. We liked the jarl while Lord Arne seemed cold and treated us as men to be used.

The jarl looked at me and I nodded. "Our drekar is healed and ready to sail, Jarl."

He said, "You have been chosen as the navigator, Leif Longstride. It was not only Gandalfr who did so but the Three Sisters. You have shown that you have skill and the mind to be a helmsman. Your share of the profits will reflect that."

I cared not for more silver. I would rather be Gandalfr's assistant but I nodded for I knew the answer that was expected, "Thank you, Jarl. I am honoured."

Lord Arne was impatient. He had not sailed all the way south just to sit on an island and feast. "Then, Cousin, we can sail and raid. My men and I itch to take the treasures of Bordèu. They have, it is said, a fine church and there are rich merchants there. We can take their ships, their town and churches. We will have slaves we can sell or ransom. And that is only the beginning. The land of Al-Andalus promises even greater riches." He laughed, "Soon we will leave the cold waters of the Great Ocean and enjoy the balmy Blue Sea where the sun always shines." Jarl Bjørn Haraldsson nodded. Lord Arne's voice was almost imperious as he said, "I will lead and *'Ægir'* will guard the rear."

I noticed that Lord Arne always commanded. The jarl seemed happy for him to do so.

Snorri asked, "When do we leave?"

Lord Arne looked at the sky, "It will be a quiet night for there is no rain. The men have eaten well and we will sail at dawn. It will take close to a day to reach the mouth of the river and then a day and a night to be close to the city. If we reach it at dawn we can catch them unawares."

Snorri shook his head, "That means we sail down a river we do not know at night."

Lord Arne oozed confidence, "I have sailed it twice and it is wide and without hindrance until we come to the parting of the rivers. By then it should be dawn and, if not, we can wait." I knew, from his voice, that he would not wait. We were dismissed for Lord Arne turned to speak to his hearthweru.

As we turned to leave the jarl took my arm, "A word, Leif."

He led me to one side and waited until we were beyond earshot. He said, "My cousin brought other news when he came. He captured some Frisians who tried to take one of his fishing boats. He discovered that the ambush on the coast, it was planned." He paused, "It was Erland Brynjarsson who was responsible. He now lives in Dorestad where he and his son have great power. Because they are rich they have influence. He chose to send men to attack us."

The news explained a great deal. We had been attacked by Frisian pirates and it had been something which had worried the men for there was no reason for it. I nodded, "Thank you for telling me."

He added, "Now is not the time but when this raid is over we will visit with Erland and repay his treachery."

"Do I tell the others?"

"I think they need to know why we lost men, don't you?" I was honoured that he had told me. He could have told Oddr.

I returned to the crew and told them our destination. Snorri did the same for his crew. Joseph looked happy for the further south we went the closer he came to his home. I said, "We have fewer rowers and that means the others might be faster. Perhaps that is why we are at the rear but we have the newest ship and the cleanest hull. *'Ægir'* will make up for the men we lost." I looked to Oddr. I was the helmsman but he commanded.

"We have the smallest crew but the greatest heart. We will triumph."

"There is more news and this pertains to the attack by the Frisians."

Every eye fixed me and I told them of the treachery of the former hersir. He was Brynjar's uncle and I saw my shield brother's knuckles whiten on the hilt of his sword as I spoke. His voice was low and filled with feeling as he said, "I swear that although he is of my blood, I will have vengeance on that snake." He drew his sword and kissed it before gripping the blade so that his blood dripped to the earth. He was making a blood oath. He would fulfil it or die trying.

Oddr nodded. We all felt the same and the Clan of the Otter would have its revenge. Now, however, we had to put that quest to the back of our minds and Oddr was our leader. "We will all

Dragon Rock

have vengeance but first we have a fortune to make. That dish will be a cold one before we enjoy it, Brynjar. Harden your heart and hone your skills on these Franks. We now have another purpose."

Snorri was also angry. "It was Erland's treachery which delayed and hurt us. Gandalfr might still be alive but for the Frisian attack. My brother will have his revenge. I will see to it."

I was not sure about that. There was no doubt that Erland's treachery had hurt us but I could not help but think that the Norns had been spinning and they were the cause of Gandalfr's death.

I had much to do and I spent the night worrying about it. It was my responsibility and it was a heavy one. Gandalfr had seemed so at ease with it and I was terrified. Perhaps it was that terror that inspired the dream, or should I say nightmare, that I endured that night.

The sea was calm and blue but it was overhung with a strange fog and the ship was not moving. The sails hung limp and listless. The only sound that I heard was that of the oars as they ploughed through the water. It was then I heard another sound. It was more oars and I looked around to see the other drekars. There were none and then through the fog I saw the prows of three ships. I did not recognise any of them. They were filled with fierce warriors. Some were half naked and had shining black bodies. I saw sparkling blades and heard fearsome cries. I urged on the crew and they rowed as hard as they could but each time I looked around they were gaining.
We were doomed.
Suddenly, from ahead, I heard a shout and saw Lars, one of the ship's boys, pointing. From the water rose a dragon. This was not a dragon ship but a real dragon. With a long, pointed snout and teeth that threatened to devour our drekar it lay on the water. It fixed us with its eyes which were red and dead. Its wings were wide as it beat a path towards us. I grasped my sword for soon I would be in Valhalla with Gandalfr. Then a voice in my head, Gandalfr's, said, "Fear not!"
The dragon swept over us and then I saw its wings dip as it plunged down to smash the leading ship to kindling. Its mouth made short work of the others and then it flew up in the air

Dragon Rock

before circling. As it descended, I watched as it headed for three rocks. When it neared them the three rocks changed and I saw that they were not rocks at all; they were the three sisters and they were spinning. Beyond the dragon I saw a cove and it was surrounded by pine trees and then it all faded.

I woke with a start. I put my hand on the ground and felt the earth. It had been a dream but one so vivid that I could have sworn it was real. It must have been a silent dream for, the sentries apart, the rest of the crew were sleeping. I was too afraid to risk returning to bed and I went to make water. I put more kindling on the fire and went to fetch some salt water to cook our breakfast. We would be eating before dawn and this would be our last hot meal until after we had raided. The water began to bubble. I saw Nils rise and said, "The water is heating. I will go to the drekar. You are in charge of breakfast."

He nodded sleepily and I went to the drekar. The two ship's boys who were on watch stretched as I approached, "Go and help with the food. I will watch. Bring my food here."

"Yes, Leif Wolf Killer." I smiled. The jarl often called me Leif Longstride, especially when Lord Arne was around, but most of the crew gave me the honorific, Wolf Killer. They all envied me the wolf skin and the teeth I wore around my neck. The ones who were most envious, however, were the ship's boys and younger warriors like my brother.

I went to the chest. It had an intricately carved dragon's head upon the top. When I ran my fingers over it I could almost feel the dragon move. It had been Gandalfr's but Snorri has insisted that I have it. His sword went with him to the next world and I was left with his compass, sealskins and the other accoutrements of a navigator including all the tools I might need to repair the ship. I knew it was the greatest treasure I had been given and when Snorri allowed me to copy Gandalfr's maps then I felt I was the luckiest man alive. The nightmare seemed to confirm that view. I donned my sea boots. They were mine and not Gandalfr's. They were sealskin and waterproof. I donned the sealskin hat I would wear and placed my sword and dagger in the chest. I would not need them. That done I closed the lid, my fingers dancing across the intricately carved dragon on the top. It was as I did so that I realised that it was the same dragon I had

Dragon Rock

seen in my dream. The dragon was Gandalfr. My fingers went to my Hammer of Thor. I now understood the dream a little more.

I walked the deck to check the ship. I needed to keep my mind occupied. The oars were neatly stacked by the mast fish. Before we had left the fjord Gandalfr had ensured that they were all straight and warped ones had been replaced. I made sure that all the sheets and lines were not frayed and were taut. There was a chest with spares and we had a spare mast and yard in the hold but now was not the time to replace them nor when there was a storm which threatened to tear the mast from the keel. We needed land to make such changes. In this land that was always dangerous for we were in a sea of enemies. The men's chests were all neatly placed. I saw mine. It was largely empty now but I would leave it there. If nothing else it gave an extra bench should we need it. The sheets were all in good condition and they would not need to be replaced. The most damage had been to the strakes and they were repaired and sealed with pine tar. We had used most of our previous supplies. The small pot that remained would be for emergencies.

I turned as I heard footsteps behind me. It was Joseph with his belongings. His place, when we sailed, was next to the prow, well out of the way. He would tuck what he had close to the prow and hope it did not get too wet. I said, "If you wish to use my chest, Joseph, it is here and empty. It will keep your possessions dry."

He beamed, "If you are sure, Master."

"I am sure." I watched as he packed his few possessions there. As a healer he was allowed knives for we had recognised that a healer needed them and we had established that the man was not a threat. When the lid was closed he turned. I said, "If you were to be landed when we raid, would you be close to your home?" I had no idea where his home lay. The maps we had ended at the mouth of the river Joseph had said was the Gironde and the town of Bordèu.

He shook his head, "I would be a dead man or a slave again if I landed there." He looked wistfully to the east. "As far as I can remember there is a passage between the land of the Arabs and Africa. It leads to the sea which ends at my home. From there it is many days of sailing."

"Then you are further from your home than we are from ours."

He nodded, "So far that it seems like a dream to me now."

He would not run, at least not yet. To be truthful I had decided that as he was my slave I would give him his freedom as soon as we were within sight of his land. Of course, that seemed unlikely, at the moment. We had to make a raid along a river first and if we found enough we would be able to return home.

I heard the camp coming to life as Oddr and the hearthweru of the two leaders roused the men. The ship's boys hurried aboard, balancing along the plank that led to the island. There was a bowl of food for me and some flatbread. They had their own food too. As they handed the bowl and bread to me, I said, "What about food for the healer?"

Before they could answer Joseph said, "I will get my own, Master. It will be good to have one last walk ashore. As you know I am not the best of sailors."

Nils said, "Sorry, Joseph." He was not treated as a slave by any of the crew. They had all seen how his ministrations had saved men's lives.

"When you have eaten, fetch the beer and the wine aboard. I want them secured before the crew arrive."

"Yes, Leif Wolf Killer."

I ate the salty seafood and meat stew. The oats and barley had thickened it. It did not look attractive but it was filling. I went to the water barrel and poured a horn of it. The water from the island was good. Who knew when next we might find such a treasure? The ale we had was lessening each day and we rationed it. We hoped that Bordèu would have such riches.

There was a tiny line of light in the east when the sails were hoisted and we set sail. The wind was from the east and we would not need to row. When we reached the river, that would be the time to lower the sail and break out the oars. I had the easiest of tasks. I just had to follow the wake of *'Byglja'*. In the twilight her wake seemed to glow. Snorri was now the best of navigators, he had inherited the mantle from his brother, and I could trust his judgement.

As we passed the sleepy land to the larboard side I knew that men would still be watching. They would see shadows moving

Dragon Rock

across the sea but that would be all. They would have confirmation, when dawn broke that we were no longer on the island and we had left. That we had hurt the Franks in our sea battle was clear from the fact that they made no attempt to attack us again. They would be interested in our destination. They might wonder if we had returned home. I had Nils on the yard of our mast and I called up to him, "Once the sun has risen keep your eyes behind us. I want to know if we are followed."

His voice drifted down, "Aye, Leif Wolf Killer."

Oddr joined me. He was eating an apple. "Why the watch behind, Leif?"

"This is the land of the Franks. I do not know if they are the same people at Bordèu but I want to know if there is a chance that the men we fought will warn them." I had studied the map and I added, "We sail south and then southeast. If they discover we have gone and know we sail south then they could send a rider south and east straightaway. We do not want a warm welcome."

He nodded, "Gandalfr chose well." He left me to go and stand at the prow.

We were following the land so the sunrise would not be the spectacular one we could expect if we were far out to sea but it presaged a fine day. Every day was hot to us but this one promised to be one that would burn the skin. The wind, however, was a good one and pushed us south. I saw boats closer to shore. They were fishing. Some might know who we were but as we had not raided this far south before that was unlikely. They would be wary of us for we had shields along the side and such adornments meant danger to fishermen.

"Nils?"

"The sea behind us is clear. The ships closer to shore are just fishing."

Birger joined me with a horn of ale, "Our father and uncle will be fishing now, Brother."

I took the ale and drank it. "Aye, but it will be colder there and unlike these Franks, they will be further out to sea. There the skrei are worth catching." I pointed to the Frankish ships. "They will have smaller fish where they are fishing."

Birger smiled, "We are the better fishermen!"

"Of course." I looked around and saw that we were almost alone. "Listen Birger, when we go ashore to raid the Franks do not try to be a hero and attain glory. I have seen others try that and their end was not a good one. Learn from each combat. Watch those who are better fighters. Oddr and Asbjørn are both mighty warriors. Watch their backs and guard them from an unwary blade."

He frowned, "Is that what you did?"

I smiled, "We were, in many ways, luckier than you for we trained and fought together. There is just you, Anders, Benni and Fritjof who are new to the crew. The rest have been on a raid already. You four should fight together and keep in the second rank."

"I am not a coward."

"No one said you were but no one will think less of you if you are not in the fore. Rather, it will be the opposite. They would prefer that you gained experience so that next time you will be better. They cannot be watching out for battle virgins."

"We could follow you."

I nodded, "Aye, you could and that might be a good thing but I believe the others I mentioned are better warriors."

He shook his head as Dagfinn and Brynjar came down the boat, "That is not what others say. They think you are a great warrior."

I was stunned. I was not a bad warrior; I knew that but I would not speak of myself in the same breath as Oddr and Asbjørn. I looked ahead and saw Snorri putting the steering board over a little. I made the same move. Perhaps I would not even go on the raid. Snorri stayed with his ship. It might be that I had to stay on board. It was when I realised that I would not want to do that I understood that I was a warrior first and a navigator second.

Chapter 2

It took, not a full day as we had expected but less to reach the mouth of the river. We had stayed further from the shore to disguise our intention. There would be watchers on the shore who would report that we sailed away but they would not know which direction we would take. We had time, as we bobbed in the waters out to sea to prepare the ship for its journey down the river. Once there we took down the sail and stepped the mast. With the mast and sails stored, we would have to take to the oars and row. We stopped well offshore so that we would not be observed while we did so. We had been told that the river twisted and turned. We did not want to tack our way upstream. With the mast stepped we would be harder to see and that was what we wanted. We would be just three hulls, low down and almost invisible as we headed inshore. Lord Arne led and we were at the rear. The other good news was that Lord Arne had said that there were no bridges. If anyone saw us from the northern bank they would not be able to take the news to Bordèu.

The crew began to row. I found it easier to see ahead without the mast but I knew we did not have a lookout who could see beyond the bends in the river. Instead I had Harland at the prow and Lars and Nils on the two sides of the drekar. They stood on the gunwale and clung to the stays. They were there to ensure that we did not hit a rock or some debris. The river was wide and, we had been told, free from rocks. I did not want to tear a hole in the keel. It was smoother than at sea. There were no waves. I was able to see that Lord Arne had been right. The river was as wide as a sea. It was as far from a fjord as one could imagine. The land was low to the sides with tilled and tended fields and on the slight slopes there were terraces. Joseph said that they grew grapes here and made wine. We saw not a single fortification. We rowed down the middle of the river and we kept a steady pace for no one wanted exhausted warriors when we arrived. We did not use a chant at first for there was no need. We did not double the rowers but had one man on an oar. We needed a steady pace for we wanted to arrive in darkness and then we would raid under the cover of night. It was an hour or so before dusk when we had changed three times that I began to sing and the rowers joined in. The river was still wide and the banks many paces away. The men needed to be revived and a chant always helped.

> *Odin had sons Hermod was one of many*
> *A bright and beautiful god and as valiant as any*
> *He rode with the Valkyrs with his spear Gungnir*
> *He was sent by Allfather Odin upon the steed, Sleipner*
> *With his mail corselet and Gambantein,*
> *He was sent to Rossthiof in the land of the Finns*
> *A horse thief and sorcerer cunning*
> *A mage known for his spinning*
> *With Odin's staff Hermod feard naught*
> *As he rode to the land of night*
> *Rossthiof could not fight the magic wand*
> *And he fell and grovelled upon the land*
> *Commanded by Hermod he obeyed the command*
> *To see the future of Odin's land*
> *His spell revealed a bloody child*
> *And the death of a son of Odin*
> *He told Hermod to see Rinda who dwelt in Ruthene far*
> *And Odin should bed her and heal the scar*
> *Odin had sons Hermod was one of many*
> *A bright and beautiful god and as valiant as any*

The song was as much to maintain the enthusiasm of the rowers as much as anything. We stopped after two renditions but the men appeared to have been revitalised. When the crews swapped over we sang it once more and then as the darkness became complete we rowed in silence. Night carried sounds and we wanted to slip silently along the river. We had just the sound of the oars slapping on the water as an accompaniment to our voyage. We heard the creak from the hull and the sound of birds from the banks. It was when darkness fell completely that I discovered the smells of the land. They had been there in the day but I had been distracted by the strange plants and birds that I saw. Now, as we rowed in the night, it was the smells and the sounds which came to the fore. There was a strange perfume in the air. Occasionally it disappeared when we passed a farm or

Dragon Rock

village for then the smell was mixed with woodsmoke and dung. We saw nothing and I could barely see **'Byglja'** ahead of me. As darkness descended Snorri hung a lamp from his stern so that we had a pinprick of light to guide us. Even if we were seen then the people would not know what we were. We might appear as ghosts or spirits and the people would shelter and touch their crosses of the White Christ for protection. We were, so Lord Arne told us, the first drekars to raid this land. They would know us better after this.

We reached the confluence of the two rivers. The sea-like river became narrower and we headed down the steerboard side waterway. It ceased to be the huge passage that allowed slight mistakes when steering. This last part would need close attention. It was more nerve-wracking and for the three lookouts more important that they were vigilant. They called out each time they spied white flecks of water. I kept my eye fixed on Snorri's stern.

I had last made water when we had stepped the mast and I knew that as soon as we stopped to land and we had taken the port the first thing I would do would be to make water. Before then I would have to don the helmet and take my sword and baldric from the dragon chest. I would not wear my mail shirt nor take my spear. If we had to leave in a hurry then I wanted to move as fast as I could.

"**'Byglia'** is slowing, Leif Wolf Killer." I had good ship's boys and the message from the prow reached me within moments.

"Lars, join me. Crew, slow the oars."

Oddr was on the front oar and he slowed. The rest took their beat from him. I peered ahead through the gloom and saw that the jarl's drekar was slowing even more. Lord Arne had been here before and would know when to stop. Snorri would simply follow our leader.

"Slower." As we slowed I said, "Oddr, I think that we must be close to landing."

He said, "Those not on the oars, dress for war. Replace us when you are ready." It naturally slowed us as half the crew left the oars.

I turned to Lars, "Hold the steering board."

I knew that he would be honoured and terrified in equal measure. I had been the same when Gandalfr had first asked me to help him. Unlike my first time this would be for moments only. I lifted the lid of the dragon chest and took out the helmet, head protector, sword and baldric. I had them on even before the first of the rowers had been changed.

Joseph appeared next to me. "Do you wish me to come ashore, Master?"

I shook my head, "You will stay here with Nils, Harland and Lars. Any who need to be healed will be brought back here." I saw the relief on his face. The last thing he wanted was to be taken by the Franks again. He had been cruelly treated the first time. He had told me that, wilder though we looked, we were more civilised as masters. "Stay here with me until we land."

We were sailing along a river which led, generally eastwards and I saw the first glow of the rising sun ahead and with it the outline of buildings. There were towers rising above the port and city. I said, "Joseph, are those defensive towers?"

He saw where I pointed and peered. He shook his head, "They are churches. They can flee there and take shelter but they are not like the towers they use further north. They will not have platforms where they can fight and hurl rocks at you."

I nodded. It made sense. The raids came from the south and it was the land which bordered Al-Andalus that was in danger from attacks by the Arabs and Turks.

I saw that it was Nils who was now at the prow and he waved for me to turn the steering board. Harland was on the steerboard side. As I did so I saw that Snorri was slowing. I said, "Oddr, be ready to pull in the steerboard oars." He nodded. In battle I would never dream of commanding a warrior like Oddr but on a drekar I was the master. I saw the ships tied up to the quay and I said, "Now, Oddr."

"Run in the steerboard oars."

As they were run in I judged the pace of the river and the approaching ship-lined quay. "Larboard oars in."

We did not crash into the trader but, like the other two dragon ships, we made a grinding and crunching sound as we ground next to them.

Dragon Rock

"Ship's boys secure us to these ships. Joseph, she is yours to command."

He smiled at the joke, "Yes, Master."

The oars were stacked and, after securing the board, I followed the rest of the warriors as they poured over the side of the trader. The crew were already dead by the time I passed them. The first they would have known of our raid would have been the grinding of the hulls. They would have opened their eyes and seen the Norsemen with bare blades and with it, their deaths. Joseph and the ship's boys would take all of value from the dead and then they would make the journey to the sea as their bodies were slipped over the side.

I did not use my wolf shield. I left it on the side of the ship. If there was a shield wall then I would be at the back and would not need my shield. I realised that I would need to get used to being at the rear in any attack. I was the navigator now. When I had been just a warrior I would have been with my shield brothers fighting at the front of the warband.

I had to run to catch up with the others. We raced through the port, passing warehouses that promised much. There had been noise when we had ground against the tethered ships but we had not cheered or shouted. Cheers and shouts were for fools. The ones who had died on the traders that had been tied to the quays had been asleep or overcome quickly and they made little noise as they were slain. Now, however, as we flooded onto the stone of the quay there was noise. Someone shouted an alarm. At least that was what I took it to be and when I heard a bell ringing it was confirmed. The noise grew as the alarm spread but by then it was too late and the damage was done. The wolves were in the sheepfold. I followed the men of Bygstad. The three ships' crews would raid in three bands and only come together if there was a defence that needed all our shields, spears and swords. Oddr led us to the right where I spied a gate with two small watch towers. Our task was to head west along the river and city.

Oddr raised his spear and shouted, "Bygstad! Wedge!"

Had I been at the fore I would have been just behind Asbjørn and Oddr. I would have stood with my shield brothers, the Wolves of Bygstad, Brynjar and Dagfinn. I now found myself with men like Birger, Anders, Benni and Frithjof. These were young warriors learning their trade. Their shields were barely marked and their weapons had yet to drink from an enemy's blood. Their helmets were still pristine and fresh and none wore mail. The four of us found ourselves in the centre of the rear line.

Anders, who had been on a raid as a ship's boy and was a friend of Birger's smiled and said, "We are honoured, brothers, Leif Wolf Killer fights with us." For some reason that made them cheer. I drew my sword and raised it. The cheer rose as those ahead saw the blade glinting in the morning sunlight.

I knew that Oddr must have seen something that needed a block of men and when he shouted, "Charge!" and then "Odin!" I knew that we were about to attack. All I heard was the crash of metal on wood and screams as our warriors hit whoever stood in their way. The sun was rising behind us and in its rays I saw the gate was close to us and Oddr was securing it. It was not closed and as we passed beneath it I saw the dead Franks. They had been the night watch. Had they barred the gates then we might have been held up for a little longer but such was our skill that our axes would have opened the gates in a flew flashes of axe. I saw none from our village who were dead. The Franks had no mail and poor helmets. The shields they had used were too small to afford much protection. Their best weapons were the fine swords that hung from their belts but against our longer spears they had stood no chance. We were all warriors. They were night guards.

Once through the gate I heard Oddr shout, "Steerboard crew with me. Asbjørn, take what you can from these buildings with the larboard crew. Leif Wolf Killer, help Asbjørn to search these buildings."

I was not sure if he was protecting me or trusted me to do a job on my own. I shouted, "Aye, Oddr. Birger and Anders, stay with me."

Fritjof nodded, "I will see you later, Birger." Fritjof was in the steerboard crew and he ran to join Oddr.

Birger said, as we headed to join Asbjørn, "Where will they be going?"

"There will be another gate. Lord Arne and the jarl will not want word to get out before we have secured the walls. I need you to be close to me, Birger. This is not yet over."

Dragon Rock

There were less than twenty of us left. The sun had illuminated the town and I saw many buildings. The ones close to the wall looked to be cruder than the ones that lay to the east of the road taken by Oddr. Asbjørn grinned when he saw me, "Good, you are not taking your leisure then, Leif." He pointed his sword at a building with a solid looking door. "We take that one. Folki, take four men and see what lies in those poorer buildings."

Folki might not have liked the orders but he obeyed Asbjørn. I knew that whatever we found in the better buildings would be shared with the whole crew. The rest of us ran and as my friend Dagfinn smashed his axe at the door we heard the smash and clash of weapons and then a cry from the men led by Oddr. They had reached the gate and there was a battle ensuing. Dagfinn's axe made short work of the door and as Asbjørn slung his shield on his back he pointed his sword and said, "Leif Wolf Killer."

I had no shield and it made sense for me to go first. With drawn sword and seax I entered the dark entrance to the house.

I could smell woodsmoke and people. The house was occupied but it was silent. That cautioned me. Who waited within? It was a narrow passage and I held my sword before me. The helmet was necessary but it restricted both my hearing and sight. When I had hunted the wolf it had been those senses that had saved me. I put my left hand to the wall. I needed to be guided down the corridor. I suddenly found something warm. It was a lamp that had been recently doused. That alerted me and I knew that someone was ahead, lying in wait. I picked up the still warm pot of oil and walked forward. It didn't matter if we made a noise but I did not want to give an enemy my exact position. A spear rammed from the dark could easily end my life. When a shadow moved ahead of me I just reacted. I hurled the lamp into the dark and it distracted the warrior just long enough for me to see his spearpoint. He had flicked his weapon at the lamp. I lunged in the dark and felt my sword grate against the haft of the spear. The head of his spear slid along the sword and passed by my belt. It was then I saw the Frank. He was clean shaven and taller than I was. My speed had taken me close to him and I carried on with the thrust of my sword. I was helped by Birger pushing into my back. The sword slid into the man's middle. He was unprotected by mail and I twisted as I stabbed. I found myself face to face with him. I pulled back my head and butted him. His nose burst as it broke and the man began to slide to the ground, from my blade. He was dead but the last blow meant he could not use a dying move to end my life.

Behind him I heard a shout. It was in Frankish and while I understood some Frankish words I did not make them out clearly. What I did know was that there was more than one man's voice. The man had clearly emerged from a door and there were others behind him.

"Birger, behind me!" I levelled my second weapon. It was a Saxon seax and could be used like a short sword.

Asbjørn appeared to my left. He nodded, "Now!"

We both pushed together through the door, our swords held before us. It was a tight fit but those within were expecting a single man and when two came through with sharpened blades it took the man waiting there by surprise. My eyes were now accustomed to the dark and I saw that there were four or more warriors in the room. The one who faced us had donned a helmet and had a small shield and a spear but he was in his underwear. His sword came at me but I had good reactions and I flicked it up. Asbjørn did not hesitate. His sword slashed across the man's throat. I pushed the shield with my sword hand and the dying man fell back. The others in the room launched themselves at us. Like me Asbjørn had two weapons while the Franks in the room had shields. A short weapon could easily slash across the top of the shield. Birger stepped to my right and his movement distracted one of the men. The room was small and one mistake could easily cost a man his life. I did not want my brother to die here. The Frank tried to turn and I slashed at his sword hand with my dagger. Birger had quick reactions and his sword ended the man's life. I sensed rather than saw the sword that came at my side and I just moved my seax seemingly instinctively. Sparks flew in the gloom as the weapons came together. I raised my sword horizontally above my head. I did not want to catch it on the ceiling and I swung it sideways at his head. I caught him just below the rim of his pot helmet and the edge sliced into his skull.

Suddenly there was no movement in the room. They were all dead.

Dragon Rock

Asbjørn said, "These were here to ambush us. There will be others. Search the rooms. Anders, fetch light. I have had enough of the darkness." I turned and saw that Birger was unhurt and there was blood on his blade.

Birger left with the others and I waited with Asbjørn. When Anders returned with the oil lamp we were able to examine the dead. The man I had killed first had rings on his fingers and wore gold around his neck. I said, "This man was a lord. Joseph said they called them leudes."

Birger was still in shock, "I did not think, Brother, I just stabbed."

"You have done well and these, from their weapons, are his bodyguards." I turned to Asbjørn. "It was good that you and I led and not men like Birger or Anders."

From the other rooms we heard screams. Asbjørn smiled, "And now we have their women. I had better go and see that the young men do not get over excited. There will be coins forthcoming from the wife of a lord." I nodded. "You collect our treasure. I will join you later."

I knew the men I had killed and who Birger had slain. The others were Asbjørn's kills. I put the rings and chain with the golden cross in my satchel. I slung the swords and scabbards over my shoulder. The one slain by Birger had a silver cross. Birger would like that. The cross went into the satchel. He also had a good sword. The last man I had killed also had a cross. This one was made of base metal. It could be melted down. I put that in my satchel and the other swords I found went over my shoulder. I was laden like a pack horse. Asbjørn had slain three and one had rings. I took a cap I found discarded on the floor and put the rings and jewels I found on Asbjørn's dead within. I took their swords too. The man I had first slain also had rings and a good weapon. I was struggling to carry them all when I emerged from the house. Outside it was now daylight. Oddr and his men were back and they were busy scavenging in the building next to the one we had taken. I saw now that there was a bench outside the house we had entered and I laid my treasure there. It was a substantial pile.

Oddr came out of the building he had searched and his sword was bloody. "We took the gate, Leif Wolf Killer. The town is ours. We have not lost a man. This was a good plan. We took them by surprise."

Asbjørn and Birger came from the house with Anders, Folki and Bjarni. They led four females. Two were not yet women but the other two looked much older. One had grey hair. She was the one who glowered and glared at us. The other three looked cowed.

Oddr smiled, "These look like they could be worth coins."

Bjarni said, "They would not make good slaves."

Oddr laughed, "And there you are right but they can be ransomed. These ladies have never done a day's work. There will be thralls somewhere. We will ask for ransom for them. Their thralls we might keep. Leif, you and your brother, take them back to the ship. Anders can help you. Have Joseph discover all that he can about them."

I nodded and pointed to a coil of rope that lay on the ground, "Birger, tie their hands and then to each other. Anders watch them."

The rest of the band left with Oddr and Asbjørn to search the other houses. This was clearly a district filled with sturdy and well-built houses and that meant there would be a fine church nearby. Inside would be treasure. Joseph had explained that to me. A church meant rich pickings. They had good doors and well-made rooves. There were good candles and candlesticks. I went back through the gates to the port side of the wall and saw a small hand cart. I took the handles and wheeled it back. Birger had done as I asked. I began to load the weapons and treasure on the cart. I put my helmet there too.

"Stay here." I returned inside. Now that Anders had lit the lamps I could see that it was a well apportioned dwelling. There were heavy curtains hung from the walls to keep the rooms warm. I first went through to the kitchen and the larder. I found a large ham which I took and an amphora of wine. I took them back outside and placed them on the cart.

"Do you need us, Brother?"

I shook my head, "Just watch these, especially the old one."

Once back inside I took all the food I could find and the best of the curtains from the other rooms. If we could find a chest they could be taken back to Bygstad and if not they would make blankets for the ship. It was when I searched the chest in the bedroom of the lord that I found something that was worth more than everything else I had taken. It was a fine chest made of a well carved wood that I did not recognise. It would be useful but the real treasure was hidden in the bottom and was swaddled in a blanket. It was the blanket that first drew my eye. When I picked it up it felt heavier than it should have. I laid it on the bed and carefully unwrapped it. Inside was the greatest of treasures for a navigator, it was an hourglass. I wrapped it again and held it like a newborn babe. I placed it inside the chest this time cushioned with the curtains. The coins I found in the small chest I carried under my arm.

The cart was well loaded by the time I had finished placing the chests on it. "Anders, you push the cart. Birger, you lead and I will walk behind." I took out my sword and pointed to the gate. Three of the captives looked ready to obey but the older woman stood defiantly. I had a few words of their language and as I poked the woman in the back I said, in what must have sounded like appalling Frankish, "Move or die!" Joseph had said that my accent mangled Frankish but she saw the look in my eye. I would find it hard to stick a blade in an old woman but all she saw was a barbarian with a blood-spattered tunic. She obeyed.

Once through the gate we saw other raiders returning with booty. The men at the gate had been stripped of weapons and their bodies disposed of. The fish in the river and the sea would feast on the corpses. I wondered if, as these were Christians who were doused in water as a sign of their faith, they would take comfort in the fact their corpses were taken by the same water. I would ask Joseph. He seemed to understand the Franks who had been his master better than anyone.

Someone, probably Joseph, had placed planks across the trader. We were able to walk the women across. "Nils and Lars, help Anders to unload our treasure." It would take time to carry the treasure and to secure it on the ship.

Joesph came over, "We have taken some of the things from the trader, Master, but I am guessing that the jarl will want to use it."

I nodded as I placed my treasure in my dragon chest. "He can send it back to Bygstad. I do not think that this one raid will be

Dragon Rock

the end." I nodded to the women. "They will be held for ransom. Find out their names and make them comfortable but, Joseph, keep them secure. The old one is defiant. I spoke to her in Frankish but I am not sure she understood me."

"Yes, Master." He smiled, "These people are related to the Franks but they are Vasconian. The accent and some of the words they use are different." He turned and spoke gently to the women. The old woman apart they smiled at the more understandable use of their own language and his tone was calming. He led them to the prow. I turned to Anders and tossed him one of the swords I had taken. "Here, Anders, a good sword for you."

He grinned and said, "A great gift. I thank you."

I saw the look of disappointment on Birger's face and I tossed him the sword I had taken from the leude. "You have one sword but perhaps you can give that one to our little brother. Here is one with a well-made scabbard for you."

"Thank you, Leif, a mighty gift." The smile on Birger's face was so wide that I thought he would split his face, "This is generous beyond words. Do you not want it?"

I patted my sword, "No, Birger. It is yours. This one will do for me. We trust each other."

Fritjof looked disappointed not to be included. I said, "I have a spare sword in my old chest, Fritjof. It is better than the one you use. It shall be yours."

His smile returned.

I then went to examine the trader. She was not a knarr for she was of Frankish design. The steering board looked similar but I did not think she would carry as much cargo as a knarr. I searched the hold and found cargo already loaded. She would have been ready to sail on the next tide. Birger joined me as I lifted the lid on the chest which had belonged to the captain. Inside was, for a navigator, treasure: maps. They were like gold to me and as Birger searched the chest for things he wanted I looked at the maps. I could not read the words but I could see where the land lay and where there were dangerous waters. Joseph would need to translate for me. I put them back in the sealskin pouch I had found them. That alone told me that the captain valued them and also that he had traded with men from our lands. It was our people who hunted the seal.

Birger took the things he wanted and said, "What will we do with this ship? Burn it?"

I shook my head, "A crew will be found to take it home to Bygstad."

"Will you go, Brother? I know you wish to see Freya and Leif."

"As much as I might want to I am now the navigator for *'Ægir'*. If Gandalfr still lived then, aye, I would sail home but the others are right. My son may be toddling or even walking by the time I see him. It will be Freya's father who raises him. My son will be in good hands."

He nodded and we headed back to our drekar, "And what do we do next?"

"That depends upon the Franks. I daresay I will be summoned, along with Oddr to speak to our leaders." I pointed south, "The land of Al-Andalus seems to me a place where fortunes could be made."

Anders was placing things in his chest when I spoke and he said, "I heard Haraldr Long Nose say that they are fierce warriors."

I put the maps in my chest along with the hourglass, still wrapped in its blanket, and said, "As are we. I fear no man and no sailor. The monsters from the deep might be a danger or creatures as yet unknown but a man is still a man no matter what his colour or his faith. The leude I slew had a good sword and was clearly a warrior yet he died. We shall see, Anders. Remember that Lord Arne and the jarl have been dreaming of this for some time. We will raid until we fail."

I found myself touching the Hammer of Thor. The dream I had came back to me. I did not want the Three Sisters to spin for me.

Chapter 3

Lord Arne was ruthless. Any who might be valuable as hostages or for ransom were kept. Some of the senior officials from the port were also retained. Those who had a skill such as bakers and their families were retained. The rest were sent from the city. They left happily for they were free. We did not need more mouths to feed. It was better that they were outside the city. The ones we released looked to be grateful for they were not killed, neither were they enslaved. When the Umayyads had come those had been the two fates for those who were taken. We also kept many of the thralls. Some were promised their freedom if they cooperated. They were the ones who could prepare food. The women who had been used by the Franks for pleasure were also kept. I would not use one but there were men who needed such women. The slaves viewed our arrival as a mixed blessing. Some might be freed but others would be exchanging one master for another.

It was evening when I was summoned, along with Oddr, to the house in the centre of Bordèu which had been taken over by our leaders and their hearthweru. A bull had been killed and it was being cooked out in the square. The men cooking it called to us as we passed and we acknowledged them. None of them were warriors who had attained fame and the two of us had.

Inside the hall I saw that some men were drunk already. Being able to hold drink was different for every man. I rarely had so much to drink that I passed out. I seemed to know my limit but others did not. I had heard of men who had died because of such mistakes. If you were drunk at home it was one thing but to be drunk on a raid could result in death. Lord Arne and the jarl were not drunk but they looked in good humour. Snorri was seated close by them. I could see, from his face, that he was still mourning his brother. The two had no other family and had been close.

Their bodyguards vacated two seats for us. We had our own drinking horns but they had Frankish thralls who brought us goblets. I looked in mine and saw that it contained wine. The jarl said, "The men of Bygstad did well. I hear you have women that can be ransomed."

I nodded, "They lived in a fine house and the man of the house was a lord."

"Good, my cousin and I see no reason to rush off. The ships we took are all traders. You and I have fought their warships and they hold no fear for us."

I had examined the trader next to us and seen that her hull was loaded. She had been about to sail, "Jarl, one of the ships was ready to sail and had a full cargo. It seems to me that she could be sailed, not back to our homeland but, perhaps, to the land of the Angles, Wessex or Mercia. There her goods could be traded and the ship return here."

The jarl turned to his cousin, "That is something new." Lord Arne nodded. The jarl seemed to wait for such approval before making a decision, "A good idea, Leif. It would need a good captain, you perhaps." Lord Arne shrugged. I had the impression that he did not particularly care for me.

I said, "Snorri, is the best captain that I know."

Snorri smiled, "You honour me but this is your idea. Why not you?"

"I have my own brother who is here to watch over and he would not relish leaving this raid."

Snorri nodded, "A good answer. If you wish me to sail, Jarl, then I shall."

"How long would it take you?"

Snorri rubbed his beard, "Hard to say but no more than half a month there and the same back. We would not have to risk the waters of Frisia or Frankia. I would sail to Dumnonia as it is called by others or Curnow as the people there call themselves. They live far to the west of the land controlled by Charlemagne and I believe they are happy to trade with men like us."

"Not Wessex?" The jarl asked.

Snorri shook his head, "We might sail a Frankish ship but as soon as we spoke they would know us for what we are, Norsemen, and they would execute us. This is safer and more profitable. They have gold in Dumnonia."

Lord Arne nodded, "Then sail on the next tide. You can also take slaves to sell at the slave market there. Ask for volunteers to be your crew. They can have a tenth of the profits and you a quarter. Fair?"

Snorri nodded and added, "And when this is done I would have the ship."

The jarl looked surprised, "You would become a trader?"

"It seems to me that the Norns have spun. I lost a brother but Leif here has brought me something to take his place. Do not worry, Jarl, I will spend this voyage training another to be your navigator. My brother did a good job with Leif Wolf Killer and I shall try to copy him."

Lord Arne seemed satisfied with the plan, "Good. Then, Cousin, we spend as much time here as it takes to be given weregeld. There are horses and we will send our men out to raid the land. By then the Duke of Vasconia or whoever Charlemagne has ruling this land will have summoned an army and try to oust us."

Oddr spoke for the first time. "Would you fight a Frankish army? I thought we came to raid."

Lord Arne, I had come to learn, was far cleverer than his cousin. I preferred the jarl as a man and a leader but I recognised the cunning in his cousin. "We still have our ships and we will be well fed. We hold the town and we will sell it back to the Vasconians. Our raids over the next days will show them our mettle and they will buy us off rather than fighting. They are not sailors and when we choose to leave we shall be able to." I was not sure about that but I was a lowly warrior and new navigator. What did I know?

Everyone nodded. I said, "And then?"

Lord Arne studied me, "And then, Leif Wolf Killer, we will head south. The Umayyads or Arabs, whatever you wish to call them, are not invincible. We will raid their lands. The slaves we take will be more valuable than Franks and we can take valuable things that do not take up much of the hold. When we have enough we will sail home."

Everyone seemed satisfied with that. The jarl said, "And then we can visit our vengeance on Erland Brynjarsson, eh?" He was looking at Oddr, Snorri and me.

I nodded. That was the best reason for staying here. We had been betrayed by our former hersir and everyone on my ship wanted vengeance.

The crew for the trader was easy to find. There were many young men who saw the chance to put not only silver in their hands but also gold. I rose in the middle of the night to speak to Snorri before he left on the high tide. We had moved our drekar in the afternoon and we were now tied to the quay. I stood at the steering board with him.

"I have the maps from the captain of this ship. Would you like them?"

He shook his head, "I have my own and besides, I am guessing that the language on them is Frankish."

"It is."

"Then they would be useless."

I had already decided that and I had asked Joseph to copy them for me. One of the treasures we had saved before Einar Foul Fart burnt everything he did not see as having value, were some pieces of parchment discovered in the church at the abbey. I knew the value of the blank parchments and I gave them to Joseph along with some quills and ink I had found. He would make copies. I could then leave the originals in my chest.

"You will not be sailing along the coast?"

He shook his head, "The shortest way is to head north and west. It is into the deep sea but there will be neither pirates nor raiders and we can take advantage of the winds. They blow southwest to northeast at this time of year and we will fly, both ways."

"And when you return you give up the way of the warrior?"

"Aye, Gandalfr had planned on doing so. He saw in you the potential for a replacement. Had he let you command the drekar sooner then he would be alive and, perhaps, trading."

I fingered my Hammer of Thor, "The Norns."

He did the same, "Aye, the Norns." He sniffed the air. I was still a novice but an old navigator like Snorri could smell the changing of the tide. "I shall see you in a month." The crew and the slaves who would be sold were already aboard.

I clasped his arm and then climbed back aboard my drekar. I unfastened the ropes as he raised his sail. Already the current was tugging him towards the sea. He was right, he would fly. Coming back it might take him as long to make it up the river as the journey to Dumnonia. I watched his wake until it disappeared behind a bend in the river. I missed his brother and now I missed him.

We had two more traders that looked as though they might be able to make the journey north to our home. We could not afford to crew them as yet but they were moved and their holds inspected. We had sent the best cargo with Snorri but there were still things that we could use back in our homes to the north. The Franks liked good pots and had cloth and linen that was far better than ours. We loaded one of the traders with it. We spent that first day stripping the churches and the houses of all that could be taken.

The next day we loaded all that we had found and could be taken home into the traders. It was a time-consuming job as we had to balance the cargo. A badly loaded ship could easily founder in the Great Ocean. It took all day. The next day Lord Arne led the first band of warriors to raid the land to the south of the river. We also had men on the walls and watching our captives. As the evening fell I realised that we had brought three ships this time but it was not enough. This land was like a tree laden with juicy plums. We had barely taken from the low hanging branches. We would be leaving more behind than we would take.

We had sent the captives we had found on the first day to the hall used by the two lords. It saved us having to watch them and I did not enjoy the hateful stares from the old woman. I know that she was a Christian but she had the look of a witch. All the ones who would be ransomed were kept under the watchful eye of the two lords. There were no men who were warriors left in Bordèu. They had all been slain in the taking of the city. There were, however, youths, the heirs to the lands and goods of the lords. Jarl Bjorn Haraldsson hoped that they would fetch a good price. There were also men who, Joseph told me, were like clerks. They kept records for the merchants and the lords of this land. They too could be ransomed. The way these people lived was nothing like our lives back in the fjord.

Dragon Rock

When Lord Arne returned he had with him animals that had been taken, gold and more captives. He had been successful for word of our arrival had yet to spread. Farms and villages had been raided and none had been able to withstand him and his men. He had the biggest crew and this was their first battle. Our two ships had fought the Franks already. We knew why word had not spread. Joseph had gleaned that we had arrived on a Sunday and people had been preparing for church. The town would become busier during the week when the market was used. Lord Arne's raid, whilst highly rewarding would now warn the land of Vasconia that a new scourge had arrived. This time it was not dark-skinned men from the south but fair skinned raiders from the north. The next men sent to raid would not enjoy the same freedom as Lord Arne and his men. Lord Arne had also taken captives from the farms and villages. We would ask for money for their lives. The ones to be ransomed were placed in the hall and the goods that were to be saved placed on the trader we had half loaded. The animals would be slaughtered as and when we needed them. If nothing else we would eat well.

The jarl went to raid a different part the next day and he raided closer to the coast than had Lord Arne. We were told by the jarl that the men of Bygstad would raid north of the river the next day. In preparation we took *'Ægir'* across the river to find a good landing place. We rowed upstream, to the east although as the river twisted and turned its direction varied. I sought somewhere that was close to a settlement. We found an island in the middle of the river and next to it was a beach. I grounded the drekar on to it. The island made the river wider and, when we had raided, we would have enough room to turn the ship around and sail back to Bordèu.

Oddr and Asbjørn jumped ashore and disappeared. While they did so I looked at the island and the banks. I was learning that a good navigator learned to use all that he found to make his voyage easier. When they returned they looked pleased. "We can use the two channels to turn the drekar and head back to Bordèu."

As I turned the ship the two stayed with me at the steering board. We had the current with us and we would only need half the crew to row. They would just be needed to keep the way on the ship and we had less than seven miles to travel. As we sailed the two men explained what they had discovered, "We found a small town. It is a large village really, just a mile from the island. They had no sentries and we were not seen. There is no wall. Between the island and the town are many farms. Some look to grow grapes but we heard animals. Tomorrow, Asbjørn and I will take most of the men to the town. You can take the new ones, the youths, to raid the farms that lie closer to the ship."

"Are you sure?"

Oddr smiled, "They will learn much from Leif Wolf Killer. They all admire you already and there should be little opposition on the farms. You can raid the ones closest to the ship whilst we clean out the town. That way you can turn the drekar when you return."

It made sense and I nodded.

Asbjørn peered to the west and the side of the river that had been raided by Lord Arne, "I cannot see these Franks sitting idly by and letting our handful of men ravage their land. They held off the fierce armies of Arabs and Turks who came here and we are far fewer. We will have to fight."

Oddr said nothing. I nodded, "And we are now tied here until Snorri returns. Within a short time we will have filled our holds and even those of the two traders." I adjusted the steering board to take us closer to the larboard bank. "We do not have enough crew for the traders as it is and if we lose men in battle…"

Oddr sighed, "Our two leaders will not settle for Bordèu. They want to test their swords against the men from the south. The lure of the Arab gold draws them thither." He looked at me and said, quietly, "Perhaps if your uncle, the hersir, was with us then he might be able to allow us to sail home. I have no voice in this council."

He was right. The headstrong Lord Arne and his cousin, the jarl, had dreams of glory. Those dreams were not shared by most of us. We wanted silver and riches to make our lives in the fjord easier.

When we reached our berth Oddr and Asbjørn went to tell Lord Arne of our plans. Joseph had stayed in the town and had spent the day copying maps. He returned aboard with his copies. They were beautiful. My slave had a fine hand. We placed the originals in the bottom of my dragon chest and the others were wrapped in sealskin and then placed in the top of the chest where they could be easily reached. I would enjoy studying them that night when all the preparations for the raid had been made.

Anders, Fritjof, Benni and Birger were honing the blades I had given them. They were keen to put them to good use. While food was being cooked on the quayside I went to join them. They had yet to be told the plans.

"Where do we raid tomorrow, Brother? Did Oddr tell you?"

I nodded, "The main band will raid the town he found but you and the other young ones will raid the farms closer to the river." I saw their faces fall. These four were the youngest and the least experienced of the crew. While they were close they saw the raid as a mark of the lack of trust Oddr had in them. It showed on their faces. I smiled, "You will be led by me."

The smiles on their faces beamed. Anders said, "Then this raid is an honour. We are not being used because we are young."

I shook my head, "You are chosen because you are young and you will obey me. Whilst Oddr and the others know that they will face men who can defend in numbers we need caution. There will be just four of us and we cannot risk a fight against large numbers."

Birger said, "Will you wear your mail?"

I nodded. I would do so if only to draw the blades of any good warriors to me. I was there to protect my little brother and his shield brothers. "Now go and make your preparations."

When they had gone I gathered my ship's boys and Joseph around me. "Tomorrow, when we land, I will leave you to guard the boat." They nodded. "It will be moored next to the island. Lars, you are the most experienced. When we return you will need to bring the drekar to the east bank. Can you do this?" If he could not then we would have a problem. We would have to leave the ship where it could be attacked. I did not think that there were men east of the river who would risk attacking a ship but I had to make a plan that would cover that eventuality.

Lars chewed his lip and then nodded, "Aye, Leif Wolf Killer, and I am honoured that you trust me."

I looked at them and said, "I know that you wish you were ashore with the others but you should know that when we return to Bygstad you will have a choice to make. Do you choose the sword or the sail? I would still be a warrior but for Gandalfr's untimely death. If one of you wished it you could be the navigator for the men of Bygstad."

Nils said, "But you do both."

"Not out of choice. The Norns spun and Gandalfr died." They all clutched at whatever token they had around their necks. I saw Joseph smiling at the superstition. I knew that he had his own beliefs but I had never seen him make any similar gesture. He did not make the sign of the cross as the Christians did. Perhaps his religion kept such things hidden.

Birger and the others returned. I said to them, "Now when we raid do not take your shields." I saw the looks on their faces. To them a shield and a sword marked them as a warrior. "We do not go to fight large numbers. We go to hunt and the best weapon when hunting is a bow. Take your bows. You will need your swords and helmets but I will be the only one who will need a shield." They still had disbelieving looks on their faces. "The reason Oddr chose us was because we are a small number who can stay hidden. He expects the battle to be in the town we found. Stealth is our aim."

Birger said, "Like when you hunted the wolf."

"Exactly like that. Now ready your bows and remember to take a spare string. Keep it in your helmet. Eat well this night and take an ale skin with you. We will not need food for we will take from the farms we raid."

They left and Joseph smiled, "The Franks paint you men of the north as wild men who care not if they live or die. I have seen that while you are brave you do care. I will not be there with you tomorrow but I know that if your brother and the others are threatened you will risk your own life to save them."

"Of course."

He nodded, "I have learned much from you. Thank you, Master."

When the jarl returned he had more captives and more treasure. He had found a good church which he had emptied. As with Lord Arne he had not lost a man. That might change when the Vasconians roused themselves.

Dragon Rock

We left before dawn and that was not necessarily out of choice but because the river was higher. We rowed upstream and when we reached the island Oddr and Asbjørn, along with the rest of the warriors, slipped over the side and with shields over their backs ran down the track. They did not look back. I wore my mail and had my shield slung over my back but I did not bother with the spear. We slipped ashore too. I waited while my little warband strung their bows and Lars and the others sculled the drekar to the island. Once it was tethered I waved my hand and headed through the small wood that lay next to the river. While I had been waiting I had caught the faint whiff of woodsmoke from the east. I soon spotted a hunter's trail and, once we joined it, the going became easier and the smell of smoke grew stronger. When the trees thinned out I saw, rising ahead, a wooden building. I stopped and watched. It was a farm. I heard the bleating of goats. They had animals. I also saw that there were the familiar vines on the slopes below the house. There was, I could see, a low fence. It was not a defensive structure. It was there to control animals. Once I had worked that out I sought a safe route to get to the house unseen. It had a good view of the trees and the land between. I saw that the land descended to the south and without leaving the shelter of the trees I led my little band down to what looked like a natural hollow. It was a place where water naturally gathered. There was a pond there and the prints around me told me that they had at least one cow who went there to drink.

I turned and spoke quietly, "We will approach the farm using the path that they employ to water the animals. Nock an arrow and walk behind me. Watch my left hand for signals. I will tell you when to loose an arrow." They nodded.

With a drawn sword I left the trees and after skirting the watering hole went up the muddy path. Had this been home it would have been wet and slippery. Thankfully the land hereabouts was warmer and we had not had rain since we arrived. It was a good surface on which to walk.

Despite my helmet I could still hear relatively well and when I heard Frankish being spoken I tried to work out the direction. I slowed as we began to rise towards the wooden palisade. Unlike some warriors I did not polish my helmet. It was slightly tarnished and did not reflect the light. My sword, on the other hand, would and I kept that low. I peered through the slats in the wood and I saw two men with helmets and swords holding a third man who had neither a sword nor a helmet. He was dressed in tattered clothing. There were two thralls and a woman watching but my attention was on the fourth man. He was dressed in a type of armour I had not seen before. It resembled the scales of a fish and came down to his knees. His sword was a longer one than mine and he held it in two hands. I saw his round shield and strange looking helmet on the ground. I was curious. I moved slightly to my left to get a better view of the man that the other two held. I saw that the two men had pulled his arms back so that his head was extended. As soon as I saw that I knew that this was an execution. I might have merely watched but the Norns were spinning. I spied, dangling from his neck, a Hammer of Thor. I studied him again. He was blond and stocky. He had a determined look in his blue eyes and he was not afraid to die. He was one of us, a Viking. The man in the fish armour was clearly taunting the prisoner before he executed him.

 I turned and pointed to the bows of my four companions. I held up three fingers and then pointed beyond the palisade. I mimed slitting a throat. They nodded. I waved my hand to make them wait and then I moved along to the opening in the palisade. As I did so I swung my shield around. As I neared the entrance I saw the sword raised. I stepped up into the opening and shouted, "Now!" I wanted to arrest the blow and draw attention to me so that my four archers could send their arrows.

 My appearance and my shout froze the man with the sword. I heard the flight of four arrows. One went towards the mailed man and that was a mistake. It would not penetrate the armour. I saw it hit and bounce off. A second arrow hit an arm and hung there. In that time I had taken three steps closer and the warrior took his helmet and shield. The woman screamed. The other two arrows had hit the two men holding the prisoner but they were not mortal strikes. I had to trust my little brother and his friends for the warrior picked up his shield and helmet before he launched himself at me.

 As he raced to me I took in the fact that his shield, although smaller, had a spike on the boss. If he punched with that then it

Dragon Rock

would be the equivalent of a dagger thrust. His helmet was also longer at the rear and gave better protection to the back of his neck but, unlike mine, he had no protection for his nose. He would, however, have better vision. He was bigger and broader than I was and he clearly thought he could cow me. I heard a cry from my right and hoped that another arrow had found its mark. I had fought bigger men before and I had a strategy. I made myself even smaller and when he swung at me I merely ducked and spun so that he hit fresh air. I slashed my sword at his back and heard the grunt as I struck. He had mail and a padded undergarment but he had felt the blow. I had used the flat of my sword and as I continued my spin I saw that the fish scales were overlapping and held not by metal but leather. Leather could be cut.

    He came at me again but this time he did not rush. He held the shield before him, the spike looking threatening. He then swung his sword at my head. It was a test. I angled my shield as I blocked the blow. His sword slid down, catching a little on the boss. It was a small distraction but it allowed me to slash, not at his shield but the lower part of his armour. The blow would not hurt him. It was not intended to. I wanted to make his armour less effective and when a piece of armour the length of a hand dropped and trailed from the rest, I knew I had the beating of him. He had not even noticed. He punched with his shield, the spike coming for my eye. I flicked up my shield and the metal edge caught the spike and lifted it above my head. I then did the unexpected. We were close together and I brought up my knee between his legs. He had no protection there and I hurt him. He stepped back and screamed in anger rather than pain. I slashed again at the other side of his armour and another piece hung down. This time he was aware of it. The two pieces of metal would act like anchors. He thought to end the contest and brought his sword down vertically at my head and helmet. I lifted my shield while stabbing with my sword. I knew I would not penetrate his armour but I managed to cut more of the fastenings and sensed the tip slip into his gambeson. He felt it too and we were close enough for me to see the look of fear on his face. It was my turn to use my shield as a weapon and I rammed the metal edge towards his eyes. He reeled but the edge still caught his nose. Blood spurted and when that happens eyes water. He lost sight of me for a heartbeat and in that heartbeat I killed him. I slashed my sword across his unprotected throat. He had no armour there and the blood spurted and arced as he fell to the ground. I heard hoofbeats. I whirled and saw that not only were the two men who had been holding the prisoner dead, but another man, who had been holding horses, also lay transfixed by three arrows. I saw another man, leading the remaining horses, galloping away. I did not sheathe my sword but looked at the woman and the thralls. The thralls abased themselves and, seeing the bloody sword, so did the woman.

The prisoner held up his tethered hands and I walked over to cut his bonds, "Thank you, friend." He was a Dane. He spoke our language but the accent gave him away. "I am Christof the Wanderer. Am I your prisoner or...?"

"You are free."

He stood and patted Birger on the back, "And thank you, young bowmen. You have saved my life."

In that brief moment I learned much about the man. He was cheerful and looked on life as half full. As much as I wanted to hear his story, the fleeing horseman had added urgency to our task. "We have little time. We have a ship on the river. You can repay us by telling us what treasures lie within."

He nodded, "In the kitchen there is a hole in the floor and a chest. The man you slew was a rich man. There is a cow and four goats. They have wine and there are two hams."

"Thank you."

"And there is more. The three thralls are Angles from the land of Northumbria. They will be willing to join you, as would I."

"Good, then tell them to fetch the hams and the goats." He began to speak to them. One or two words I could understand but I had too much to do. "Birger, fetch the horse and gather all the weapons. Take the armour from the dead Frank. He has rings too. Fritjof, secure the woman and take her to the drekar. Get Lars to bring her over to the shore. Benni and Anders come with me."

After slinging my shield over my back, I went into the farmhouse. Knowing that there was a hidden hole in the kitchen helped me. I saw the edge of the top and used my seax to lift it. There was a chest inside. I opened it and saw that it had both gold and silver. There was more silver than gold. I put it under my arm. "Search the house and take whatever you can carry. We want things that are valuable. We have no time to waste."

With the weapons, hams and food loaded on the horse we left the farm and headed to the river. I would have liked to have taken the cow but that would have slowed us down and we would have struggled to get it aboard. We had enough from the one raid.

By the time I reached the river Lars had brought over the ship and we were facing downstream. The woman was already aboard and I saw Joseph speaking to her. He was more valuable than any warrior. I knew his words would calm and reassure her. The last thing we needed was a woman who was screaming and upset.

I put the treasure in my dragon chest and the youths secured the weapons and armour in their chests and my old one. Christof the Wanderer had brought a large amphora of wine and he placed that by the steering board.

Anders said, "What do we do with the horse?"

As much as I would have liked to keep it we did not know what Oddr and the rest would bring. I said, "Take off the saddle and let it go. The saddle might prove useful."

Once the horse galloped off I took my drinking horn and poured myself some wine. I nodded to the four men we had brought. "Welcome, and help yourselves. There are beakers by the ale butt."

Christof the Wanderer did that first and he raised his beaker and said, "Thank you…"

"I am Leif Wolf Killer, my brother, Birger, Anders, Fritjof, Benni, and the man speaking with the woman is Joseph our healer."

I saw the questions written all over the man's face but he just said, "These men are Aedgar, Allan and Gurth. They are Northumbrians and follow the White Christ but other than that they are good men."

I nodded, "And I can tell that you have a tale to tell but that will have to wait. The rest of the band are raiding further upstream."

He frowned, "Cambas?"

I shrugged, "All I know is that it is upstream."

He nodded, "There are no defences and the men there do not have a good leader. Now, if you had raided further west you would have found a place that could be defended; Crion has a good wall and the man you slew is the brother of the leude there. The man who fled will be bringing horsemen." He was warning me.

"Lars, Nils, Harland, untie us. Christof, have the men use the oars to push us into the middle of the river."

As they all ran to obey me I went to the stern and picked up the anchor. It was a large stone secured by a rope. It would not stop us moving downstream but it would slow us and keep us in the middle of the river. I looked at the sun. It was gone noon and I expected Oddr and the others back well before dark. No one wanted to risk the river at night. This was not the broad one we had travelled when we had arrived.

The first of the warriors returned not long after we had moored. Nils saw them coming and, after raising the anchor, we sculled back to the shore. By the time we had secured the ship to the trees the two men had arrived. We put the gangplanks down to make it easier to board. The two had been wounded and as soon as they came aboard Joseph tended to their wounds. I asked how the raid had gone.

"They fought but as they had no mail and we outnumbered them then it was over quickly."

"Then how did you two get your wounds?"

Galmr shrugged, "Just bad luck. They had some boys hurling stones. We were both hit."

"And is there much treasure?"

"Plenty of food and a little silver. There are a couple of pigs and two goats too. It was a poor church but they had fine linen and candlesticks as well as good candles."

"Did Oddr take slaves?"

He shook his head, "He said we could always come back for slaves if we needed to."

The Norns had been spinning for as Oddr and the main body began driving their animals up the path I heard the thunder of horses. Birger shouted, "Horsemen!" He pointed towards the west and I saw a line of horsemen galloping along the path. They were on the northern bank. Perhaps they had come from the place Christof had mentioned.

I took action immediately, "Use your bows, all of you." Arrows would be more use here as a wounded horse would discourage riders. I cupped my hands and shouted, "Oddr! Horsemen!" I pointed to emphasise my point. I looked at the three Northumbrians. There were no weapons for them. I said to Christof, "Here is a sword for you!" I threw him the one I had taken from the leude. "Tell the three thralls to stay out of the way."

He spoke to them as he twirled the sword in his hand. From the way he spun it in his hand he was a warrior as well as a wanderer. The first of the arrows flew from Birger and the bowmen. It was a poor return from the first arrows. One horse was hit but not slowed. What it did do was to make the horsemen transfer their shields from their left hands to their right to protect themselves. It meant they had no weapons in their left hands.

Christof suddenly shouted, "It is time for me to pay back the Franks for their treatment of me." Before I could stop him he bounced down the gangplank and with the sword held in two hands ran towards the horsemen. His appearance came as a shock to the leading horseman. It also spurred Birger and the others. My brother shouted, "Bowmen, aim at the leading horse. Now!"

This time the arrows hit their mark and one struck the leader in the neck. I am not sure if it was a mortal wound but the arrows that struck the horse made it rear and in its rearing it overbalanced and the horsemen was plunged, along with his mount, into the river. The second rider stared in horror at his companion. I heard the cry, "Odin!" and saw the flash of blade as Christof the Wanderer hacked through the warrior's left leg. His horse joined the first and entered the river with the mortally stricken warrior. The others, having seen the fate of the first two and fearful of the wild man with the sword veered towards the trees. It was only a slight delay but it allowed Oddr and Asbjørn the chance to organise.

"Wedge!" There were just fifteen men in the wedge but, as they headed up the path the horsemen, there were just twenty of them, reined in. Birger and the bowman sent more arrows and men were struck. When Christof roared and charged them again then their resolve ended. Perhaps the first two warriors had been their leaders. They turned and fled. Oddr and Asbjørn joined Christof and watched the horsemen until they had disappeared from sight.

The Norns had been spinning. Had we not rescued Christof then who knows what the outcome might have been? I looked at the three Northumbrians. Would they prove as useful?

Chapter 4

It took time to load the ship and then row back to Bordèu. There was no time for talk but questions could be seen on the faces of everyone. I just concentrated on steering carefully down the river in the late afternoon sun. Things had happened so quickly that I had not even had time to take off my mail. We slipped quickly down a river that was eager to get to the sea. We tied up and the animals were taken ashore.

While they were unloaded Oddr and Asbjørn joined me. The four men we had rescued had travelled down the river by the steering board. Oddr smiled and said, "Now is the time for introductions. What is the name of this wild berserker who drove off a band of horsemen?"

I said, "He is Christof the Wanderer and like these three he was a slave of the Franks. Christof, this is Oddr and his shield brother Asbjørn. They lead the men of Bygstad for the hersir."

Christof bowed and said, "And I am no berserker, Oddr of Bygstad, but I did not relish being captured by the Franks a second time. Leif Wolf Killer saved my life and I wanted to repay him. I saw that the Franks had no weapons in their hands. It was a calculated move." He had a calm way of speaking. He was not given to angry outbursts and he always spoke with a smile on his face and in his blue eyes. The longer I was with him the more I realised that he measured his words. He also had, as I discovered, a sense of humour.

Oddr laughed, "It was indeed and these three?"

"These are Northumbrians who were enslaved with me."

Oddr looked at me and said, "Have you invited them to join our crew? We could do with such men."

"There has been no time."

Christof said, "For my part I owe you a life, Leif Wolf Killer, and I will happily join you. As for these three..." he turned and spoke to them. I noticed that the slighter of the three, the one named Allan, did the speaking. At one point he shook his head and at another pointed north. Christof turned and said, "They are happy to sail with you, Leif Wolf Killer, but they say that one

Dragon Rock

day they would like to return home to the land of the Northumbrians."

I looked at Oddr who nodded, "That suits us and when we return to Bygstad we will sail to the coast that is their home and leave them there."

Christof explained. Their smiles and nods showed their approval. I said, "But Christof, we need to teach them our language."

"Of course."

Oddr asked, "Apart from the bounty of men was there anything else you took?"

In answer I lifted the lid of the chest we had taken from the Frankish farm. The rest would remain on board. Oddr nodded his approval and then closed the lid. He took it and said, "We took another one from the town. We will take our share and I will take the rest to the jarl. He needs to know what happened today." Although the jarl had not raided with us he was entitled to his half of the treasure for we were his men and we sailed his ship.

I pointed to Joseph, "And we have the wife of a leude. Joseph can escort her to the other captives. Christof thinks that she can be ransomed."

"Leude?"

Christof explained, "It is what they call their lords."

"Good." He waved Joseph forward.

They left the ship and I called over Birger, "Help me to take off my mail." He did so and once relieved of the burden I stretched. I had not been hurt by the encounter and my mail and undershirt had protected me. I pointed to the slop chest and said to Christof, "In there are clothes for you and the Northumbrians. We took them from the Franks. They will be better than what you have. Birger, have Anders and Benni bring the chest of helmets and swords we took."

As the Northumbrians began to search for garments that would fit Christof asked, "Do you wish the sword returned to you?"

I shook my head, "We took it today and I have a blade that is special. Take it with thanks. Whilst I know you did not go berserk, you showed great courage and you saved the lives of some of our men."

He smiled, "It is easy to be brave when the alternative is to return to a life of slavery. I endured it once but no more." There was determination in his voice.

I left them to it and went with the ship's boys to examine the ship. I did not think that we had suffered damage but it was something that Gandalfr had instilled into me and I did it every time we docked. I checked each rope and peered over the side to look at the hull. We had not used the sail and so that was one task less. It did not take long to confirm that we had suffered no damage and I returned to the plank that led to the stone quay.

Dagfinn and Brynjar had begun to cook some of the food we had taken. One of the pigs was slaughtered and already the smell of cooking pig was making me hungry. Joseph had returned and he helped to make a stew to go with the pig's meat. The jarl and Lord Arne had deliberately left the bakers in the city alone and we had fresh bread each day. This type of raiding suited me. There were no seas to fight and we slept under cover. We had plenty of food and we had as much to drink as we wanted. Lord Arne had been right. Whilst we missed our families, wintering in the warm and living off the land kept us fed. If we just raided the land of the Angles or the Franks who lived closer to our home we would endure gales, cold food and frozen fingers. We had already taken more treasure in this one day than on the raid so far. These people were rich.

Oddr and Asbjørn returned with the news that our leaders were more than happy with both our news and the results of the raid. As we sat and ate from the pewter platters we had taken from the houses we had raided, and with the juices from the pigmeat running down our beards, Oddr told us what Lord Arne had told him, "He expects that the Franks will now come to remove us. There is no need to risk more men in raiding. Those horsemen who tried to stop us will have spread the word north of the river. We will defend the walls and make them bleed. When they realise they are losing men they will be forced to pay us to leave and have the captives returned to them. He will send his men out each day to scout for signs of the enemies but other than that we stay within these walls."

Dagfinn said, "And then go home?"

He shook his head, "We have to await the return of Snorri and then the plan is to go to the Blue Sea. If any wish to go home then the jarl will give them a trader. We have goods to send back to Bygstad. You can sail on the trader if you wish."

Bjarni said, "Lord Arne does not wish to make a quick raid and then return home. When we sailed south he kept speaking of the Blue Sea and the treasure of the east."

Dagfinn shrugged, "What do our two leaders plan?"

"As they have said since we arrived here, to sail to Al-Andalus." This was not something to be debated for each man would make his own decision. This was not a Thing but it was a place to make views known and Dagfinn had done that. I did not think that we had to make a decision quickly. It would still be many days before Snorri returned.

Asbjørn had refilled his beaker with wine. He was developing a taste for it, "Christof the Wanderer, we need a tale. Regale us with yours."

Christof was a natural storyteller and something of a show off. He happily stood and after downing his wine he began to speak. Some men tell stories which, no matter how exciting the theme, become dull in the telling. I think that Christof had the skills to make the raising of a mast seem exciting. I noticed Birger, in particular, watching the way he told his story.

"My brother, Axel, was the captain of a knarr. Along with five men from our village we traded with, first the men of Frisia, and then Frankia. We made a good profit for we were the only ship doing so. The *'Anya'* was fast and we had ten men to sail her so that we could take to the oars whenever we were chased. For five years that did not happen. It was when we sailed up the Liger that we were undone. We had traded well. The jet we had sold to the merchants was so valued that we were given a chest of silver. We left with the intention of picking up a cargo in the port at the mouth of the river and then returning north. The lord of that land was a cunning man. The Liger has many bends. He sent horsemen ahead and as we sailed down that river he had a chain placed across it. We did not see it until it was too late. The keel was torn from our ship." I heard the emotion in his voice. He felt the same about his ship as my father did about our snekke. Its destruction would have been like the loss of a family member.

Dragon Rock

"Only my brother and I made it ashore. A blow from a cudgel sent me into a black pit and when I awoke I was shackled. I never saw my brother again. I learned, as I began to speak their language, that he had been executed. I still do not know why I was spared but I swore vengeance." He turned to me, "The lord who executed him was the man who was going to take my head, Leif Wolf Killer." He bowed, "I am in your debt. He took me and other slaves back to the home where you found us. These three Northumbrians had been taken further north when their ship was taken by Frisian pirates. We have spent the last one and a half years suffering at the hands of these cruel Vasconians. I have a broad back and I was used as a pack horse." He gave a wry smile, "And I am now an expert in the clearing of dung and avoiding coating myself in it." He shook his head, "We do not treat thralls the way that they treated us." He bowed, "And that is our tale. If nothing else it is a warning not to surrender to these people."

Men applauded and he sat. They liked that he had survived and sworn vengeance. That was our way. If you hurt us then you would pay. I asked, "Why were you to be executed?"

Christof refilled his horn and after taking a drink he said, "That was the doing of the witch you took. She lusted after me. Whenever Lord Lupus was away, and that was often, she would try to get me to go to her bed. She wanted a child and Lord Lupus, well, he seemed unable to sire children. I was no fool and I did not fall for her charms. Lord Lupus knew he could not father children and if his wife fell pregnant…" He pulled his finger across his throat. "When he returned," I saw him calculating, "was it only yesterday? She told him that I had tried to take her. He flew into a rage and determined to have me beheaded. He wanted to do it in daylight and that also gave me a night to await my fate. Your arrival, Leif Wolf Killer, was timely. He had been with his cousin, the Duke of Vasconia, who had summoned his leudes. They were concerned about raiders along the coast. Not long before you arrived he sent his captain, Geoffrey, to tell his cousin that men had attacked Bordèu." He smiled, "Word of Norsemen on the river has spread." He gave a rueful smile, "I suspect that even if the witch had not made a false accusation then I would have paid the price for your raid."

Brynjar said, "I am surprised that you let the woman live."

Christof shook his head and clutched his Hammer of Thor, "When I said that she was a witch I was speaking the truth. She was a Christian but she spun, much as our volvas do. No, I would not harm a hair of her head. I would not upset the Three Sisters and, besides, if she had not falsely accused me then Leif here would not have been able to slay Lord Lupus." He smiled, "You know what Lupus means, do you not?"

I shook my head. Joseph said, "It is Latin, Master, and means wolf."

Silence fell and men fingered their hammers. Christof was right. The Norns had been spinning. I had been meant to save him. Dagfinn put his arm around my shoulder, "*Wyrd*, eh, Leif?" He waved his hand above my head, "I cannot see the spirits that are close to you but I know they are there."

I did not like the attention and the news had shaken me and I needed to ponder what it meant. "Will you sail home in the trader?" We knew that our leaders would offer berths to any men who chose to return to our homeland. I knew that if Dagfinn went then so would Brynjar. I was destined to stay as I was the navigator.

He smiled, "I do not know. Christof's story means that your presence here has attracted the attention of the Norns. If I sail home do I risk their displeasure? We have until Snorri returns in any case."

We would not be needed to raid but we knew that we would need to fight. The Northumbrians did not need a shield but Christof did. As much as he wanted to make his own there were no materials close to hand. Instead he decided to use the shield of Lord Lupus. He decorated it himself to make it look more like our shields but as it was smaller it would not be used on the side of the ship. The spike also marked it as different. The three Northumbrians had weapons but they had been sailors and not warriors. I knew that they would prove more useful when we sailed. They could not only row but they could also aid my ship's boys. Their coming would make my crew better sailors. *Wyrd*. Joseph was the one who taught them Norse and, in return, his language skills were improved. He seemed to have a natural skill in languages and learned them easily. The first week that they lived with us saw them able to communicate with us and I knew that soon they would be able to understand my commands and communicate with me.

Our raids around the local area were the first indication that the Duke of Vasconia had raised an army. We still sent men out each day to see if enemies were approaching. Some of Lord Arne's men clashed with his scouts and when they returned to Bordèu we closed the gates and prepared for a siege. We learned that at least one of our scouts had been taken and so the scouting ceased. We could ill afford to lose men. We had food aplenty for we had thrown out the extra mouths. We now had just our crews, the captives and those who made bread, ale and cooked our food. There were wells and the river gave us fresh water. We were confident. The walls of the city circled the heart of it. Lord Arne had his hearthweru guard the captives but the rest of us were allocated a place on the walls. Each crew had one third of the walls. There were three gates and we had the one on the northern side. We had ten men watch the walls at night and during the day another ten would take over. We spent five days watching and awaiting the arrival of the Duke of Vasconia, Felix.

When he did arrive it was with an army, half of which were mounted. Christof, who rarely left my side, laughed, "These men of Vasconia think that horses can win any battle. I showed that a man who does not fear them can defeat them." He was not boasting. He said it modestly. We had all seen the way he had done so. "How does he think that they will scale the walls?"

He was right. We had more than half of our men armed with bows. We had found a good supply of arrows in the armoury and if they charged the walls then the sky would be darkened by their flight. I was dressed in my mail and I had my spear. If they tried an escalade and used ladders to breach the walls then that would be a better weapon than my sword. I counted and studied the men before me. As Christof had observed there were as many horsemen as foot soldiers. I also noted that few wore mail. The fish plate armour seemed to be the style they liked. We did not. Even Birger did not want the leude's armour. He had asked if he could take it back to Bygstad and have Alfr melt down the metal and make it into a mail byrnie. I was happy for him to do so. My share of the treasure we had already taken would make me a rich man. I knew that when we returned home I would never need to go to sea again. I would not say that I would never leave Bygstad. The Three Sisters liked to weave spells and upset the plans mere mortals made.

There looked to be an army of six or seven hundred that were gathered outside the walls. We would be well outnumbered but I knew that it was not just about numbers. We had stout walls we could defend. We had captives we could use to bargain with and we had the means to escape. We had left men with the ships and there appeared to be no sign of a Vasconian fleet. We were not discomfited.

One of the jarl's hearthweru, Erik Three Fingers, came running down the walls. "The jarl needs Joseph the Healer. The Franks wish to speak."

Joseph looked at me and I nodded. He bowed and left. After they had gone Christof said, "Joseph is a thrall, Leif Wolf Killer, but he is almost like a free man. Had I enjoyed such freedom then slavery might not had been so onerous."

"He is not really a slave. If we ever near his home then I will land him and set him free."

"And where is his home?"

I waved a vague hand to the east, "Somewhere many leagues away in the Blue Sea. It may even be close to the place where the White Christ was nailed to the cross." I shrugged, "I cannot comprehend such distances."

"Then it is unlikely that he will be fully granted his freedom."

I clutched my Hammer of Thor, "Who knows."

"Aye, still, he has a good life and he is treated well. I have noticed that the crew are very protective of him."

"He has saved many lives and they know his value. I like him. He is a clever man."

"That he is."

Noon came and went. We took it in turns to leave the wall and to make water although some men used the walls to foul the ditch with both dung and piss. The baring of their buttocks brought angry jeers from the Vasconians. We ate at the walls and we waited. In the middle of the afternoon Erik Three Fingers returned. He was alone. "Lord Arne and the jarl need Joseph to stay with them, Leif Wolf Killer."

Dragon Rock

"Then the talks are ongoing?"

He smiled, "Lord Arne asked for the weight of the Duke of Vasconia in gold." Laughing he said, "He is as big as Einar Foul Fart." Einar was one of Lord Arne's crew and my men had joked that balancing the ship with such a one aboard would be hard. "The duke refused and will return tomorrow. Lord Arne knew they would refuse but there will be another offer."

"Thank you."

His face became serious once more as he spoke to Oddr, "The jarl says to keep a good watch this night. He fears the Franks may try to take the city under cover of darkness. They know the city better than we do."

"I had planned to do so already."

When Erik had gone Oddr said, "Steerboard watch first and then larboard watch."

"What about me and Christof. We are not in a watch."

"You will want to be with your brother. The two of you can watch with him."

"Thank you." I would be with the larboard watch. It meant Asbjørn was the watch commander. That was good. He had a sharp mind.

We did not return to the ship to sleep but descended the walls. The people who lived close to the walls had been ousted. Most had been evicted from the city. We slept in beds with a roof and with kitchens. It was a luxury.

Although Birger and the other young warriors had not yet gained any mail they now had much better swords and all had a good dagger taken from the dead Franks. Birger had the padded shirt worn under the mail from one of the dead Franks. It would not stop a blade but it might slow an arrow and would protect him from a blow by a stone. Had the two men wounded in the raid had such clothing they might not have been hurt.

"Sleep in your clothes. If we are roused we will have no time to dress."

Fritjof said, "You will sleep in your mail?"

"It will not be a restful sleep but I am a navigator and we are used to going without sleep. I will rest my body and it will suffice."

Dragon Rock

We were not woken by the sound of an assault in the night and when we were shaken awake by Oddr, Asbjørn and I roused our men. We took our weapons and went directly to the walls. As we arrived the men we relieved descended for food and sleep. Asbjørn was in charge and he spread us out. He took the gate and had me at the corner tower. I heard the hiss of water as men emptied their bladders into the ditch. I had Birger and Anders with me as well as my new shadow, Christof. We had our spears and our shields. Anders laid his down.

"Pick it up and hold it over your arm."

"But I do not need it."

I nodded, "Suppose we were going to attack the walls. How would we do it?"

I saw Anders screw his face up, "We would take out the sentries."

"How."

"With a bow or a stone."

I said nothing. Anders was a little slower than most. Birger shook his head, "And if you have a shield before you and a helmet on your head then the places an arrow or a stone can hurt you are lessened."

He smiled and picked up his shield.

I said, "Now, stand five paces from me on that side. Birger, five paces on the other. You look for movement. If you see a shadow moving then tell me."

We could see the pinpricks of light that marked the Frank's camp. If they came from that direction then they would be seen against the light. I looked to the black parts. If I was going to sneak up on the walls I would use the darkness to hide me.

It was not me who saw the arrow that came towards us but Christof, standing ten paces from us. He shouted, "Arrow."

I pulled my shield around to cover my whole body. Half of me was protected, in any case, by the wooden palisade that ran around the stone walls. An arrow slammed off the wall. Horns sounded. Each leader, Oddr included, had one. As the ones who had been asleep raced to the walls, stones and arrows began to rattle off our shields. I knew that the men on my section of the wall were protected but a cry from towards the main gate held by Lord Arne told me that someone had either been unlucky or

Dragon Rock

careless. I peered over the top of my shield. It would take a highly skilled archer or a very lucky one to send an arrow that might hit the gap between my helmet and my shield. I saw the men advancing behind oblong shield shapes. They were not shields as such but boards to protect the men advancing. I also saw ladders. The one thing we did not have were forked poles to push them away but we did have rocks.

I shouted, "Save your arrows until they try to ascend the ladders then we have them." I heard other warriors, further down the wall, wasting their arrows. The large, improvised shields protected the advancing men. I saw the first men appear in the ditch below me. We had been remiss in not clearing it and they planted their ladders. One slammed against the wall next to me. Men, at the bottom, leaned against it and it would not be easily moved.

"Ready with rocks and arrows." I laid my spear against the wooden palisade and hefted a large rock. The trick would be to wait until the men had climbed a little way up to us. Birger and the ones with the arrows sent them at the ascending men. The Franks held their shields above them but arrows sent at the side had success. I saw one climbing close to Christof the Wanderer. Fritjof sent an arrow to slam into his side. He screamed and fell but another continued to climb up the same ladder. The man climbing my ladder had two men below him when I raised my hands and dropped the rock. It was a heavy one and it hit his shield hard. He began to overbalance and, as he fell, took the other two with him. An arrow pinged off my helmet and I swung my shield around again. I had been lucky. The success of Fritjof's arrow showed the others how to do it and soon men began to fall as they were hit in the sides by arrows. That some managed to reach the top was clear from the clash of metal and wood. All we could do was to hold our section and hope that the rest did so too.

The horns of the Franks told us when the attack was over. We cheered and banged our shields. It was a victory. We stood to until the sun rose in the east and then it became clear that the Franks had no stomach for a continuation of the fight. An emissary who was bareheaded and with open palms approached the main gate. I was too far away to hear the words. Joseph was still with Lord Arne and when, a short while later we were given a message to allow the Franks to take away the dead, we knew what had been said.

I was still in command and I said, "The rest of you go and get some food. Birger and I, along with Christof, will watch this wall."

There was no danger. The Franks looked to have lost many men. I counted eighteen bodies close to our gate and as the main fight looked to have been at the main gate then the enemy would have been hurt.

Christof was in a good mood, "I enjoyed that. The Franks think they are the finest warriors but they are mistaken. They ride horses and that means they look down on men that they are fighting. That is always a mistake. Now we shall see the Duke of Vasconia make a more attractive offer."

"You are sure?"

"It is a rich land, Leif. The wine they make here is sent to Byzantium, Wessex and Saxony. The Emperor Charlemagne is said to enjoy it. They do not have winters like we do and they can grow crops when our homeland is covered in snow. It is their weakness. We fight harder because we are used to fighting nature."

We had lost men in the attack although not on our section of the wall. The Vasconians had made their strongest assault on the main gate.

I chatted to Christof while we waited, "Did you navigate with your brother?"

He shook his head, "I stood a watch for I can follow a course but he was the one who knew how to use the sun and the stars. He had the maps and charts in his head. I was the one who led the crew to fight."

"And was that often?"

"At first it was. There were pirates who saw our ship as an easy victim. I had a fine sword and good mail. We drove them all away and they learned to leave us alone. One day I would have such mail and such a sword." He patted the hilt of the sword of Lord Lupus. "This one will do but it belonged to Lord Lupus. Does your home have a swordsmith?"

"We do. Alfr makes good weapons."

Dragon Rock

"Then when we reach your home I will ask him to melt down this sword. I will have it tempered with some of my blood. That way the spirit of my enemy is contained in the blade and yet the sword will belong to me."

As we continued to watch I took in what he had said. He wanted to join our clan. It made sense. Those who lived in his world were now dead and he was reborn.

The Vasconians did not come again and that night we had our normal watch but we were undisturbed. We had another day before the emissary returned and this time he came with the Duke of Vasconia and a man dressed in fine robes. Christof said that the man was a bishop, one of the priests of the White Christ. There were armed mailed men who were behind the leaders. Haraldr One Eye and Einar Foul Fart came to fetch, not Oddr, but Christof, Joseph and me.

I had no idea why but we obeyed and we made our way down the fighting platform. As usual Lord Arne did not even look at us. The jarl said, "The Franks wish to speak to us. My cousin needs Joseph to translate. He understands most of their words but Joseph's translation will give him time to think."

I said, "But why Christof and me?"

"You because Joseph is your slave and Christof because the Duke of Vasconia asked for the Viking we rescued from the farm."

Christof said, quietly, as Lord Arne instructed Joseph in the words he would use, "I like this not. Duke Felix was Lord Lupus' cousin. This does not bode well."

As we walked down the wall I asked, "Have we lost men?"

Haraldr One Eye nodded, "A couple. They were young warriors. One was dragged from the walls and another was hit by an arrow. Both had swords in their hands. All is well, Leif Wolf Killer."

Christof's fears were confirmed when Duke Felix spoke. I had time to study the man for the conversation, in Frankish, seemed to take a long time. I understood perhaps one word in four. The duke had mail like his cousin but it looked to have been lacquered to make it look like gold. I knew it would not be. Gold was valuable but no one fought in such armour. His helmet was also richly adorned but, to my mind, was impractical. There were what looked like two wings at the side. In a fight they could be struck and the helmet torn from a head. The description of him was right, he was as big as Einar Foul Fart, however he looked to be taller.

Joseph turned and spoke, "The Duke of Vasconia will not pay his weight in gold for he says, Lord Arne, that you maggots are not worth it. He will, however, make a trade. He wishes the return of the man who violated the wife of Lord Lupus." I turned to look at Christof and wondered how the duke had learned of that.

Lord Arne asked, quickly and before Joseph could continue, "And why would we do that?"

In answer and almost as though the duke had been studying the men on the wall the guards parted and there we saw one of Lord Arne's crew, Ulf Larsson. He was on his knees and his hands were tied behind his back. His head looked bloodied. He lifted up his face and I could see resignation upon it. He was like Birger, a young warrior on his first raid. He must have either been the one who fell from the walls or one lost on a scouting expedition. Either way he had been taken.

Lord Arne looked at his cousin who turned to me, "You rescued him. It is your decision."

Before I could answer Joseph said, patiently, "Lord Arne, I had not yet finished. He wishes the wife of Lord Lupus also returned or this man will be executed."

Lord Arne frowned and snapped, "I might have let him have this man but if he wants the wife of a valuable lord then he can think again." He turned to Joseph, "Tell him that I have no intention of giving anything away. If he wants the wife of the leude then he has to pay."

After Joseph had translated, the duke looked to be furious and he turned and spoke. One of his men took out his sword and beheaded the luckless Ulf. The body fell in a pool of blood and the head rolled to stare at the walls.

Lord Arne turned to Haraldr One Eye, "Fetch me one of the port officials, the younger one."

We had the hostages and the remaining people of Bordèu in a warehouse. We all stood and watched the blood from the young warrior pool by his corpse. He would not be in Valhalla. There was no sword in his hand. He had been unlucky. Had he died when he had fallen he might have had a sword and now he would be in Valhalla. I could not help but touch my Hammer of Thor and pray for a better fate than the luckless Ulf Larsson.

The young man was dragged to the wall by Haraldr. He was little more than a youth. His occupation meant he did no physical labour and he had smooth hands. He was not a warrior like Ulf. His hands, like Ulf's, were tied behind him. He screamed in his language as he was brought. Ulf had remained silent during his ordeal. Lord Arne reached down for the rope that lay at his feet. At the end was a grappling hook. It was there in case the Vasconians used towers or rams to attack. He fastened a noose around the other end of the rope and slipped it around the young man's neck. The young man looked to be Birger's age. I saw that his smooth fingers were ink stained. The youth was a clerk and not a warrior. I saw the water puddling by his feet and knew that he had wet himself.

Lord Arne turned to Joseph, "Tell the fat bag of pig's grease that I will hang one of the hostages each day until the ransom is paid." He waited until Joseph had finished translating and then nodded to Einar and Haraldr. They picked up the young man who struggled in vain and then hurled him over the walls. They grabbed the rope and jerked. I think that the two were being kind for in their jerking they broke his neck and he had a quicker death than a slow one of strangulation.

"Tie him there and leave him." He turned to me, "Leif Longstride, leave your slave here. You and Christof the Wanderer can return to your men."

As we walked down the wall Christof said, "I know now how Lord Arne feels about me. I am disposable."

I said, "I think that Lord Arne feels that way about everyone who does not sail in his ship, me and our crew included."

"Yet you follow him."

I shook my head, "We are the men of the jarl and that is who we follow. That the jarl is under the spell of his cousin is another matter."

Oddr and the others had seen little thanks to the curve of the wall but they had heard the scream. We told them what had happened.

Bjarni said, "Lord Arne has one thing on his mind, becoming rich. Nothing will stand in his way. I just pray that the jarl asserts himself or we may all find a grave at the bottom of the Blue Sea and I do not wish to spend eternity as a screaming gull."

That evening Oddr went to meet with Lord Arne and the jarl. He came back with the news that we had been offered the duke's weight in silver. The duke had realised how ruthless his enemies were. Whilst still a compromise we would all be richer and as it would take some time to collect the ransom we could continue to search the city for treasure and to fill the holds of the two traders that remained. Lord Arne had been proved right. This would be the most successful raid made by our people. If we sailed home when we were paid then we would be the stuff of legend. I knew we would not be sailing any time soon.

Chapter 5

The silver took longer to be gathered than was expected. We did not mind. We kept slaughtering the animals we had taken in the raids. We had even found three Saxon thralls, women, who were able to brew ale for us. They had worked for one of the Frankish lords and done the most menial and demeaning of work. They were happy to be given something that they enjoyed. We promised them their freedom when we left. The three Northumbrians had told them that they were going home and they wished to join them.

The mood, however, amongst the hostages was tense. The young man hanged by Lord Arne had been popular and resentment brewed amongst the remaining captives. It was Lord Arne's men who guarded the hostages and they reflected their lord. I was glad that we were seen as unimportant by Lord Arne. He saw us as fodder for swords. We had no hersir with us and the jarl seemed happy to let his cousin make all the decisions. We kept to ourselves. I made sure that we had full water barrels and, thanks to our rescue of the Saxons, we had more than our fair share of ale. There were many barrels in Bordèu for they sent wine to Frankia and Wessex. The ale we put in them was not harmed and, if anything, it was imparted with a better taste. We were content. We caught fish in the river and we were well fed. It did not matter that we were, apparently, trapped in the port. As raids went we were well off. We scavenged from the warehouses and homes. We took barrels that could be filled before we left. We took ropes that could be used. We found treasure in the form of iron nails and trenails. The yards and spars we found were of no use to us. They were intended for Frankish traders and not Norse warships. We used the time when we were not on watch to take everything that might be useful. We even found some of the spices Joseph had said were worth more than gold. We stored them.

Snorri and the trader arrived back before the silver was delivered. He had a tale to tell when he arrived. As luck would have it I had returned to *'Ægir'* to check on the crew. All was well on the ship and so I slept aboard. Nils woke me, "Captain, there is a ship sailing down the river. We heard her sail flapping."

I did not think immediately that it was Snorri. My first thought was that it was an attempt by the Franks to end the conflict through a raid.

"Arm yourselves." I drew my sword and went to the prow for we were facing downriver. I saw the distinctive shape of a fat bodied trader and I relaxed immediately. It was not a warship. As it drew nearer so it became clearer it was Snorri's ship but when I saw a man at the prow I did not recognise I did not sheathe my sword. It was only when I heard Snorri's voice ordering that the sail be lowered that I relaxed. "It is Snorri. Be ready to take his ropes and secure him to our side."

I stayed at the prow so that I could speak with him. As the ship passed me I saw that there were not a handful of men as she had when she had left but there looked to be almost twenty men crammed aboard the stubby trader. They were warriors.

Snorri gave orders and the ropes were thrown. I caught one and Snorri beamed, "I thought you would have been abed in Bordèu, Leif Wolf Killer."

"I just wanted a night aboard my ship. That I am here when you arrived is good. I can see that you have a story to tell us."

"Aye, but it can wait until we are fed. With your permission we will use both ships as accommodation."

"Of course." I turned, "Lars, ale and food."

I went to the steering board. We would sit on Gandalfr's chest while we spoke. Lars brought us some ale and a platter with the remains of the pigmeat we had enjoyed that night. There was plenty left for it was a boar. The farmer who had lost it would be cursing the Norsemen who took it. I said, "Some of the men with Snorri will be sleeping aboard. Move the chests to make room and find skins for them."

"Yes, Leif Wolf Killer." He turned, "Nils, we have work to do."

When Snorri joined me I waited until he had drunk a horn of ale. His eyes widened, "This is good ale and it is fresh." I saw that the men he had brought, when they were given food and ale, stayed on the trader. There was more room on the deck. Snorri and his crew slept on ours.

I nodded, "Some Saxons made it for us."

"Saxons? I can see I am not the only one with a tale to tell."

I laughed, "You are my guest so you go first."

He nodded and Lars refilled his horn for him. "Well, the voyage back was both fast and without incident. We were welcomed in the land of Dumnonia for King Geraint has to contend with the West Saxons and they raid his lands. He was happy to be given the chance to trade with us. The weapons we had aboard were better than he had and the other goods were needed. He made an offer for me to bring to Lord Arne. If we would fight for him he would pay us."

"Mercenaries?"

"Aye, it is worth thinking about."

I pointed my horn at the men who, having eaten, were rolling into their animal skins. They were clearly either Norse or Danish, "And those men?"

"They had been employed as mercenaries by the king but only until such time as they could leave. When they heard of Lord Arne's raid they asked if they could come. They are warriors. There was no bad feeling."

"And their story?"

"Charlemagne now wishes to destroy all those he calls Vikings or barbarians. He has a fleet and they sail between Frankia and the land of the Angles. Any who are not Christian are killed and their ships destroyed. Danni the Dane and his men were survivors from a battle that took place off the coast of Dumnonia. They managed to beach their stricken ship and he and fourteen survivors were rescued by King Geraint of Dumnonia. Their ship foundered and was taken by the sea. They have spent the last six months serving King Geraint. When they heard of our raid they asked if they could join the jarl." He shrugged, "I can understand it. They need to be afloat and with Charlemagne's circle of ships strangling the passage south we were a godsend."

If there were ships barring the way home then it was a major problem. "That does not bode well for us getting back."

"I know, but there is a passage to the west of the land of the Angles. It means a more difficult voyage around the land of the Caledonians but it can be done. King Geraint let me view some

charts which I had copied. I will have Joseph make one for you."
I nodded. "There is more. The Franks have ships at the mouth of this river. We took longer to get back than I expected as we had to dodge the Frankish ships. There are many of them and they all seek Norse and Danish ships. We were lucky that there was a fog and we sneaked past under its blanket. They were looking for more drekar, I think, and not a Frankish trader. I also think that they were still assembling the blockading ships. There were just five there when we spied their masts. The jarl will have trouble getting out to sea." He held up his horn and it was refilled, "And now your tale."

I told him everything. When I told him the name of the man I had killed he grasped his Hammer of Thor. "And when the silver comes we will leave but bearing in mind what you told me that may not be as easy as Lord Arne thinks. He now has three more ships to serve him and they will each need a good navigator."

"Aye, for the sea is empty on the route I took. You could do it but there are few others who would be able to. I will give you copies of my charts when we leave." He yawned, "And now I will sleep. Tomorrow is time enough to speak to the jarl. I will do whatever is commanded of me but I confess my heart is no longer in this venture."

His voice sounded flat. The death of his brother had affected him more than he was letting on.

Snorri, his crew and the new warriors left for the Great Hall not long after the sun had risen. He asked me to ensure that the trader was ready for sea, "She is a good ship and I like her. She responds well to the touch and whilst not as speedy as a drekar, she is livelier than a knarr. I have called her **'Gandalfr's Heart'**. It is a good name."

"That it is."

She was the largest of the three traders that had been in the port when we had taken it. I noticed that the hulls of the Frankish traders were slightly narrower than our knarr. It meant less cargo but, with a good navigator, more speed. Now that our time in Bordèu was coming to an end we would have to think about manning them. However, what was uppermost on my mind was the news that the Franks would be waiting at the mouth of the estuary. It was a wide piece of water but our fleet of six ships, this time with masts and sails to mark their position, would be easily seen. I remembered the last time the Franks had tried to take us, at Guedel. We had suffered damage. If our lords and masters chose to take us further south then the last thing we needed was to do that with damaged ships. While the ship's boys went about their daily tasks I walked along the quay to examine the keel and the prow. The front of the ship was the place that there would be the greatest risk of damage. Christof had mentioned a chain. If they did that here then how would we avoid the fate of his ship? I studied the well-made bow. How best could we protect the front? Whatever I used had to be light for what we did not need was to make the front too heavy. Heavy seas could flood her that way. We needed a protection which would be light and yet effective.

 I missed Joseph who spent much time with Lord Arne. He was not a sailor but he had a mind that seemed to enjoy seeking the answers to seemingly impossible questions. He would have enjoyed the challenge and I know would have come up with a clever solution. His language skills would keep him from me until we sailed. It would have to be the mind of Leif Wolf Killer that came up with the answer to this question. I looked up and down the quay and saw nothing that would help me. I wandered into the warehouses to see what lay there. We had taken, already, the goods that could be sold or used. What remained were not without their use but we had decided to leave them. At the chandlers I saw the spare masts, eight of them. We had left them there because they were too short for our drekar and were too thick to be used as oars. There were other pieces of ship's furniture but they were for their traders and not drekar. The steering boards might be taken and used for the traders but they would not help me. It was when I came to the coils of thick rope that were used to tie ships to the quay that the solution came to me. These were not the sheets we had taken already to be used as replacements on our ships. The six ones I saw were thick hawsers. They were heavy and made up of smaller ropes bound together. I walked to one and picked it up. It was almost too heavy to lift but it was also thick and could absorb blows. I hefted the hawser on my shoulder and went back to the ship.

Dragon Rock

I studied *'Ægir'* as I walked towards it. I looked at the drekar as though I had never seen one before. The shields no longer lined the gunwale and I stopped to examine the hull. The advantage of the ropes was that they were long. I realised that they would fit along the gunwale and reach around the bows of the ship. All that we would need to do would be to secure them to the side. If we struck anything they would absorb the damage and our hull would not be torn. Even if they were ruined it would not matter as they would have done their job and could be discarded. If they had no hurts then they could be taken aboard and reused.

"Nils, Lars, go to that warehouse and bring all the ropes like this one. Place them on the quayside." I saw the questions on their faces. I smiled, "Humour me and obey."

As they hurried off I went aboard and dropped the rope by the prow. We had nails. That was one of the first things we had taken from the chandlers. There was a large box of them aboard each ship. They varied in length from some the length of my thumb to longer ones the length of my forearm. The ropes could be attached as we sailed down the river. It was as I placed the rope at the prow and stroked the figurehead that I remembered the attack from the Franks. I also thought back to the attack by the horsemen at the river. I smiled. I knew how to use some of the spare masts and make *'Ægir'* not only harder to sink but a more offensive weapon. When the boys had stacked the ropes I sent them back for two of the masts. This time they just obeyed. They would speculate and might even think that I had gone mad but I did not care. My mind must have taken lessons from Joseph for it felt as sharp as a seax's blade.

I headed for the walls at noon. Snorri had not returned and I was curious about the plans of the two lords. Would they change their minds about raiding further south and choose to head home? The silver we would take was a huge sum. A large part of me hoped that they would. There was a time that I might enjoy sailing further south but I had been away from my family long enough and now, I wanted to return home. I envied Mikkel. He would not be as rich as we would be when we finally reached Bygstad but there were riches that were not silver.

Dragon Rock

I joined my men on the walls. Christof was speaking with Oddr and Asbjørn. He got on well with the two warriors. He was an affable man and good company. His time as a slave had made him want to make up for the time he had spent alone. Oddr pointed to the Frank's camp. There was movement and I saw a wagon. "Could this be the silver?"

I said, "It might be but the reason for its arrival might not be a good thing."

The three turned to me, "Surely it is good."

"Snorri arrived back last night. He brought not only more warriors but the news that there are now ships at the mouth of the river. The Franks are blockading us. It seems suspicious to me that it took so long for such a rich people to gather enough silver to pay us off. They might have been waiting for them to seal off our escape."

Christof nodded, "Aye, now that you come to mention it that is true. Lord Lupus' cousin has much wealth. His armour and that of his bodyguards is the finest I have ever seen. They have eating knives, spoons and goblets which are made of silver. The wife of his cousin is a captive and we know how desperate he is to have her back." He grinned, "Duke Felix's wife, Duchess Mathilde, is rich in her own right but she has the face of a wild boar. The Duke Felix lusts after the wife of his cousin. The Franks will try to take back the silver and to take us."

Oddr said, "That is a risk, is it not? What if they sink us?"

Christof shrugged, "You are the first ships to raid. This will have come as a shock to them and they will not want a repetition. The last thing they need is for you to return home and encourage more men to come to raid."

Asbjørn said, quietly, "But we do not go home. The jarl wishes to raid Al-Andalus."

Christof showed his surprise, "A bold, not to say reckless venture. I have traded down there but we did it only once. The seas are more benign than the Great Ocean we sail but the men there have nimble boats which they fill with men. They do not care how many men they lose and they take any ships with those who have skin like ours."

Oddr said, "But it will be profitable."

"If you survive. We barely escaped with our lives."

I fingered my Hammer of Thor, "And yet, even though you escaped, the Three Sisters spun and you were taken anyway."

Christof laughed, "By Thor's Hammer you are a thinker. I can see that sailing with such a captain as you will be interesting."

I shook my head, "I am not the captain. That is Oddr. I am the navigator and helmsman. If Gandalfr had not been killed then I would still be taking an oar."

Oddr put his arm around me, "You were never just an oarsman, Leif."

Asbjørn pointed as horns sounded, "Look, they wish to speak." We saw the Vasconians approaching.

Christof smiled, "They have the silver. I think Leif is right. They had the silver all along but they wanted to wait until their trap was in place." He turned to me, "Did Snorri say where their ships were?"

"At the estuary."

He shook his head, "They will not be there now. They know were Bordèu lies and they only need to block one river." He pointed to the river, "This one. You might have been able to break past them at the wider mouth but at the confluence? We will have to fight to get out."

I do not know what the other two thought but I agreed with Christof. This all made perfect sense. If I was the duke then I would choose a place to attack that ensured victory. He intended to destroy our ships and display our heads on the walls of Bordèu.

The exchange took place that afternoon. There appeared, as the captives were all released, to be no attempt to cheat us of silver. The Vasconians had scales and the duke, without his armour, was weighed. We had a fortune in silver. Haraldr One Eye, clearly one of Lord Arne's chosen warriors, came to us. Oddr was summoned to the Great Hall but a short time later I was also sent for along with Christof. Haraldr One Eye led us there. He was not happy to be a messenger, "I am a warrior!" He shook his head, "I do not like sitting behind these walls. I like a deck beneath my feet."

Christof asked, as we walked to the hall, "How did you lose your eye?"

Dragon Rock

He shrugged, "I would like to say it was earned in combat but it was not. It was bad luck. We were raiding the Frisians and *'Nidhogg'* collided with one of their ships. A shard of wood flew up and took my eye."

The eye was an empty red wound and I said, "Why do you not wear a patch?"

He laughed, "Because this way I terrify those that I fight."

The hearthweru were enjoying ale and wine. There was much laughter and noise but the two leaders, along with Snorri and Oddr had serious faces. We approached and Lord Arne stood and bellowed at his men, "We have not yet escaped this Frankish land. Curb your tongues or leave. We wish to speak to these men." Lord Arne had a frightening reputation. I had yet to see him fight but I had heard that he had no peer in battle. All the hearthweru became subdued and a hush fell over the hall.

Jarl Bjørn Haraldsson said, "Leif Wolf Killer, Oddr tells us that your new warrior and you have ideas about the payment this day."

I nodded. Christof was new and so I spoke. I explained what he had told me and my conclusions. I saw Joseph, standing behind the jarl, nod his agreement.

Lord Arne smashed his hand against the table, "Treacherous dogs! I will slaughter everyone left in Bordèu and burn their port to the ground."

Jarl Bjørn Haraldsson shook his head, "Cousin, that is the worst thing we could do. For one thing it would tell the Franks that we were leaving and would be a marker for their ships. The blockade would know when we were coming." I realised that the jarl was asserting himself a little more. It boded well.

"Then what do you suggest?"

"That we sneak away at night." My voice sounded almost too quiet after Lord Arne's shout.

"And as soon as we do then the people we leave behind will tell those outside and they will send a signal." Lord Arne's voice was almost mocking as he dismissed the suggestion made by me.

Joseph coughed and Lord Arne and his cousin looked at him. I could see that the two men had come to respect him as much as I had during his time as a translator. The jarl said, "Yes, Joseph?"

He bowed, "My lord, if you release all the people from the city and then bar the gates they will not know we have left. We could leave whenever it suited us. By the time they entered the port we would be downstream."

The jarl turned to me, "This slave is worth his weight in gold. We shall do that."

Snorri had not spoken but now he did, "It matters not. They will have men and ships across the river. They might even have it barred with a chain or a rope."

Christof nodded, "That is how we were taken. They used an iron chain."

Lord Arne growled, "Then we would fight."

Snorri shook his head, "We have to do this without fighting so that our ships are not damaged for the traders have a long voyage home and if you and the jarl are to raid Al-Andalus then you need ships that are whole." I think that I was the only one who noticed Snorri's choice of words. He had said you and the jarl. He would not be raiding.

"That is impossible. We have to fight and break through a wooden wall of ships. There will be damage."

There was silence. I said, "There might be a way." Every eye swung to me. I was aware that the hall was silent. The hearthweru had been listening. They were as enthralled as they would have been had it been a song they were hearing.

"Go on." The jarl's voice was encouraging. I think if Lord Arne had commanded me to speak I might have been less confident.

"I think we can protect our ships with ropes tied around the gunwales and the keel. There are many thick hawsers in the warehouses. There are also spare masts from their traders. If we fixed them to our prows they would act as lances. It would be unexpected and they could cause damage to the enemy ships. If we angled them to strike down they would drive into their hulls. We use a wedge of three ships to drive through whatever defences they have."

I saw from the looks on their faces that they thought it was a good idea. The banging of the hands of the hearthweru on the table was also confirmation of their approval. The jarl said, "And as this has never yet been done it would come as a surprise. It could well work."

Snorri shook his head, "I think that this is an inspired idea but," he paused for effect and you could have heard a pin drop in the hall, "what if they have something in the water? It could be a chain, a rope or logs tied together with ropes."

He was right and I felt deflated. Christof's voice was filled with hope, "Then if you give me three or four men we could sail ahead of the drekar and eliminate any danger. We could sail in a trader. They have a smaller shadow and we could use the riverbank to disguise our approach." He gave a sad smile, "It is the least I can do for Leif Wolf Killer. He saved my life."

Snorri nodded and smiled, "That might work. I have sailed downstream. We could use *'Gandalfr's Heart'*. My brother would like that." There was a cheer in the hall.

Lord Arne said, "We leave as soon as we can. It cannot be today. We will send out the people in the afternoon of tomorrow." He smiled, "Tell the men that we will have a great feast. The Franks will hear what they want to hear. That will give us the day to make the changes that Leif Wolf Killer has suggested." He stood, "We keep our plans in this hall. You are all hearthweru. Keep still tongues in your heads." His words were filled with unnamed threats.

"Aye, Lord Arne." Every one of them chorused an answer.

There was a hubbub of noise and at the table where we sat, Joseph topped up our horns. Snorri said as we all thought about what we planned, "Jarl Bjørn Haraldsson, I will not be raiding Al-Andalus with you."

The jarl said, "But you are the navigator."

He shook his head, "I do not know those waters. You do not need my knowledge there."

Lord Arne nodded, "Snorri is right. We will all have to learn what the seas are like. Cousin, you could be the navigator. I am the navigator of *'Nidhogg'*. You could be the one on *'Byglja'*

I saw the jarl studying Snorri and he asked him, "Why?"

"I had time on the voyage to Dumnonia to think about Gandalfr and about myself. I would take the trader and return home. With your permission, Jarl, I would trade with the men of the west and give you a tenth of the profits." He paused and drank some ale, "I would be able to lead the other traders safely home. You now have more men to fight and there are those who wish to sail home." He glanced at me. "Leif has told me that the three Northumbrians wish to go home and they would be good warriors to protect the traders. It would satisfy all for you do not want to lose a large number of your crews to man the traders."

It was Lord Arne who made the decision. He smiled, "And that is a good idea. We divide the silver and other treasure into three. That way each of the three settlements will benefit." He nodded to Oddr, "Bygstad will have, naturally, the smaller amount." I knew why that was. The hersir was not with us. Had he been we might have argued for an equal share.

Oddr nodded, "Of course." The tone of his voice told me that he was not happy but he would not argue.

The jarl said, "Then I will navigate. We will spread the new men out in our two ships. Oddr, is that satisfactory?"

"We have enough men on the oars and we now have Christof the Wanderer. We are happy." I knew why he had refused the potential offer of more men. We did not know the mettle of these new men and he did not want the harmony of the ship upset.

As we headed back to our ship Snorri walked with me. "I might have stayed for you, Leif, but your idea to break the blockade shows me that you have the mind and heart of Gandalfr. He might have thought of that but I have too dull a mind. I will speak with your family."

"And I still have so much to learn."

"You have what is needed. Remember those things that Gandalfr lived by." He held up fingers as he named them, "Keep a tidy ship and tie things down. Check the ship every day and replace anything that is worn or might be worn. Teach your crew to be sailors and you will have an easier time. Most importantly, trust your ship. *'Ægir'* was built by my brother. His blood is in the keel and his spirit, even though he has gone, remains within." We were crossing my ship for him to reach his and he pointed to the steering board. "That is where he fell and there will be where his spirit is the strongest. Sleep there and know that when you steer and your feet are on the deck that he helped to build, he is with you."

Dragon Rock

I looked down and felt a shiver run up my spine, "Thank you. I shall miss you, Snorri."

"And I you but the Norns have spun and this is meant to be."

As Snorri went to **'Gandalfr's Heart'**, I felt as though I was being cast adrift. My father and uncle had been my rocks in Bygstad and since we had raided, the brothers Gandalfr and Snorri had been there for me. Now I would be left to my own devices. When I climbed aboard the ship and saw the dragon on the chest, the dream of the sea dragon came back to me. Was it good or ill?

Chapter 6

To ensure secrecy all the people who lived close to the port side of the city were removed. They had been the bakers and cooks. They were allowed to leave. Although they had not been mistreated I think that they were happy to be away from us. It was clear that we would be setting sail and I think they feared we would do something barbaric before we left. Snorri knew ships better than any and it was he who fixed the ropes in place. Once we had evaded the blockade they could be easily removed. The securing of the masts was a little trickier. They had to be placed at a precise angle. The shape of the bows ensured that the two masts would converge and each ship was slightly different. It was Joseph who worked out the best angle. He was clever. We used a couple of the longer nails we had found to fix them. Snorri was confident that once the masts struck, the force of the blow would shear the nails and the masts would drag down the bows of any ships we hit.

That done Christof told the three Saxons what he wanted them to do. They were more than happy to go along with his plan as it meant they would be leaving the land of the Franks and the voyage north would take them closer to their home. The Saxon women chose to go with them and that also provided two of the crew for the trader. Two of Lord Arne's crew wished to go home and they had grown close to two of the Saxon thralls. It was *wyrd*. The other two traders were crewed with smaller crews. They each had just four men on board along with thralls who chose to live either in the land of the Angles or in our home. The slaves who wanted to leave Bordèu had endured enough Frankish hospitality. We were seen as fairer masters. The three ships would be reliant on Snorri and his skills to get them home. He was the only real navigator amongst them.

After fitting the masts and sails we then loaded the traders and the three dragon ships. The holds on the vessels were opened and I made sure that *'Ægir'* was well balanced. We were like carrion crows. We took everything that we might need or want to use. The traders had holds that were large enough to accommodate pots, cooking utensils, bolts of cloth, sacks of

Dragon Rock

dried beans, amphorae of oil and wine and all the food that could be found. Anything that might go off on a long voyage would be eaten or salted. The day did not have enough hours for us. I hated deceiving my men but I told the lie that we would have a feast and leave the next day. As the crew were also in the port gathering what they could there was always a chance that the Franks who remained would come to hear of our plan. The jarl and Lord Arne, along with their hearthweru, continued with the illusion. They stayed in the great hall where they pretended to be drinking and to be getting drunker and drunker. When the Franks were released they would confidently tell the duke and his leaders that the Vikings would be too drunk to do anything. It might encourage him to attack the walls but it would not matter by then for we would be on the water and we feared no man when we were on the water.

We used most of the men, armed with spears and swords, to ensure that everyone who was still in Bordèu was sent through the gates towards the Frankish camp. Freed from their acting role the hearthweru, when the gates were closed, checked every dwelling. When that was done the three gates were barred and carts piled inside them. We would make it as hard as we could for them to enter their own port. Men were left on the walls as sentries so that they would think we were feasting. The reality was that most of our men were preparing for the voyage to the sea.

As darkness fell men made as much noise as they could whilst loading the ships. The illusion would be kept up for as long as possible. Snorri and his trader left first for they had to ensure that if there was a chain it was removed. We would not leave for at least an hour. We were dependant on Christof doing that which he had promised. Gradually, men boarded the ships. The handful who remained made even more noise and when the sentries were summoned they, too, sang and made as much noise as they could. When silence descended the Franks would think we were all asleep having succumbed to the drink. As Oddr said, they might even try to scale the walls but by then it would be too late. We would be heading downriver.

I never left my ship. I had too much to do. It had taken me a long time to balance the ship's ballast after fitting the rams. The crew all knew what they would do. Oddr might command on the land but on the drekar it was Leif Wolf Killer who made the decisions. Bows and bags of arrows were laid by the shields that ran along the sides of the drekar. While the crew would be at the oars we needed to have signals passed and to that end Joseph had volunteered to be at the prow. It was the most dangerous position but we needed someone who was both calm and clever. The ship's boys would be spread out between him and me to pass on directions. We would have a light from the stern to signal the others who would follow us.

We would be the leading ship in our nautical wedge. To that end we would head into the river first. We would be ahead of the other four ships. The other two drekar awaited the last of the hearthweru who would board at the last minute. When we were ready I gave commands. We untied the ropes and the oars sculled us into the centre of the river. We had to back water for the current wanted to take us to the sea. The other two traders would follow *'Nidhogg'* and *'Byglja'*. Both ships were held to the land by a single rope. I saw the last dozen or so men race for the two ships. The jarl waved. He was ready. The two traders were untied and we were about to embark on a race to the sea.

"Oars!"

I did not use the sail. The wind was not with us yet and we would have to row downstream but as the current was with us it would not be hard. I glanced behind and saw the other two pull away from the quay and take station on our steerboard and larboard quarter. That was all part of the plan we had discussed in the Great Hall. The idea was for me to strike the first ship. We did not know but we hoped that the other Franks would be panicked and if they moved to avoid our charge then *'Nidhogg'* and *'Byglja'* would be able to ram them amidships and that would sink them. The two traders and Snorri would have to pick a course through the debris that we knew would fill the river. It was thirteen miles to the confluence of the rivers and the place we had assumed they would try to stop us. If they chose somewhere closer to the sea then we would escape without the rams. Joseph would be looking to the steerboard bank. When Christof and his Northumbrians cut the barrier, if there was one, they would signal to Joseph and then follow in our wake. We

Dragon Rock

would pick Christof up once we were at sea. He had chosen his course and it was to follow Leif Wolf Killer.

The river was silent. When we heard the distant noise from astern I worked out that the Franks had broken into their city. They would search for traps and for us but no matter what they did they could not catch us. There were no ships left for them to use. Even horsemen could not match the speed we attained on the river as it sped to the sea. The men at the oars were pulling regularly. They were not exhausting themselves for they were to help me steer. I kept sniffing the air for the breeze which would fill our, as yet, furled sails. At the moment it was blowing east to west. When we reached the sea that would help us but until then the sail would be more of a hinderance. The wind was the weakness in the Frank's plan. We could keep moving but the ships that awaited at the blockade would need the wind.

The message was passed from Joseph. Lars was the closest of the crew to me. He said, "The trader is ahead. The barrier is clear."

I nodded. "Signal the others." We had a pot with a burning light hanging from our stern. At the moment it was hidden by a piece of water-soaked leather. As soon as Lars revealed it then the others would know and the light would continue to hang there to give the other ships our course.

A few moments later Lars said, "*'Nidhogg'* and *'Byglja'* are pulling closer."

I looked to steerboard and saw Snorri. He waved. He would join the other two ducklings who would follow the three bigger warships. They would have to use their sails and have to tack back and forth. I did not envy them their task. Soon, if we were successful, they would have not only the wind to contend with but spars and planks.

Lars had just resumed his position when the message came from Joseph. "Frankish fleet ahead!"

From now on it would be hand signals that we would use and we would need to travel at a greater speed. "Oddr, pick up the pace."

He began to sing and I stamped on the deck to give the beat. The crew joined in and I felt us surge forward. We were not as fast as we would be without the extra weight of the cargo, rams and ropes but we were going fast enough.

> *We are the clan of the otter*
> *We live where no one else can*
> *We fish the seas and water*
> *We serve the goddess Rán*
> *We are the clan of the otter*
> *We live where no one else can*
> *We fish the seas and water*
> *We serve the goddess Rán*
> *We are the clan of the otter*
> *We live where no one else can*
> *We fish the seas and water*
> *We serve the goddess Rán*

    I heard horns from ahead as we were seen and, perhaps, even heard. They would assume that their barrier would tear out our keels. Dagfinn was close and he shouted, "I see the logs in the river." I risked a glance to steerboard and saw the logs they had used as a barrier. They were floating towards the sea. Christof and Snorri had succeeded. If we touched them we would just brush them aside and they would be another obstacle, floating downstream, to damage the Franks.

    When I looked back to the prow I saw Lars pointing to larboard. I gave the slightest of adjustments to the steering board. A moment or two later he made the same sign. I moved the steering board again. When he put his hands together I knew that Joseph was happy with our course. I saw the ships ahead. They were shadows but their masts with the furled sails made them unmistakeable. The oars and the river were racing us as though we were on a headstrong horse. Arrows flew in the dark from the Franks. I prayed that none would hit the younger warriors who were closer to the prow. That was not the way to die. I heard arrows striking the deck. The boys crouched. I saw Joseph kneeling at the prow where he was afforded some protection by the dragon. I saw the Frankish ships looming closer. I would aim for the nearest one. There looked to be just enough room to pass between the two Franks before us if we ran in our oars. I did not need Joseph's directions now. I would use my skill and my eye. I

Dragon Rock

did not want to hit the ship bow to bow. I wanted a glancing blow. I turned the steering board a little more to larboard. I waited a few moments and then shouted, "In oars and brace!"

The ships behind would see my move and know what was coming. Their captains would make their own decisions and choose their own course. My task was to break the blockade and theirs was to exploit the breakthrough. The arrows were still flying but the sight of the dragon ship galloping towards them must have unnerved them for we bore a charmed life and I heard no one cry in pain. Perhaps the others, like me, had a woven spell that protected them. The crack when we struck was like Thor's thunder. I was prepared for the collision but had I not been holding the steering board I might have been knocked from my feet. The masts struck first and there was a terrible tearing sound. A few moments later our hulls ground together. I hoped the ropes would absorb the collision and prevent us being damaged. The bump was gentler than I had expected. The masts had absorbed most of the shock and, I guessed, caused the most damage to the enemy.

Snorri was proved correct. I heard Birger shout, "The masts are freed." I knew what he meant. The force of the blow had made the nails and the wood break. The masts were no longer attached to us and the Frank was holed. I felt the bows lift as the weight disappeared. The blow had succeeded in not only knocking one crew from their feet but also holing the Frank. I heard a second crash to larboard and knew that the jarl had rammed a second Frank. I did not have the luxury of time to observe it. I had to concentrate on the sea before us. I saw, in the darkness, that there were smaller boats beyond the larger warships. I shouted, "Out oars! Bows!" I would have to rely just on Joseph now and hope that his eyes would identify any danger. Those who were not on the oars would grab a bow and send arrows at the smaller boats that would be like dogs trying to bring down a stag.

I began to stamp my foot.

We are the clan of the otter
We live where no one else can
We fish the seas and water
We serve the goddess Rán

We surged through the water. We were more like a horse than a ship. As each stroke of the oars bit into the water, the bows, now freed of the weight of wood, lifted. We rose and fell. The current was faster here for the other river had added its power to the force that would take us to the sea. We still had many miles to travel but the river would be much wider and we could outmanoeuvre any Frank who tried to take us by conventional means. Seeing a dark expanse of water before me I risked a glance behind. The two other dragon ships had spread out. I saw two Frankish ships that were sinking and a third was trying to make the shore. It had been damaged. The other Franks were either turning or trying to rescue survivors. The three ducklings were in a second wedge and looked to be safe.

Suddenly there was a crack from the bows. Joseph shouted, "We have rammed a fishing boat."

I nodded. The ropes would have absorbed the damage but I would need to check below the waterline when next we landed.

Brynjar shouted, "Joseph, we have a wounded man."

I said, "Nils, get to the prow." There were no arrows flying and the boys needed to become sailors once more. I glanced ahead and saw nothing but water. "Oddr, you can slow down. Just one man to an oar and the rest can have some ale. They have done well."

Oddr shouted, "Slow the rate. One man on an oar." The men on the oars were shield brothers and they would decide who drank first. Oddr kept rowing while Angmar stood and went to the ale butt. Others did the same. I looked astern and saw that we were all whole and we were two wedges. The drekar sailed in a straight line but I saw Snorri weaving the traders to take advantage of the wind. If nothing else it would familiarise the two men skippering the other traders with their ships.

Lars brought me a horn of ale. I drank left-handed. I handed him back the horn. "Have the ropes removed from the gunwale and stored. We will have to wait until we stop to take the others down."

He nodded and headed down the drekar to tell the others. The ropes had served their purpose but now they were extra weight. The river had soaked them and made them even heavier. If we did not land soon then I would have them cut into shorter lengths. They could dry on the deck. In these waters the sun soon dried out anything that was damp.

It was not long after the hawser had been retrieved that I felt the change in the wind. It had moved from east to west to southeast to northwest. We could run in the oars. "Hoist the sail." As soon as the sail was filling I shouted, "In oars." The oars were run in, "Stack oars! Well done." They all cheered. It felt like a victory in battle.

We had made the run up the river to Bordèu in one long day and night. By dawn we were already nearing the mouth of the estuary. Rán had favoured us and the wind and current had sped us along the river. I spied a fishing village and a beach on the steerboard bank. We needed to remove the hawsers and it seemed as good a place as any. There looked to be little threat there.

"Oddr, I am going to land. There are people in the fishing village but I do not think that they will be a danger to us."

He nodded, "Front four oars arm yourselves. We go ashore."

"Lars, signal the jarl what we intend."

He stood on the gunwale and held the back stay. He waved to the north. After a few moments he said, "He has acknowledged, Captain,"

"As soon as we land have the rest of the ropes removed. Do so carefully. I do not want the ship to be damaged. Place the ropes on the deck. They will need to dry out before they are stored." The thick hawser by the gunwale had been easy to remove. The others were harder to reach.

"Aye, Captain."

Joseph and Birger joined me, "How is the wounded man?"

Joseph said, "An arrow to the shoulder. There was blood but his leather byrnie stopped the head from penetrating too deeply. A week or so and he can row."

"You did well, Joseph."

He smiled, "It was good to be useful but I knew I could not make a mistake. Your skill was greater. You hit the Frank at a perfect angle."

I shook my head and clutched my Hammer of Thor. Arrogance never pleased the gods, "Luck."

I saw the villagers fleeing. They took to the land beyond the shoreline. "Lower the sail." The fastest way to stop us would be to lower the sail, yard and all. I had timed it well. The boys and some of the oarsmen, now freed from their task, had the sail and yard down quickly. We ground up on the beach and Oddr led his men to check that it was safe. The boys leapt into the water and drove the metal stakes into the earth. When the ropes were tied we were fastened securely. I did not need to give any more orders. Lars knew what to do and as soon as the ship was tied to the land, our stern drifting out a little into the river, he and the others began to remove the ropes from around our keel.

'Byglja' ground on the beach next to me. The jarl had not judged it as well as I had and more of his ship was on the beach. Snorri had more experience of the drekar. The jarl was still learning how to handle his vessel. He would struggle to take her off. We might have to tow her.

"That worked, Leif Wolf Killer." He leaned on his gunwale as his boys secured his ship.

"The gods were with us and we suffered no damage."

He nodded and, after ordering the removal of the ropes, went to speak to his cousin.

Oddr came back leading a pair of goats. "Do we slaughter them or take them for milk?"

"Bring them aboard." I pointed to the fish drying on the racks. "We will feast on those."

Lord Arne had pulled up on the other side of *'Byglja'*. I did not hear the conversation but a few moments later the jarl came over to our side again and said, "We will not risk the Franks coming. When we have taken off the hawsers and you have your man aboard we sail south."

"Yes Jarl." It made sense. We might enjoy a hot meal after a row but the risk of being taken was too great. The plan had worked.

Snorri came with Christof and both climbed aboard. I had already given Snorri the things he would take to my family. I needed no treasure where we were going. He came to say goodbye. Who knew if we would meet again.

Dragon Rock

He nodded and smiled, "Gandalfr would be proud of you, Leif Wolf Killer. That was as smart a piece of sailing as I have ever seen. Your plan was a good one."

"And you, Snorri, have done all that you promised."

He shrugged, "I did little but sail down the river. Christof and his Northumbrians did all the work." I nodded. "I will miss you, Leif Wolf Killer. Know that until you return I will, when I am in Bygstad, watch over your family."

I knew that he and his brother hailed from Askvoll, "You would live in my village?"

He lowered his voice, "I prefer the hersir there."

"I am pleased and tell my family that as soon as my duty is done I will come home."

"Of course."

The jarl's voice drifted over, "It is time."

I nodded. We clasped arms and just nodded. There was much unsaid by words and spoken by eyes. Neither of us trusted our voices. The man who joined us together was Gandalfr and, while he was dead, he would be the invisible bond that would mark us as brothers of the sea. He left the ship and headed for the trader, his new home. Would we meet again?

I knew that I had been used in the river. Lord Arne and his cousin had allowed me to risk my drekar and the crew of *'Ægir'*. It was why I had led but once we began to head west, to confuse any who watched us, we were relegated to the rear. Lord Arne would lead and we would have to follow. We sailed west until the coastline disappeared and then we turned to head south. The wind, which had reverted to an east to west direction helped us and we would not need to row. I had my maps. Snorri had given me copies of all of his but no one, not even Lord Arne, had good maps and charts of the seas into which we would be sailing. This was a risky venture. If we succeeded then there would be riches beyond compare. They would dwarf the fortune we had sent home. The three traders had holds each containing chests of silver. Bygstad's was the smallest. However, if we failed then death was the option we would choose for the alternative would be slavery and the Umayyads, as Joseph had impressed upon us, were cruel masters.

I waved Birger and Lars closer to me. "I will need to be relieved at the steering board. I have chosen you two to be that relief. Between the two of you, you can learn to steer. Do so now while I make water. Birger, take the steering board. It is like our father's snekke but just a little bigger. Keep the other two ships in a direct line with our mast. Do not move the steering board too much."

I saw him lick his lips, nervously. He had steered the fishing boat at home but then there had just been a handful of men aboard. Now he had a full crew. "Yes, Leif."

Christof came towards us, "Leif, I can navigate. I would join these two as your relief."

"Of course." I could tell that my brother and the warrior we had rescued were both pleased with that decision.

I saw that Lars was relieved that someone else would be the first to hold the steering board. I waited until he had his hand on the board and then I went to the larboard side, dropped my breeks and relieved myself.

Joseph came from the prow. "Food, Master?"

I nodded, "And ale." The Saxon ale wives had spent the last few days using all the barley in Bordèu to make ale. We had a full barrel as well as water. The water would keep while the ale would not. I dropped the leather pail into the sea on the steerboard side and hauled up some seawater. The lesson I would give the two youths would be a short one. I would only risk letting them sail later, after the sun had passed its zenith. Then I would risk a sleep. I took off my clothes and laid them at the side. I doused myself in the bracing sea water. The sun would both warm and dry me. I sat on the dragon chest and Joseph handed me one of the platters we had taken in Bordèu. On it was bread, still slightly fresh, cheese, ham and grapes. The food would get worse until we raided again and we had no idea when that might be. This was a feast compared with what might await us. Even Joseph was in the dark about that. Christof had a slightly better idea for he had sailed the waters once but that memory was not recent. Lord Arne would choose the place we raided. I savoured the food. The bread was not stale and Joseph had smeared it with butter. The southern Vasconians had liked to use oil on their bread. We were more familiar with butter. We

Dragon Rock

made that at home and anything that reminded us of home was a good thing. When the platter was clear I drank the ale and then dressed.

A navigator learns to feel the sea and the weather. The wind was changing direction. I said nothing but I watched the jarl and Lord Arne. When I saw their sails flapping I looked up at the pennant flying from the mast head and said, "Birger, ease her a little to larboard. Just a touch."

He obeyed but Lars said, "The jarl has not changed course yet."

I smiled, never taking my eyes off the mast, "But he will."

Sure enough a few moments later the two ships ahead made the same turn and our masts aligned once more. I saw that Lord Arne had moved first. The jarl could sail but he was not a navigator. I hoped he was a fast learner.

Birger asked, "How did you know?"

Christof's voice came from the larboard quarter, "Because, Birger Eriksson, your brother is a navigator. He knew the wind had changed."

"You are a navigator?"

I looked at Christof the Wanderer and answered Birger, "Christof helped his brother. It is why he helps you now."

"However, Birger, there is world of difference between steering a ship in the day and navigating. Could I sail at night?" He shook his head, "Nor could I steer her in battle. My brother was the navigator. He could steer a course in the darkest of nights. I was the warrior."

"It is good to know. Lars, your turn. Birger, you did well."

By the time the sun was high in the sky and the wind had not changed for an hour I decided I would risk a sleep. Lord Arne had not headed closer to the shore. To all intents and purposes we were in the middle of the ocean but the land of the Franks and Al-Andalus lay to the east of us. Joseph had made me a bed on the larboard quarter.

"Christof the Wanderer, if you would watch these two I will risk a sleep." He nodded, "Birger and Lars, take turns and get used to the feel of the drekar. Wake me if we head southeast or, if we continue with this course, when the sun dips in the west."

"Aye, Brother."

Dragon Rock

I rolled in the wolf skin I would use. I covered my head with it to keep the sun's glare at bay. Facing the stern it was as dark as I could make it. The tension of the race down the river had taken its toll and I was exhausted. The oarsmen had, largely, spent the day dozing. Christof, Lars and Birger would enjoy a night of sleep but I would be awake. I was soon in the comfortable darkness of sleep.

I do not know where dreams come from. I had not learned to predict when they would come. Often, when I slept, images and faces would appear. They were normally my family. The face of my child was a blur for I had never seen him. Sometimes, and this was one such night, it was as though the gods were telling me a story or perhaps it was the Three Sisters giving me a glimpse of the future. I did not know the reason but that afternoon, rocked gently by the motion of a drekar flying over the waves, I dreamt.

It was as though I was in a cloud. I saw nothing. I felt the deck rising and falling but I saw nothing and I did not hear a sound. I peered ahead and saw, in the water, the snout of a dragon. Its eyes were black. It had savage teeth ready to rip out my hull. I turned the steering board but it seemed to take an age. We came so close to the teeth that I was sure I would be eaten and then the clouds appeared once more. I called out but no one answered. Then I saw three shapes manifest themselves before me. They were bigger than the waiting dragon. I tried to turn but the steering board seemed unwilling to move. The shapes became women and I saw that they were huge, old, time ravaged creatures. Even in my dream I recognised them as the Three Sisters. The largest of them held up a hand and spoke. I heard the words but her mouth did not move. The words came into my head, 'I am Verðandi, Leif Wolf Killer. Turn around and seek the cove. Heal your ship and return home. Your family needs you.' Just then her mouth did begin to open as though to swallow me but instead she blew and the clouds disappeared. The Three Sisters vanished and I saw a stand of pine trees and a cove that looked barely big enough for 'Byglja'.

Dragon Rock

"Brother!" I was awoken from the unfinished dream by Birger who said, "The sun is dipping below the horizon."

I leapt to my feet and looked ahead. The three ships were in a perfect line. I smiled, "You have done well. The two of you can sleep. Christof, take the steering board while I make water and then you can sleep too."

The two youths headed to their chests. Christof spoke as I made water. He did so in a low voice, "You dreamed, Leif Wolf Killer."

"Did I call out?"

"You did but I could not make out the words."

I took the steering board, "I saw a dragon and the Three Sisters."

His hand went to his Hammer of Thor. "They have chosen you."

I shrugged, "I do not know but even though I called out I think they were trying to help me."

He spoke, almost in my ear, "When the Norns do that then beware for there is always a price to pay."

I sighed, "Christof, you know we can do nothing about it. I know that I would rather be in Bygstad than sailing into these unknown waters but what can I do? This is not my ship and we serve the jarl."

Christof nodded and said, "Aye, I can see that I am part of this web too. We shall share the adventure."

"Let us hope that we can survive."

Chapter 7

For three days we continued our course into unknown and empty waters. Each night we would reef our sails and Lord Arne and the jarl would hang lamps, taken from the port of Bordèu, from their sterns. Each day the sails would fill and we would continue our journey. Part of the reason for our course was the wind. We took advantage of it and headed further and further south. The sun burned a little hotter here and men's skins reddened in its heat. Each day I would use the hourglass we had taken in Bordèu and with the wooden compass, plot our position. Joseph helped me to keep a chart that would guide us when we eventually turned for home. The blank piece of calfskin I used would become as valuable as gold once we reached Bygstad for it would give others a way to reach the riches of the south.

On the fourth day I was with Oddr and Asbjørn at the steering board. The men trailed fishing lines along the side for we augmented our diet with a fine array of fish. They were devoured uncooked and, fresh from the sea, there was no finer taste. Nils had just given us the three red-gilled fish he had caught and we were eating them when Harland shouted, "Land to larboard."

We could see nothing. He was at the masthead but I trusted my lookouts. Oddr tossed the bones over the side. We had known for some time that we were close to land for gulls were with us. They swooped to pick and squabble over the tossed treat. The spirits of drowned sailors appeared to be quite belligerent. They had not died in battle and were denied Valhalla.

Oddr joined me, "So it begins. Leif, you are the navigator, do you know where we are?"

I shrugged, "I know where Bordèu lies and how many miles we have sailed. I know that the coast of Al-Andalus lies to the east of us. I also know that it cannot be Africa for we have not sailed for long enough, other than that you know as much as I do."

Asbjørn asked, "But you could find your way home from here?" It was a question and not a statement. He was thinking of getting home. We were in strange waters and he did not want us to be lost for the Great Ocean looked huge.

Dragon Rock

I nodded, "Even without a map. We would turn and sail due north until we spied Wessex. The sun, even on a cloudy day, would guide us. Then we would sail up its west coast and round the rocks of Caledonia."

"You would not sail the more familiar waters of Frisia and Denmark?"

"No, Oddr, for Snorri told me of the fleet that waits in those straits. We broke through once but I would not try that again at sea. Hopefully when we do return home we will be laden and I would not risk losing our treasure." I smiled, "I can get you home, Asbjørn."

Oddr asked, "And then what?"

"I will see my family and see if we can make a brother or sister for little Leif. I will go fishing with my father and enjoy our newfound wealth."

"I meant will you go to sea again?"

I looked at the waters. They had been most benign since we had left Nervouster. There were no mountainous troughs and crests. We were not tossed about and the wind was helping us. Sailing was pleasant and I enjoyed the power of steering such a fine ship. "Some time in the future then aye but I would like to spend time with my family. My father is not getting any younger. When I left home I was not the man you see now. I have learned much and I would like to talk to him and my uncle. I am now a father and there were things I did not ask of them when I was a single man. That was a mistake. I want to know more about them. I thought I knew all that there was to know but now I know differently. I want to be a good father as they both are."

"You have grown wise."

"And you two, what about you?"

"You are right, we need to spend time at home but the silver we took, it beggars belief." Asbjørn's eyes were wide, "We lost a handful of men and made the Franks bleed hacksilver. Imagine sailing these waters with more ships. There is no one who could face us. We could take all that we wanted and become as rich as..." he had nothing to compare it with for in our fjord we were all poor, "a king!" We had no king but the Saxons and Franks did.

I knew then that while most of the crew would relish going home, silver and success had planted a seed in their minds. The seed would grow and it would mask the dangers and its flowers would promise more treasure. They would want more. I thought of Lars Greybeard, my father-in-law. He enjoyed his life and he was not a rich man. He was content. Who was right: Lord Arne or Lars Greybeard? Or was it that every man had to choose his own path? Were we all navigators of our own destiny?

The next day we turned and headed more south and east for now we had sight of the land. Within a few hours of dawn we saw the coastline grow from a thin line to rising cliffs. What we did not see were other sails or the smoke from settlements. Lord Arne changed course and sailed a parallel course to the coast. It was late in the afternoon when we saw the other two ships reef their sails and signal for us to close with them. With reefed sails we let the wind ease us next to the other two.

Lord Arne had a powerful voice but he cupped his hands to speak to us, "We think that there is a river to the east of us. We will sail due east until we reach it. We need fresh water and we need to know where we are."

We knew that there was now a kingdom in Al-Andalus called the Asturias. They worshipped the White Christ. Christof had told me that were was another river, the Porto and there was a land with a fortress called Portus Cale. It appeared to be the border between the Christians and the Muslims. I had told this to the jarl and, no doubt, it would influence Lord Arne's decisions.

He shouted, "Does your slave speak the language of these people?"

I turned to Joseph who shook his head.

"No!"

"Then we will try to enter the river and see if we can get water. We have enough food." The jarl and I nodded. "We sail in under reefed sails. It will be dusk when we reach the mouth of the river."

As we sailed Christof shook his head, "And that means we will be lit against the setting sun. Even under reefed sails they will see us."

"What do you know about these people, Christof?"

Dragon Rock

"That they are Christian and were strong enough to take the land back from their Arab conquerors. I do not think that they will have treasure and if they do they will guard it more fiercely than the men we fought in Bordèu. They have not had enough time ruling this land. I would just take water and then depart."

"That is all we have time for."

I could see that something troubled Christof but he said no more and returned to his bench. He had taken my oar next to Birger. I was pleased for he could continue to train Birger as I had done when Gandalfr had been the sailing master, a lifetime ago. I said, "Christof, instead of rowing, go to the prow to spy out danger."

Oddr had heard the words and the men were readied to land and, if needs be, to fight. I knew that the water in the river mouth would be too salty to be of any use. To ensure water we could drink we would need to sail some miles up a river that we did not know, in the dark.

I was happier with Christof at the prow. He could use his eyes, nose and his experience. I knew that Lord Arne and the jarl would be doing the same but this was my ship and I wanted nothing to harm her. The mouth of the river looked alarmingly narrow although it was not guarded by rocks but beaches. If we went aground we had the ability to float her off. We saw no buildings and there was no smell of woodsmoke. Once through the river's mouth I was relieved to see that it widened from four hundred or so paces wide to more than a Roman mile. There were no whitecaps to mark rocks and we edged sedately up the river. The reefed sails meant we had to have the oars manned by half the crew. The other half were armed and ready to fight but this felt even more deserted than the river we had used in Vasconia. As the river was wide and appeared to have no settlements we continued to sail up it. When the sun finally set it was though a curtain of darkness had descended. I ordered the sail to be completely reefed and we relied on the oars. The light from the jarl's ship guided us but it appeared to be moving away from us. I did not make the mistake of ordering more speed. There was no need.

Christof came down the centre of the drekar, "Lord Arne has stopped, I think there is an island."

"Slow oars. Let us edge in."

It proved a wise decision. There was no beach and trees overhung the river. I saw that the jarl and Lord Arne were in the process of anchoring as close to the island as they could manage without fouling their yards. I did the same but left a ship's length between us. When the anchors were out I walked to the prow and the jarl came to the stern of his ship.

He pointed to the river, "The water is drinkable. We can fill our barrels."

I pointed to the island, "And is there anything on the island we can take?"

"I do not know. We can explore it in the morning. This looks like a safe anchorage."

It did look safe but Oddr was taking no chances. He had men to watch at the prow and the stern. While the barrels were filled I took advantage of a night without a watch. I slept.

I woke just before dawn. It was Asbjørn who had commanded the ship during the night. After I made water I went to speak to him. He pointed to the other bank, "There is another island there, smaller. We did not smell smoke in the night. I think that if there is a settlement then it is further upstream. Dagfinn's watch caught some fish."

I roused Nils and Lars, "The two of you, swim to the island and see if there is anything there that we can eat. If there is we can land men and take it."

They stripped off and with a blade between their teeth lowered themselves over the side and swam the ten paces to the shore. One of Asbjørn's watch brought two silvery treats, "Fish."

I took one and used my seax to gut it. I threw the entrails in the water. It would encourage more fish and we would be able to catch them. The fish was small but sweet. I crunched the head and enjoyed the slightly salty taste. As the sun came up so more men woke. Oddr and I would not begrudge them their sleep. Everyone but me had endured a night watch.

The jarl came to speak to me, "Are your barrels full?"

"Aye, Jarl, and I have sent men ashore to see if there is food."

"Good. We will leave when the tide is right."

Nils came racing back and waved. I went to the prow to speak to him. "Captain, we have found food but there is a small boat on the north side of the island. They are fishing. Lars is watching them."

"Return to Lars. Wait near to the fishermen." I attracted the attention of the jarl. "There is a fishing boat on the other side of the island. If you were to sail around the north side and we the south then we could speak to them." I was never sure how Lord Arne would react to suggestions but the jarl seemed to have a more open mind.

"A good idea."

I said, "Hoist the anchor. Oddr, have the oars manned."

It took the jarl longer to be ready to sail and I waited. He had to be in position before us. When I saw him pass Lord Arne's ship I nodded to Oddr and the men rowed. As we cleared the island I saw the fishing boat. It looked like a fatter version of our snekke. They saw the jarl before they saw us and they immediately hoisted the sail to escape downstream from the dragon that appeared upstream. By the time they realised their dilemma they had almost bumped into **'Byglja'**. They stopped and waited. They would be terrified. Our dragon ships were well painted and the figureheads frightening. They lowered their sail and waited. Our ship nudged up to them and then I had the men back water.

I shouted, "Christof and Joseph, go and try to speak to these men. I know you cannot speak their language but the two of you know more words in Frankish than we do. Tell them we mean no harm. Find out all that you can."

Christof nodded, "Come Joseph."

The sculling of the oars kept us in the same position. Christof came back from the prow after a short time. "There is a town upstream. It is fortified."

I nodded, "Anything else?"

"We learned the name of this river. It is the Minho and there is a larger one further south called the Douro. That is a well defended river. They have a mighty stronghold there, Portus Cale."

Oddr had been listening, "Was he trying to put us off attacking them?"

Dragon Rock

Christof nodded, "He was but from what I have heard they are a fierce people and not worth attacking. I have heard of this Portus Cale."

"You did well to speak to them."

He nodded, "There were enough words we both understood and your slave has a gift for languages, Leif."

I looked at Oddr who said, "Then let them go." He hurried forward. I saw the boat raise its sail and head away. The jarl let them pass. We edged our ship closer to him and Oddr reported what had been said.

I saw Lars and Nils. They were at the side of the island and the trees there did not overhang. There was a small beach and I waved them towards it. "What did you find to eat?"

"Berries and nuts."

I saw that their hands were empty, "Were they good?"

Lars beamed, "Yes, Captain."

"Then swim back and board."

The jarl sailed back to confer with Lord Arne and by the time we had picked up our two crew the decision had been made. We would sail beyond the river called the Douro. Lord Arne was convinced that greater treasures awaited us there in the land of the Arabs.

That afternoon while Lars took a turn at the steering board I sat with Christof and Joseph. I said, "You spoke with the fishermen a long time."

Joseph nodded, "It took some time for me to find the common words. Once I did then between us we were able to understand almost everything that they said."

"And did you learn anything useful?"

Christof said, "That the men Lord Arne wants us to raid are a mixture of pirate and horseman. They sail well and rule the Blue Sea beyond the Pillars."

"Pillars?"

Joseph explained, "The name they gave in the ancient world, Master, to the water that separates this land from Africa."

"Then let us hope that we do not have to sail beyond these pillars."

Now that we had a better idea of the coast we sailed closer to it. We saw the entrance to the river that the fishermen had described. There was a stone fort at its mouth. It was defended and the fishermen had spoken the truth. I think it helped Lord Arne to finally decide that we would not raid there. I think he reasoned that in Al-Andalus there would be softer targets. The winds stopped being as generous and we made slower progress but we had food and we had water. Almost a week after meeting the fishermen we saw what appeared to be an island and a channel. Lord Arne stopped his ship as did the jarl and we drew alongside.

Lord Arne commanded us as though we were his ship and not the jarl's, "Oddr, your ship has the shallowest draught. Sail down the channel. It looks like it may afford opportunities."

Oddr shook his head. I was being insulted and he did not like it, "Lord Arne, Leif Wolf Killer is the navigator of this ship and he makes those decisions not me."

"He is little more than a boy and besides the ship belongs to my cousin."

The jarl had been placed in a difficult position. He was slightly in awe of his cousin but he respected the men of Bygstad. He called over, "Leif, do you think you could sail the channel?"

I knew my ship by now and I was confident that we could but I did not want to make it easy for Lord Arne. "We could but Lord Arne should follow closely in case we become grounded. He can tow us off."

"A reasonable idea, Cousin, eh?"

The answer was given with an accompanying scowl, "Of course, now get on with it."

I had the sail reefed and used just one man on each oar. Christof and Joseph stood on either side of the prow to look for shallows and we entered what soon became clear was, not an island but a marshy lagoon. Birds teemed on the shallow waters and I knew that if nothing else we would eat well. Birger and Lars came to the steering board. I said, "Birger, look for signs of houses. Smell the air for woodsmoke. I will be a little busy with navigation to notice such things."

"I will." He went to the mast and began to climb.

The channel headed east. My two lookouts used hand signals to steer me safely down the water. After a hundred or so paces I saw that the channel split and one arm led north but ahead I could see a wider patch of water. I chose the latter. The channel became as large as a tarn.

Christof shouted, "I can no longer see the bottom."

"Birger."

"There is a fishing village ahead and to the south. There are no more than a dozen houses there and they have boats drawn up."

"Then we head for the boats."

Oddr was next to me and he shouted, "Those not manning an oar arm yourselves. Shields, swords and spears will suffice."

As we approached we could see the panic amongst the fisherfolk. Grabbing children and driving animals, they ran. I shouted, "In oars!" when we were just thirty paces from the beach. I timed it right and we ground softly up onto the sand. The warriors leapt ashore and I waved Lars and Nils to take the stakes with which they would secure us to the land. They knew what to do without a command.

Oddr shouted, "Stack the oars. Join the others."

Oddr and Asbjørn led the men from the drekar. Nils and Lars looked expectantly at me. I waited until the current took the stern back into the lagoon. Once the warriors had left us we were lighter. "Drive in the stakes now." It meant we would float and be able to leave in a hurry if we had to. The delay meant that Lord Arne and *'Nidhogg'* ground next to us just as the first stake was driven in.

I was left with just Joseph, Christof and my ship's boys as the rest of my crew joined the other two crews to secure the village. We went to the beach and I sent the boys to find kindling. We would eat hot food. I waved an arm around the lagoon, "A pleasant enough place but hardly a fabled land of riches."

Christof nodded, "I fear that anything that is valuable will be well guarded." He turned, "Come, Joseph, let us see what they have left for us."

He and my slave left the ship as did the boys. I walked the drekar to check for damage. There was none and I celebrated our successful landing with a horn of ale. I had deserved it. That done I landed and lit a fire under a pot that was found in one of the houses. I used sea water and set it to heat. The sea water was

Dragon Rock

bubbling and the boys threw in the shellfish they had found as well as greens found in the small vegetable plots close to the houses. Joseph and Christof had been into the deserted village and found the pots as well as dried, salted fish and a salted goat's leg. I stripped the meat and threw the bone into the pot. The other two ships had been left with just their boys and they just lounged on the ship. I knew that the most senior of them would enjoy standing at the steering board pretending to be the helmsmen. It was what boys and youths did. They played at being the men they wanted to copy. Our crew would have hot food.

The water was bubbling away well and there was a good aroma rising when we heard the first of the men returning. It was Oddr and the crew of *'Ægir'*. Their spears were in the backs of the villagers that they had taken. They were mainly the women and the children who had fled and been easily caught. There were some youths but the men were not with them. They must have resisted. Oddr did not look happy. He waved over Christof and Joseph, "Tell them that they are now our prisoners." He shook his head, "What we are to do with them I do not know. Brynjar, take four men and guard them. I will have you relieved."

My shield brother nodded. Christof and Joseph went and spoke to the captives. They huddled together in fear.

Oddr and the others stacked their weapons. "Have you searched the houses, Leif?"

I shook my head, "Joseph and Christof searched the kitchens for anything that we could eat. I had food to prepare."

"Good. The rest of you, come with me and we will search the houses before the people return." He added, as Joseph returned, "Do the people know they are captives?"

Joseph nodded, "They are terrified, and will not run."

"Then you two come with us. Joseph and Christof you can show us where you searched."

I watched the captives. The women ranged in age from women who were toothless and grey, to their granddaughters. The boys were all younger than the youngest ship's boy.

Christof and Joseph returned at the same time. They had some food as well as pots and jugs but little else. Joseph said, "Poor as I have seen. Lord Arne will not be a happy man."

Dagfinn and Brynjar along with Erik Broken Nose and Bjorn Larsson came back with what they had found. They dumped what they had collected by the fire. It was a motley collection but I did not see the glitter of either gold or silver.

Christof said, "These people are not Arabs. They are the people who lived here before the land was conquered but as that was generations ago they do not resent their masters. They are left alone."

Dagfinn said, "Until we came. Why do we not go home now? We have treasure in the traders. We could catch them before they enter the fjord."

Brynjar shook his head, "Until we are released by the jarl then we stay. I like it no better than you do, Dagfinn, and if the hersir was here we might be able to go home." He shook his head, "I, for one, want to have vengeance on my uncle, Erland. That seems to me more important than this robbing of the poor."

There was no criticism yet I felt obliged to defend my uncle, "We chose Brokkr because he was a good leader and not because we wanted him to lead us to war."

"I know, Leif, but like Dagfinn I feel that we are wasting our time here in this land." The three of us had trained together and we could be honest with one another.

Oddr and the rest of the crew returned with a haul of pots, some copper coins as well as wooden furniture that would be used as kindling. The village had not been a source of treasure.

It was a good while later that the jarl and Lord Arne tramped in. I had sent for the boys from the other ships and commanded them to begin to cook. It meant there was some food for the two crews when they returned. The jarl and his cousin ignored us and ate together. I did not think that anyone would thank us for the food we shared with them. It was after we had eaten that Oddr and I were summoned.

There were no thanks from Lord Arne but the usual scowl, "We should have taken the channel to the north when we entered the lagoon. The good settlements look to be to the north of here."

Dragon Rock

The jarl was not exactly criticising me but I felt obliged to answer him, "This lagoon looked safer and I did not want to tear the hull from another ship." I did not point out that Lord Arne had chosen my ship because we were expendable and, having chosen me to lead, it was my decision to make.

The jarl smiled, "And it is a good place to make our home." He pointed to the channel that led north. It was not the one I had ignored but another. "Tomorrow we take, *'Nidhogg'* and the best warriors. We spied a town with walls and we will raid it. You, Oddr, will guard *'Ægir'* and *'Byglja'* and the captives."

Oddr said nothing for I knew he was angry.

Lord Arne was dismissive, "We will be away but two days and a night. When we return we will sail south with enough food and water to keep us and we will voyage into the Blue Sea." His patience was clearly at an end. He wanted more riches than we had gathered so far. He waved a hand for us to leave.

We did not move for it felt as though we were being treated as thralls. His eyes narrowed. The jarl said, quickly, "Thank you for preparing food. Your crew, Oddr, will have to watch the captives this night for the other two crews will need to prepare for a raid."

We nodded and left. Oddr mumbled, "We are now herders of men and not warriors."

"Let us make the best of it, Oddr. This lagoon teems with life. There are birds whose eggs we can take and flesh we can eat. There are fish for us to dry and," I pointed at the fenced area that was tended, "there is fresh produce for us to harvest. We can make cheese from the goats' milk and I think I spied some beehives. If we are able then we should make mead."

He clapped his arm around my shoulder, "The pot is always half full with you, Leif Wolf Killer. We will make the best of it."

The ship, *'Nidhogg'*, heavily laden, sailed north just after dawn. There were no waves in the lagoon and the waters would not capsize her. Some of the ship's boys and older sailors were left with us. Oddr organised the crew into three. One third hunted for birds and their eggs, one third fished and one third watched the prisoners. He chose Angmar and the younger warriors for that task. Christof went with the hunters. I had Joseph stay with the captives and my brother to learn their language. Lord Arne might bring back treasure that could be weighed but I wanted the treasure of knowledge. If Joseph could discover where the people of this land had treasure worth taking that would speed up our return home.

Birger, of course, was less than happy with his role as people herder. I tried to make the best of it, "Stay close to Joseph and try to learn their language. If you can speak some of their words then when we find ourselves close to a stronghold we might use you as a spy."

That appealed to his sense of adventure and he was a little happier. I had deceived him. It was not Lord Arne's way. He liked to use force of arms and not his mind to achieve what he wanted. Had he been at the farmhouse where Christof was bound then Christof, along with the wife of the leude and all the thralls would have been slain. That was his way. He would use his sword first and then worry about the consequences after. I believed that my way was better for we had gained the Saxons as well as Christof and they had enabled us to escape from Bordèu.

The Three Sisters were spinning still. Birger stayed to watch the captives even after his watch was changed. Anders came to fetch food for him. "Where is my brother?"

Anders shrugged, "He said he was enjoying the closeness of the buildings and he would spend the night there. He does not seem to mind being a watchman."

I wondered about that but dismissed the thought. I had a ship to worry about. I had the responsibility of watching the ships and I could ill afford the luxury of finding out why Birger was absent. Part of me worried that he was becoming distant. He had come on this voyage to be a warrior like me and all he had to show for it was a sword. I hoped he was not brooding. Bad thoughts could affect a man who was far from home. I checked that the ropes securing the ships were taut and that the stakes would not move. I went to the men making the mead from the honey we had found and ensured that they would also keep watch on the ships and then I went see the ones who were preserving the fish and the birds we had hunted.

When I returned to the fire I saw Joseph pouring ale into Christof and Oddr's horns. Oddr said, "Sit, Leif. You are working harder than any of us and that is not right. We are ashore and this is the time you should be able to enjoy life."

Dragon Rock

I nodded, "I know but Gandalfr and Snorri expected much of me."

"Sit." It was a command, "Joseph, pour your master some ale."

I sat on one of the upturned fishing boats and Joseph filled my horn and then waited at my shoulder. "And I am fretting about Birger."

Christof and Oddr gave me a quizzical look but Joseph smiled as he leaned in, "You need not worry about your little brother, Master."

"What?"

"He is content." He said nothing more.

Christof said, "Joseph, you cannot just make a comment like that and leave us hanging. What do you know?"

Joseph was loyal to my family and I knew he did not want to speak to any other than me but we had taken this carrot from the ground and we could not put it back. I said, "Speak. Oddr and Christof are friends."

He nodded, "There is a maiden with the captives. She had no mother and her father was slain by Lord Arne. She is alone and Birger took pity on her. She smiled when he tried to speak to her. The young woman is unhappy. I do not have many words of her language but she was alone even in this village. None of the other women offered her comfort. Birger did. He is showing her kindness."

Oddr nodded, "I remember the maiden of which you speak. Her father tried to protect his daughter. He was a brave man. He fought when the others laid down their weapons and he died well. Now I know why. There, Leif, you can put one worry from your mind."

I smiled, "Thank you, Joseph. Let me know how my brother fares."

"I will, Master."

Oddr and I were worried when, three days later, *'Nidhogg'* had still to return. We were about to sail *'Ægir'* to search for her when a voice called, "Sail, ho."

We saw the masthead of the drekar as she came down the channel. She was overloaded and the water was almost up to the shields that lined the gunwale. As she neared the beach I saw that some men sported wounds. "Joseph, your skills will be needed."

He hurried to fetch his medical kit.

The boys from *'Ægir'* ran to catch the ropes thrown from the drekar. Lord Arne and the jarl leapt ashore first. The jarl said, "We have wounded."

"Joseph is ready."

The two men strode to the fire and the pot with the bubbling stew. The jarl said, "Hot food. I am ready for this."

Oddr frowned. This was not the way a leader should lead. Oddr would have ensured that the men were all off the ship first and he would certainly not have eaten before them. The more time the jarl spent with Lord Arne the less we liked him. "Was the voyage a success?"

Lord Arne laughed, "Aye, the jarl and I have gold and silver in our holds."

He did not say that we would share in the bounty. Oddr's eyes narrowed.

I asked, "Do we have enough to go home?"

Lord Arne ignored me. As I was coming to realise he did not particularly like me. The jarl said, "No, Leif. The Blue Sea calls us."

"And did we lose men?"

"Yes, Oddr, six men died and there are another eight who have wounds."

"Then do we have enough men to face the dangers that we will find in the Blue Sea?"

Lord Arne stopped eating and wiped his mouth with the back of his arm, "We do and as your crew has yet to lose a man then you will have the honour of leading us through the straits. We sail tomorrow. Navigator, you will need your maps." We would be the bait and we would take the risks. Lord Arne would learn from our mistakes and our losses.

The jarl said, "And we will use your luck, Leif Wolf Killer, to take such treasure that men will speak of it long after we are in Valhalla."

What worried me was that we might be in Valhalla before we took any treasure.

"Yes, Jarl. And the captives?" I looked at Lord Arne.

"Leave them. They cannot do us harm."

I went to find Christof. He had learned some of the words of these people and as Joseph was busy, healing, he would be the one to speak to them. I waved him over. "Christof, we are leaving tomorrow. You can tell the people that this is the last night they will be held. Let them know we intend no harm to them before we leave." I wanted to leave with as little fuss as possible.

He shook his head, "They will struggle to make a living here, Leif Wolf Killer. The youths were just learning to fish and forage."

"It cannot be helped, Christof. Their men are dead and we cannot raise corpses." The people looked apprehensive as we approached. My eyes were seeking my brother and I found him. He was apart from the rest and his arm was around a maiden with long dark flowing hair and almond eyes. He would find it hard to leave them.

Christof spoke. He was halting in his speech. Joseph would have been more fluent. When he finished there were smiles. The exception was Birger who stood and, holding the maiden's hand, came over to me. "Brother, I wish to take this woman with us on the ship. Her name is Maria."

I shook my head, "You know, Birger, that we sail the Blue Sea. It will be dangerous for her."

My brother was now a different man. He no longer looked and sounded like a youth. He had come of age. "Leif, if she stays here she will be shunned and no one will look after her. Her father was not popular. She would die. I will care for her."

"Care for her?"

He put his arm around her shoulder and kissed her on the head, "I would wed her and make her my wife." It was a shock but Birger was not me. Who knew how a pretty face might affect a man? He had made his decision and I would have to live with it.

The look the girl gave him told me that she was happy for this. I clutched my Hammer of Thor for I saw the cross of the White Christ around her neck. I nodded, "Then bring her aboard this night for we shall leave early tomorrow."

Chapter 8

I had little time to think about my brother's choice of wife for I was tasked with navigating for our little fleet. Thanks to the raid on the fortified hill fort Lord Arne and the jarl now had a better idea of what lay ahead. We had more than five hundred miles of open sea to sail before we reached what Joseph had called the Pillars of Hercules. We had taken and filled water barrels from the village and also made mead. We had plenty of food but we were sailing into the unknown. Birger did not neglect his duties as assistant helmsman but that was largely thanks to Joseph who took Maria under his wing. He made a bed for her at the prow. As it was me who was on the night watch Birger could lie beneath furs with Maria and during the day, when Birger steered, Joseph would watch out for her and teach her our language.

As I stood on the steering board feeling the wind and the current I wondered what my mother would make of a Christian coming into our home. This was not the same situation as Joseph, who had come as a slave. This was the woman who would bear her grandchildren. She did not believe in the same gods as we did. How would she fit in? I put the thought from my head. That meeting lay lifetimes ahead. The winds did not help. I was loath to use the oars and so I tacked to take advantage of them. I was rewarded, two days after leaving the lagoon, when two dolphins appeared on either bow and seemed to lead us south. I took that as a good sign and when more benign winds blew the next day I felt more hopeful.

The other problem I had to contend with was the proximity of the coast. We had to keep it to larboard as we sailed south. At night, even under reefed sails, it was a nerve-wracking experience for we knew not where rocks lay. We were, by my rough estimate, halfway to the straits when we were surprised by ships pouring from the coast. It was not long after dawn. When the sun fully rose above the horizon, I saw that the coast was closer than I had expected. I had just put the steering board over to take us further west when Harland, who had just climbed to

Dragon Rock

the masthead and was straddling the yard shouted, "Ships, many of them, to larboard."

I saw the lateen rigged ships heading for us. There looked to be more than ten of them although it was hard to make out true numbers. I shouted, "Let fly the sail!" We needed as much canvas as we could manage. I turned and waved to the other two ships but I could see their sails being loosed. They had seen the danger too. The little ships were racing like hunting dogs keen to nip at the stags that would soon be at bay. I put the steering board to take us away from the coast.

Oddr shouted, "To arms!"

Glancing behind I saw that the other two drekar were copying my manoeuvre. I had worried that Lord Arne might seek glory and take on these enemies but he appeared determined to take the treasures of the Blue Sea, no matter what.

The sail filled but it was not yet pulling as much as I would wish. "Pull on the larboard backstay. Loosen the steerboard one." As my boys raced to obey me and while the warriors picked up bows and donned helmets, I adjusted the steering board. I had learned that getting the best from a drekar needed delicacy. When I looked ahead and saw the sail fill I knew I had judged it aright.

I glanced behind. Lord Arne was the better sailor. His ship was just three lengths astern of us but the jarl's sail was flapping a little. He was losing way. He was already five lengths behind Lord Arne and seeing his isolation the boats all converged on him. We were safe but if the two of us continued on our course then the jarl would be taken. I had many friends on his ship and I could not allow them to die.

"Oddr, the jarl is in trouble." I pointed and Oddr shaded his eyes. "Man the oars and we will go to his aid."

"Aye, we are oath bound, Leif Wolf Killer, but our lives are now in your hands."

I knew what he meant. I was risking our crew in an attempt, which might prove to be in vain, to save another. I felt the weight upon my shoulders. "Ship's boys, prepare to come about. When I give the command furl the sail faster than you have ever done so before."

They raced to the sheets. I knew they would not let me down. The men had their oars in their hands and they were ready at their chests. The oars were not yet run out and they awaited my command.

Joseph brought a terrified Maria to the stern. He gestured for her to sit between the dragon chest and the other chest. "What will you do, Master?" I gave him an irritated look for I did not have time for this. He said, "I have a vested interest in this for if you fail in whatever you plan then I will be a slave once more and the Moors, Umayyads and Berbers are fearful masters."

I nodded, "I will do what they do not expect. I will sail towards the coast and then, after turning, use the wind to plough into them. Their eyes are fixed on the jarl and Lord Arne. They can see that Lord Arne has abandoned the other ship and they will be overconfident."

"A good plan and thank you for sharing." He then said something to Maria and she smiled. I could see why Birger had lost his heart to this almond-eyed beauty. The jarl had corrected his course and his sail was now billowing well. He was not, however, outrunning the hunting dogs. They were fast little ships who knew these waters. *'Byglja'* would soon pass our stern.

"Furl the sail. Out oars." I began to bang my foot.

We are the clan of the otter
We live where no one else can
We fish the seas and water
We serve the goddess Rán

As the crew sang and pulled I began to increase the speed of my foot. We were not aiming for the small boats yet. I was still heading for the coast. I looked at the piece of cloth flying from the masthead. We were still sailing into the wind. The lateen-sailed ships were more than a thousand paces away. They had passed us and as their attention was on the jarl I doubted that any would be looking astern. I saw my chance and shouted, as I put the steering board over, "Loose the sail!" Such was the extreme nature of the move I made with the steering board that we heeled alarmingly to steerboard. Maria and Joseph had to cling to the chests.

I shouted, "Let Fly! Let Fly!"

Dragon Rock

As soon as the sail snapped and cracked we leapt forward like a horse about to take a fence. I wanted as much speed as we could manage but we also needed men to man the sides and loose arrows.

"Oddr, keep the strongest at the oars. Have the rest take bows. We are about to harvest sailors!"

He was laughing as he shouted his orders. Then he said, "If we survive this then my sons will have a tale that will have their hearts racing."

We were a well-trained crew and there was barely a missed stroke as half of the crew stood and fetched their bows. I saw the bowmen judging the range as they strung their weapons. This would be a finely judged attack. The jarl had his men lining the side ready to fend off his attackers. Already one boat, faster than the rest, had grappled his prow and there was the flash and clash of swords in the morning sun. The ship, tied to their bow, would act as a sea anchor.

The ship's boys were at the stays and they needed no commands to righten and loosen them to best effect. Nils was at the steerboard forestay and he shouted, "We are about to hit a boat."

I shouted, "In oars!" As the oars slid in I said, "Brace." I feared what the collision might do to *'Ægir'* but the fate of the jarl's ship lay in my hands.

We heard screams first and then the grinding of wood on wood. The bows came up and out of the water. Then we crashed down and there were even more screams. "Out oars!" As soon as the oars bit we raced on. I heard the sound of bowstrings as arrows were sent, not at the men in the water, but those in boats that were trying to get out of our way. I saw that the fight at the bow of the jarl's ship was over. The lateen-sailed boat was drifting away. I aimed our drekar for the stern of **'Byglja'**.

"In oars! Prepare to come about." My command was for the ship's boys who knew what I intended. We passed the stern of **'Byglja'** and I saw that it was Halfdan who was steering. The jarl was fighting. As we came about I saw that my seemingly mad charge had worked. Sinking one ship had made the others turn away and having lost the wind they had lost their only advantage. We were the faster ship and I pulled ahead of *'Byglja'*. As we passed I shouted, "Follow us."

I heard the jarl shout, "We will and we are in your debt, Leif Wolf Killer."

Some of the boats tried to turn and follow us but it was a waste of time. Halfdan had the sails trimmed well and we were both flying away from danger. Oddr and the crew banged their feet on the deck and cheered. Dagfinn ghosted up to me and said, "You showed Lord Arne what he should have done. I do not think he will appreciate the lesson."

"I long ago learned that this," I patted my heart, "is my best advisor. When I do that which it wishes all turns out well."

Once we had outrun our pursuers I had the sail lowered and we had changed to rejoin Lord Arne on the original course. He had not made any attempt to come to our aid. The problem was that there would be no time to have a meeting and clear the air for we had no plans to land before we passed through the straits. It would not bother me but I wondered about the cousins. By the time the sun had passed its zenith we were the leading ship once more and I was heading for the coast again. As soon as I saw the land to larboard I turned to run a parallel course.

"Christof, hold her steady on the course. I will go and see if we were damaged."

He nodded and took over. I went to the prow. After stripping off, I picked up a length of rope and looped it around the prow. Then I fastened it under my arms so that I was supported. Birger and Anders had come with me and they stood watching as I clambered over the side. Spray showered me immediately as the bow dipped and then rose over the waves. This close to the coast they were not the troughs and mountains that might have drowned me out in the ocean. I walked my way across and down. I kept one hand on the prow. I could see where splinters had been shaved off by the collision. When we had time they could be sanded smooth. I needed to get lower.

"Birger, throw me the end of a piece of rope. Get Anders and Lars to help you to hold it."

"Aye, Brother."

Dragon Rock

As he went to obey me I walked along the hull to the other side of the bow. It was the same story. There were just a few grazes. She could handle that.

"Here."

They threw me the rope. I put my feet against the ship and leaned back. It was the most frightening thing I had ever done. I had to trust my own knotting skills. The rope held me. I was still showered with sea water but I could live with that. I then tied one end of the second rope around my waist. When I was happy with the knot I shouted, "Lower me in the water. If I tug on the rope then haul me up."

"Are you sure?"

"No, but we need to check."

Birger nodded when he was ready and I slipped out of my rope harness and walked down to the waterline. I held up my hand and Birger and Lars held me. I saw no damage but it was below the waterline where the danger lay. I was about to signal to Birger to raise me when the two dolphins reappeared on either side of me. They leapt from the water and then descended. I took it as a sign. I waved and the rope began to lower me into the sea. The foaming force of water was almost too powerful and it twisted and turned me. I had to fight to hold my position but I managed. I could see nothing but I was able to run my fingers along the keel, seeking a crack. I found none. I pulled on the rope and I found myself rising. There were more faces than just my brother, Anders and Lars peering down at me. They all looked fearful. I shouted, once I had my breath back, "There is no damage on the larboard side. Give me more slack and I will test the steerboard."

This was much harder and as I slipped beneath the waves I had to fight the sea again and I feared I would not be able to do it. Suddenly, I was pushed in the back and I found myself in the right place. I had been under longer than the first time and I worked quickly. There was no damage. I pulled on the rope. My journey back was fearful. I bumped against the prow and I knew that I had taken skin from my back. Once my head broke water I gulped in as much air as I could. I was hauled aboard and landed on the deck.

Birger's face was filled with awe. He shook his head, "If I had not seen it with my own eyes I would not have believed it."

Joseph came over and said, "You are hurt. I will tend to it."

I nodded and said, "Seen what? I just went to check the hull."

Oddr had been watching and he said, "A dolphin helped you to round the prow. Did you not feel it?"

"I did but I did not know whence came the aid."

Birger said, "Rán was watching over you."

I nodded, "Aye, she was."

No one would let me dress or resume my duties until Joseph had worked his magic. That one act of some would say, madness, changed the crew. It was the talk of the ship for a long time. It was not only what they saw as my courage in risking the sea but the intervention of Rán that made them realise we were special. Perhaps it was a reward, some said, for having gone to the aid of the jarl. Others thought that I was favoured by the gods. Whatever the reason the crew all became much closer. There are always disagreements on a small ship like a drekar and often they can boil into conflict but that did not happen from that moment on. Whatever hardships we had to endure were all seen in the light of the dolphin that had helped the navigator.

When I finally took over at the steering board it was late afternoon. I had eaten whilst I was being tended to. By the time darkness fell we had reefed the sails and hung the light. I knew that within the next days we would reach the Blue Sea. As I watched, with just Anders for company, I wondered if Lord Arne would continue to use us as expendable bait once we reached the dangerous waters of the Moor and the Berber. That was a hard watch. My back, despite the salve applied by Joseph, hurt and I was tired beyond words.

It was the next day that the storm began to brew far out to sea. Christof and Birger were at the steering board and I was sleeping. They let me sleep longer than they ought to have done, for when they roused me the ship was moving more wildly than when I had retired. I looked to the west and saw the storm clouds there. There was, as yet, no rain, but the clouds looked to be laden.

"Reef the sail!" The boys hurried to make the sail so that there was the smallest canvas for the wind to hit.

Dragon Rock

By my reckoning we were still a day away from the waters that promised to be a little gentler. We were now committed to this course for the wind would drive us east. We had to continue and pray that the storm would not be as bad as it looked or that it would blow itself out quickly. I took the steering board. As I took it, I glanced astern and saw that Lord Arne had also reefed his sail. He was now three lengths behind me and the jarl's ship was so far away that it was barely visible. Christof and Birger had improved their skills when given the chance to steer but I knew *'Ægir'* better than any living man. I made the slightest of adjustments to the board and we moved a little easier.

"Birger, give me my sealskin cape and hat. Bring Maria here with Joseph. Make a nest for your little bird here." He nodded. The prow would soon be bearing the brunt of the seas and Maria would be soaked there. I also reasoned that she might take comfort if she was close to the man who was steering the ship.

Oddr made his way back to me. The growing strength of the seas was clear to be seen. He lurched along the deck like a drunken man. "A bad storm, Leif?" It was a question and I nodded. "What are our choices?"

I did not turn my head but jerked it westwards, "We could try to turn around and not broach and face the waves."

"We might capsize."

"Probably." I was having to almost shout above the noise of the seas crashing against the side. "We could hove to and run out a sea anchor and ride it out." He nodded, "Or, we could use the wind and let it push us east. It is the direction we wish to take."

"And you favour the last."

"It gives us a chance of survival." He nodded, "I cannot see the jarl, can you?"

He peered astern and, shaking his head, said, "I can barely see Lord Arne. He is rising and falling into troughs."

I had never seen the seas as high as they were. Even the masthead of the drekars that were following us disappeared under waves that were higher than a mast. The waves were crashing over us and soaking us with icy salty water. Even a sealskin cape was of little use.

"Then my plan is the only one which gives us a chance of survival."

Dragon Rock

"And you are aiming for a strait which you will barely be able to see and you know not where it is." We were having to shout above the noise of the wind. Men were tying down anything that might be swept overboard or would cause damage as it slid down the canting deck of the drekar.

I gave him what I hoped was a positive smile, "I have a rough idea and, unless it is nightfall, we should be able to see the land, even against the storm."

"Then, Gandalfr's heir, we are in your hands. What would you have us do?"

"Secure everything that can be secured, even the men and if I call for oars then they will need to be ready quickly."

He put his hand on my arm, "May the Allfather be with you."

"It is Rán who needs to watch over us and her husband."

He hurried forward and spoke to men as he passed. Birger and Joseph brought a terrified looking Maria to join me and Nils and Lars stood waiting behind. I saw that she had brought the bleating goat with her. "Make the nest between Gandalfr's chest and the chest with the tools. There is a spare sealskin in Gandalfr's dragon chest. Joseph, get under it with her." I was having to shout now and he just nodded. Between them they lowered the girl down and Joseph jammed himself next to her. It was not easy for the motion of the ship was so violent that men were falling to the deck. Soon they would have to tie themselves to whatever they could. For me it would be a battle against the storm. The chests were secured to the stern and would not move. Birger took the sealskin and, after kissing Maria, covered them. The goat gave a little bleat but I knew it would be comforted by both Joseph and Maria and give them the warmth of its body.

Birger smiled as he tucked in the sealskin and shouted, "Watch over her, Brother."

"You know I shall and take care of yourself. This will be a test of both our wills and our skill." I would have clasped his arm but I dared not take my hands from the steering board. I had to steer a straight course and avoid us being beam on to these seas. They would roll us over and we would all die. He nodded and headed back up the drekar. I said to Nils and Lars. "You two, stay by me. I may need your weight on the board and if anything

Dragon Rock

breaks then it will be you that tends to it. Tell Harland to watch from the prow."

They nodded and Lars shouted, as the wind screamed around us and Nils went to find Harland, "I have never seen a storm like this. Have you?"

I said, "Once. Now sit on the chests and hold on."

I had been in a storm although it had not been as bad as this one. It had been when I had been fishing with my father and uncle. Birger had not been with us and when the storm had blown up, this time from the land, he had headed out into the darkness of the sea and let the wind push us far out to sea. I had been terrified but my father and my uncle had told me to trust to the snekke. My father kept the snekke straight as an arrow before the wind and when it died and we were still whole, he turned us around and we headed back to our home. We arrived late and my father made me swear to keep the adventure secret. He did not want to frighten my mother. This storm was worse and I could not help but feel that this was all part of a spell woven by the Norns. The storm, the wind and the sea were driving us where we wanted to go but they were threatening to devour us. I had to keep us directly before the wind. If we deviated from that course then we might be swamped and sunk by the storm which drove us east.

I had my feet well apart. I smiled, Snorri and my uncle were made for such seas. I was too tall and I was not broad enough. I had to rely on my strength. The withies on the steering board were new and that was a good thing. The steering board had been made by a good shipwright and was new. If the withies were severed or the steering board broke then we would lose way and we would be doomed. The ship bucked like a wild horse but *'Ægir'* was not wild, she was my ship and was merely driven wild by the wind and the sea. She wanted to live and so long as she did then there was a chance for us to survive. She rose with the crests and then plunged almost vertically into the troughs that seemed like chasms. It was both terrifying and exhilarating. I had the fate of the whole crew in my hands. *'Ægir'* and I would have to be as one if we were to emerge from this chaos.

The rain began to pelt and it bounced off the deck. I was protected by my sealskin cape. There was a hat in my chest but

Dragon Rock

Birger had not given it to me. The hood on the cape kept the rain from pouring down the back of my neck but my face was pelted with sleety rain that would have been more at home in Bygstad than here close to the land of Africa. I knew then that the Three Sisters had sent this storm. Already my hands were like icy claws that clung on to the smooth wood of the steering board. There was a wrapping of rope I could use to keep a firmer grip but for the moment I was content with the place my fingers gripped. I could almost feel the heart of the drekar beneath my feet as she fought the storm and the sea. It was like the battle I had fought with the huge, mailed Frank. I took heart from that. I had survived and I prayed that my ship would too. If she did not then we would all become seagulls doomed to fly the seas forever. I comforted myself with the knowledge that the rain would fill the barrels. As soon as it had begun to rain the tops had been taken off. I smiled at my optimism. We might never need the water.

The rain pounded on my back as the storm intensified. There was no point in looking around for Lord Arne or the jarl. I could barely see the prow. I was trying to keep the mast and prow in line. That gave me, in the darkness, even in the blackness of the storm, my direction. I was helped by the men who huddled with their backs to their chests. They helped me to focus my eyes on the middle of the drekar. This storm would test the keel. I had examined the damage after the collision with the small boats and found none but if there was the slightest of weaknesses then the storm would find it. I took heart from the dolphins. The Three Sisters might have spun but the dolphins were a sign that the goddess of the sea wished us to live. I also felt, and I could not explain why, that Gandalfr was with me. My hands did not feel like my own. They felt as though another was keeping them fixed to the steering board. This had been Gandalfr's ship and part of him remained.

The sky was so black that, when night fell, I only knew because my bladder needed to be emptied. It had been long hours since I had done so. However, the rain began to ease and I took that as a good sign. As the wind lessened for a few moments, I heard from beneath the sealskin, the sound of Joseph singing some song in a tongue I did not understand. It did not matter that I did not know the words for the song was calming.

Dragon Rock

In the brief lull Lars said, "Is the storm ending, Captain?"

"Not yet but the wind does not feel as strong as it was and the bows are not rising and falling as much."

My face and hands were rimed with salt and my skin felt red raw. This was not the leisurely cruise that Lord Arne had promised. This was a storm that was trying to deny us entry to the Blue Sea. If I could have risked it I would have clutched my Hammer of Thor. A sudden rogue wave came from larboard and struck me full in the chest. I was almost knocked from my feet but I managed to remain upright. The wave smacked me hard and the spell made by my mother before I had left home pressed against my chest. I felt hope soar. If Thor could not help me then the spell woven by my mother and my aunt would. Birger had one too and that comforted me. Despite the wave the storm was abating.

"Lars, ale. My throat is as dry as a desert."

He clung on to my waist as he pulled himself up and held the ale skin to my mouth. I gulped down the ale. When I had enough I nodded. It was little enough but as the ale soothed my throat I thought I saw the sky becoming a little lighter ahead. There were fewer clouds there. The partial easing of the wind had given me the hint that we might survive. I suddenly laughed. The ale had eased my throat but now the need to make water was overwhelming. The wind was marginally easier. I needed a focussed mind.

"Lars and Nils, take the steering board while I make water." The two of them slid over and then stood. They grabbed the steering board. I said, "Hold the part wrapped with the rope and keep the prow and the mast in line." They looked fearful. I smiled, "You can do this and think of the tale you can tell your children when you become fathers."

Nils said, "Then you think that we will survive?"

"I know that we will survive." I sounded more confident than I felt for who knew what damage had been caused by the storm. "Now do you have her?" They nodded and I let go. My hands hurt as the blood rushed to fingers that had gripped the steering board for so many hours. I went to the larboard side, lowered my breeks and felt the joy of making water after holding it in for so long. It made me smile. I hurried back and took the steering board. "Thank you. Now drink some ale and resume your seats. The storm is abating but we have not the luxury of relaxing."

Over the next hours the storm grew progressively weaker. The skies were still dark but the rain had stopped. When a weak line marking the eastern horizon told me that dawn was almost upon us I said, "Nils, Lars let us risk a little more sail. Take out a reef."

I noticed, as they scurried forward to obey me that the ship was not moving as violently as it had. Oddr and Christof noticed it too for both came staggering towards the steering board. Oddr said, "Is the storm over?"

"Not quite but it is lessening."

Christof pointed to the sail which now had one less reef in it, "Is that not a risk, Leif?"

"If I am right then we are close to the straits. We will need steerage and I want to be able to control the drekar. At the moment we are at the mercy of the wind and the sea. *'Ægir'* sails better when she has some control." They both nodded. "When you are able let the men make water, drink and get some food. If I call for oars then I do not want men on them who have not eaten for almost a day."

Christof said, as Oddr went to the larboard quarter to make water, "And you must eat too." He shook his head, "You have a hidden strength, Leif Wolf Killer. I watched you in the storm and you barely moved. You were like a lonely rock. Your eyes were fixed and the storm could not shift you."

"You did not know Gandalfr but this was the ship he steered and he taught me. I felt his spirit in me and the drekar. I was not alone."

Christof touched his hammer.

As soon as the ship had more sail our motion became easier. It was still a wilder sea than we had seen so far but it was not the wild beast it had been in the dark hours of the night. That was manifested when men began to be able to move around the deck. They still sought handholds but it was easier.

"Nils, Lars, another reef."

"Aye, Captain."

When they came back and our movement was smoother I said, "Can you see the jarl or Lord Arne?"

Dragon Rock

They peered behind me and Lars said, "The sea is empty and the sky to the west is still black."

"Nils, peer under the sealskin and see how Joseph and Maria fare."

He did so and said, "They are sleeping!"

"Good. Now take out another reef and tell Harland to pull himself onto the prow. He can seek the straits."

I knew that a lookout on the masthead would give us a better view but the sea was still too rough for that.

When the sun rose we only knew because the sky was marginally brighter. The skies were still grey and filled with malevolent looking clouds. The seas were still white tipped and while the troughs were not as deep as they had been, this was still the time for caution.

Over the next hours the wind, which still came from the south and west, pushed us ever eastwards but our motion became easier. Oddr and Asbjørn joined me along with Birger. Birger looked meaningfully at the sealskin and I said, "They were asleep. You can wake them if you wish. She is your woman." He peeled back the skin and we saw that Maria was cradled in the old slave's arms. As the light struck them they both opened their eyes. When Maria saw Birger her face lit into a smile that brought a sunrise to the stern. She stood and they hugged.

I said, "Thank you, Joseph."

Asbjørn held out a hand to help the healer to his feet and Joseph said, "Despite the storm that was as comfortable a night of sleep as I can remember." Then his face became serious, "But I would not wish to endure such a storm again."

I said, "Birger, take Maria and Joseph back to the prow. The seas are no longer crashing over us."

As they left us Oddr said, "And what now?"

I glanced astern at an empty sea but one still filled with white tipped crests and troughs. There was no sign of any other vessel. I shrugged, "I would still stay on this course for those clouds tell me that the storm is not far away. We are on the edge of it and if we turn we might have to endure it again."

"We sail to the straits?"

"That was the plan. The alternative is to turn around and sail back into the storm to seek the others."

"Then what should we do?"

I sighed. Asbjørn was asking me to make decisions that would affect everyone on board. "When we reach the straits, we will stop and wait. We know that Lord Arne and the jarl will try to reach them. We have food and we have water enough for six or seven days at least."

"We just wait?"

Oddr turned to his shield brother, "He is right. We do not want to risk the Blue Sea without the others and we cannot seek them. Leif, could they be ahead of us?"

I shook my head, "We were the fastest of the three and the one with the smallest crew. They will still be in the storm. If Snorri was at the helm of *'Ægir'* then I would be looking for them even now but the jarl…"

Oddr nodded, "A good leader and a brave warrior but not a great navigator. Your plan is a good one. When we see the straits we shall wait."

I felt a sudden shiver down my spine. The Norns were spinning.

Dragon Rock

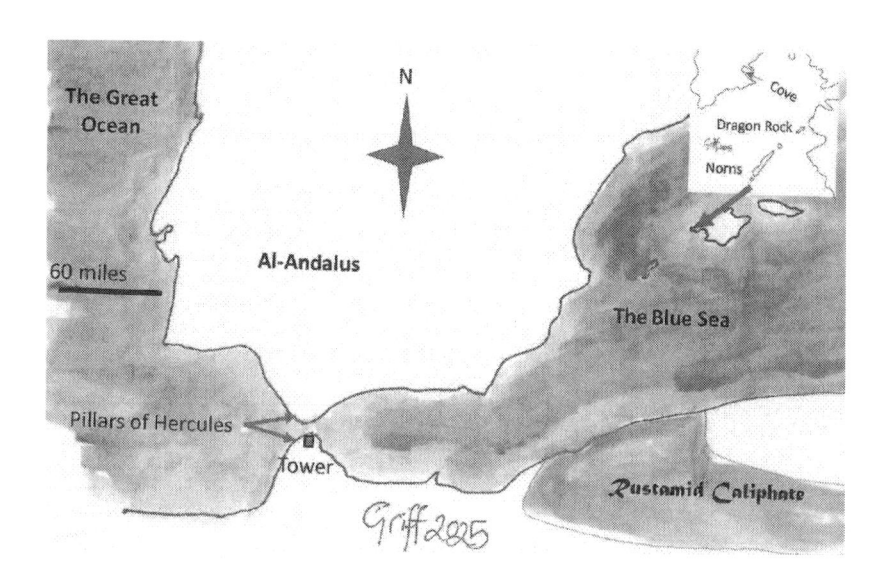

Chapter 9

I did not use any more sail. The wind was still strong from the south and west and pushed us, a little more sedately now, where we wished to go. I ate and my ship's boys went to check on damage. There were ropes that would need to be replaced but that would need to wait until the seas and wind were calmer. I looked to the mast, the sail and the yard. Alarmingly the yard supporting the sail looked to have a crack in it. The storm had been a violent one and the yard had twisted in the wind. The weight of the sail and the power of the wind had damaged what was, effectively, a new piece of timber. We had a spare but that was in the hold and we did not dare to stop to replace it. When the wind abated enough I sent Lars up the mast with some thin rope to bind the yard. Pine tar would have held it but the tiny amount we had was also in the hold and needed to be heated to be truly effective.

Suddenly Lars shouted, "Sails."

"Where away?" I was hoping he would point astern but, instead, he pointed to the south and west. I saw four sails. They were the lateen sails we had encountered before and they were heading for us. Sometimes you have to make an instant decision. I was the navigator and while Oddr was in command I needed to save the ship and the crew. If I turned and headed west, they would catch us. It would be the same if I headed due south. Our only chance was to risk the damaged yard and head north and east. We were due to head east, to the straits, but we were now alone. The jarl and Lord Arne were nowhere to be seen and as navigator I wanted to wait.

Even as I was about to give the order Lars shouted, "I see the straits!" He pointed. It was due east. The Norns had been spinning.

"Full sail! Oddr, oars!"

Oddr shouted, "Man your oars!" but he ran to me as he gave the command. "What do we do, Leif?"

"There are just four ships but they are behind us and to the southwest. If we try to head back towards the jarl we will struggle against the wind and they will catch us. They may be friendly but I would not like to gamble on that."

"No, I agree."

"The ships are to the south and west. With the wind the way it is our only chance to save *'Ægir'* is to break into the Blue Sea. We use the oars and outrun them." I pointed to the repaired yard, "The yard is weakened and I dare not try manoeuvres that might break it. If it fails then so does the sail and then we are doomed."

He looked astern, "And the others?"

I shrugged, "My concern is *'Ægir'*."

"Aye, you are right." He turned to leave.

I said, "Oddr, this will be a long and steady haul. Once we pass the straits then I will turn south and east. Unless they have oars we can lose them."

"And that will take us to Africa." I heard the resignation in his voice. Once we entered this Blue Sea would we be able to escape? We were in a trap with just one way in or out.

I kept my voice as calm as I could, "We need to find somewhere safe where we can repair the ship. From what Joseph has told me there are more empty places in Africa than anywhere else he has seen." I shrugged, "It is all that I can think of. We need to repair the ship and then worry about how to escape."

As soon as the sail filled we began to race. Had it still been the wind we had endured in the night then we might have heeled over and capsized. I pushed the steering board over as gently and slowly as I could. Luckily the wind had lessened and the water lapped towards the gunwale but did not flood over it and then *'Ægir'* righted herself. I kept glancing at the yard which creaked but Lars' repair appeared to work.

Oddr shouted, "Out oars." The oars were single manned. This was a long haul and we would keep a steady speed and replace the rowers. He looked at me.

I called, "Oars in the water and row!" I stamped my foot to give the beat. I glanced to the lateen-sailed ships and saw that they had not closed much since we had turned. Our oars would give us the edge. It was now a race and a test of my skills and of their captains. The advantage they had was that they knew the waters. They knew the pitfalls and the dangers. They knew where the rocks lay. My hope was in my ship which had a shallow draught and was lithe and responsive. Lars, Nils and Harland ran to me to await orders. "Harland, go to the prow. I want your eyes to watch for danger." I would normally have sent him to the masthead but the yard was damaged and I dared not risk his weight breaking it.

"Aye, Captain."

"Nils, take off my cape and store it." While he did so I said, "Lars, the yard?"

I saw the youth who would soon have to choose if he wished to be a warrior or a navigator as he wrestled with his answer. "The rope should hold it, Captain, but…"

"But I need to be gentle with it." He nodded. "The two of you stand by the stays. We may need to adjust them quicker than we normally would."

It felt better to be out from under the sealskin. The clouded sun might not have made the skies blue but the air felt warmer already. After the icy waters of the dark sea and the wind and the rain this felt positively balmy. I glanced to the ships that were pursuing us. They were gaining but not at a great rate. I knew that I could increase the speed of the rowers any time I chose but that moment was not yet. I could now see the land on either side of the straits. I had been told that the straits were wide. Some said ten miles and some eight. Both gave me a little room to manoeuvre.

We were not winning the race. The boats that chased us were as lively and fast as a snekke and their captains knew both the winds and the waters. The ships that had attacked us before had been packed with men. The vessels themselves were small but they posed a great threat. These would be the same. As we closed with the straits I saw that they were very wide; the trick would be plotting the best course. The closer I aimed for the centre the more chance they had of catching us. I took a decision. As soon as we had changed the rowers I shouted, "Faster until I say otherwise."

Asbjørn commanded this half of the crew. Oddr would take over when they tired. I saw that Birger and Anders were amongst the crew at the oars. My little brother would be sorely tested. As I banged my foot to give a beat, Asbjørn began to chant the saga of Gunnlaug the Worm Tongue and Raven the Skald. It was a long song but part of it leant itself to a fast pace and that was what he used. He had a good voice and the crew soon joined in.

> *Bade I the middling mighty*
> *To have a mark of waves' flame*
> *Giver of grey seas' glitter*
> *This gift shall thou make shift with*
> *If the elf sun of the waters*
> *From out of purse thou lettest*
> *O waster of the worm's body*
> *Awaits thee sorrow later*

I could feel the ship surge forward and after a few moments I looked back and saw that we had increased our lead. I gave another four renditions before I shouted, "Well done. Steady as you go!" The oars slowed to a regular pace that would maintain our lead and give the rowers a little respite although the muscles on their backs would be burning.

The smiles told me that they were pleased with themselves.

"Rocks a mile to larboard," Harland had good eyes. I saw his hand pointing slightly ahead of us. He must have seen the white foam marking rocks on the larboard side of the prow. I eased the steering board slightly to head more to the east than northeast. We would still be getting closer to them but I wanted the clear water beyond the straits to be in sight before I made my turn. I glanced astern and our pursuers had not changed course. They knew what lay ahead.

A short while later Harland shouted, "Rocks, four hundred paces, to larboard." This time his voice was urgent, almost fearful. I adjusted the steering board more violently. Harland turned and waved his arm to steerboard. When Joseph, also watching at the prow, made the same move I put the steering board hard over. Nils and Lars ran to adjust the sails which had begun to flap. Looking astern I saw that the move had lost us the gap we had created. I did not panic for I saw the wider expanse of water beyond the straits. It would be close.

Lars was on the steerboard side and he had just finished adjusting the back stay when he shouted, "Tower to steerboard." The sail had obscured my view of the headland. A tower suggested a structure for defence. I did not move the steering board. I waited until I could see the headland. It was more than a mile away but our course would take us to within five hundred paces of it.

"Harland, are there rocks to steerboard?" I called down the ship which was now silent. No one had the voice to sing and they were just sucking in air. Oddr and the replacements were all on the steerboard side staring at the tower.

Harland went to the other side and pulled himself up on the forestay and balanced on the gunwale. He turned, "No, Captain, clear water." My ship's boys had learned to differentiate between the two.

That meant the tower was there to defend the passage through the straits. Five hundred paces was too long for a bow but Joseph had told me of machines used by the ancient Romans and now the Byzantines that could send a bolt a mile or more. The tower would give elevation to the machine and, if they had one then, who knew the effect? I moved the steering board to sail more east than south and east. Immediately our pursuers caught up with us. I thought about ordering more speed. I would have to wait until we changed crews. By my reckoning that would be once we were through the straits and in the open sea once more. The slight change brought us more wind and that helped the rowers.

I saw movement from the tower. I saw the flash of colour and the light glinting off helmets. Shiny helmets and swords did not worry me but I wondered what danger lurked in the tower. We were, by my reckoning, six or seven hundred paces from the tower when we heard a crack like thunder. Every eye went to the stone structure. The bolt that they sent flew over the top of our mast and splashed into the sea a hundred paces from us. Even though it was fast we could see that it was the length of the body of Harland. If that hit us below the waterline then we would sink.

Oddr came racing down, "What in Odin's name was that?"

Thanks to Joseph I knew the answer, "A machine of war. We are in trouble. Have the oars double crewed. When you are in position I will order full speed."

He nodded and hurried back. Poor Asbjørn and my brother were exhausted already. This would be a hard pull. There was another crack and this time the bolt struck the water forty paces

Dragon Rock

from our steerboard side. They were getting the range. The crew were still settling into their oars. I moved the steering board to larboard to try to confuse those using the weapon. The crack told me the bolt was on the way. It flew alarmingly close to the front of the mast and fell into the sea just a ship's length from us. My slight adjustment had saved us but they were closer with each missile.

"Row for your lives." I began to stamp. The oars bit into the sea and we leapt forward. The sound of the oars in the water almost drowned out the next crack but I saw the flight. This time it struck. It did not hit the deck or the passengers but it hit the yard. There was a loud bang followed by a creak and then the sail and yard came crashing down to the deck.

My ship's boys and Joseph raced to move it for it had fallen on four of the rowers, one of them Birger. This was a disaster. The two oars were in danger of fouling the ones around them. Lars was quick thinking. He shouted, "Nils, pull the oars inboard." Between them they pulled the oars in and then set about tending to the men and the sail. We had slowed for a heartbeat but thanks to Lars we were now able to row once more. I glanced behind and saw that the ships which pursued us had closed. I pushed the board over to move us closer to the shore. Although it moved us closer to the tower it meant that they might not be able to see us properly. The lookouts had said no rocks and we were shallow draughted. I also thought that if we were hit again and started to sink we could get ashore. After a few moments and when there were no further cracks of doom I realised that the bolt thrower appeared not to be able to traverse or to change its angle enough to hit us. There were no more deadly cracks. The open water ahead was inviting. The ships behind relied on the wind. We were powered by warriors. Until the sail could be cleared we would not have full power but half of the crew were relatively fresh.

There was plenty of open water but the question was which direction would keep us safe? I headed south and east. That would mean the ships behind could not use the wind as well and if we rowed hard we might escape them.

We could only keep up this speed for a short time. Joseph had a clever mind and he joined Lars and Nils to free the yard and the sail. The yard was shattered and so the broken yard and sail were laid down the centre of the drekar. He called for Maria who hurried forward. The only one who looked hurt was Birger. He and Maria moved him closer to the prow. I heard Joseph say, "Lars, take an oar!" Lars was the strongest of my crew. My ship's boy obeyed. The healer had taken command.

They needed the beat again and I shouted, "Asbjørn, sing!"

As soon as he began and I stamped the beat we surged. I saw that we had almost passed the southern arm of the straits and I began the turn.

> *Bade I the middling mighty*
> *To have a mark of waves' flame*
> *Giver of grey seas' glitter*
> *This gift shall thou make shift with*
> *If the elf sun of the waters*
> *From out of purse thou lettest*
> *O waster of the worm's bedy*
> *Awaits thee sorrow later*

It took just four verses for the ships to fall back. We kept going until I could see that they had stopped. They were heading into the wind and did not have oars.

I shouted, "You can slow to a regular beat."

I knew that the hands of the crew would be raw and the muscles in their backs burning but they had saved us. Now it was my job to save the ship. We needed to get as far from the straits as we could. Who knew when the wind would change?

When I saw that Asbjørn and the ones who had been rowing the longest were tiring, I shouted, "Half crew!"

The relief on their faces was clear. The relieved crew went to the water barrels. Having been topped up by the storm the water was fresh. The ale would keep. When he had drunk Asbjørn joined me. He was puffing and panting. When he managed to find his voice he said, "Are we in trouble?"

I nodded, "We need shelter so that we can repair the yard. The men need food and we all need rest."

"You need rest. While we cowered before the storm we were not working and you were."

Dragon Rock

"When Gandalfr gave me the task I knew the burden I took on. I think that if and when we ever get to Bygstad I will give the steering board to another."

He laughed, "Bygstad is a lifetime away. The moon is closer."

While the yard was down and broken I could see that the mast had not been damaged. I wondered at that. Perhaps the damage to the yard had saved the mast. A broken mast would be harder to replace. "Nils, shinny up the mast. I need a deserted beach."

He bravely climbed. There was no yard upon which to perch and he had to cling on when he reached the top. Holding on with his right hand he pointed with his left. "Due south. There is a sliver of sand and I see no smoke from fires."

I nodded, "Come down and direct me."

We found ourselves sailing south. There were patches of sand that we passed but none was big enough for a safe landing. I needed a wide expanse of beach. There were other places with low cliffs. What I did not see was a single tree of any size. The ones that I did see were strange looking ones with frond like foliage. It was good that we had a spare yard for without it we were stranded. Our repairs, however, were using up all that we had. What we needed was a stand of pine trees and where would we find them here?

The closer we came to the beach the more hopeful I was. We had disappeared from the line of sight from the tower very quickly. The ships and the tower had seen us heading south and east. Nils' sharp eyes had made us take a direct course to the south and so I hoped that any search for us would be to further east of our present position. It was a cloudy day but I saw, ahead, the sun beginning to break. Visibility would improve. We needed a sea fret and that appeared to be unlikely.

"Slow oars. Asbjørn, you will need to take men ashore to see if it is clear."

He turned and chose his men. I saw that one of them was Christof. I wondered how he felt about our dilemma. He had fled from one danger into another.

Nils and Harland went to the prow with the stakes that would keep us tethered to the shore. I saw that Joseph and Maria still tended to my brother. I had almost forgotten him. Gandalfr and Snorri had experienced the same problem. They had to care for the ship before their family. I nudged us gently onto the soft white sand. Asbjørn led the men who would go ashore and they landed in the sea at the same time as my ship's boys. Oddr ran in the oars. I stayed at the stern. If there was danger then we would have to move quickly. Asbjørn and his men disappeared and I heard the sound of the hammering of the two stakes that would secure us. Joseph had said that in the Blue Sea there was little tide but I would have to make that judgement myself.

It seemed an age before the scouts returned. Asbjørn cupped his hands and shouted, "It is safe."

I nodded, "Oddr we need a fire and hot food. Dagfinn and Brynjar, we need the yard from the hold." I called to the boys on the beach. "Drive in the stakes as deep as you can and secure us."

Oddr nodded and said, "Go to see your brother. You have done all that you could for us."

I left the board and walked down the deck. Men patted me on the back as they headed to the beach. Already Lars was removing the sail from the yard. I said, "Can we use any of the yard?"

He shook his head, "No, Captain."

"Then it is firewood. We waste nothing."

Birger was sitting up and was awake. He had a bandaged head, Joseph said, "He will live but I would like him to rest for a day. You need not concern yourself, Master, Maria and I will tend to him. He can stay here."

Birger said, "Thank you, Brother. I know that you have saved us."

"Safety is a long way away, Birger." I turned, "Joseph, what do you know of this land?"

"It is part of the Rustamid Imāmate. The Umayyads who rule this land have local rulers who are given much autonomy. They are pirates and slave traders. If we are lucky they will be busy fighting one another but slaves such as us are valuable and females…"

He needed to say nothing more.

Dagfinn and Brynjar had the yard. I said, "Go ashore and search for trees. I doubt that you will find any for I cannot see any from here but we need to know."

Dragon Rock

Nils and Harland had come back aboard. "We need to fit the sail and lift the yard into place as soon as we can. The crew did well today but we cannot have them rowing again for so long. *'Ægir'* and her speed are needed."

I was exhausted but I could not afford the time to eat and sleep would be a dream for the foreseeable future. I smelled the fire as it was lit. The old yard had been used as kindling. The men ashore had set sentries and I saw men foraging for shellfish.

I shouted. "Joseph, see if you can identify food that can be eaten."

"Yes, Master." I knew he would not be happy to go ashore. He feared being enslaved by a crueller master than me.

Tiredness makes a man clumsy and the fitting of the new sail took far longer than it should. The smell, first of the woodsmoke and then the drifting aroma of salted meat mixed with fish made my stomach realise how long it was since we had eaten. The sun rose into the sky and the deck became so hot that it seemed to burn even through sealskin boots. It made us hurry but I suspected that the sand ashore would be just as hot. Maria rigged a shade over Birger at the prow and the two of them were cooler than anyone else aboard. They looked like cooing doves in a nest. It made me smile. By the middle of the afternoon we were ready to hoist the sail into position. I sent Harland ashore to fetch men to help hoist the yard and while he was away Nils and Lars took the opportunity of replacing every rope and stay. It was not wasteful. The old ones would be stored in case one broke. The storm had frightened me and I did not want to risk more damage through a frayed rope.

Dagfinn was amongst the ones who came aboard to help, as did Oddr. I think they both wished to speak to me but I was glad of their strength. With stronger arms than my ship's boys we soon had the yard in place. The sail was furled and I smiled for the first time in nearly two days.

"Well Oddr, we can sail."

He looked at me, "No, we cannot, at least not yet. You are too tired."

"But we are amongst enemies."

He sighed, "And if we sail we will still be amongst enemies. You are the sailing master but we need you to be alert and to use

Dragon Rock

your quick mind. We have scouted the land around and there are no people. Men have slept so that they can keep watch tonight. You can eat and have a full night of rest. We will leave when the sun has risen and when we have decided our course."

I looked at Dagfinn who nodded his approval of the idea, "Leif, Brynjar and I searched for trees. We found none that were suitable nor did we find tracks either of men or animals. We have landed on a desolate part of this land. Joseph says that there are many such places and, to the south of us, stretches a sea of sand. We were guided here for this is as near to a sanctuary as we could have found. Let us use it."

I wanted to do as they said and I nodded, "But I will sleep aboard the drekar."

Dagfinn laughed, "As if you would sleep anywhere else."

"But first I will check the hull." I had taken out the small pot of pine tar. It was too small a quantity now as we had used most of it when we had repaired the ship at Nervouster. I saw the split seam straight away. It was good that I had checked. The tar I had would be just enough to seal it.

"Lars, heat the pine tar."

"Aye, Captain."

"Nils, there are fronds on those stunted bushes that can be cut and used as a brush."

It took an hour to heat the tar and another hour to cover the wound but the pine tar covered the strake and I hoped it would dry overnight.

I walked along the beach back to the ship. It was my intention to climb aboard but my body refused to obey me. I do not know if it was the storm or the length of time at sea or possibly the sand but for whatever reason it was as though I had forgotten how to use my legs. I stumbled as I walked along the beach and Dagfinn and Oddr had to support me when I began to fall. My legs would not move. I saw the looks of concern as we neared the fire. I felt foolish. I was not wounded. The fire and the pot were close to some rocks which made convenient seats. I was lowered gently, like an invalid, to sit on one.

Joseph came over, "What ails you, Master?" He gave me a horn of ale.

I said quietly, "I know not, Joseph, but I cannot use my legs." I drank the ale which tasted like nectar.

He smiled, "You stood for more than a day and this hot sun is not what you are used to. I think that a night of sleep will see a full recovery."

I looked at him, "You think a sleep will help me to recover?"

"Of course. A man cannot do what you did in that storm and not suffer as a result. I slept for most of the time and yet I still felt as tired as I had ever felt. You had the burden of the ship on your shoulders." He saw my angry look and sighed, "Master, there is danger in this land and on this water. But right here and now we are safe. When we leave then there will be danger and the others are right. Leif the Wolf Killer will need to be at his best to help us to survive."

He was saying what Oddr and Dagfinn had and they were all right. It made sense and the walk from the ship had made me feel like a newborn lamb. "Then bring me food."

There was a surprisingly good mood around the fire as we ate. We had lost no one and that was a miracle. It was when we spoke of the other ships that the mood darkened, "We have not seen either of the other ships. Have we been abandoned?" Falco's words reflected the view in the crew. Others began to voice their disquiet and I sensed ill feeling creeping into the camp.

I was full and, if truth be told, ready for sleep, but I needed to calm the fears of the others, "Falco, there are a dozen or more explanations of where the other two ships are. We can speculate as much as we like but the truth is we do not know. They could have turned to ride out the storm. They could have followed us but be further north. I know that when Lord Arne spoke of this raid he wanted to sail north once we passed through the straits."

Oddr nodded, "Aye, he did and Leif is right. We are on our own." He smiled, "We no longer have to do what the jarl and Lord Arne decide. We make our own decisions."

In an instant the pot was no longer half empty but had become, miraculously, half full. "We could go home!"

Oddr nodded, "Aye, Frode. We could." Frode was like me. He had a young family he was desperate to see.

Falco asked, "Leif, you are the navigator, what do you say?"

Every eye swivelled to me, "I would like to go home. Leif Leifsson awaits his father and my mother and father do not know that Birger has found a woman." That made them all smile. Birger and Maria were aboard the ship but everyone approved the joy that they shared.

Oddr said, "So, Leif and his crew apart, we will all stand a watch this night and on the morrow we sail. It will not be easy to pass through the straits with that tower and that machine they use but we can only try."

I said, "I had almost forgotten the tower but there is a solution. We sail north and east for a day and then sail west to pass through the straits when it is dark. They saw us on the way here because it was daylight."

Oddr clapped me on the back, "And that is what we need, Leif, your mind as sharp as ever. Now return to the ship and sleep. Let us bear the burden of this watch as you did in the storm."

Birger and Maria were standing when my ship's boys and Joseph followed me aboard the drekar. They were looking west to the setting sun. It seemed to be setting the sea on fire. Birger must have seen my earlier stumble for he said, "Should he be standing, Joseph?"

My slave nodded, "He has rested enough and his colour had returned. This is good. Now is the time, Master, for you to sleep. I have a potion if you wish."

Shaking my head I said, "As soon as I lie down I will be asleep."

When I reached the stern I saw that Nils and Lars had made a bed between the chests for me. They had laid a fur and my wolf skin was on my chest. Lars said, "The nights can be cold and Dagfinn said that the wolf would protect you."

"You all fret too much but I thank you."

I had made water and emptied my bowels whilst ashore and as I pulled the wolf skin over me I felt safe and cosseted. The drekar rolled gently in the surf as though *'Ægir'* herself was rocking me asleep.

I dreamed.

The lateen sails came once more. They were like angry moths but unlike those flying insects these beasts had a sting. Arrows

flew and we fled. They seemed to be attached to us and we could not shake them. Then I heard Gandalfr. I could not see him in my dream but I heard his voice. 'The Norns, follow the Norns.' It was then I saw the Three Sisters rising like giants from the sea. I did as I was bid and headed for them. I heard the cries of 'Rocks!' I headed for the Sisters and sailed between Urðr and Skuld. I heard the screams and the crash as the Sisters tore the hulls from the ships that followed us. Then I saw Gandalfr but this was Gandalfr the dragon. This was the carving I saw on the old sailor's chest. His head rose from the water and one eye peered at me. He began to swim through the water and when he disappeared beneath the waves I saw a stand of pine trees. Suddenly there was a flash of sunlight from behind the trees and I was almost blinded.

"You are awake, Master, good. I fear the bright sun of this fine morning has given you less sleep than we might have hoped."

I stood and saw the men trooping towards the ship. We had survived the night but Gandalfr had given me a warning. There was danger ahead and there was sanctuary.

Chapter 10

Joseph had brought me food and it was hot. I ate my fill and by the time I had finished we were ready to sail. I looked at the masthead and saw that the sail was still furled. The wind was southwest to northeast. It was a warm wind and it felt dry. There were no clouds to the southwest. My plan had been to sail north and then north easterly. It seemed that the Norns wished that too. I would say nothing about my dream. If I did then who knew what the consequences might be?

Oddr stood, "We are ready, Leif Wolf Killer, and we are in your hands."

I nodded, "Joseph, take the compass from the chest and the map." The skin map was still largely empty. The straits were marked and the long sweeping bay where we had spent the night but little else. I had taught Joseph how to use the compass and he was quite skilled. That, allied to his scribing skills, made for a neater and better map. "Harland, release us from the land. When he is aboard, Lars, then let fly the sail. *'Ægir'* needs to spread her wings."

I went to the steering board and looked down the drekar. The crew had bows, not yet strung, at the ready and they lined the sides. Maria stood at the prow and she looked like the spirit of the goddess of the sea. She was looking north for Harland had released the tether holding the bow and the wind and the sea had swung the bow around. I leaned gently on the steering board to centre us. The ship was keen to leave the land and Harland had to cling to the rope. Falco and Gudmand hauled him aboard. He landed laughing and dripping.

Falco laughed, "We have caught our first fish of the day!" There was a good mood amongst the men.

"Lars!"

I almost held my breath as the sail was unfurled. My tired clumsiness the previous day came to my mind. If I made a mistake then this could end in disaster. My head was filled with doubts. Would the yard hold? Was the sail secure? When it filled and billowed I was answered. We leapt forward as though the drekar herself was weary of being tied to the dried and desiccated desert. I clutched my Hammer of Thor. It was a good start.

The storm had clearly passed for there were just a couple of small scudding clouds against a blue sky. The waters showed why the sea was named. It was the blue of my mother's eyes. This was not the dark and threatening water on the far side of the straits. There were neither troughs nor crests. The waves were tipped with white but they were so small as to seem inconsequential. The wind was strong enough to move us quickly and yet not strong enough to damage the new and, as yet, untested yard. That was always my fear. We had a spare mast but no spare yard. I knew now what I had not known in Bygstad, we needed two of everything.

Harland sat atop the new yard and kept a good watch. The blue skies and clear air meant he could see a long way away. A sail from any ship that might pose a threat would soon be seen. The crew relaxed in the sun. All had stood a watch in the night and the chance to doze in the warm sunshine was not to be spurned. Oddr, Asbjørn, Brynjar and Dagfinn did not rest. Although they lounged by the gunwale they were keenly watching larboard and steerboard. They were the leaders of our ship and until we reached home they would be alert. Our course, we had decided, would be north and east. That would take us deeper into the Blue Sea but we needed to be much further north when we turned to sail west. We did not want to risk the machine in the tower. We needed sea room as we could predict neither the wind nor the currents.

I had retired early the previous night but Dagfinn told me, when he brought me a horn of water, that when the men had spoken the desire to return home was unanimous. We had all felt loyal and supported the jarl but if he was not with us then we could make our own decisions.

"And what if he joins us here in the Blue Sea?"

Dagfinn clutched his Hammer of Thor, "Then the Norns would indeed be spinning. I am sorry, Leif but the jarl is no navigator. If he was at the steering board when the storm hit then he is dead along with his crew." He waved a hand at the seabirds above, "And their spirits would be there."

Dragon Rock

It was cruel but nonetheless true. I knew that if Halfdan was at the steering board then they might have had a chance. Would the jarl's pride have allowed him to make such a decision?

The hourglass we had taken at Bordèu had survived the storm because it had stayed safely wrapped in the chest. When the sky was thick with cloud then there was little point in using it. Since we had landed, where the sun shone, we had used it. The ship's boys enjoyed being the ones to turn it. They hovered by the board when they saw the last grains slip to the bottom. I was still learning to get the best use out of it but Joseph assured me that it would make our maps more accurate and help us to know our position. The map was still more than a little sketch. We had the bay marked and the straits but the north side of the strait, apart from the rocks we had seen, was bare. However, Joseph assured me that we were moving well. He had devised a way of measuring our speed by dropping a knotted rope over the side. To me it was still a mystery, so he made squiggles on a wax tablet to explain. I smiled and nodded but I had no idea what it meant. I took his word. He was invaluable. He was able to provide a more accurate assessment of both our speed and position. Here, in these strange waters that might make all the difference.

It was after the noon sighting that I broached a matter that needed to be given voice, "We are sailing away from your home."

"Yes, Master."

"Are you happy about that?"

He studied me and said, "You deserve the truth, Leif Wolf Killer for you are an honourable man. No, I am not happy but neither am I unhappy. My life is better with you than it was in the land of the Franks. I have been away from my home for so long that my real reason for wishing to go there is to spend my last days in the place where I was born. I do not think there will be either family or friends left there for me and if there were we would have little in common. I am still hale and who knows, Snorri may decide to trade in this sea, and if he does..."

I did not think he would but I was pleased with his answer. Men rarely had the chance to be happy. There were too many other people making decisions about our lives not to mention the

Norns. Had we raided these waters then I would have tried to land him near to his home.

Oddr and Asbjørn joined me an hour after the noon sighting. Lars was beaming when he turned over the hourglass. We were still sailing north and east. Oddr said, "When do we turn?"

"I planned on waiting until dark. I have seen no sails but this way, if we are seen then our intention will not be clear. We will reef the sail and slip quietly west. The wind is kind and Christof and Lars can keep this course while I take an hour of sleep."

Asbjørn said, "This sea is so empty and flat. It is like we have entered a different world."

Oddr said, "We have. The land smelled different last night. I found it disturbing. The land in Bordèu smelled strange too, but not as different as this hot land." I adjusted the steering board, "I wonder if they worship the same gods as we do here?"

Joseph had finished making his marks on the compass and shook his head, "The men here worship the same God. He has different names but it is the same deity. He is called Jehovah by the Jews and some Christians and Allah by the Muslims."

Oddr rubbed his beard, "Then why the different religions?"

Joseph hung the compass from the hook and smiled, "The man who can answer that will bring peace to this land."

Asbjørn nodded, "It is strange. I, for one, like some things about it. I could get used to the warmth and the gentle seas but I would not like to live here for the air seems to dry a man out. The sooner we get back the better."

I waited to take my short sleep until the wind was steady. I pointed to the hourglass. "Three hours is all I shall need. If the wind changes or we sight a sail then let me know and wake me."

"Yes, Captain."

Christof just smiled.

I went to my chest and took out the wolfskin. I did not need its warmth, just the protection from the glare of the sun. I also found the smell to be comforting. It reminded me, somehow, of home. Mercifully, I did not dream. It was not a deep sleep. I was aware of the conversation between Lars and Christof. They kept their voices low and I heard not a word but I heard the rumble as they spoke. Even so I rose refreshed. I would manage the night without sleep. Lars would watch with me and so I sent him to enjoy some sleep and I ate some fish caught by Harland and enjoyed the luxury of a horn of ale. We still had a small barrel of mead left from Bordèu. That would only be opened when we escaped this beautiful trap.

The days and nights were roughly the same length in this part of the world and, as we watched the sun begin to set in the west, I turned the ship. I had the sail reefed so that only half of it was catching the wind and my plan was to sail slightly north of west to take advantage of the wind that still blew from southwest to northeast. If it did not change then when we sighted the coast of Al-Andalus, we might have to row. I wanted men who were ready to fight and not oarsmen.

The sun seemed to set more quickly in these southern realms. One moment the west was bathed in a blue tinged orange light and then it was just a glow that disappeared. During the storm we had not spied the moon but we did now. It would be full in a day or so. Lars brought us ale and some salted meat to eat while we watched. Nils was on duty as the lookout at the prow. Birger and Maria still had their nest there and Joseph had vacated his place and joined us. He slept between the chests. There were no birds and the only noises were the sound of the keel as it slid through the water and the creak of timbers. Occasionally there was the snap of a sheet or a sail but we had trimmed them well and that only happened twice in the watch. The ship seemed to float serenely on this sea. Joseph had told me that this sea was saltier and that would make the ship float higher. How he knew these things I did not know but he was right. We seemed to be a fraction higher and the passage was much smoother.

I spent the watch teaching Lars how to navigate. I needed a substitute. The storm had demonstrated that. He was older than Nils and he seemed to want to be a navigator. He also wanted to be a warrior. After a lesson in how to make the most of an awkward wind he said, "You are a warrior and a navigator, Captain, I would be like you."

I shook my head, "A navigator has a harder, more arduous life but a warrior can expect a shorter one."

"We have not buried many men."

"One shield brother is one too many. The shield wall is an unforgiving place. In the heat of battle you can be struck by an enemy you never even saw."

"I would still like to try."

"Then when we are in Bygstad I will train both you and Birger to become warriors."

"Surely Birger is a warrior already?"

I shook my head and moved the steering board a little. I had felt the wind shift. "This is his first raid as a warrior. He has yet to fight in a shield wall. My shield brothers watched over him when we took Bordèu."

My words gave him something to think about and he was silent. It allowed me to sail the ship and to plan what we did next. Joseph said that we would hit the coast of Al-Andalus by the next afternoon. It could be an hour or so earlier or later. Earlier would be perfect as that might allow us to slip through the straits unchallenged. Once we reached the coast we would hug it to the west. It was some days since we had endured the storm and been attacked by the men in the tower. They might have forgotten us. I felt a sudden chill. Was it the breeze or had my thoughts disturbed the Three Sisters?

We kept turning the hourglass and so we had a better idea of when to look east and see the sun rise. As soon as Lars saw the greyer light he went to rouse Harland. Joseph seemed to have some extra sense that I did not possess for he woke and rose. He looked astern. "It promises to be a fine day."

"How can you tell? There is just a hint of light."

He smiled broadly, "I spent the early years of my life close to these waters. In that time I learned to tell the weather from the sky. Your land and the land of the Franks were both mysteries to me but since we have returned I feel that I am as one with the land."

"As one?"

He nodded, "We have a word for it, attuned."

I smiled, "I think I know what you mean. My father and his brother are like that. They know the waters of the fjord and the weather. We were only caught out by the weather once and that, I think, was Loki playing tricks to test us."

Dragon Rock

The sun suddenly flared up a bright orange and pink behind us. He said, "I will make water and then fetch you food."

Harland had joined us, "Wake Oddr and tell him it is dawn." Oddr would rouse half the crew to watch for dawn in case we found enemies.

Oddr must have been rising already for he soon joined me. I said, "Joseph thinks it will be fine weather today."

He gave a rueful shake of the head, "This is one day that I wish we had a sea fret from home or a squall. I would sneak out and not risk that terrifying machine ending our voyage."

We all watched as the sea before us came to life. The light picked out the white tipped waves. They seemed like miniature versions of the seas we were used to. Birds appeared, as though by magic. They would follow us all day looking for any treasure we discarded. I sent Harland up the mast and he called down, "The sea is clear."

I nodded, "We can use the full sail now, Oddr."

I was asking his permission. He nodded. As soon as the sail began to billow then we would be visible for many miles. "Aye, Captain, full sail."

The moment the wind caught us we flew once more. *'Ægir'* loved these waters. To my mind she flew over the sea like a bird seeking prey. Her keel barely touched it. She would be sorry to leave the Blue Sea. The rest of the crew were roused and men made water, emptied their bowels and then breakfasted. Lines were run out for fish and Nils and Lars found their beds. Our voyage had a rhythm to it.

Birger and Maria came down to the steering board. I had yet to hear her speak more than a couple of words. That morning I heard her first utterance in Norse, "Thank you for saving us."

Her voice was as beautiful as she was. She had not butchered our words as I knew we did when we tried to speak Saxon, English, Frisian or Frankish.

"You are welcome." I was unsure if she understood everything I might say and so I spoke to Birger, "Is she comfortable? I mean it must be hard with so many men on board and some of them can be a little frightening."

"They have all been more than kind to her, Brother. They treat her as a little sister. She was terrified in the storm but she said that Joseph gave her comfort."

I was relieved, "Good."

He had his arm around her waist and she was leaning into him. He said, "Brother, we would be wed as soon as we can."

It was not unexpected I suppose. He had spoken of this the moment he had come aboard but I hoped that it was a whim. This still felt like a surprise. "Is there a rush?" I had thought they would wait until we reached home and the marriage could be held in Bygstad.

He looked a little embarrassed, "When we lie together, I am, well, aroused and it is not right. If we are wed then it will be better."

"And how does Maria feel about this?"

"She wishes it too. She has no family and…Brother, this feels right."

"And when we reach Bygstad I will not have to endure the sharp edge of Mother's tongue not to mention our aunt. They would not approve. They will expect me to be as a parent to you."

He laughed, "There you have no fears for you are the favourite of both of them. I am prepared for the tears and the recriminations."

"Then you shall be wed but we will have to wait until we land. That may not be until we have passed Al-Andalus."

"Just so long as we are wed then I will be happy. We will both be happy."

He put his mouth to her ear and after he whispered some words she squealed so loudly that the crew all turned. When she grabbed me and kissed me there was a huge cheer. I realised then that this was *wyrd*. The two were meant to be together and that would not have happened had we not sought the Blue Sea.

I turned the steering board to head further west. The wind made us move marginally slower on that course but I was anxious not to lose sea miles. Once there was time I would sleep but, for the moment, the ship needed me. It was not long before noon when Fritjof, who had a fishing line run from the larboard bow, shouted, "Sail to the south."

I looked up at the masthead. Harland peered south and he nodded and pointed, "She is due south of us, Captain." He paused, "She looks to be alone." There was another pause. I looked up at our huge sail that was filled with an almost perfect wind that was driving us toward the coast of Al-Andalus. "She is turning."

I shouted, "Thank you." I would not leave the steering board for a little longer.

Oddr came to join me, "Do you think it is good or bad, Leif?"

"We were hidden and now we are seen so it cannot be good. We look different to the ships of the people of these waters. The Franks have similar sails and hulls. I think that the ship will report our presence."

He nodded and rubbed his salt rimed beard, "Then we make the most of this time. I will ensure that the men eat and rest." He nodded to Christof and Lars, "You must rest too."

"I will." He was right. Even if no ships appeared I needed to sleep for pursuit or not I would be on watch all night. I waited until half of the hourglass had been filled and when no more reports of sails came I said, "Lars, Christof." They came over, "I need to sleep."

"Yes, Captain. Any special orders?"

"Watch for sails to the south and west. Wake me if even one appears."

I slipped beneath the comfort of the wolf skin and dozed. I did not sleep for I had a fertile mind and it was filled with dire predictions about what lay around us. The last thing that filled my mind before I slipped into a light sleep, was a picture of Joseph's map and the sketchy outline of the eastern side of Al-Andalus.

"Captain!"

Lars' voice woke me and I threw off the cloak and stood. The sun was beating down and the gunwale, when I touched it, was burning to the touch. Lars pointed, not to the south but to the south and west. There were lateen sails ahead and they were heading, like a shower of arrows, directly for us. I looked at the masthead pennant. The wind still came from the south and west. They would be faster than we were.

Dragon Rock

Just then Harland shouted, "To the north and west, I see land."

It had to be Al-Andalus. We were so close to the straits and yet our way there was barred. Christof said nothing but I saw the questions written all over his face. Joseph and Oddr were making their way towards me. I needed time to think for I would soon be bombarded with questions. In addition my head felt as though it was being burned. I picked up the wolf skin and draped it over my head and shoulders. It felt better and, surprisingly, calmed me. I put my hand on the steering board, "I have the board. Lars, make water and drink. Then bring me a horn of ale."

Oddr and Joseph had reached me. Oddr said, "There are eight sails, Leif."

I nodded, "That is too many to fight." If there was one thing we had learned from the straits it was that the men who sailed these ships packed them with men. There could be almost a hundred men aboard eight such ships. "Joseph, open the map." He unrolled the precious map and I said, while he held it, "Where do you think we are?"

He glanced at the compass hanging from the hook on the gunwale and then at the map. He pointed at a spot close to the coast but north of the straits. "I think here. We would have reached the coast by dark and then had all night to slip through the straits. This is bad luck."

Oddr and I looked at each other. It was not luck it was the Norns. Oddr deferred to me, "So what do we do?"

"The wind brings them closer to us and we need speed. We will have to turn and use the wind."

Oddr said, "And that takes us away from the straits."

I had already calculated all the dangers and I spoke honestly to him, "This will be a long chase. These are not the stormy waters where they first met us. These are their home seas and they know them. They will hunt us just as we hunt deer. They are like a pack of hounds. There are eight of them and they can stop us from turning. They will follow us until they catch us."

Christof said, "Then night fall is our best chance to lose them."

I nodded, "It is six or more hours until dark. We head north and east to stay as close to the coast as we can and when

Dragon Rock

darkness falls I will turn due east. I am hoping that they will expect us to turn and head for the straits. I pray that by dawn we wake to an empty sea and then we can try the straits once more."

Oddr nodded, "We have food and, thanks to the storm, we have water. The ale will run out in two days."

I shook my head, "Until the men take to the oars we use water. The ale will be for when the crew bend their backs." I looked at the masthead, "Prepare to come about!" Lars, Harland and Nils ran to the sheets. The sail was billowing well but as soon as we turned it would be as taut as a woman about to give birth.

I pushed over the steering board and we heeled to steerboard. My warning meant that men grabbed anything they could to keep their feet. Christof was still by the board and he was staring west at the sails which could now be made out. "Leif, there are two big ships amongst the smaller ones. They look to be almost as big as we are. The other six are little more than large fishing boats." He paused, "They have armour for I saw the sun reflecting from blades, helmets and armour."

It was not that we needed confirmation but we now knew that these were warships and that they meant to take us.

The delay I had created in turning brought them to within a couple of sea miles of us. As I glanced from the masthead to the seas behind I saw that we were using every puff of wind. We could travel no faster unless the men took to the oars and that would be a last resort. The two larger ships could be seen now and they were in the centre. The smaller ships flanked them. After an hour, Joseph turned the hourglass. I tried something. "Lars, Nils, stand by the sheets. I am going to make a move and see what they do." I needed to know how the ships behind would react if I changed course. I turned to head due north. Our speed did not change but after a few moments, when I glanced astern, I saw that three of the smaller ships carried on with the original course while the other five copied ours. I now knew what they would do. They would use their numbers to counter any move I made. I stayed on the new course for an hour and when the hourglass was turned I resumed our original course. My move had done two things. It had shown me what they would do and it had increased our lead. It was only by the length of a couple of ships but, in the dark that might be enough. My plan had a chance of success.

The lead we had gained was lost in the next two hours as they used their nimble hulls and ships powered by galley slaves to close with us. They were doggedly determined. They would have more men at the oars and they would be slaves. It did not matter to them if the men died so long as they rowed. As darkness fell we continued our course. The moon was our problem. Although not as bright as the sun it still gave them an idea of where we were.

"Oddr, take to the oars. Lars, I want the sail furled in the blink of an eye."

They both hurried to obey me. No acknowledgement was needed. I waited until the oars were run out. Every member of the crew, Birger included, was at the oars. They were not yet in the water. Sound travels at night and so we could not use either my stamping foot or a song to keep the beat. Oddr and Asbjørn would have to do that. I nodded and the oars were lowered into the sea. They bit. The crew had, in the main, rowed together for a long time and as soon as the ship leapt forward with their power I said, "Sail!" I had to imagine what the ships behind would see. We were hull down on the horizon. As soon as the sail was furled we would vanish. The one time I had changed course it was to head to the coast. I now had some sort of idea of what they would do. Three ships would follow this course and, I hoped, the rest would change course and head to the coast. They might not and that was a chance we had to take. As soon as the sail was down I put the steering board over to head east. This was a leap into the unknown. We had to vanish and that meant disappearing into the vast empty waters to the north and east of us. I would still use the wind but not for at least an hour. The crew would row for that time. It would seem longer than an hour to the crew.

Joseph stood by me. I said, "I no longer need the wolf skin, Joseph, put it in my chest. It kept the sun from me."

He did so and then poured me some mead. We had some we had made at the lagoon. It was not as good as what we had from home but the honey it was made from would give me energy and feed my mind. I drank it and stared ahead into the empty black night. When I peered astern I saw nothing. The sails had disappeared but I had to keep to my plan. We would row. The men had not had to row since the storm and they were not yet tired. They would be able to sleep in the night and if we had to row again they might be ready. As for me? I had steeled myself to another night without sleep. The mead had helped.

After an hour I said, "Let fly the sail. Joseph, watch astern." Once the sail filled I said, "In oars."

This time there was noise in the night as the oars slid in through their ports. I hoped that our pursuers were many miles astern.

"Joseph, can you see anything?"

"It is still, so far as I can tell, an empty sea."

Oddr and Asbjørn joined me, "Have we lost them?"

I shrugged, "Hard to say, Asbjørn. I would hope so but we will not know until dawn. Harland and I will watch this night. We may need the crew in the morning."

"And our course?"

I smiled, my teeth would look white in the moonlight, and I hoped a smile would reassure them, "The gods determine that. So long as the wind is from the south and west we sail north and east. If it changes…"

Oddr put his hand on my shoulder, "We are in safe hands."

As the crew rolled into blankets or simply curled into balls the ship fell silent. Harland stood with me but his task would be to watch astern and turn the hourglass. Each turn was marked on the wax tablet next to the compass. We knew the passage of time. Mine was to save the ship and the crew. Gandalfr could not have known this would happen but his presence in my dreams told me that he knew now. I took comfort from that. His spirit was in the ship. His blood, now scoured from the stern was also in the ship. When I gripped the steering board I felt him close by. The others could steer the ship but they would not be tied to Gandalfr. That was our hope. We would have help from beyond the grave.

Chapter 11

It was three hours into the watch when the wind shifted slightly. I could have woken Lars and Nils to help Harland to trim the sails but the shift was a slight one. The wind came more from the south than the west and was warmer. I could smell the warmth. I turned so that we kept the strength of the wind. We were heading more northerly than east. We had gained a lead and if we slowed we might lose it. I intended to keep the sail full and billowing. We had a keel free from wildlife and *'Ægir'* was fast. I knew that our pursuers could keep up with us but I had one advantage. Our course was in my mind. We ploughed on through seas that felt as though I was on a tarn and sheltered by hills. There were no troughs and the drekar rode the waves as though she could fly over them.

I wanted the crew to be ready by dawn and so I used the hourglass. Thanks to the records kept by Joseph we knew when the sun would rise and I had Harland wake the boys and then the crew. He woke Oddr and Asbjørn before he woke the crew. It would allow them to make water and dress. I needed to empty my bladder but this day that would have to wait until the sun rose properly and we were in an empty sea. Harland would have to wait for his rest and I sent him up the mast to be ready to scan the sea when the sun rose. The ship was alert when the glimmer of light appeared in the east. Everyone peered out to sea. We had no idea if any sails would appear and every man stared into the dark sea to watch for the first flash of light.

I waited with bated breath as the sun flared brightly in the east. It would be a hot day and I would need my wolf skin. Of course, if there was no sail then I could enjoy a short and blissful sleep. I was the only one whose attention was not on the sea around us. I was watching the pennant, the sail and the sea ahead. When Christof's voice came from the larboard quarter it almost made me jump. "Sail away to the southwest."

I shouted up to Harland, "Can you see her?"

"She looks to be alone, Captain."

Dragon Rock

If we could see her then she could see us. I said, "Let us see if she is an honest trader or a hunting dog. I will change course. Let me know what she does."

I turned the steering board so that we were heading east by north. I waited.

"She is altering course, Captain, and she is following."

"Oddr, take to the oars. We will keep this course until we lose her and then turn to head due west."

My sleep would have to wait. As Joseph turned the hourglass I said, "Fetch me the wolf skin and some water."

He placed the skin so that my head and shoulders were covered and handed me the horn of water. The skin was not for warmth but shade. I downed the water, knowing that I would need to drink regularly if I was to stay alert. He took the horn and handed me some figs we had taken from Maria's village. They had dried a little but that would not impair their taste. I felt better after the food and water.

The oars were run out and I nodded. They slid into the water and bit. This time we could chant and I could stamp. The men were refreshed and we sped over the water as though we were a sea bird seeking fish. Harland shouted, after a few strokes of the oars, "She has disappeared."

It would not do to stop rowing, at least not for a while. I glanced at the hourglass and estimated a quarter of that time. It was a rough and ready guess. I then said, "In oars. Eat while you can. We may not have lost them." After the oars were stacked Oddr approached and I said, "I will head due north and then ease us back to our course to the west." He nodded. I looked at Joseph, "How far do you think we are from the coast, Joseph?"

He frowned. He knew as well as I did that I was being unreasonable. He took out his chart and looked at the marks he had made on the compass. It was early yet and there were just two marks. He said, finally, "Anything between fifty and a hundred miles."

I nodded, "Then that would take us twelve turns of the hourglass, a whole day."

"Yes, Master but it is a guess and assumes that the wind stays where it does."

"Let us be positive. If it was night when we reached the coast then we would be hidden." I looked at the pennant. The wind was still blowing from the south. I shouted, "Coming about." This was not the hard heeling we had endured earlier. It was a gentle change but the wind was stronger and pushed us forward. I waved over Lars, once the sails had been set, and said "Take over while I make water and walk the ship. Due north." He nodded. A straight course was relatively easy. All he had to do was to keep the prow and the mast in line and hold the board in the same place as me.

I made water and then walked down the drekar. Gandalfr had always done this at least once a day and when I had spoken to Snorri I had discovered that he had too. I had learned it gave me a feel for the ship. I could touch the mastfish and gunwale. I could peer over the prow and see the cut of the ship through the water. Another reason was to stretch the legs that had been braced for more hours than was good for them.

At the prow I saw Maria was nestled in Birger's arms. "You know that you may have to row more today. The Norns are spinning Brother and these pirates are persistent."

"I know and I am ready." He nodded down the ship, "The crew believe in you, Brother. We all think that no matter how dark things are you will save us. The storm showed us that."

It was a faith I could do without for that faith was also a burden. I was not Gandalfr and I was just reacting to the sea, the wind, the Arabs and, of course, the Norns.

When I reached the steering board I took a moment or two to scan the horizon. It was empty. There were no sails and no land. After taking the steering board I said, "Joseph, keep a watch here, astern of us."

He nodded, "We are like the fox trying to hide from the hounds, Master." He turned to look behind us. "You should know that the further north they chase us the fewer are our choices."

I nodded, "The same is true going south. If I were the hunter I would wait at the straits."

"But then, Master, you know that we wish to return home. The hounds think we wish to raid the henhouse. They will not stop until we are caught."

Dragon Rock

He was right and they would continue to hunt us. They were trying to keep us from the henhouse.

We could not see what was below the horizon. It appeared to be an empty sea. Then Harland called from the masthead, "Sails to the southwest of us. There are four of them."

I had to assume that the one that had found us still trailed in our wake. That left a turn to the east as my only choice. I was about to order it when Lars shouted, from my right, "Sails to the east of us."

The net was closing. "Harland, how many sails to the east of us?"

He peered and after what seemed like a lifetime said, "Four. One is one of the big ships we saw before."

They had gained one ship at least and had us pincered.

Harland shouted, "The other big ship is to the west."

Joseph did not shout for he was next to me but he said, his voice flat, "There are two sails astern of us."

We were being driven north. They had spread their net wide during the night. I could not see but I guessed that there had to have been at least three ships searching for us. When Joseph said, "Three ships astern," it was confirmed. The three scouts had been sent to find us.

Oddr came to the stern. He had donned his mail. I saw that the rest of the crew who had mail were now donning it. He said, "Do we take to the oars, Leif?"

I shook my head, "They are not gaining. We have the best of the wind and the three behind us, the ones who might catch us, are small vessels."

Asbjørn and Christof had joined us. Asbjørn said, "The others will join the ones behind and then close with us."

Christof said, "I do not think so. Such a move would allow us to sail either east or west and escape. They want us to go north." He paused, "They know the waters better than we do. They are driving us somewhere that they think will trap us."

I said, "Joseph, what lies north of us?"

"There are some islands. They are called the Balearics but I do not know exactly where they are. As I recall they are to the east of Al-Andalus and south of the County of Toulouse and the Land of the Franks."

Dragon Rock

"Then that is where they want to catch us. If they lie across our path then we will have to turn either east or west and when we do there will be four ships, including one the same size as us, waiting for us."

Asbjørn said, "Are you saying that we are doomed?"

I shook my head, "We are afloat. We have not lost a man and we have water and food. So long as that is true then there is hope."

Oddr said, "Joseph, how do these people fight?"

"They have good bows. You saw how skilled they are from the machine they had in the tower. They will not be wearing much mail. They will try to kill the helmsman and close with the ship when you are in disarray and then they will board you. Warriors will be slain and the boys, Maria and I will be enslaved." He added, sadly, "Birger and Anders may not be killed. They might be taken…" He shook his head, "It is better you do not know the reason."

I nodded, "Then Oddr, we need to think about resting men who might have to row. The ships that shadow us, if the wind remains as it is, cannot catch us for an hour or so. Have the men rest. My crew and I will watch until we need you." I was exhausted and I feared that, as with the last time I had gone so long without sleep, my body might fail me.

Oddr nodded, "Lars, fetch Leif's shield from the side. Your task is to protect him when the arrows rain down upon us."

Oddr and Asbjørn went among the crew. Christof laid himself down close to the steering board. When Lars brought my shield he placed it next to him. "A good shield and a well-made design. You made this yourself?"

"I did."

"Good, that marks you as a good warrior."

"Master, the ships following are closer."

I turned and looked, "They can come as close as they like but once they are in arrow range then they will learn of our skills." I looked at the masthead, "Harland, are the ships to the east and west any closer?"

"A little, Captain."

Christof said, "They are hauling us in gradually. Whoever commands these vessels is clever."

It was another hour before Harland reported that they were clearly closing with us and were getting close to bow range. He added some new information, "Of the three who follow us, one is larger than the others and is a little low in the water."

Christof said, "Then she is laden with men and that is why they are not closing with us."

"Land to the west."

I looked up and saw Harland's arm pointing to the northwest. I said, "They must be your Balearics, Joseph."

He nodded, "They are a string of islands."

"The ships to the west are closing."

That made sense. They would not wish to risk the rocks that lay to their larboard sides. I was about to turn a little to steerboard when Harland shouted, urgently, "The ships to the east are closing too." The jaws of the trap were closing.

I made a quick decision, "Oddr, take to the oars. They are closing on us."

It was clear to me what they had planned. They had gradually closed the net and once they passed the first of the rocks and islands they knew what to do. It meant that there was something ahead that could hurt us. I knew we had to get sea room and the only way to do that was to be faster than they were.

Oddr gave commands and the oars were manned and run out so quickly that even as I looked to see where the enemy ships were we were ready. We needed a steady but powerful beat and I began to stamp my foot as I sang.

We are the clan of the otter
We live where no one else can
We fish the seas and water
We serve the goddess Rán
We are the clan of the otter
We live where no one else can
We fish the seas and water
We serve the goddess Rán
We are the clan of the otter

We moved forward quickly but the three sets of ships all closed with us. They were a good eight hundred paces from us and I was happy with that distance. As we began to row we

Dragon Rock

would extend our lead. We would row for an hour and, hopefully, I would be able to avoid whatever they thought was an obstacle.

Joseph was still next to me, looking astern, and he said, "The larger ship, she has oars." It was said in such a manner of fact tone that he could have been asking me if I wanted a horn of ale.

My heart sank when he spoke. If they had oars then they could row and they could keep up with us. They would be right behind me when we reached the point of danger that I knew had to lie ahead. Even when I asked the question I knew the answer, "The other large ship, does she have oars?"

I did not take my eyes off the mast and the prow as I steered as straight a course as I could. His words, when they came, were like a death knell, "Yes, Master, she does."

I just nodded and said, "Thank you."

The Norns had spun and I was being tested, again.

I kept glancing to the two sets of ships and was relieved when they began to drop astern. That relief was short lived as they were able to use the same wind as we did and form a long line. I could only sail my own course and worry about my own ship. Lars and Nils were now experienced enough to know when to trim the sails and we lost not a moment thanks to a flapping piece of canvas. The men at the oars were pulling as hard as they could. If we were destined to lose we would go down fighting. I was determined that would not happen.

Harland at the masthead shouted, "Captain, rocks ahead."

I was momentarily annoyed for that was too vague a call and then I remembered that he was little more than a youth. "What size? Are they a reef or do they stand proud?"

"There are three of them, Captain. One very large one and two smaller ones."

Both a shiver and hope sprang in my heart as the dream came back to me. I needed to see for myself. Only I would know what to look for. "Lars, come here!"

He raced to my side and I saw the fear on his face, "What is wrong, Captain?"

"Take the board and hold this course." When he had it I ran the length of the ship. I saw the shock on his face and Joseph's as I left the steering board. That shock was reflected on the faces of the oarsmen as I hurtled up the deck. They stared in disbelief.

Dragon Rock

Maria's mouth dropped open as I climbed onto the prow where I peered ahead, with my hand shading my eyes. The rocks were a blur at first but such was the speed of the drekar that they soon became clearer. They were the rocks from my dream. It was the Norns. Gandalfr had sent me the message. How, I did not know but I trusted him. He might have been a dream but I now saw the reality.

I ran back down the drekar and shouted, "When I give the command run in the oars and hold on."

Oddr shouted, as I took back the steering board, "What is happening?"

I pointed ahead and said, "The Three Sisters."

He could see nothing but he smiled. He trusted me.

I said to Lars, "I have little time to explain so listen and do exactly what I say." He nodded. I could see that he was both mystified and terrified for I must have sounded like a wild man. "Ahead are three rocks. They look like the Norns. I intend to sail between the larger one and the two smaller ones, Urðr and Skuld. You have to guide me there. Use your arms to move me larboard or steerboard. We will be travelling fast and there will be rocks. When we are heading directly for the gap, and there will be a gap, hold your two arms up in the air." He nodded, "Do this, Lars, and you will save the ship."

"I will not let you down."

"You will know the safe passage when you see the dragon in the sea." I could not see his face for he had turned to run but I knew that he thought I had gone mad. I was trusting Gandalfr and the Three Sisters.

Joseph could now see the rocks and he said, "Are we sailing to our doom, Master? Will you turn?"

I shook my head, "We are going to turn the trap on our enemies. They will tear out their hulls on those rocks."

He said, quietly, "How do you know? You have never sailed here before."

"I have dreamed it. There is a rock and beyond the gap is a dragon in the water and beyond the dragon there is a sanctuary."

He said nothing for a moment or two and I was too busy gauging the moment to run in the oars to notice. He finally said, "You are a most interesting people, Master."

Dragon Rock

I saw that the ships were now in a long line and were less than four hundred paces from us. They were anticipating a turn and no matter which way we did so there would be arrows waiting to rain upon us. The ships would be able to shower us along the length of the ship and there would be carnage. They had, so I had been told, good bows. Within a hundred more paces they would be in range and I would be their target. I had to hold my nerve.

Lars held up his left arm and I moved the steering board accordingly. He held both arms up. I saw that the rocks I thought of as Urðr and Skuld were closer. I said, "Oddr, run in the oars."

There was hesitation for he could see, as well as any could, that the enemy were closing. He said, "Are you sure?"

The chanting had stopped and every eye was on me. I roared, "Run in the oars and brace!"

They obeyed.

I was counting on them closing with us and being so determined to get to us that they would not realise their danger. They knew the islands were ahead, it was part of their trap, but our sail obscured the distance to the rocks. I hoped that they had forgotten the danger the rocks represented. They would see their trap closing and be eager to close with us. When the oars stopped pushing us forward so their speed increased. Joseph said, "One of the ships with oars is gaining, Master. It is almost within bow range." I knew that they thought they had us.

"Let me know when you see men with bows, Joseph."

There was silence as he studied them. "I see a warrior with golden armour. It reflects the sun and he is urging them on."

To me that sounded like either a very brave man or an incredibly foolish one, or both. A man wore armour on a ship at his peril.

My eyes did not leave Lars. I was sweating beneath the skin for although the sun had disappeared the air was still warm. I did not need protection from the rays and now the wolf skin was too hot. "Joseph, take my skin from me."

As soon as it was removed it felt better because the air felt cooler. I had not noticed the sun disappearing and I also felt something else, the wind was dropping. It explained why the enemy ship with the oars was catching us and leaving the others in its wake. I flicked my eyes to the sail. It was still full but it was no longer stretched. This was a race to the rocks. If we lost then we would be surrounded and the pirates would swarm all over us.

Lars' left hand moved and I moved the steering board a little. His arms came up together. The rock I thought of as Skuld, loomed large ahead. It seemed like a mountain and it told me that we were very close to the rocks. The wind was still dropping. Now that I had discarded the skin I could feel the difference. I saw that Oddr had ordered bows to be strung and the best bowmen, the ones with the strongest pull, came towards the steering board. I knew why. Now that the wind was dropping they had more range. They would not be loosing into the wind.

The first of the enemy arrows fell before our arrows were released. Joseph was quick thinking and he lifted my wolf shield and held it at an angle over our heads. Joseph did not want to tend to his own wounds. The arrows did not hit the shield but they struck the gunwale and two clattered to the deck. The six bowmen before me drew and Oddr said, "Release."

Their arrows flew together. I did not see either their flight or the result for Lars had moved his hand to the right. The slight change in wind direction had deceived him. I corrected my course. If nothing else I would be putting off their archers. While their men with bows would be aiming for me our bowmen could just rain arrows at their deck. They had men rowing and they would have their backs to our arrows. Those backs would be bare.

Oddr shouted, "Good hit. We have struck an oarsman."

It would be little but enough. One oar not pulling could not only slow the ship up but also change its course.

Lars' voice screamed down the drekar to me, "Rocks ahead!"

I shouted, "Brace!" I knew that even if the gods guided my hand there was still a chance that we could catch a glancing blow from the rocks.

It was then that Lars put both his arms to steerboard. It was an urgent message and I put the board over. Lars seemed to merge into the rock and almost disappear. I felt us strike. It was the slightest of touches but it was followed by a long grinding noise that almost sounded as though *'Ægir'* was screaming. The drekar

Dragon Rock

lurched to larboard and the bowmen were almost thrown from their feet. Joseph grabbed at the nearest thing he could for support. It was me. My stance, wide legged and braced held us. The grinding stopped and I shouted, "Take to the oars and row for your lives."

There were no rocks before us but Harland shouted, from his precarious place at the masthead, "Land ahead."

Lars shouted, at the same time, "Fog bank ahead!" Harland had mistaken the fog for land. Lars would make a good navigator.

Joseph's voice was full of awe as he said, "That is rare in these waters."

I had no time to think for the oars bit and we surged ahead. There was clear water and I glanced behind. It was marginally brighter and I saw the larger ship as it struck the rocks. We had been damaged, that I knew, but I saw the bows of the leading enemy ship rise as it smashed into the rocks. They had not enjoyed a man at the prow. The mast fell forward and I heard the screams as men began to die. I turned back to look at the bows and, peering ahead, I saw that the wind had died completely and that we were now in the fog bank. I could barely see Lars.

I shouted, "Slow the oars." My mind was confused. Had I seen the fog in my dreams? Then the vision came to me. I needed to find the dragon in the sea. How could I do that in this fog? This needed my eyes. I shouted, "Lars, Christof, to the steering board. Oddr, one man to an oar and as slow as you can manage."

Lars arrived and Christof, when he had relinquished his oar, joined me. "I need the two of you to steer. I will go to the prow and shout commands."

"Captain, it was open water until the fog rose."

I said, "There is a sign there that I will be seeking. If I find it then we will be safe."

Lars asked, as he took hold of the board, "And if not?"

"Then the enemy will find us and we will battle until we are no more."

As I passed Birger he asked, "Are we sinking?"

I shook my head, "We are hurt and land is close but I cannot predict if we will stay afloat." Oddr joined me and Birger as we

Dragon Rock

went to the prow. I said, "Birger take Maria to the stern. It will be safer."

He looked down as he took Maria's hand, "Brother, the deck is wet."

I nodded, I had seen it as we had neared the prow, "We have sprung strakes. Fear not, *'Ægir'* is fighting for her life."

I hung from the steerboard side of the prow and Oddr did the same to the larboard. He said, "Leif, you know what we seek but I do not."

"You are looking for a dragon in the water. When you see one then sanctuary is close."

"A dragon?"

"Verðandi came to me in my dreams and the dragon we seek has the same head as the one carved on Gandalfr's chest." I knew without looking that Oddr had clutched his Hammer of Thor.

It was an eerie feeling as we edged through a fog which would have been more familiar to me in the fjord in Gormánuður. This was the Blue Sea but the sea was anything but blue. There were no waves but it looked dark and threatening beneath the veil of fog. This had not been in my dream. I recalled the fog but not the threatening water. Had I been duped? Were the Sisters playing with us? Perhaps the dragon would not be a guide but would devour us.

When Oddr spoke, it was almost a whisper, "Leif, look ahead. Am I dreaming or is that not your dragon?"

I pulled myself up to rest my body on the prow and that allowed me to see what Oddr could see. There was the dragon. It was a long low rock but it resembled a dragon. More, I saw the eye and through it, far in the misty distance, I saw a single pine tree. It was almost like a beacon. The fog was thinning. It was sanctuary. Then the fog closed in again and the tree disappeared.

I shouted, urgently, "Lars, Christof, a turn to larboard." The oars were still pulling steadily. "More!" I saw the snout of the dragon a length away from us and I knew we would miss it. I was clutching my Hammer of Thor when we passed the snout. I saw the rocks that were the dragon's teeth. They were just fourteen paces from us. As soon as we were clear I shouted, "A turn to steerboard."

Dragon Rock

I knew that those who were on the steerboard side saw the dragon when I heard a collective gasp. I ignored it. We were seeking safety and thus far my dream had been a good guide. I prayed that it would continue to be so.

"Centre the board." Only my voice could be heard above the crack of the oars and the flapping of a sail that no longer pushed us. I was aiming for the single pine tree that I had seen through the eye of the dragon.

Harland's voice came from the masthead. "Land a mile ahead, Captain," He could see above the fog. I heard the incredulity as he added, "I see pine trees!"

"Steady at the oars."

"Aye, Oddr." Asbjørn led the men at the oars and they would know nothing of the dragon or what lay ahead. They were trusting to the eyes of the lookout and the skill of a young captain.

Oddr hissed, "I see water breaking on rocks."

I shouted, "I want to go as slowly as a wolf approaching a flock of sheep."

We were now reliant on the skill of Asbjørn. He had to control the speed of the ship. It was then I noticed, as we slowed, that the sea was closer at the bows. We were taking on water more rapidly now. We had been holed. It was as I looked ahead I saw the water that was free of rocks. "To steerboard, a touch." The two men on the board were listening and we moved. "Enough!"

Oddr said, "I see rocks to larboard."

"And there are some on my side. If my dream is right then we are in a cove of some kind. Back water and hold."

I stood and stripped off. "What are you doing?"

"I am seeking shelter. When I am in the water then throw me a rope. Tie the rope to the prow."

He nodded, "I hope you know what you are doing."

"So do I, for all our sakes."

I did not jump but lowered myself over the side. The seas had been warm hitherto but the fog had made them seem almost icy. As I passed the steerboard bow I saw the scrapes and gouges. We were sinking. I could not find the bottom. I thought back to the time I had swum with the jarl and his hearthweru. Had that been preparation for this? I swam ahead of the now stationary ship and turned on my back and sculled. Oddr threw me the rope. I shouted, "Edge us in!" I caught it and swam along what I hoped was a channel. It was not easy with a rope but I managed it. I saw sand to my right and risked putting down my feet. I touched bottom. I turned and saw that I could barely see the prow of the drekar. The rope was just twenty paces long.

I shouted, "I am going to pull us in. Let the oars ease us in. Have some oars ready to push us away from rocks. We need just four oars to steer us. Keep the steering board centred."

Oddr's voice seemed to be disembodied and eerie, "Aye, Leif Wolf Killer."

I put the rope over my shoulder and pulled. There were rocks on the seabed but they were not large enough to hurt the drekar. My feet were a different matter. I noticed that the beach was shelving and soon I was walking on sand. The drekar was moving well. I found myself knee deep and I shouted, "Stop rowing and take down the sail. I need men to help me."

Even though there was fog I saw that there were rocks, stunted trees and bushes lining the beach but the channel seemed to be a perfect width for the drekar. I could see, as men jumped over the side to join me, that there was a gap of at least four paces on both sides.

Dagfinn and Brynjar were the first to join me. Their faces had expressions of both wonder and joy. Dagfinn said, "Life is never dull with you, shield brother."

They both took hold of the rope and when another six joined us I said, "We are holed at the bows. We need to pull the drekar as far up the sand as we can manage. On three. One, two, three."

We are the clan of the otter
We live where no one else can
We fish the seas and water
We serve the goddess Rán

We pulled until half of the drekar was out of the water and then I saw a wall of rocks covered with undergrowth before us. I shouted, "Hold! We are safe." I sat on the sand. "Thank you Verðandi." I clutched my Hammer of Thor.

Chapter 12

Dagfinn and Brynjar secured us to a large rock and a tree so that our stern would not swing while we repaired it. I stood and Nils brought me my clothes. He was grinning. "Snatched from the jaws of our enemy, we pass a dragon and Leif Wolf Killer finds us a safe berth."

As I began to dress I said, "We are not yet safe. I want you and Harland to cut as many branches as you can. We need to disguise the ship. When the fog clears then our enemy will search for us."

Brynjar said, "It will soon be night."

"Then all the more reason to be hidden." I went back to the ship and hauled myself aboard. The crew cheered as I passed. I hoped that the sound would not carry to the rock called Skuld. We had disappeared in the fog and had been heading to the dragon rock. I hoped they would think we suffered the same fate as their ship.

Oddr grasped my arm, "I began to doubt that we would survive. You did well."

I smiled, "But we are holed. I need the mast to be stepped. Then we disguise the ship. The Norns sent the fog but already it is disappearing. By dark I want us to be part of the land."

"Aye. Leave that to me."

I went to the steering board. Joseph and Lars looked full of wonder. Maria was being cuddled by Birger and Christof said, waving a hand at the trees that rose on both sides of us, "I do not know how you found this place but I am happy you did. This is a perfect berth for us."

"Christof, take some men and go ashore. I need to know if this place is safe. My dream said it was but …"

"It will be good to step on land." He waved to two warriors, "Halvard Halvardsson and Siggi the Smiler, come with me. We go ashore." He went with the two warriors to explore the trees that rose above us. I heard Oddr shout to others as he ordered the mast to be stepped.

"Birger, take Maria and Joseph. We need a camp. I found a beach but I am not sure that it will make a good camp. Do not forget to take the goat ashore. The grazing will make for better milk."

He nodded and said, "Brother, you have done enough. Let the rest of us do this."

I shook my head, "I will rest when we are hidden." As they left us I said, "Lars, we need to make the ship invisible. Go and help the others to cut down branches and small trees. Use them to disguise the stern." When I was alone I took out the lengths of rope we had used in Bordèu to protect the hull. They would be used once more. I cut the thick rope into usable lengths and then made it into thinner strands. By the time the boys began to arrive I was ready. I sent Harland over the side and he held the bottoms of the branches while we tied them to the stern. Once the stern was covered we fixed more to the mast fish. The rear of the ship was now covered in vegetation. I hoped that from the seaward side we would blend into the trees and bushes of the cove. The rest of the crew had stepped the mast and gone ashore but it took time to complete our disguise. By then night had fallen and the fog was rapidly disappearing. I even felt a slight breeze. It was now coming, not from the southwest but the east. *Wyrd*.

Birger came down the drekar for me, "Oddr asked if you have finished."

I nodded, "We have."

"Then I am ordered to bring you ashore. We all think that you have done enough. Christof has scouted. We have a place where we can camp and we have a fire going." He saw my face as I was about to object. He shook his head, "The fire is hidden by the trees and Christof said, when they scouted, that they could not smell woodsmoke. We are alone. Oddr has men who will sleep aboard the ship and others to keep watch. You and your boys have earned a night of rest."

I was weary. I could not remember the last time I had made water, eaten, drunk some water. All that I could remember was gripping the steering board and staring ahead. I did not go directly to the camp. Birger pointed up the narrow path to the top of the small rise but I shook my head, "I need to view the ship." Instead of using his path I walked around the side of the drekar. I had to paddle through ankle deep water but, after twenty or so paces, I found myself on a beach that curved around. I walked on

Dragon Rock

the sand. The land above me was easier to climb. Birger followed me. When I reached the far side I saw that I would be able to view the stern of the ship. Although it was dark I would make out the trees. I knew where the ship was and I was less than a hundred paces from it and yet I could barely see it. A ship out to sea would not be able to make it out. Instead of walking back the way we had come I climbed up to inspect the stand of pine trees that stood there.

"These are perfect."

"For what, Brother?" Birger was not a sailor and he did not see what I saw.

"We can make pine tar and we can cut another mast and a yard. They will need seasoning but in any case they are better than nothing."

"Can we use them to make strakes?"

"We could but there is no need as we have some on the ship and we have nails we took in Bordèu. Who knew that the greatest treasure we brought from there would be not silver or gold but iron!" I looked around, "Which way to the camp?"

"Up the slope a little way. The ground rises and then falls." He led me through the trees and we soon saw the fire and the men making beds amongst the trees. I had not seen it from the beach nor the ship. Christof had found a good campsite.

The crew who were there cheered when I arrived. Oddr said, with a smile, "Are you happy, Captain Leif? Is *'Ægir'* tucked up for the night?"

"She is and I am content. Tomorrow I will cut down two pine trees and dig out their roots. We will make pine tar."

"How long will it take to repair the ship?"

I shrugged, "We will need to use levers and wood to raise the bows from the sand. We struck the rocks by the prow and I hope that there is no more damage further aft. We take out the damaged strakes and replace them. We seal them with pine tar. That could take six or seven days or we may do it in three."

"Then we must hope and pray that our enemies do not find us for we are stranded here like a fish."

Asbjørn said, "Then I will take men tomorrow and hunt. We need food and we will need water. We can also look for signs of those who seek us."

Joseph said, "And before all of that my master needs food, ale and sleep."

He was a slave but he spoke with the authority of a lord and Oddr nodded, "You are right, Joseph the Healer. This day has shown us that without Leif Wolf Killer we are like babes in the wood."

I smiled, "It was Gandalfr and his spirit along with the Three Sisters that saved us."

After I had eaten and drunk some mead Joseph put me to bed. He had brought my furs and wolf skin from the drekar and I was given a cosy spot close to a large pine. Dagfinn and Brynjar flanked me. They were still my shield brothers. We had trained together and in that training was formed a bond that could not be broken. I think that, had not Birger found Maria he would have slept close by too. As it was they sought a nest away from the main camp. We all knew why. Before I retired I said, "Oddr, tomorrow you must wed Maria and Birger."

"I am not a hersir."

"No, but you do lead us. My mother would wish it as would his aunt, the wife of the hersir."

He nodded, "I will do so but this voyage has shown me one thing, I am not meant to be a leader. Unless Brokkr sails on the next raid I will not stir from home."

As I lay down on the bed of pine needles and my fur I nodded, "I do not think that many men will wish to raid again, with or without Brokkr. That we have not lost more men is a miracle."

He stared across the bay to the west, "I wonder what happened to our other two ships."

I had thought about that too. "I do not think that they will have passed through the straits."

"Why not?"

"Firstly, because we would have seen them but more because those ships would not be pursuing us if there were two such ships abroad in their waters." He looked at me to continue. I sighed, "They are either sunk or they have sought a landing somewhere. There will be damage in either case."

"You may be right, now rest. We will watch as you watched in the night."

Dragon Rock

I was so exhausted that I was asleep before I even knew anything about it. I woke because of the lack of motion and the smell of the pines. For some reason it made me homesick. That we had found such a stand of pines was nothing short of a miracle. The land of Africa had yielded nothing longer than a branch the length of a sword and the trees with the fronds looked nothing like a tree. These trees were perfect. When I woke the rest of the crew were up. Food was being cooked.

Joseph brought me some ale and food. He said, "I think we can make some ale, Master. When Christof was scouting he found some wild cereal. I will go with him this morning and explore the possibility. We may be able to use it to make a palatable brew. Unless, Master, you need me."

"No, Joseph, I am just going to do things that my father taught me to do."

I saw Christof waiting. He would watch over my slave. His real intention would be to watch for danger from those who lived on the island. Joseph was uncertain if it was the Byzantines or the Arabs. Neither would be happy to have Norsemen on the island. Lars and the boys had slept on the ship. As I passed Oddr, heading down the path to the water, he said, "I have men on the headland watching for sails. Do you need men to help you?"

I shook my head, "The boys and Birger will be enough." He nodded. "The marriage?"

"Tonight after we have eaten."

I waved to Birger, "Come with me, we have work to do."

Unsurprisingly Maria came with us. I saw that she carried Birger's water skin.

The boys saw us descend and came to the prow. I said, "Harland, stay aboard and keep watch. Lars and Nils, fetch the tools from Gandalfr's chest."

Gandalfr would be helping us once more. I let the three of them carry my tools up to the stand of trees. I had decided that the trees I would choose would not be visible from the sea. I had spied the pines through the eye of the dragon and I did not want a curious sailor to see men hewing trees. The two trees I chose were straight. More importantly, their roots looked like we could dig them out easily. It was the roots we needed for the pine tar. We had two good wood axes and I made sure that they were sharp. Birger and I had done this back in Bygstad and we stood on either side of the tree and began to swing. It was competitive. I won and by that I mean that I reached the middle before Birger did. I waved him and the others to stand behind me and then I made the last cut. The tree fell where I wanted it to. As it fell nature did half of our work. The smaller branches broke off.

"Lars and Nils, use the hand axes to take off the smaller branches. The smallest can be taken back to the ship. Give them to Harland and he can add to the disguise. The really small ones will be needed for the fire."

Birger and I then began to chop down the second. I knew that Birger was trying to impress Maria. I let him win this race and I stepped aside to let him fell the tree. We now had the two trees we needed. Lars and Nils took down the spare branches and then we cleaned up the second tree.

"Birger, we need a kiln for the pine tar. Do you remember how to make one?"

He nodded, "Of course."

"Then go to the cove and find a flat patch of sand above the waterline that will do. There should be plenty of rocks to build it with and I passed on the beach, some limestone. When you have made the shape of the oven with the rocks then take the limestone and break it up. Do not mix it with the sand. I will do that." He was happy to do that. It meant he would be with Maria.

When the boys had finished with the trees the three of us took them, one by one, down to the cove. They would be something we would shape while the pine tar was made. We left most of the tools at the cove and headed back to the pine trees with mattocks, picks and spades. I took off my top. It was hot already and the work we would do was hard. The boys copied me. "What we need to do is to dig out the pine trees' roots. We need to do so carefully. We want as few roots damaged as we can. The trees are not deep rooted. We have all day to do this."

By noon we had one root already out and the boys had heeded my advice. Only one small root had been broken. We manhandled it down to the cove. The stones were already in the shape of a kiln and the limestone was broken up. There were channels in the sand and they led down the slope to one of the Frankish pots we had taken from Bordèu. The handle on it had

Dragon Rock

been broken and rendered it useless as a pot but we just needed something to hold the pine tar.

"Ask Maria to fetch us food, Birger, and I will finish the kiln." Maria spoke some of our words but when I had tried to speak to her she had not understood more than half of them. She and Birger communicated more easily. He told her what was needed. She smiled and their fingers touched as she headed up the path, which was becoming increasingly well worn, to head to the camp.

I was giving lessons to Lars and Nils. I needed to explain what we were doing and why. "What we are doing will make pine tar but we will not be as successful as if we were back in the fjord using ground limestone, good sand and fresh water. The salt in the sand and the water will not make as strong a mortar. It will, however, be better than just packing sand around it."

I showed them the proportions we used to mix the mortar and then I added the sea water. The salt in it would make it less useful. I used a sloppier mix at first. I poured the mixture on the top. It poured through the crevasses. I was satisfied.

"Now we start work on the trees."

"Is the oven finished?"

"No, Nils. We let the mortar dry first. I need some pine bark cutting neatly. We need a few pieces and they will form the channels that run down the sand to the pot. Birger, we need the pine tar pot to be as level as you can make it before we put the channels in."

By the time it was level we had cut eight good lengths of pine bark. There was more scrap than channels but nothing would be wasted. The bark would dry out and we would use the resiny bark as kindling. While we waited for the food and the kiln to dry out a little more I took out the shaping axes and I showed the three of them how to shape the tree into a mast. The smaller one would be used to make a pair of yards. As we shaped it the pile of shavings was gathered. We needed fuel for the oven. By the time Maria arrived with the food we had a mast that was beginning to take shape. One end was narrower than the other but we still had much work to do.

We ate. Our foragers had found berries and some nuts. Hunters had managed to kill some birds and other small animals.

The stew, flavoured with herbs and greens found by Joseph, was an interesting taste. More importantly it was hot and filling. The four of us then split the last tree. It would be a harder job to shape it but we had time. I let the two ship's boys continue to shave off wood from the mast while Birger and I shaped the two yards. It was almost evening when I resumed the work on the oven. I mixed the next mortar to make it firmer. I added ground up shells too. I used my hands to mould it around the rocks. I set Maria to collecting as much dried wood as she could. It was something, Birger told me, that she had often done at the lagoon.

I stretched. "We can do no more here. Come, we have one more root to dig out."

"And then we make pine tar."

"No Nils, we then light a small fire and dry out the oven. If I did it right then tomorrow we can begin to make pine tar."

Lars asked, "And if not?"

I smiled, "We start again!" Light was against us and by the time we reached the last root and began to dig it was too hard to see. We would have to resume the next day.

By the end of the day we were dirty and sweaty but we had one root we could burn. Before we left for the camp I lit a small fire in the kiln to dry it out. The real fire would be on the next day and that would be much hotter. That might be the one that destroyed all our work.

I had forgotten about the marriage but when we walked into the camp Oddr was ready. Birger and Maria were excited beyond words. I doubted that Maria would understand either the words or the ceremony. She was a Christian and their marriage ceremonies were different. The actual wedding seemed to take a heartbeat but it was a little longer. The two of them stepped over Birger's spear and Oddr bound their hands together. He pronounced that they had chosen to be wed and were now married. They were not the same words as would have been said at home but there we had volvas to direct the ceremony. That was it. Had it been in Bygstad then our mother and aunt would have woven a spell and that would lie beneath them when the marriage was sealed. In a ceremony back at home there would be more words but Oddr had said all that was necessary. Anders, Benni and Fritjof had made a bower for the couple away from

Dragon Rock

the rest of us but still guarded by the sentries and they left to cheers and banter. Luckily most of it went over Maria's head.

I slept on the tiny beach at the cove. That way I was close to the fire and to my ship. Joseph stayed at the camp for he found some cereal and was brewing ale. He told the waiting warriors that he could not attest to the taste but it would be ale and would be ready by noon the next day.

I slept alone. The boys were on the drekar and the rest of the men were in the camp but I lay under my wolf skin warmed by the kiln and comforted by the sound of the water lapping around the stern of the drekar.

When I woke the fire had gone out and it was still dark. I made water and then walked around to the larger beach in the small cove. I would not be seen unless there was a ship actually offshore. I peered out into the night. Even in the dark I saw the huge rock that was, in my mind, Skuld. I saw no vessels and no fires to indicate men camping on the rock. I wondered if they had given up. I did not know these people. If they were Norse or Danish then they would not give up until either we or they were dead. Men had died. It was not in battle, at our hands, but we had caused their deaths.

When I reached the kiln once more the sun had risen and I was able to examine it. There were no major cracks. It meant we could make the tar. I put the bark and the kindling in the ashes of the fire and lit it. I took all the dried wood that Maria had collected and slowly built up the fire. There was fresh wood and that I placed around the back of the kiln to dry. We had to wait now until the fire was hot enough to burn the pine roots.

Lars, Nils and Harland came down the side of the drekar. I waved them over to me, "We are almost ready. Let us go and dig out the last root."

We were more refreshed and it took less than an hour to dig it out. It helped that it was slightly smaller. We carried it down and laid it next to the first.

"Make water, eat food and then fetch me food and ale. We will spend the day here. We have much to do."

The kiln was still not hot enough and so while I waited I chopped the pine roots into smaller pieces. I had examined the keel and knew that the area we had to slaver with the sticky tar was not large. This morning would also be the time we used the crew to lift the bows higher so that I could work on the keel more easily. The boys returned and we ate. I told them what I would do and they nodded. This was a lesson. My father had taught it to me and Birger. In a perfect world Birger would be with me now and watching but I understood why he was not here. He and Maria were still in their bower. I deemed the fire was hot enough and I threw in the chopped-up roots. I had stones close by and I packed the opening with them. I used wet sand and the last of the ground up shells to mix with water to make a rough seal around the oven's mouth. I was improvising for at home we would have used clay to make a solid seal. When I had finished the tendrils of smoke and steam that came out told me that it was not completely sealed but it would have to do.

"Go to the stand of trees, we need four long thin trees to use as levers."

They hurried off. We had enough branches hewn from the two larger trees to support the keel but we needed long levers to lift it. I continued to pack the openings and then I watched. It would be a trickle of tar that came out first. It would never be a torrent but it would be a steady flow…if I had made it correctly.

Oddr and the other senior warriors came down before the boys had returned. "Leif, the lookout spied a ship out to the southeast of us. It did not close with this bay but it shows that we are being hunted."

I knew that they had not yet done with us. "Then we have to work quickly. I need the whole crew today. We must raise the ship and put it on timbers so that we can repair the damage."

Oddr shook his head, "We need lookouts. You can have all but four of the crew."

Falco said, "My father is a carpenter, Leif, and I have some skills if you have the tools." I pointed to Gandalfr's fine array of tools. Falco smiled, "Then all is good."

Birger arrived. He had a sheepish smile upon his face. Anders, Benni and Fritjof gave a long, 'ooooh'. The others said nothing. "Birger, I need the tail of one of those squirrels we hunted yesterday. If there is more than one that can be used then all to the good."

Dragon Rock

Pleased to be away from the looks and leers from his friends Birger hurried back to the camp. Lars, Harland and Nils returned with the first of the levers. The crew began to strip to the waist. Despite the shade of the ship, the trees and the rocks this would be hot work. I had the spare strakes and nails ready. They would need to be cut precisely. As soon as we had the four long levers we divided into four. It would take the whole crew, me included, to lift. We used rounded rocks to act as fulcrum.

"Lars, you and the boys have one task. When the hull is clear of the sand then place the branches beneath it. There are eight. Place four on the bottom and then another four at right angles and above the first four. That should be enough." I had spent enough time on this tiny beach to realise that the sand was a thin covering and there was rock beneath.

"Yes, Captain."

We slid the spars under the keel and then placed the rounded rocks close to the ship to allow us to lever. Had we had the time I would have lifted the deck and removed ballast. The presence of an enemy scout prevented that. This would need the brute strength of the crew. We all took the strain and every eye was on me. This was as much about working together as anything.

"One, two, three!"

On three we all pulled down the levers. The tallest men were at the end and the shorter ones at the front. *'Ægir'* cooperated and she rose. The boys did as I asked and the eight logs were placed beneath her.

"On three gently lower. One, two, three."

The weight of the ship pushed the logs down a little but there was still enough of the hull for Falco and me to work.

"Thank you, we can take it from here."

Oddr said, "Today we hunt and gather food whilst looking for enemies. Joseph said he believes that there is a port a few miles away. They may send men to search for us."

We had been lucky thus far and I knew it.

I glanced at the tar which was gathering in the pot. "Lars, light a small fire next to the pot to keep the tar warm." Birger arrived. "Brother, make the tails into brushes. Use some of the pine we cut."

I found the damaged strake. The ones around it were scratched and scraped but they could be smoothed. The pine tar would help to protect them. The one strake we had to replace was curved. We had to take all of it out. It was the length of a tall man's leg. With Falco at one end and me at the other we prised it out. I put the damaged strake on the sand. We might be able to use it for firewood when it had dried out. While I cleaned up the area where we would replace it, Falco measured the gap and marked the strake.

Falco said, "Leif, you have skills with the steering board but I have skills with the adze and shaping axe. Let me do this."

I nodded, "I will prepare the hammer and the nails." Had we been in Bygstad we might have bored holes and used trenails. They would have lasted longer. We had no time for that and the cruder method of hammering in iron nails would have to do.

"Lars, you and the boys, along with Birger, can continue to shape the yards and the mast." I looked at the pine tar. It was gathering well.

The difference between what Falco would do and what I would have done was the difference between a makeshift repair and the work of a man with skill. He made a joint at either end so that the strake would be held firmly in place before we used the nails. It took him at least two hours to make the strake and then he turned and nodded, "We can hammer the strake into place, Leif." I saw that he had cut his hand while working on the repair and some of the blood had smeared on the raw wood. That was good. It meant part of Falco was now within the drekar's hull.

We did not rush as we hammered in the nails that would keep the strake in place and when it was done we took handfuls of sand and rubbed them along the edge to make them smooth. The sand would also help the pine tar to stick. We smoothed the gouges and scratches caused by the rock and then stood back. The ship was ready for the tar. The boys and Birger stopped their work to watch Falco and me as we took the brushes and covered the new strake in the tar. We then worked our way up and down from the strake. We used all the tar but the damaged area had enjoyed a good, thick coat of tar. There was still tar oozing from the kiln. We would have enough to give a second coat, the next day.

Dragon Rock

There were still some hours in the day and after Maria and Joseph had brought us food we finished off the shaping of the yards and spars. I had the boys place them on the deck.

Dagfinn came for me as the sun started to set, "Oddr needs to speak to the men. Have the boys watch the tar and the ship." I frowned. He said, "I think they are ready, Leif."

"They are. Lars, I leave you in command."

He looked as proud as anything. He nodded, "I will keep her safe."

The men were gathered around the fire. As we made our way through the trees Dagfinn said, "Oddr wants to hold a Thing."

That made sense. We had some serious decisions to make. Oddr was neither jarl nor hersir. Joseph had Maria close to him. He knew that a Thing was for men only. He, Maria and the ship's boys would not be part of the debate that would take place. Joseph understood the concept and approved of it.

"We are all here. Joseph, fill the horns with your newly brewed ale. This seems a fitting occasion to taste it."

He and Maria took the pot they had filled around the waiting men and scooped ale into the horns. It would be put in a barrel and kept aboard. Oddr raised his horn and said, "The Clan of the Otter!"

We raised ours and chorused, "The Clan of the Otter!"

The ale was good and had an earthy, lemony flavour I liked. I saw Joseph looking expectantly at me and I nodded and raised the horn in approval. He smiled.

Oddr stepped into the middle of the circle of warriors, "We have decisions to make. The Norns have spun and while we have repaired our ship it is not yet ready to sail." He looked at me and stepped back.

I stepped forward, "We will apply the last coat of pine tar as soon as we can. We can lower the ship into the water tomorrow but I know not when it will be exactly. We need it to dry as much as possible. We could sail the day after or even, if all goes well, after dark." I rubbed my chin as I thought, "That might be the best solution." I stepped back.

It was Christof who moved forward, "We may not have that time. Brynjar and I went many miles today and we saw scouts. There are men who are hunting us. We saw them searching the bays that lie to the east of us. They will reach us within a day or so."

He stepped back. Brynjar stepped forward, "We counted forty of them. Their leaders were mailed."

Frode stepped forward, "I would not come so close to be taken prisoner and made a slave." He nodded towards Maria, "And I want to see the face of Birger's mother when she sees the beauty her son has brought home." That brought a smile and a ripple of approval around the circle. He stepped back.

Oddr looked around and when no one else stepped forward then he did so. He sighed, "When the hersir asked me to lead the men of Bygstad I did not think that I would have so many decisions to make. I thought we would just be following the jarl. That is not meant to be. When we hunted I saw a place we could meet these hunters and ambush them. It is six hundred paces to the east of us. There is a slope and we could hide in the trees so that we would be above them. Leif, you and the boys need to make sure the ship is ready for sea. As soon as it is then I want the mast stepped and the sail ready to be raised. Our lookouts report that there are still ships hunting us. We will need to fly." I nodded. "Tomorrow morning we take all that needs to be loaded down to the ship. Joseph and Maria will stay by the ship. We will then wait at the place where we will ambush those who hunt us. Leif, you will fetch us as soon as the ship is ready."

Although I nodded I saw a problem. The drekar was not in the water. I would have to find an answer myself. Every eye was on me. My decision to risk the rocks had saved us and hurt us at the same time. It would be up to me to save us again.

Dragon Rock

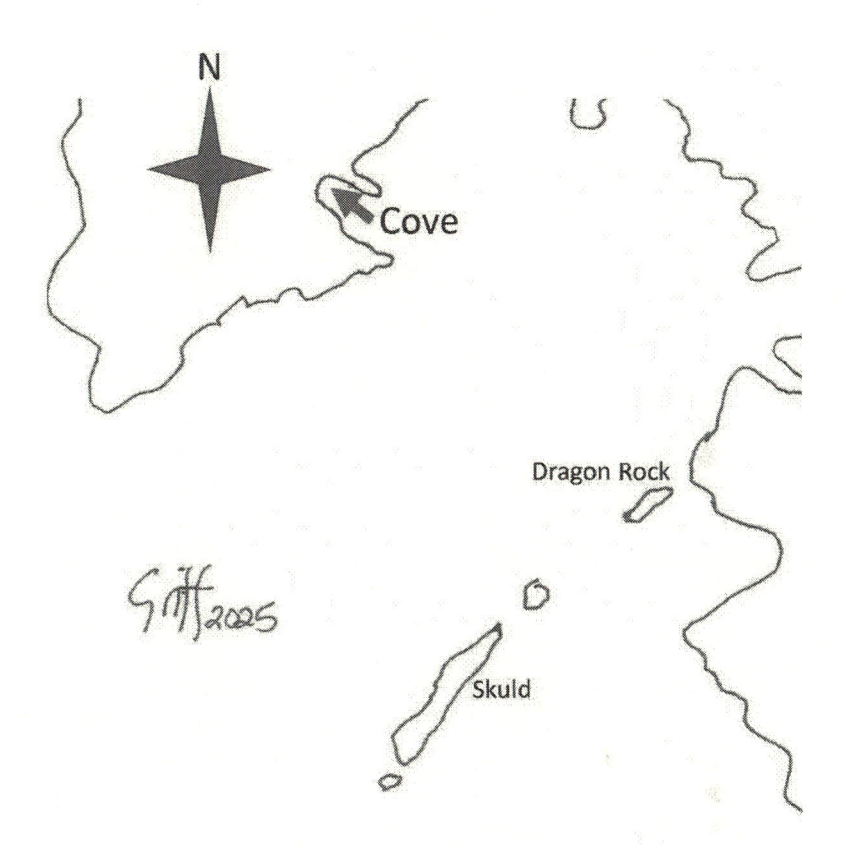

Cove

Dragon Rock

Skuld

Chapter 13

It was dark when I reached the ship but there was a glow from the fire that was warming the tar that lit my way through the bushes and trees. By its glow I saw that the flow of tar was now barely a trickle. My boys had been joined by Birger, Maria and Joseph. We had brought some of the things to be loaded on the ship. I said, "Joseph, make beds. Birger, we will finish the covering of the tar." It would have been better to wait until daylight but the presence of potential enemies changed all of that. The damage had one coat and that would be almost dry. I was in unknown territory. Back in Bygstad we had used pine tar when we had the time to let each coat dry before applying the next, and we could then let the whole hull dry out of the water for seven or more days. Here I was making makeshift repair.

The hourglass was still in use and it took two hours to complete the sealing. The tails we had used had shed some of their hairs on the hull. I hoped that they would help to bind the strakes. When we had finished we sealed the last of the precious pine tar in a pot. If we were damaged again we could seal the hurt.

We were exhausted when we finished. Before we rolled into our beds I said, "We will be up before dawn. I want to be able to remove the logs from underneath and be ready to move the ship into the water by mid-morning."

Birger said, "Just us?"

I shook my head, "No, we will need the crew but Oddr plans on having them rise early to clear the camp and set up the ambush."

Joseph asked, "Will the tar be dry?"

"I hope so."

My sleep was fitful for I bore the weight of the lives of everyone on my shoulders. If I made a mistake then we could still all end our days dead or as slaves.

The need to make water and my fitful sleep meant I woke well before dawn. I made water and then made my way to the ship. I gingerly touched the strakes we had coated. They were tacky rather than sticky. By dawn it would be drier. I made my way up to the camp. I saw that it was Dagfinn and Fritjof who were on watch.

"You are up early."

I nodded, "The tar should be dry by morning. When we have carried the supplies to the camp I want to float the drekar, if the tar has dried."

"That is sooner than we hoped."

"We are not yet on the water and we have a mast to fit too." I spooned some of the stew from the pot into a bowl. The night watch had filled the hours by cooking. One thing we would not miss from this land were the flies. The use of fires kept them at bay and helped men to enjoy a night of sleep.

After eating my breakfast I headed back to the sea and, after rousing the others, watched the sky begin to become lighter. It was as it did so I saw that the three branches we had placed around the stern of the ship now looked to be dying. Their colour would be different from the trees behind them. A scout or a curious lookout might come closer to investigate. Time was running out and I could almost hear the Norns spinning. They enjoyed teasing men, especially resourceful men who challenged their webs. We had to leave as soon as we were able and trust that our repair had worked. It would not be the Blue Sea that would test our handiwork but the mighty ocean beyond the straits. I went to the strakes and touched them in a different place to the one I had before. It felt less tacky. It was drying. I picked up a handful of sand and threw it on the pine tar. It stuck. The weight it might add was marginal and the sea would soon wash it off but if it helped to dry the tar a little quicker then it was worth the attempt. While the others rose, made water and ate breakfast I gave the thinnest covering of sand as I could to the tar.

The others were ready for work when I heard the men coming down from the camp. They carried the supplies we would take. The ale was now in a pair of barrels. Bordèu had yielded many such containers. I thought of it as Bordèu treasure. Oddr laid down his load. He said, "Christof and Benni are watching for the scouts. We will join them when all is brought here."

I went to the hull and touched the sand. It was dry. "We can float the ship now, Oddr. It will take two hours or more to ready her for sea but I believe that we can leave before noon."

"The dark would be better. The scouts report the ships still seek our hiding place. Night is our friend and will hide us."

I shrugged, "Whatever you wish but I will be happier when *'Ægir'* is in the water once more."

By the time the supplies were all down an hour or more had passed. I climbed aboard the ship for we would need someone to steer when we put her in the water. Harland came with me to stand at the prow and to throw the rope to the ones on the small beach. This time it was Oddr who gave the commands. I heard him shout for the levers to lift. I felt the prow rise a little as the wooden poles lifted the front of the ship from the supporting timbers and then were gently lowered to kiss the sand. We did not yet move.

I shouted, when my ship's boy had thrown the rope to Lars, "Harland, ask Oddr to have the men push the ship gently back so that the stern is in deeper water."

This was the time for our chant. The crew needed to push together. They had to be firm and strong yet gentle.

> *We are the clan of the otter*
> *We live where no one else can*
> *We fish the seas and water*
> *We serve the goddess Rán*
> *We are the clan of the otter*
> *We live where no one else can*
> *We fish the seas and water*
> *We serve the goddess Rán*
> *We are the clan of the otter*

I felt the bobbing motion as Harland, peering over the side, shouted, "We are afloat, Captain."

I heard the cheer from the warriors. "Tie us off and then begin to load the ship, lift the deck." Men went to tether us to two trees. There was little tide in this sea but it paid to be cautious.

I went to the prow and lowered myself into the sea. Oddr said, "Do you need men to be left here?"

I shook my head, "If you wish to leave this evening then we have all day to balance the ship and I would be happier if there were men between us and the hunters."

"We will let you know if we are found."

Dragon Rock

"And I will come for you when we are ready for sea."

I put my hands to the repairs. I was feeling for the bubbles that would tell me the hull was still damaged. There were none.

It had taken an hour for the crew to bring our pots and supplies to the beach. With just a few of us left, Joseph, Maria and my ship's boys, it took twice as long to load the ship. Eventually, after almost three turns of the glass, we had the ship loaded and the deck replaced. Fitting the mast and the sail could normally be completed in a short time but that was with a whole crew heaving. It took us more than an hour to fit the mast and another to attach the sail. What I now feared was that, with a furled sail, we might be seen. I did not raise the sail. That could wait until the crew were all aboard.

The sun had passed its zenith two hours earlier when we had finished. The goat had been brought back to its home at the bows. We had cut grass for her and Joseph had the mash from the ale making in pots. She would enjoy that too as we headed for home. The chests were made ready for the oarsmen. The barrels were all secured and we were ready for sea. I sent Harland to the masthead to keep watch and, after strapping on my sword belt and donning my wolf cloak to protect me from the sun, I set off to let Oddr know we were ready. Once at the camp I saw the evidence of our short occupation. When the hunters who sought us found it they would know where we had been but by then we would be at sea and safe. Oddr had said that the site of the ambush was six hundred paces or more to the east of the camp. That was a little vague. A navigator would have been more precise and given bearings.

I could not find the path that they had taken and so I made my way, carefully, through the trees. I kept stopping to look ahead for any signs of the warriors. When I did finally see one it was not a Norseman. It was a man wearing a hood. He had on a rough tunic and breeks. On his feet he had sandals. None of those things marked him as a threat but the small round shield he held in his left hand, the short sword hanging from his belt and the fire hardened spear he had in his right hand did. He was seeking us. When he glanced to the left I saw that he was darker skinned than we were. He was one of those who were hunting for us. I drew my sword and my seax. I had no mail and no helmet but neither did this potential enemy. I had to slay him or else he might summon help. Before I could move closer to him I saw movement in the trees beyond him. There were others. The ambush was about to be ambushed and I dared not shout. If I did then I would draw every enemy to me. I had to use cunning.

I calculated that I still had time before I needed to utter a warning as the men were sneaking up the slope to the waiting warriors. I moved steadily towards the man whose attention was on the higher ground ahead. I managed to get to within eight feet of him and I was ready to strike. I was undone by the twig snapping beneath my feet. It cracked and his head whipped around. I had almost forgotten that I was wearing my wolf cloak but the look of horror on the man's face and the shocked silence told me that I had scared him. Before he could shout I ran to him and hacked sideways into his body. It was his shocked silence that doomed him and his shield did not save him.

His falling body tumbling down the slope was, however, heard and I saw a face as a warrior who had been hidden by bushes, turned. Now was the time for a shout, "Bygstad! Stand to! Ware danger from steerboard!"

Two men rushed at me at the same time as I heard a horn that was not ours. The enemy leader was ordering his attack. I crabbed my way sideways up the slope as I sought to escape the attention of these two men and join my shield brothers. I wanted to be closer to our men and above these two. They had spears and swords. They also had the same small shield the dead man had held. There was a roar from below the hill and a wave of warriors raced up. Christof had been right, they were not mailed but they had numbers.

I heard from my left, Oddr's voice as he ordered a shield wall. That would ensure that the ones who faced the attack would be the best warriors and they were both mailed and experienced. The ones like Birger, Benni, Anders and Fritjof, would be in the second rank.

The two men coming to get me were eager for what they saw as an easy victory. Their heads were down as they charged up the slope. I saw a flat space between two trees and it was there I stopped and turned. It was when they looked up and saw, not a man, but an armed wolf that they halted and looked in horror at

Dragon Rock

the apparition before them. I laughed and roared. They flinched. I think I could have risked walking backwards up the slope but this was too good a place to vacate so easily. I had two trees that would protect me almost as well as shield brothers. Added to the fear they obviously felt, the trees gave me confidence. I would stay and fight them here. It would be two less men for the clan to have to fight.

They came on together and that was out of lack of confidence. They held their spears before them and nervously tried to negotiate the slope as one. I stepped from the safety of my arbour for a single swashing swing at their spears. The sharp edge of my sword hacked off a foot from the end one of one of the spears and I stepped back. The warrior threw the now useless spear at me. With no end to balance it, and as I was stepping back it was easy to deflect. As he drew his sword his companion lunged at me with his spear. It had no metal tip but was fire hardened and as I was not wearing mail it could kill. I used my seax to block the spear and lunged at his face with my sword. I was above him and the end of my blade came out of the back of his skull. His companion ran to rejoin the rest of the enemy soldiers racing up the slope to get at me. He was not a real warrior. I turned and risked showing my back as I ran up to join the shield wall that was forming just forty paces behind me at the top of the slope. I was ahead of some of the enemy but another twenty had taken an easier route and they were about to charge the spears of our skjaldborg.

Dagfinn shouted, "Leif, stand in the second rank. Guard the end."

I reached the second rank and turned. I was behind Frode and Angmar and next to Anders. Anders had his spear between Frode and Angmar. The enemy did not strike as one. To do so they would have had to halt and I think whoever led them was afraid we might run. Our spears were thrust at heads and the enemy spears struck the solid walls of shields that were much bigger than they would have seen before. Their spears were, in the main, fire hardened while ours were made of iron. Even the enemy ones that struck did no damage and most broke while I saw Anders' spear go into the eye of a warrior who had a leather cap. The man made barely a sound as he died. The ones who had been chasing me now reached the skjaldborg. They had a slope and bodies to contend with and they endured the same fate. Men fell in the first encounter and those that reached us first were the bravest and the best.

Oddr was neither hersir nor jarl but he was a warrior and seeing a chance for victory he shouted, "Charge!" The wall of shields became a flood of warriors as we broke the shields apart and charged. I was at the end and I stepped beyond Angmar to hack into the side of a surprised warrior. They outnumbered us and the last thing they expected was for us to charge. We had to kill as many as we could. I knew, even as I slashed through the leather cap and skull of another warrior that we wanted them to flee back to their homes in terror. We needed them to wait to gather a larger army to come for us and by then we would be gone.

We were warriors and knew how to fight. Even Benni, Fritjof and Anders had fought Franks and Vasconians. We slashed and stabbed. I used my sword and seax to carve a path through them. I struck confidently and quickly. I had sharpened blades that were well made and when they struck they made savage wounds. It was made easier when some turned to try to flee. The slope and the undergrowth proved as deadly as we were and many tripped and fell. Wearing no mail I was as fast as the men I chased. Half of their men were already dead or wounded and the rest obeyed the horn. They fled back down the slope. Oddr shouted, "Hold!" We held the line. Men were breathing heavily and that was all that we heard except for the sound of men slipping and sliding down the slope.

Oddr said, "Is anyone hurt?"

Brynjar said, "Fritjof was speared in the leg."

"I have a wound that needs to be stitched." I turned and saw that Falco had a long scar running down his cheek.

"Leif, take them back to the drekar and have Joseph look at them." He wiped his sword on the tunic of a dead enemy and sheathed it. "We are ready to sail?"

"We are." I glanced up at the sky. "It will be sunset in two hours."

"Then when we have ensured that they are gone we will join you. Thank you for the warning."

Dragon Rock

The wounds to the two men I led back to the ship were not life threatening and when we neared the ship I shouted, "Joseph, we have wounded." I left the two of them on the beach and climbed aboard. "Lars, have the foliage removed. We no longer need it."

Harland shouted down from his lofty perch, "Captain, there is still a ship out there. It is close to the dragon rock."

We dared not move the foliage for the ship would see the movement and the ship. "Then leave the foliage where it is. We are leaving at dark, Lars. I want the ship ready. As soon as the sun sets then remove the foliage."

"Yes, Captain."

Nils asked, "Were others hurt?"

"No, just these two." I took off my wolf skin, "This terrified them." I put it in the chest along with my sword and seax. I would clean them later. I saw that Joseph had hung the hourglass in its usual place and it had been turned. The hourglass gave order to the ship as well as information.

The crew arrived in ones and twos. Oddr did not need the whole crew to scout and the more men we had on board the better. We had time for the men to take off their mail and clean the blood from their hands and faces. They ate and were able to make water before we took to the sea. The presence of the enemy ship could have been seen as a problem but now it seemed as though it helped us for it made us stay in our cove. Oddr and Asbjørn came to the stern as soon as they boarded.

"So, Leif, what is your plan?" Oddr led the men in battle but now he needed advice from the navigator.

When Gandalfr had been killed, in the eyes of the crew, I had been forced to try to become the man who had more experience in one hand than I had in my whole body. My father had taught me that a man does not shirk his responsibilities. He faces up to them. "The ship is patrolling the waters between the large rocks I see as the Norns and the land beyond. I think that there is clear water between Skuld and the dragon to sail."

"But we do not know those waters."

"No, Asbjørn, but then do we know any of the waters? It is a risk and there may come a time when we have to challenge one of their ships but I would make it later rather than sooner." There was still enough light to study a chart and I waved over Joseph who held a map in his hands. "This is very rough and ready but it is all we have. You can see that there are gaps but the coast of Al-Andalus appears to be the west of us. If we sail south and west we should keep it to steerboard and these islands to larboard. We need to keep out of sight of the land. They may have towers and even if they do not have a machine which can destroy us they can give a warning and send other ships to take us. We need to get as close as possible to the straits and do so unseen. We will stick to the original plan and sail as far from the tower as we can and pass through the straits at night."

Oddr nodded, seemingly satisfied. He put his arm around Asbjørn, "And when we do reach home we shall see our wives and family eh?"

Asbjørn nodded, "Aye, I have almost forgotten what my son and daughter look like."

I said, "And I have never seen my son."

Oddr nodded, "And that is why I know we will get home. You are driven, Leif Wolf Killer. You endure hardship because you have one task and one end. The crew trust you. I trust you. I do not always understand the decisions you make but you were chosen and for good reason. When we sailed over those rocks I thought we were doomed but we were not. Continue to do as you do, Leif, and we will all see Bygstad again."

I was left with just Joseph. The ship's boys had learned to eat and drink while they could and they were young. They had still to grow into men. "Joseph, can I do this? We have to sail through largely unknown waters against a fleet of enemies."

"Oddr is right, Master. I had not seen it amongst the men when I lived among the Franks but I see it in you. You have been chosen. Oddr put it in words when he said that you make the right decisions. Do not doubt yourself."

I liked the gentle slave, "Joseph, I promised you that I would take you to your home and I cannot. I am sorry."

He nodded and I saw sadness in his eyes as he looked eastwards to the darkening sky, "Yes, Master, so close and yet so far. Perhaps the Parcae keep me with you for a reason. My life is better than it was, much better. Had you asked me two years ago if the life of a slave could be fulfilling then I would have said no but now my life seems almost that of a freeman."

His words sparked an idea in my head and I suddenly said, "Then you are free. I free you."

His mouth dropped open, "Free?"

I nodded, "I will tell the crew now."

He held up his hand, "First, Master." He emphasised the word, "Do you mean I can leave now? I can go where I wish."

"Of course. We will be sailing close to the coast and I can land you there."

He nodded and said, carefully and clearly, "And if I want to stay?"

"Then we shall pay you as a healer. You will share in the profits from the voyage. If we ever reach home." I saw him thinking, "You would stay?"

He nodded, "Until you said those words I never thought about being free. I know you once promised me freedom but I never expected to get close to my home. I like your family. I confess that life aboard a ship is not enjoyable but I like Bygstad and I enjoy the life on the farm with Lars Greybeard. I do not know if my family live or if they have been made into slaves. This life I know and with the clan I can make a difference. I will stay with you, Leif."

I held out my arm and he clasped it. I realised this was the first time we had done so and it felt right. I said, loudly, "I have given Joseph the Healer his freedom. He is no longer a thrall. I have promised him a share in the profits." I saw Oddr smile and nod. The crew cheered. It was a special moment for it meant the crew, for some reason, were in a good mood. It almost seemed as though I had made a blót. I knew it was not for to be a real sacrifice it had to be something you thought was valuable and you were losing it. Joseph was invaluable but I was not losing him.

I was able, then, to put my mind to the task in hand. The sail had yet to be unfurled but in the sky that was growing darker as evening approached I saw the pennant. The wind was from the north. We would be sailing south and east first and then south and west once we passed between Skuld and the dragon rock. The wind would still help us as we headed to the straits. The

Dragon Rock

danger would be if it continued to blow from that direction going through the straits for it would take us closer to the tower. That was in the future. Now it was almost time for us to leave.

I said, "Lars, Nils, untie us and Harland, remove our disguise." I had learned that tides were negligible in this Blue Sea. We would not move very much. However, I did not want the rocks at the side to be an issue and so I said, "Run out the oars. Keep us away from the rocks and be ready to back water when I say." The oars would need to push us away from the cove and then turn us around. Once that was done they could be stacked on the mast fish and it would be up to me, the sail, the ship's boys and, most importantly, *'Ægir'* to save the clan. As I put my hand on the gunwale I knew that she was ready. She was now healed and rested. I said, to her, "Now is your time, my sweet. Take us home."

I waited until the sun had set completely and the foliage had all been removed before I hissed, "Back water." I knew how sound carried across the sea at night. The boys were ready to unfurl the sail. I had told them that until we passed the dragon rock we would use half sail. We did not need speed, we needed care to tiptoe though the rocks and to pass the guard ships that would now be moored as sentry ships. Joseph and Maria were at the prow. They would be my eyes when we headed for the channel I hoped was both wide enough and deep enough for our keel. I did not want to hurt *'Ægir'* again. Harland was at the masthead. When Joseph raised both arms I knew we were clear of the cove. "Steerboard oars, back water. Larboard oars row." We turned around in our own length. I waved to the boys and the sail was unfurled. "In oars." The oars had been greased and they slid silently in. The wind filled the sails and we began to move, steadily and silently across the darkening waters.

Skuld was the best marker for the rock was huge while the dragon lurked with its head just above the sea to larboard. It would need a wary eye to be kept on it. I knew that the guard ship would have anchored. There were too many rocks for a ship to risk sailing in the dark. For all I knew there were a number of sentry ships watching for us. I wanted silence. I kept one eye on the pennant and sail and the other on Joseph. I had to trust his judgement. I saw that Birger had joined his bride and they were

Dragon Rock

watching too from the prow. It was Birger who told me I was sailing too close to the dragon. He waved an arm and I shifted the steering board. As we passed the huge rock I thought of as Skuld I glanced along the rocks. I was shocked to see that what I had seen as three islands, the Three Sisters, were in fact two islands. One large one and a smaller one. There was no gap between Urðr and Verðandi. I had chosen the right passage. I touched my Hammer of Thor. Had I picked another then we would be dead or slaves.

Once we were through I had to watch for two things: the land to larboard and the guard ship to steerboard. When Birger and Joseph signalled that we had clear water I said, "Full sail!" *'Ægir'* was ready to fly. With the wind filling her sail she leapt forward. As our bow rose and fell I could not help but think of the dolphins.

As soon as Lars came to the steering board the other two went to adjust the sheets and ropes so that they were all taut. Our time tied to the land had allowed us to replace any that looked damaged in any way. Lars turned the hourglass. I looked at the sky. There were a few scudding clouds. We would be dancing in and out of moonlight. I hoped that the sentries on the guard ship were watching the island. It was night time but we would be seen if any was looking.

It was Nils who would have the first watch atop the masthead and when he had checked the ropes he clambered to the top. Harland descended. He would be the one who fetched ale and food while we sailed. The crew would sleep. The day had been a busy one and while we had won the fight it had to have had an effect on both bodies and minds. Nils looked astern and to the west first. That was where the guard boat watched. I caught a whiff of woodsmoke from the east that told us there was a settlement there but as I could see nothing I assumed that there was no tower. The land was a darker shadow well to the east.

The night passed. Lars marked its passage with the turning of the hourglass. I marked the compass when I caught a sight of the stars but it would be a rough guide. We were now sailing south by west and the wind from the north was a good one. A navigator could ask no more.

The hourglass, allied to our eyes, told us when dawn would be soon upon us. I sent Harland to wake Oddr and then to relieve Nils. Both Harland and Lars had enjoyed an hour of sleep. Nils, like me, had been awake all night. We needed the full crew ready for dawn. The night had hidden us but now the full glare of the hot sun would mark us.

Oddr, Asbjørn and Christof came to the steering board. All had food in their hands and horns with ale. "How went the night?"

"A good passage and we saw nothing. That, however, is no surprise. This morning will be more of a challenge and," I pointed to the pennant, "the wind is changing. It still blows from the north but it is a little more westerly."

Asbjørn was the one who struggled to read the wind and its effects, "How will that affect us?"

I shook my head, "It will make little difference for now but if it continues to change and come from the west then our speed will slow. We might have to tack and turn more frequently."

Oddr looked at his friend, "And if it switches to blow from the south or south and east then we would have to take to the oars."

"Then let us pray that it does not change."

The sun rose and we breathed a collective sigh of relief when we saw neither sail nor land. We had passed beyond the rocks and I hoped that we were out of sight. The sea was barely flecked with white and that meant no rocks. I stayed at the board for an hour and then handed it to Christof and Lars. Birger would relieve Lars after an hour and Nils an hour after that. I would be woken. Two hours of sleep would refresh me and I would have another sleep in the afternoon. When I reached my home I would enjoy whole nights of sleep without waking.

I rolled into my fur and covered my head with my wolf skin and was soon asleep in my nest by the larboard quarter.

Chapter 14

There was too much noise and the time was too short for a really deep sleep and I did not dream. I no longer dreaded my dreams for what I had thought was fearful had been sent to aid us. I woke because my bladder needed to be emptied. That and the call from the lookout, "Land to the southeast." However, as soon as I stood I knew that the wind was changing. It was more from the west than it had been. It still blew strongly from the north, I could see that from the pennant, but we were being pushed slightly to the east. I said, as I lowered my breeks, "Christof, push the steerboard to move us more to the west."

He did so but said, "It means we are moving more slowly."

I nodded and said, "We need to be as close to the coast of Al-Andalus as we can. Joseph." Joseph the healer came from the prow, "You have marked the course?"

"Yes, Captain." He took out the chart and the compass. He said, "The last large island in the chain is to the southeast of us. Ahead and to the west lies the mainland, Al-Andalus."

When I had finished I showed them to Christof and to Nils, "See, we have moved a mile further from the coast and that is why we can see the island."

Christof said, "I am sorry, Captain."

I smiled, "Do not be. I am the one charged with sailing the ship and it is just a mile that we have veered off course. We will soon recover distance lost." I put the wolf skin over my head. Not only did it protect me from the sun but it also gave me comfort. It was a reminder of Lars Greybeard and his sheep. The wolf had brought Freya into my life.

As the day progressed the wind kept veering but the changes were so slight that I think only I knew the full extent of them. I let Lars sleep until noon. Despite his youth he was the most reliable of my replacements and he understood the need to keep a steady course. While we were back on the course I had chosen, Christof and Nils' mistake had cost us time and put us where we could be seen from the islands.

We ploughed on for an hour or so through seas which appeared to be empty of sails. The hourglass had just been turned and I had enjoyed a horn of the ale brewed by Joseph when Harland shouted, "Sail to steerboard."

I looked but knew that I would see nothing. He had a much better view than I did. "Can you see the land?"

There was the slightest of pauses and he called down. "There is a smudge that might be the land, Captain."

That explained the sail. We were on course and sailing where I wanted to be but that meant we would see more ships. Some would be harmless traders keeping close to the coast and safe havens but there could also be hunters looking for us. Even harmless traders could be boarded and questioned and our sail, not to mention the distinctive shape of our hull, marked us as a ship that was foreign to these waters. I was not worried about the land. We might see the land but it would take someone on a very high tower with perfect vision to identify us as a Norse ship.

Christof asked, "Do we change course?"

"There is no need and I fear that we might have to take to the oars soon in any case. The wind is still veering. I want to head as far south as we can before dark."

"Then I will take the opportunity for sleep. You will need relief sooner rather than later and if we are to row…" I knew that Christof felt guilty about his mistake.

We were not a large ship and Christof let others know what I had said. Men prepared in their own ways. Some slept and some sharpened weapons. While there was not an immediate prospect of combat many of the men on the ship thought of themselves as warriors first and sailors second. Danger in these waters meant that we might have to fight.

I did not want to rest but I knew that I ought to. Lars had enjoyed two hours of sleep and I woke him, "You can relieve me for a couple of hours." I whistled and Birger looked up. I waved him to me. "You and Lars can watch for two hours. Christof is sleeping too. If the wind changes to be in your faces then wake me but other than that just keep as much of the wind as you can. I will trim the sail now but it may need more work."

I went to the stays and adjusted them so that the wind still filled the sail. We were not sailing as fast as when we had passed the dragon rock but the speed was acceptable. When I was satisfied I laid down and covered my head with the wolf to protect it from the sun.

I barely had an hour of sleep before I was woken. "Sorry, Brother, but the wind is now coming from the south and west. We are almost stopped."

I rose and smiled.

He asked, nervously, "Do we take to the oars?"

"Not yet. The two of you, I am going to make a turn. Trim the sails while I do so."

I had not really been sleeping but dreaming and planning our course. I turned the steering board so that we were sailing south and east, away from the coast and from the straits. The wind now pushed us, albeit slowly. It meant I was delaying the inevitable, the moment we would have to take to the oars. I wanted to get as far south as we could. We needed sea room away from the coast and the islands that now lay to the north of us. My manoeuvre had little effect until my brother and Lars adjusted the sails. I waved my hands to direct them and when the sail billowed a little and we started to move I held up my hand.

"Now the two of you sleep." I waved to the healer, "Joseph."

Joseph hurried up to me and he brought the chart and compass. "How far to the straits?"

He held up the map and pointed a thin finger, "We are here. I estimate between three and four hundred miles from us." He paused, "We are now travelling away from the straits."

"But still heading south." I now knew how fast we could travel. "At best speed, with the wind as it was when we left then that might take two days, perhaps less." He nodded. "This," I waved my hand around my head, "could take five or six."

"But, Captain, the wind will change again."

"We know not when." I sighed, "We need to take to the oars. Ask Oddr to join me."

When he came aft I said, "We are within two days of the straits or we would be if the wind was with us. I intend to have the crew row south and west until dark. They can sleep and we will then use this smallest of winds to head south and east. We pray for a change in its direction."

"And how long until we reach the straits if we do that?"

"More than two days and nearer to four. I would row hard, Oddr. The men have enjoyed a night and day of rest. We are fed and there is still ale."

"You are right."

I said, "We will continue on this course for an hour so that the men can prepare for a hard row."

After they had prepared and when the glass was turned we furled the sail and with men heaving and straining at the oars we resumed our course to the straits. The sunset helped me to steer a safe course. I kept the mast and prow in a line. When it dropped below the horizon we stopped rowing. Men leaned over the oars to suck in air. Joseph had been measuring our speed.

"How far?"

"We travelled thirty miles, Captain, and the men did well. With just the wind that would have been ten and those ten would have taken us further away from the straits."

"And that is what we will be doing now." I smiled, "Rest." We were sailing away from safety but it was all that I could think of.

I had decided that I would stay awake all night. The slight mistake north of the last island had cost us and I wanted to be on deck to be in tune with the wind, the sail and the ship. Lars had slept while the crew had rowed and he would be fresh enough to aid me. The rest of the crew would sleep. It would be the sleep of the exhausted. Before I had left Bygstad I would not have believed that I could do without sleep but I now knew that my body could do things that had seemed impossible. Snorri was right, Gandalfr's spirit was in this ship and he was giving me strength. I did not know how but it was the only thing which made sense to me. When I stood with my hand on the steering board, the wood carved by Gandalfr, I felt as though his hand was on mine.

By dawn the wind had turned so much that it was now blowing from the north and the west. It would drive us away from the straits. The longer we spent in this sea the more chance we had of being caught. I would have to take to the oars again. I did not want to but we had no choice.

I waited until the sun had risen and then had Lars wake the crew. One look at the sails told them all that there was to know. I

Dragon Rock

said, "I am sorry, Oddr, but we have a long day of rowing ahead of us. This time we grind out the miles."

He nodded, "Single oars and relieve the oarsmen every hour."

I nodded. We would not be able to make as much distance as with the whole crew rowing but we could keep it up for longer. "That is the only way we can do this."

He came to the stern, "When we get home I must tell my son that the life of a warrior is not all glory and gathering silver."

The sail was furled as the men began to row. I was in need of sleep but this was not a task for Lars or Nils. Christof or Birger might have managed but they were on the oars and we needed their arms and backs. I steered due west. The oars dug in and the drekar slid though the water. We turned to head west. If nothing else I now knew that our repairs had worked. There was no sign of water and we rode the seas well. Nils was cross legged on the masthead and yard and Harland was with me. I had allowed Lars an hour or two of sleep. Joseph and Maria kept the men at the oars supplied with ale and water.

The sun bore down as the morning passed and men's skin continued to redden. Some had already darkened to a light brown and I knew that when we returned home, if we returned home, then there would be much comment about the colour of our skins. We rowed on under an almost cloudless blue sky.

Nils was at the masthead and he shouted, "I feel the wind turn. Look, Captain, see the pennant." We were saved. The wind was turning and even as I watched the pennant it turned even more so that it was blowing from the southeast to northwest. The wind had died while we rowed and now came to our aid. It was a wind that would take us to the straits.

"In oars. Lars and Harland, unfurl the sails!"

The wind was with us and, as it increased, it made us fly. Men cheered and patted each other on the back. I let Lars take the steering board and I went to make water.

The wind had been steady for two turns of the hourglass when Nils shouted, "Sails to the south and west, Captain." There was a pause. "It is the large ship with the oars and her pups!" There was another pause, "I can see another large ship but they have no oars."

Dragon Rock

We had the wind but they had a line of ships waiting for us. If we continued to use the wind we could be on a converging course and they would take us. They had known we had left our hiding place and anticipated our course. Instead of wasting time searching for us they simply waited closer to the straits. Our men were tired and there was only one thing to do. We had to sail into the wind that would aid our enemies. I said, "Oddr, we cannot rely on just the wind. This wind serves our enemies more than us. If we are to escape we must row once more."

He shook his head, "You are right but the men have had a hard morning of rowing."

Brynjar said, "The Norns are spinning. Do they enjoy toying with us?"

Oddr said, "Do not tempt them, Brynjar. We had all better prepare for war. We are in the hands of Leif Wolf Killer now."

"Furl the sail and prepare to come about." I wanted them to think that we were fleeing when all I was doing was drawing them close to us so that when we made our turn we would fly past them.

In the time it had taken to furl the sail and for the men to take to the oars the fleet of ships had closed with us and were all clearly visible. Such was the power of the rejuvenated wind that even with the oars we were barely keeping ahead of them. I estimated that they were less than a mile from us and by the time we had turned they would be even closer. We heeled over and the canted decks made anything not tied down slide.

"Joseph, keep an eye on those ships behind. I want to know when they are closing with us." We were heading into the wind. The enemy had so many ships that they could tack and turn and use their nimble hulls to stay with us. The ship with the oars could do exactly as we had done.

My mind was already working as hard as I could make it to come up with a plan that would see us escape this trap.

Joseph's voice was like a regular beat as he told me of the closing distance. The smaller ships were spread out in two arcs. They were there to stop us from turning. The ship with the oars also had her oars run out and she was rowing and using the wind by tacking and turning. She had the luxury of the smaller ships and they were easier to turn. The fleet behind was gaining more than a hundred paces an hour. Soon she would be upon us. Looking ahead I saw some hope. Twilight was two hours away. Perhaps darkness might help us. The brief hope flashed like a candle before the Norns snuffed it out. After dark the small boats would simply close with us and board us. We needed to disappear but here we had no convenient bank of fog.

I glanced astern and saw that the larger ship with the oars was well ahead of the other large ship. She was powering through the water. The ship which had just sails had to keep turning. I was clutching at that straw but I knew that even without her aid we were still outnumbered.

"Joseph, I know that we are some days from the straits but how far are we from Al-Andalus?"

He picked up the map and I saw his face as he calculated. "With the wind or with oars?"

"We could use the wind to head north."

"Then four hours."

I knew then that I had to take a chance, I had to risk *'Ægir'* again. "Oddr."

He came to join me. He was a clever man and he knew that we were in a most precarious position. "It looks grim, Leif. They are catching us and the men are weary beyond words."

I nodded, "And I have a plan. It is risky but it might work." I laid out my plan and he smiled. "It means a hard row for you all."

"Better than enslavement or a watery death. I want to see my family again." He turned and shouted, "One man in two don your mail and then retake the oars. We need helmets and swords strapped to our waists. The men of Bygstad will show these pirates what we can do."

No one appeared downhearted as they took to the oars.

"Lars, unfurl the sail." I banged my foot whilst beginning the slow turn that I hoped would catch the enemy unawares. Oddr began to sing the marching song we had used in Frankia. It made me sad for Gandalfr had been alive the last time we had given it voice. When we turned we would have the wind once more but we would be sailing directly at them. I just hoped they didn't realise that. If they turned beam on and made a long line then we were doomed.

Dragon Rock

We come from Bygstad, brave and strong
We stand together as we march along
Beware our blades for we can slay
And do so all the battle day
We come from Bygstad, brave and strong
We stand together as we march along
Beware our blades for we can slay
And do so all the battle day

The men put their backs into it and we began to turn. The enemy would think we were escaping to the northeast. It was what we had done before. "Joseph, tell me what you see."

"They are following, Captain. The smaller boats are no longer in a continuous line. The large ship without oars is falling behind." He paused, "She is turning north." That made sense for she had wind she could use.

"Good." They were trying to anticipate my moves. "Nils, I need you down here."

"Aye, Captain."

"Lars, I want you three boys to string your bows. You will be the only warriors who can strike at the enemy. If we get the chance I want you to take out the helmsmen on the ships."

He grinned, "Aye, Captain. We shall not let the ship down."

I had to judge my moment well. I kept the long slow turn from southwest to north. The ship was building up a good speed. I shouted, "Prepare to come about. On my command run in your oars quicker than you have ever done before."

There was a roar as they answered me.

I put the board over and once more we canted. The goat bleated her objections and I saw Maria clinging to the prow. The move made some of the smaller boats panic. They had, like the larger ship with no oars, not anticipated something we had not done before. We were going to charge them. It would be like Christof and the Vasconian horsemen all over again. Hope sprang into my heart when two of the ships to the northwest of us collided as their captains made an error of judgement. Their prows were entangled and they were, effectively, out of the chase. The turn finished, I pointed the prow at the large ship with the oars. The other large ship was trying to turn but the wind was against them. The captain who faced me had courage. He matched my move. We would strike bow to bow. Timing was everything. I glanced at the masthead and then the enemy ship.

"Joseph, the shield."

He took the shield from the side of the ship and laid it close to our feet, he knew why we needed it.

I shouted, "In oars!"

We had built up so much speed and momentum that while we slowed a little it would not appear so to the enemy for *'Ægir'* was flying. I moved the steering board slightly. If I got this wrong then both ships would be destroyed. The enemy did not turn but kept the same course. We were less than one hundred paces apart when I moved the steering board again. It was the momentum of our ship and the little help the wind gave us which moved us where I wanted to go.

I heard Oddr shout, "Arm yourselves."

It would not just be my ship's boys who would fight. I breathed a sigh of relief when I saw that we would not strike the enemy bow to bow. We would not even scratch her side but what we would do was crush every oar on her larboard side. Unless they managed to stop the steerboard oars then the ship would slew around. I wanted her dead in the water for as long as possible.

When we struck their oars we felt the judder throughout the ship but I did not think we had been hurt. You can feel damage through the deck and I felt none. The crashes and cracks not to mention the screams from the Arab ship told me that we had hurt her. Some oars would have splintered and the deadly shards would fly and when they hit would be like arrows. Other oarsmen would be impaled by the shattered oars.

I moved the steering board to take us into open water. "Full sail!" I was heading for the coast and I wanted to be there by the time it was dark. I heard the arrows as they were released and I glanced at the steering board of the Arab. There were half naked men there and we were so close that I could see that one had jewels on his fingers and gold around his neck. I saw no mail and when our arrows struck men, one of them the helmsman, then I knew that one enemy was out of the fight. That left the bigger ship that had tried to cut us off north. She was now turning. As our warriors sent their arrows at a smaller ship I looked at the last potential enemy. She was a big ship but she did not have the sleek lines we did. In a stern chase we would win but I wanted certainty.

"Oddr, I am going to sail across the stern of the big ship. Clear her stern."

"You heard the navigator."

I now had the wind and the freedom to choose my own course. The Arab was just reacting to my moves and when he blinked and moved the wrong way I aimed my ship north and headed for his stern. They sent arrows at us but we had more men ready to loose. The Arab ship suddenly veered to larboard. We had hit the helmsman. As I put the steering board hard over I saw that the sky in the east was getting darker. Night might just save us…for the moment.

It was the small ship that was almost our undoing. She was little bigger than our snekke but she was in the wrong place at the wrong time and packed with men. No one had noticed her for our attention was on the larger, more dangerous ship. The smaller vessel suddenly loomed up on our steerboard side. No one had seen it for we were looking for more dangerous foes. I had been looking for open water and a chance to escape. The first I knew was when I was almost knocked from my feet as something struck the steering board. I leaned over the side and saw the small ship packed with more men than I thought was safe. They were already clambering up the stern. A grappling hook flew up and secured us to the boat.

"Oddr, we are being boarded." I turned to Joseph, "Hold the steering board." As he took it I picked up my shield. My sword was in my chest and the only weapon to hand I had was the shield. I straddled the gunwale and brought the edge of the shield down to smash into the skull of the first man who was climbing. He fell in a heap in the bottom of the boat. A spear jabbed up at me and I used my boot to kick the head away. I watched in horror as an Arab archer pulled back on his bow. I had the shield but I was holding it by the edge. There was no way I could use it effectively. The arrow that came from behind me smacked the man squarely in his face. From the fletch it was Fritjof who had saved my life.

Oddr shouted, "Leif, take the steering board. This is a task for men with swords and spears and not the edge of a shield."

As I lifted my leg over the gunwale I saw the effect on the other Arab ships. Thanks to the ship that prevented the steering board from moving effectively, we had slowed and they were now converging like sharks on a stricken whale. I took the steering board with my right hand and gave the shield to Joseph. I pushed on the board. It had to fight the ship that was jammed against it. Oddr was decisive. The most effective weapon we had at the stern was the stern anchor. It was a large rock secured by a rope. He shouted, "Christof, help me lift this. The rest of you slay as many as you can." Some of the enemy ships were close enough now to send arrows at us. They clattered and crashed on the deck.

Dagfinn called, "The large ship is turning and she is closing with us."

I concentrated on my task. I pushed the steering board as hard as I could and managed to put it in the right position but the ship that had grappled us was swinging around our stern. She was acting as an anchor. The sail was flapping and we were losing way. Brynjar brought his sword down hard and sliced through the rope holding the grappling hook. It was at that moment that Oddr and Christof dropped the anchor to smash into the ship. It did its job but did it too well. Our own anchor threatened to halt us. I shouted, "Cut the rope." It was just a rock and we could find another.

Oddr took his sword and hacked through the rope. We surged forward but, at that moment one of the men in the sinking ship hurled a weighted dart at Oddr. He did not see it coming and it slammed into his helmet. Still holding his sword, he fell back to the deck.

"Joseph, see to Oddr. Lars and Nils, trim the sails. The rest of you man the sides. We have to fight our way out."

The small boat was gone. Its crew were either dead or doomed to be eaten by the sharks that were already gathering but it had done its job. For the briefest of times we had almost escaped and now the Arabs saw their opportunity to catch the elusive prey that was *'Ægir'*. Our ship was fighting just as hard as we were and as soon as the wind filled the full sail she leapt forward. The setting sun was drawing her on. The large ship without oars was the greatest danger. She had managed to turn while we had fought the small ship and was now bearing down on us and aiming at the middle of our steerboard side. I still had the wind and I trusted my ship. I kept going in a straight line. The Arab saw his chance for we were on a converging course. He thought his ship would strike us and I was gambling that I knew my ship better than he did. I predicted that the smaller ships would stay out of the way of the two larger vessels. We were like two stags charging at one another. The hinds would steer clear. They would wait to pick up the pieces. The Arab rode much higher in the water than we did. That helped me for I could see better than their captain. Sailing a drekar meant using your hand and eye together. I had sailed the ship since Gandalfr died in Frankia and I knew her. I was part of her and I urged her on, "Fly, my beauty, fly."

Christof gave a gasp, "Leif, they will strike us."

I laughed. It sounded like a mad laugh even to me, "No, we will not, Christof the Wanderer, Leif Wolf Killer is not destined to die here."

I made the slightest adjustment to the steering board and moved us slightly to larboard. The Arab did not see the move and I knew that his crew would brace themselves for a collision. The bows seemed to tower over me but I knew it was an illusion. We raced beyond the prow. It took them some moments to realise we had escaped and by the time they sent arrows at us I had turned the steering board to steerboard and we had the full wind. The sky behind was dark and we headed for the golden glow of a setting sun as the large Arab tried to turn and follow us. I risked a glance behind and saw that the oared ship was catching up with her consort but neither would catch us before sunset.

When the sun disappeared I maintained our course for the remainder of the hourglass and when Lars turned it so I changed course. Joseph had told me that the coast was to the north of us and so I decided to head south and west for an hour before turning and heading west again.

"Nils, check the ship for damage and for any who are hurt."

Asbjørn knelt next to Oddr. Joseph had taken the helmet from our leader and was using vinegar to clean the wound. "How is he, Healer?"

Joseph nodded to the helmet. There was a large dent in it, "The helmet stopped the dart from penetrating but it was a heavy weighted weapon. These are designed to kill. It has cracked his skull and there is blood." He sighed, "This is not a wound I can sew. It is not a limb I can remove. All we can do is to make him comfortable until I have a better light to see. We need to make sure he cannot choke and give him water."

"That is it? You can do no more?" Asbjørn sounded accusatory.

I snapped, "Joseph did not wound your friend, Asbjørn. The man who did so is dead. The Norns were spinning and Oddr was unlucky but he is not dead and so long as he lives there is hope. Would you have us make a light so that our enemies can follow us?"

Asbjørn looked up and nodded, "You are right, Leif. I am sorry, Healer."

I said, "Carry Oddr to the mastfish. Birger, ask Maria to watch him."

Nils came back, "Fritjof is dead. Anders has a small wound but they were the only ones apart from Oddr. We were lucky, Captain."

He was right but one death was one death too many. Fritjof had saved my life and I had not had the chance to thank him. It was just one death but it made me sad and angry at the same time. Lord Arne's lust for silver and gold had cost us dear. "Cover Fritjof with his cloak. We will send him to the deep when we have time. Was there any damage?"

He pointed to the sail, "Three arrows struck the sail and there are tears."

That could prove disastrous in a storm. "Then when we stop we must sew them." I raised my voice, "Rest while you can. We are still far from the straits but we are alive and our enemies are not." As a cheer filled the ship I patted the gunwale. My fingers found the gouge made by Brynjar's sword. I saw the raw wound left by the blade of Oddr. He had saved the ship but had it cost him his life? Would he see his wife, sons and daughter? It was then I saw Birger, Benni and Anders kneeling by the cloak covered corpse of Fritjof. They had lost a friend. The four had come on the raid together but now just three would be returning home and only then if I managed to steer a course through enemies and across a sea that might yet hurt us.

Chapter 15

Joseph came down a silent ship with a horn of ale. The two of us were the only ones left awake. Men slept when they could and after the hard rowing and the fight they all needed their sleep. Even Maria was exhausted and she lay close to her patient, Oddr, and her husband, Birger. How I managed to keep my eyes open I will never know. Perhaps it was the ship giving me powers I did not know I possessed. I drank the ale. It was good and I found myself smiling. It was such a simple pleasure. "How are Oddr and Anders?"

"There is no change in Oddr. He breathes but there is no sign yet of his awakening. Maria is attentive and cares for him as though he was her child. Anders will just have a scar to impress the girls."

"Will Oddr wake?"

Joseph was silent for a while and then he said, "There is a swelling where the skull was cracked. It is too dark now but when the sun rises I would examine him more fully. Last night the sun was setting and I knew you would not want a light."

"No, a light would not do." I sensed that he had more to say but was reluctant. "Is there anything you can do for him?"

"There are two things we can do. One is to do nothing and let his body heal him."

"And if it does not?"

He paused and said, baldly, "Then he dies."

That was the more likely outcome of doing nothing. I could tell that from the tone of Joseph's voice, "And the other?"

He measured his words. This was not his language and the words he was using were not the ones he would have chosen. "I can shave his skull and then drill a small hole. I would relieve the pressure on the wound." He saw my frown at what seemed a drastic action. He smiled, "It is not as bad as you think. The skull is cracked already. Think of it as a boil filled with pus. Lancing it can be painful but it heals once the poison has gone." He had lanced many boils since we had left Bygstad.

"And if the operation goes wrong?"

"Then he will die and men will blame me." He shrugged, "In their eyes I am still the foreigner. They like it when I heal them but if I kill one…" He spread his hands, "I have heard of this technique but I have never seen it done. I will do it if asked because Oddr is a good man and if I can save his life I wish to do so. It is not just his life but his wife and family. They deserve this warrior to return home. I will bear the rancour of the crew if I fail."

He was right. "Sleep, Joseph. If you are to do this then you need your sleep. I will watch alone."

The night was the longest one I had ever endured. We had not reefed the sail but the wind was not as strong. We rose and rolled across waves that would barely be noticed in the Great Ocean. The danger was that we were sailing without a lookout but Joseph was reasonably confident that we would not see land until later that next day. He said there were neither rocks nor islands before we reached the straits. He had studied the maps and the compass and I had to trust him. It was a risk but a calculated one.

Birger was the first to rise. I had been turning the hourglass every hour and I estimated it was three hours until dawn when he rose. I saw him at the side, making water and then he came astern, pausing only to put his hand on the cloak covered corpse of his dead friend. I knew what he was doing. He was praying. He reached me and said, "Let me stand a watch with you."

I nodded. Birger had left Bygstad a youth but now he was a man. Marriage, death and the dangers of the raid had all changed him. I waited until he had control and then took my hand from the board. It felt like a claw for I had held the board through a long night. I flexed it. I took the opportunity to make water and then stretched my whole body. I sat on the dragon chest. Until I did so I had not realised how weary were my legs.

"Will we get home, Brother?"

I chuckled, "Am I now a galdramenn who can predict the future?" I shook my head. "I do not know if we will even see the end of this day. The Norns are spinning and we have a cunning and determined enemy. Perhaps when we led that ship over the rocks they lost someone who was as precious to them as Gandalfr was to us. I do not know. All I know is that they are determined in their pursuit of us and I have to assume that they

Dragon Rock

will follow us to the end of their world. I have no time for such idle speculation. I am simply doing all that I can to try to take the crew home. I want our mother to meet Maria. I want Oddr to see his children and I want to see my family too, but we are far from home and we are surrounded by enemies. We have no friends in these waters. We take each day as it comes. Once we have passed the straits I will be happier but those waters are more dangerous than these. There may be fewer enemies there but the seas are more ferocious. Birger, we have a long way to go and I cannot be certain that we will survive."

He nodded, "Then we have to be as one. The clan of the otter must fight for one another and hope that our ship can continue to save us."

Gradually, the ship came to life. It might have been our conversation that woke them I do not know but by the time the sun rose behind us everyone was awake and Harland was on the masthead seeking a sail. When he saw none then we were relieved. I shouted, "It is time to say goodbye to Fritjof." I nodded to Asbjørn, "Asbjørn, would you say the words?"

"But you are the captain."

"And my place is here watching the sail and steering the ship."

Birger said, "I will do this for he was my friend."

The body, still wrapped in his cloak and with his dead fingers around his sword, was brought to the stern. The body was lifted above the now scarred gunwale and Birger said, "Rán, Fritjof was not yet full grown and he had yet to lie with a woman but he was a warrior. His family will miss him as will his friends. He will no longer laugh and light up our lives. I know that he will be in Valhalla with Gandalfr and the others. We consign his body to your care." He nodded and the body slid beneath the blue waters. "Farewell, my friend. We will never forget you and when we are home we will recall your name with a song." It was Birger's coming of age. He then closed his eyes and sang.

Fritjof son of Beorn the Strong
You found a place where you belong
We fought together, brothers four
And faced the enemy at our door
You saved the Wolf with an arrow true

Dragon Rock

You stood firm on the sea that was blue
Now you are gone to the warriors' home
Wait for us there until we come

My brother had a fine voice and it was not until that moment that I realised it. He also had skills as a skald. The looks on the rest of the crew told me that his words were right and he had touched them too. I let the silence hang.

Apart from Harland at the masthead and Maria and Joseph with Oddr, the crew were all close to me and so I addressed them while there was silence, "There is something else. Joseph thinks that there is a chance to save Oddr but it means cutting a hole in his head. It is dangerous and Oddr might die."

Asbjørn nodded, "And if he does not do this?"

"Then Oddr will remain as he is or perhaps die in any case."

"I am his friend and shield brother. I say we do all that we can to save his life." Everyone nodded. Asbjørn added, "And while the healer does this we will put Oddr's sword in his hand. If he is to die then I want him to go to Valhalla." He smiled at Joseph, "We trust you but if he does die we want him to be assured of a welcome from Odin. Do your best, Healer, none will blame you. This is *wyrd*."

"Aye!" The crew gave their approval. Perhaps Birger's words had made them realise how frail were our lives. They could hang by a thread and if Joseph could strengthen that thread then it was worth the risk.

I waved Joseph forward, "We wish you to heal Oddr."

"All know the risks?"

Asbjørn said, "We do."

The healer took command, "Then Captain, reef the sail for I want the ship to be as still as we can make it."

"Lars, make it so and I want every eye but Joseph and Maria's on the sea seeking a sail." The truth was that I did not want them to watch the healer as he worked. My task was to keep the ship as stable as I could. The sail was reefed so that we had way but we were just floating gently before an easy wind. The ship was silent apart from the creaking of the hull and the ropes. It meant that when Joseph began to drill with the small bone drill we could all hear it. I could not conceive how he would judge what he was doing. I saw Maria's face pale but she

Dragon Rock

cradled Oddr's head in her arm as though it was a newborn babe. Birger had chosen a strong woman and that would be needed back in the harsh lands of the north.

"Sail to the northeast."

I said nothing. The whole crew, Joseph included, had heard but we were in his hands. We dared not move until he said that it was safe. The good news was that with a reefed sail we would be barely visible but if the ship came closer then she would know us for what we were. That she would be a hunter was clear to me. The Norns had spun and we were a mouse to be played with by not just a single cat but a pack. I held the board steady. Since we had entered the Blue Sea and on the long night watches I had recorded in my mind all that had happened. I did not think that the ships that followed us had come from the tower where we had been attacked. Ships that braved the seas to the west needed to be more rugged than the dancing boats that had chased us. If we were seen then I would head south and west. I would make the ships following us think that we intended to cross at the southern end of the straits. The truth was my original plan was still the best. We would find Al-Andalus again and cross through the straits at night. Joseph had marked our rough position on the map and we were within a day of the passage that would lead us home. The time spent in the cutting of the skull would not harm us. Being found while he was still working would. There was a strange silence as we bobbed along the water and while Joseph performed what, to me, was magic.

We turned the glass once and were about to turn it a second time when we heard, "Two sails to the northeast."

I tried to picture our enemies. They would have had to reorganise in the night. They would have spread out in a long line so that when dawn broke they could see a large area. The question was were the two ships at the north or the south of the line?

"Sail to the southeast!"

I had my answer. We were in the middle of their line and as soon as we were seen then they would close with us.

I was relieved when Joseph said, "We are done. I have bled the wound and sewn back the skin. We are now in the hands of

Dragon Rock

God." He turned to Maria and spoke to her in her own language. She smiled.

"Let fly the sail. We will run before the wind. Eat while you can for we may have to fight before too long."

It was like a blur as the whole crew set to work. The sail was lowered and men who had last tended a stay when they were a ship's boy now did so again. The sail filled and we increased our speed. The ship had been as still as possible but now knew that we had to run for our lives.

Christof and Asbjørn joined me. Asbjørn said, "The plan?"

"The wind is still pushing us west. We know that we have the sea legs to outrun these Arabs. I want them to think we sail to the southern end of the straits. As soon as we have a clear sea and we have extended our lead and are hidden from the hunters, I will change from a south westerly course to a north westerly one. I want to be at the northeastern horn of the straits by dark and we shall try to sneak through then."

Christof said, "And when will you sleep?"

I said nothing.

Asbjørn said, "Odin knows that you have done all that you can but even a hero needs to sleep. The ships are astern of us and we now fly. Sleep for two turns of the glass and then we will wake you. That is not enough sleep but it will refresh you."

Christof said, "He is right Leif. Birger and Lars can help me. I swear we will still be on course when you wake. I learned my lesson on the watch near the island."

They were right. During the cutting of the skull I had felt dizzy. I had put it down to what Joseph was doing but now I knew it was exhaustion. I nodded. I handed over the steering board. I did not even have time to slide my skin over my head before I was asleep. When Nils roused me awake I saw that someone had covered me with the skin. I looked at the sky in panic. It felt like I had enjoyed a full night of sleep but the sun was not yet at its zenith.

Christof said, "We have not seen any sails for one turn of the glass. The weather still blows from the east."

Asbjørn's voice came from the mast fish, "And Oddr breathes more easily."

Dragon Rock

Birger said, "And now Leif Wolf Killer is on hand to steer us to safety."

I ate and drank ale. I doused my head in a pail of sea water and then I donned my wolf skin. I was ready. "Give me the board. We stay on this course for another two hours. Send Joseph to me."

When the healer arrived, I smiled, "You did well and Oddr lives."

"He does and every moment sees a better colour. Maria has skills and she has fed him ale and honey even though he slept. They are working."

"And now I need to know where we are."

"I am afraid that cutting open the skull meant I did not attend to the compass. I have done so while you slept but my news is not as accurate as it might be."

"Your best guess then."

He pointed to the south, "I think that we are thirty miles north of our first landfall."

I looked at where he pointed, "And that puts us within thirty or forty miles of Al-Andalus."

He nodded, "Perhaps forty miles from the straits."

"Then it is time to make our turn. Thank you." I looked at the pennant and the sail. I called, "Prepare to come about." We had done this so many times that everyone knew what to do. I eased the steering board over. There was no need to heel the ship. A long slow gentle turn would serve us best and speed us through the water. It would also be better for Oddr. We moved marginally more slowly but that would not hurt us so long as we saw no sails.

It was a nerve-wracking afternoon as we edged closer to the land. It was Nils at the masthead who spotted the coast to the north of us. "Land Ho!" It was five turns of the glass past noon. Darkness would be upon us in less than three or four more turns.

I found myself grinning as I put the steering board over to sail due west. The crew were not on watch. The watch was made up of the ship's boys. Asbjørn, Christof and Birger had all enjoyed rest and sleep as had Joseph. I said, "Lars, rouse Joseph."

Dragon Rock

The healer was awake almost instantly. He was in the nest between the chests, "Yes, Ma...Captain." I smiled. He was still coming to terms with his freedom.

"Wake Asbjørn, Christof and Birger. My three boys and I will need to stand the night watch and it will be a hard one. We will have two hours of sleep."

"Of course."

I instructed the four of them on the course we were to take. It would be due west. If land was spotted to the north then we would steer more south westerly. Before I slept I went to Oddr and put my hand on his shoulder, "Come back to us, Oddr Gautisson, we need you and your courage."

Somehow just speaking to the unconscious warrior made sleep easier. Oddr was alive and if we had not enjoyed the skills of Joseph then he might be dead. Joseph was with us because of me. *Wyrd*.

The motion of the ship and my exhaustion meant I was asleep quickly and I did not dream. The wind was gentler when I woke. I felt it immediately. I went to the steering board and saw that we were still heading due west. "Any sails?"

Christof shook his head, "Not from astern. Frode spotted one to the southeast but it was sailing east and was a bare speck."

"Did it turn?"

"No."

"Then all is well." The boys had made water as had I and we could now take over. "I want the crew rested. The four of us are enough to watch. If danger comes I will rouse you. I intend to head for the coast. If we can reach it before dark then we can follow it around to the straits. It is then we will need the crew. I want to furl the sail and row into the ocean. There might not be a tower but there may well be watchers."

They left us. "Nils, you have good eyes. Masthead."

"Aye, Captain."

"Harland, go to the prow and watch for rocks."

"Aye, Captain."

"Lars, you will stay with me. This watch will see me give you more skills."

Dragon Rock

I had come to realise that I needed someone to share the steerboard with me. Lars had shown that he was calm and skilful.

"Aye, Captain."

I spent the first hour watching him with the steering board. He had learned much already and I just needed to tease out the odd bad habit. When Nils shouted, "Land to the north!" then I took the board.

"Rouse my brother and put a reef in the sail."

It was not yet time to wake the rest of the crew but the movement of my brother and Lars woke some. By the time the sail was reefed the only one not awake was Oddr. Harland peered ahead as the sun began to dip. I had already seen the shape of the land but in the setting of the sun, as the light from the setting sun splayed out across the water, I saw the straits. They were slightly to the south and west of us. The smell of woodsmoke drifting from the land bespoke homes but neither Harland nor Nils saw the tell-tale signs of surf flecked rocks. As soon as the sun disappeared I called down Nils. We needed him with Harland.

"Another reef." As they did so Joseph turned the glass. Before he had turned it again we had the sail reefed so that any more would see it completely furled. We were barely moving and that was the way I wanted it. "Have the oars ready."

Nils came running down the ship, "There are rocks ahead and a beach."

I nodded as I put the steering board over a little to head for the gap that marked the straits. "Run out the oars."

We had greased them so that they slid silently out. As we had no Oddr, Dagfinn did not sit with Brynjar. Instead, he stood by me. We needed balance and we had just two men on the two front oars.

"In oars." I heard the slight splash as the oarsmen slipped the blades into the sea. "Row." We were too close to the shore for a song and I stamped on the deck. Dagfinn copied me and I was able to stop. He would maintain the beat. It was an eerie passage along a dark coast that marked the edge of the Blue Sea. I saw the waters ahead and aimed the ship for the gap.

Nils raced down the ship, "Captain, there is a ship beyond the straits."

"Back water!" The rowers backed water. I said, "Are there rocks ahead?"

"No, Captain, but there is a small beach."

I turned the board to head for the beach. "Asbjørn, creep us closer to the beach."

I knew that Nils and Harland would watch for danger. They clambered up on either side of the prow. If their hands rose I would order the men to back water. They did not and as we slid onto sand I said, "One stroke of back water." They pushed the oars in and we moved back into the sea. Nils and Harland leapt ashore. I said, "Lars and Joseph stay by the steering board." I opened the dragon chest and took out my sword and belt. I might need it. I also donned my wolf skin to hide my white flesh. I saw that there was a patch of water and to my left lay a low island.

The boys had not driven in stakes but they had secured us to two large rocks. I whispered, "Where is the ship?"

Nils pointed, "On the other side of this spit of land."

Dagfinn and Brynjar joined us. I said, "We will scout the ship. You two search to the north."

I raced across the sand and reached the high point of the spit as the two of them headed north. Asbjørn and Christof had followed me. I saw a small ship. It lay in the lee of the island and was about forty paces from us. I heard voices coming from it. They had a watch aboard. I waved my hand for the others to take cover while I studied the ship. It was longer than the small boats that had chased us and it had oars. There looked to be ten oar ports on each side. That meant it had a crew that could be almost as big as ours. It had higher sides than our ship and the oar ports were low down, just above the water. I saw one sentry at the steering board and another at the prow. It was their voices I had heard. The one at the prow looked to be fishing.

I waved my hand and we backed down to the beach. I waited until we were by the sea and the prow of the ship before I spoke. I did so quietly. The sound of the water on the shingle would disguise our voices.

"We have a problem."

Christof nodded, "Those sentries will see us if we pass them and raise the alarm."

Dragon Rock

Asbjørn said, "If this is the only ship then there is not a problem. With the sail billowing and the crew rowing, by the time they raised their sail and manned their oars we would be far away."

Just then Dagfinn and Brynjar came racing from the north. They must have landed and explored. Dagfinn said, "There is a small harbour to the north of us. There are ships there. They are silent and appear to have no crew but there is a fire and a watchman."

I nodded, "Then there may be other ships or even a tower further around the bay. We have to eliminate these two sentries and disable the ship. That means entering the water and climbing aboard."

Asbjørn said, "I cannot swim."

I nodded, "I know but I can."

Christof said, "As can I."

I knew Brynjar could not swim either but Dagfinn could. He nodded, "I can swim."

"Then the three of us will take out the sentries. If we do it silently then we might be able to disable the ship, swim back to ours and escape. Asbjørn, have Lars and Birger take the drekar to the southern tip of the island and wait there. When we have disabled the guard ship we will cut her moorings and move her to the end of the island. We will swim back."

Asbjørn shook his head, "You are the navigator."

"And the best swimmer. The Norns have spun. We are wasting time." I handed my sword and belt to Brynjar and then stripped off. The others did the same.

Brynjar said, "At least two of the wolves of Bygstad will wreak havoc." He picked up the clothes and weapons.

"And you are there in spirit." I took the seax that had been in my sealskin boots and made my way back up the slope. The other two joined me. "You two take the sentry at the steering board. It is a longer swim to the bow and I can swim underwater. Strike quickly for there may be a splash if I can take him."

We crept down the beach on the other side. The stern of the vessel was facing us and that meant the one at the bow could not see us and as the one at the steering board had his back to the gunwale then he could not see us either. I was a strong swimmer and knew that I could swim with the seax in my hand. The other two chose to put their weapons between their teeth. As I slipped in I found that the water was cold. I realised that we were on the ocean side of the spit. This was not the warmed Blue Sea. Allied to that it was night. I swam a few steady strokes and when I neared the stern I dived down below the surface of the water. It was not pitch black for the sand was white. I was a strong swimmer and I knew I could hold my breath for a long time. The shadow of the boat above me guided me and when I saw the fishing line ahead I knew where I was. I came up on the spit side of the bows. After taking a couple of deep breaths I looked up and saw the man who was fishing. He was sitting with his feet through the rail by the steerboard side prow. I took another breath and dived down. I saw the line and also saw a small rock on the seabed. The current was a gentle one and I dived down to pick up the rock that was the size of my hand. I loosely tied the line around it. My gentle movements would suggest to the fisherman that a fish was nibbling at his bait and it would grab his attention. I then swam back and, after sucking in air, began to climb up the side of the ship. I used the anchor rope to help me. The man was tugging at the line and, of course, the rock suggested not just any fish but a big one. The rock would move in the current and encourage him. He pulled and I heard him say something, presumably to his companion. He was not looking behind him where I would silently approach, but at the line. If Dagfinn and Christof had not disposed of the other sentry then this could all end disastrously. I had to trust my friends. I pulled myself up to the gunwale. I saw that the sentry at the stern was lying at a strange angle. He was dead. The fisherman spoke again and when he had no reply turned his head. He would see his dead companion and warn the rest of the crew. I reached over and I put my left hand around his mouth. I pulled him backwards. The rail held his legs and I tore the seax across his throat. He fell forward held in place by the gunwale and prow. I took his sword and walked down the deck.

 The other two naked men rose like wraiths. There was no one sleeping on the deck but as I moved down I heard and then saw men sleeping below. There were ten of them. This was not an oared ship like ours. This one had a rowing deck at the bottom. It

Dragon Rock

explained why it had high sides. I saw the glint of metal and knew then they were slaves and shackled. As much as I wanted to free them I knew that it was an unnecessary risk. I was about to wave the other two to head back to our ship when Christof made a slight noise and one of the galley slaves awoke. He looked up and, seeing me above him said, "Leif Wolf Killer."

I looked down. It was Haraldr One Eye, one of Lord Arne's men. There was no mistaking the scarred face. The Norns had spun and we could not leave them.

I said to the others, "Cut the anchors and find an oar. Paddle us to our ship."

Dagfinn shook his head, "We have pushed our luck enough. Stick to the original plan."

I pointed at the slaves and said, "Haraldr One Eye is here."

He nodded and while Christof went to the prow he went to the stern.

I asked, "How do I free you?"

"One of the men has a key. There are others here from Lord Arne's ship."

As I went to search the men for the key I heard him wake his companions. It was the one at the stern who had the key. I returned and tossed it down to him. "When you are all freed then come on deck. *'Ægir'* can pick us up."

I went to help the other two. The anchors were cut and we were drifting in the current which, unless we did something, would take us west. I grabbed an oar and used it to scull us towards the prow of our drekar as she edged around the spit. Christof waved to attract the attention of those on our ship and I heard Asbjørn order the larboard oars to start to row. It was a whispered command. It brought the prow of *'Ægir'* closer. I saw Nils at the prow and I hissed, "Toss me a rope. We have passengers."

His eyes widened but he obeyed. I caught the rope and pulled. We bumped gently into my ship. Christof said, "They are free."

"Get them aboard *'Ægir'* and be quick."

Dagfinn helped me to hold the rope. *'Ægir'* was still being pushed by the wind out to sea and we were moving with her. The last of the slaves jumped aboard and Dagfinn and I followed. Our feet pushed the ship away from ours and it began to drift. I clambered aboard and, naked, ran down the ship. "Lars, Harland, full sail."

Dagfinn was right, we had pushed our luck and the Norns had spun. I needed to get us away from their web as soon as I could. I stood on the deck and watched the sentry boat as it drifted aimlessly in the straits. It would be seen and our presence soon detected. The Norns had spun and their web had trapped us once more.

Chapter 16

We tumbled aboard the drekar and I hurried to the steering board. "Lars, half sail."

"Aye, Captain. Good to have you aboard, again."

There were more questions that needed to be asked than there were explanations but we had no time for that. My plan had been to simply disable the ship. We had wasted time sculling back to our ship and transferring the slaves. By the time we were moving the sentry ship would be seen floating aimlessly in the straits and someone would notice and raise the alarm. I was shivering. It was always the way when you came from the water. Joseph dried me and I dressed. I nodded and, after a swig of ale to take away the salt, took the steering board. I said, "Joseph, we have ten galley slaves we freed. There may be injuries that need to be tended."

He nodded and taking his bag went down the ship where the others were drying off and the released slaves were waiting to see what would happen next.

"Birger, one of the slaves is Haraldr One Eye, from Lord Arne's ship. Fetch him here. He may have answers that will help us to escape."

All that Birger had seen was the three of us and ten men board. He had not known, until that moment, of their identity. His mouth opened with a question and then, after touching his Hammer of Thor, nodded and hurried down the deck.

I studied the sea ahead; it looked to be empty but this was the ocean I knew so well. We were in the straits and yet the troughs were already bigger than in the Blue Sea. I saw lights to my right that marked houses and villages and, mindful of the rocks we had seen when we had entered, I steered a little more to larboard to head for the middle of the channel. I guessed we were still within range of the tower but it was night and we had just half a sail. I hoped that we would merge into the darkness of the sea.

Haraldr One Eye joined me. I saw that he had a beaker of ale in his hand. He was grinning, "Thank you, Leif Wolf Killer. I owe you a life."

I nodded. There were more important things on my mind than thanks. "Your story and that of Lord Arne can wait. What I need to know is where does the danger lie? Is there a guard boat?"

"There is. We were its crew."

"The boat we just set loose in the straits?"

He nodded, "The crew sleep ashore. There were ten of them and they row the ship back and forth across the straits each day. This is the eighth day we have been aboard."

"There are no other ships that do this?"

"The tower at the southern end of the straits has a powerful weapon and there are ships in the northern port. They can be quickly summoned. They use a light and a horn to raise the alarm."

There were more questions than answers but I had all that I needed to know, "Lars, full sail."

The wind was still blowing from the north and east but it felt weaker. The winds in the ocean we were about to enter normally came from the south and west. They were also stronger. I steered as close to the wind as I could. We needed to be clear of the coast by dawn. I could still see pinpricks of light and that meant people who could mark our passage. The floating, empty ship would tell them that we had been in the straits and they might know we would head home but the ocean we had entered was far bigger than the Blue Sea. We had defeated the ships that were happier in that sea and I did not fear them in my ocean. It was the Great Ocean that was more likely to be the enemy.

Asbjørn came aft along with Brynjar. "The Norns have indeed spun, Leif. There are five men from Lord Arne's ship. The rest of the crew…" he waved a hand in the air. They had drowned.

"A tale I will need to hear but what of the others?"

"They are not Norse but they are slaves taken by the Arabs. There are four Franks and a Saxon."

"Franks?"

"They are just grateful to be rescued but they have asked to be landed when we near their waters."

I shook my head, "We will need to land, Asbjørn, but I do not intend to land anywhere that is close to places where people live."

He smiled, "One of them, Charles, has been a slave for two years. All he wants is to land and kiss the ground wherever it is. They were cruel masters. They are all grateful to us."

"Lord Arne is dead?" I asked the question just to make it clear in my mind.

He nodded, "It was the storm and the tower that did for them. I will let Haraldr One Eye tell it."

"And how is Oddr?"

"He sleeps easier."

"Good."

"And you, Leif Wolf Killer, you will need sleep too."

I shook my head, "When dawn comes we will change course and head…whichever way the wind chooses. I am hoping that it changes and that there are no more storms. When we are on a better course and if the wind is kind then I will let Lars, Birger and Christof, take the board."

"You cannot carry the weight of the crew and the ship on your shoulders, Leif."

"And I do not want to but when Gandalfr was killed that weight was given to me." I had a sudden thought, "The jarl…"

"I asked the same question. Haraldr did not see him once the storm struck. We do not know." He turned to return to the mastfish. I was left alone at the steering board.

Lars and Nils came to join me. I said, "My wolf skin." Lars took it out and draped it over my shoulders. "When dawn comes I want Harland on the masthead. After we have trimmed the sails then I need you, Nils, to tend to the sails. Lars, your lessons continue. We have many days before we are in waters that are remotely safe and I need you to become more skilled." He nodded, "You still wish to be a navigator and a warrior?"

"I do."

"And you, Nils?"

He smiled but shook his head, "I have enjoyed being of value to you, Captain, but I have grown stronger on this voyage, I took a sword from the Franks and I would make a shield like yours. This is my last voyage as a member of the crew. When next we sail I will take an oar."

"You know that may not be for some time."

Dragon Rock

"I have growing to do and skills to learn. I have spoken to your brother, Benni and Anders. I would be like them and not suffer a fate like Fritjof and slip over the side to a watery grave. Your brother knows that he has learned much on this voyage. I would learn to be a useful warrior before we sail."

Lars nodded, "And I will learn all that I can from you, Captain, and then, back in Bygstad, I will learn from everyone who can spare me the time. My father died before he could teach me and I am the eldest. Birger has said he will pass his skills to me and my brothers."

The future of the clan was assured. The crew who returned to Bygstad might not wish to raid soon but they would tell others of our adventure and trials.

"Good. You should know that we will be tested again before we reach home. The barrels we filled in the Blue Sea and the ale we brewed will not last the whole voyage home. We will need to land and whenever we do that there will be danger. I have this watch to steer our course and from then on, Lars, you will hold the steering board when I sleep." I smiled, "And I do need sleep. You will have Birger and Christof with you but they are there for you to ask questions. For the next watch ask me."

I saw, in his eyes, that he was beginning to understand the enormity of his decision. He began to ask questions about what I did. The questions did not irritate me. I remembered doing the same thing with Gandalfr and I realised that in answering them I was coming to understand myself more. I had to put into words what I did almost naturally.

The crew slept. For the slaves it was with full bellies and ale on their lips. For the rest of the crew it was with the hope that we were on our way home, at long last. We had passed the barrier that was the straits and escaped, for the moment, from the trap. The storm and the bolt now seemed a distant though painful memory. Whatever else happened we were on our way home.

Nils brought us both ale and that, in itself, was significant. He was seeing Lars not as an equal but as a superior. His decision had made the change and he was happy with it. Harland did not need to be told to ascend the mast when the first rays from the east began to spread across a mercifully empty sea.

"Take the board, Lars, I need to make water."

Dragon Rock

As I did so I noticed a new confidence about Lars. When he had done so before he had kept a nervous and watchful eye on me until I returned. I saw that this time he looked from the pennant to the prow as we headed into waters and a sky that had still to be lit by the sun. I did not rush back to the board. Joseph had risen and came over to me with a fresh horn of ale.

"How are the men we rescued?"

"The ones from Lord Arne's ship only had days of suffering but the Franks and the Saxon are in a bad way. I learned that the others who were taken died and were fed to the fishes." He hesitated, "We can land them near their home, can't we?"

I sighed, "I can try, Joseph, but you should know that my main aim is to get the Clan of the Otter back to Bygstad. We need to land in Frankia but I cannot guarantee that it will be near to their home. The fleet of the Franks also means that as we have to sail the long way home we need to land in the land of the Angles, but it will be more likely to be Dumnonia rather than Wessex."

He smiled, "They do not mind that and I will make sure that they are stronger. We still have food."

I glanced up at the pennant. The wind was shifting and I realised we must have cleared the coast of Africa, hidden to the south, for the wind was stronger and the seas had slightly deeper troughs. Those troughs would become even more chasm like. I went back to the board, "Well Lars, what should the navigator do?"

He knew that I was teaching him and he frowned, "The wind is changing and the seas are stronger. We should turn the board to compensate and take in some sail."

I nodded, "Almost right. We will change course but the wind is only a little stronger. We use the wind while we can. Bring her round to take advantage of the wind's bounty but remember to warn the crew."

He smiled as he realised what I had said. I was the one who normally gave such a command. He shouted, "Prepare to come about." I saw Nils turn and grin. He hurried to the stays. As Lars pushed the board to larboard we heeled. Water splashed over the side. We were no longer in the gentler seas of the east. These were the waters of the western ocean. The goat bleated a complaint and the former slaves clung on.

I said quietly, "Unless we are in a fight, then a slower turn is kinder to the crew, Lars."

He shook his head, "Sorry, Captain."

"Do not worry, Lars, it was a small error and next time you will be smoother." I looked at the sky. There were clouds but they were few in number and scudded high above us. They were not rain filled and, even better, they did not hint at a storm. That one could blow up suddenly was not unusual but I did not think one was due.

By the time we had taken the noon sight I was happy with the way Lars was sailing the ship and I went to my bed. The motion of this ocean was more conducive for me and I was soon asleep. I had told Lars to give me just three hours of sleep and when Joseph roused me I saw, from the sky, that he had done so. The skies still had just a few fluffy clouds and the wind was still blowing from a south westerly direction. I mouthed a silent thanks to the goddess Rán.

I saw that Lars now had the look of a sailor. The salt from the sea had rimed his hair. His hands, arms and face were red from the wind and his eyes showed his tiredness. I made water and then went to the board. "You have done well, Lars."

He nodded, "And Joseph has shown me how to use the compass. Our position is marked."

"Then when I have the board get some rest. I will have you woken before dawn. You will need the experience of sailing at night too."

I took the board and saw the relief on his face. I was pleased when Nils came over and clapped him on the back. The two were friends and he was pleased.

"Nils, sleep too. Tell Harland he can rest as well. I will send another to the masthead."

When Harland came down we had no watcher and I called Birger over. He was at the prow with Maria. "Yes, Brother?"

"You can stand a watch with me." He nodded. "Have Benni take the masthead watch until dark."

"Aye."

When he returned I asked, "Maria is well?"

He beamed, "She is glad we are not threatened any longer. She feared, not for herself, but for me. She was worried I might be killed and then she would be alone."

"When next you talk to her, Birger, tell her that she will never be alone again for even if you were gone then she is part of our family and we would care for her." I glanced up to check the wind and adjusted the board marginally. "But, of course, we will all do our best to ensure that nothing happens to you." We both self-consciously touched our hammers.

Haraldr One Eye had been watching us and when we stopped talking and Birger leaned on the gunwale he came over.

"Well, Haraldr, this is better is it not?"

"It is, Leif, and we are all in your debt."

"What happened? We have time and a good tale will help pass the time."

"It was not long ago that it all happened and yet it seems like a dream. I feel as though I had another life." He shook his head. "The storm came, well, you know that. We saw you disappear in the sea. We thought you had sunk and men begged Lord Arne to turn. He did not. Two men were swept overboard. No one saw them go. We lost sight of the jarl and it was as though we were alone in the sea. We spied the straits and we all thought that we had reached our destination and the danger was passed for Lord Arne cheered and shouted in triumph."

"Were you at the oars?"

He shook his head, "Lord Arne relied on the sails and that was our undoing for the storm took us closer to the southern shore. We saw the land and the straits. Men grew hopeful for the winds abated a little and then we saw the tower. Lord Arne was not afraid of it for it looked like the towers we saw in Frankia and they did not hurt us. The first bolt hit the mast and shattered it. When it fell it struck men. We raced to free it but we lost way and we were motionless. The next bolt pinned the jarl to the gunwale. His hand was frozen in death and he pushed us to be beam on to the storm. As we reeled we all felt a shudder as another bolt hit us but this time it was the keel. We began to sink. I was lucky as were Dargh, Erik, Hrolfr and Sven. We had no mail and when we were in the water I managed to grab the yard. The sail that hung from it acted as an anchor. The others clung on too and we watched *'Nidhogg'* slip below the waves." I saw the pain on his face and his voice became quiet. "I saw our shipmates as they followed her. The hardest deaths to bear were the ship's boys. Poor Bjorn Dannisson almost survived but the ship that came to take us prisoner, the one from which we were rescued, smacked his tiny head. They did not see him."

I nodded, "The Sisters."

"Aye, the Sisters. We were dragged aboard and shackled. We spent two nights in a hole with neither food nor water until we were led out and put below the deck of the ship where you found us."

"Where was the hole?"

"At the bottom of the tower. I cursed that place as we were led away. It cost me my friends and my ship. Lord Arne should have returned home with Snorri and the traders."

I said, "But that would never have happened. You know that. The Blue Sea was his dream and his curse."

"It was and we have all sworn that from this day forth we stay in our home. I have done with raiding. The silver we took and sent home with Snorri will suffice. I have tales to tell and a family to raise. I thought I was doomed to end my days rowing for barbarians. Each night I dreamt of home. I beg you, Leif Wolf Killer, take us there and we will honour your name forever."

"And I will do all that I can."

"And the others?"

"Tell them that we will land in Frankia and the land of the Angles but in both cases it will be to take water and food. We will not be near to people."

"Christof the Wanderer has told us that there will be weapons for them to take. They just want to put their feet back on home soil."

We sailed north but kept the western coast of Al-Andalus well to the east of us. We had more crew but none of us relished another fight. It was the next day, after I had endured another night watch, that two things happened that were important. We ran out of ale and Oddr awoke. It was Oddr's awakening that brought home the lack of ale for we had all wanted to celebrate the return from the dead of Oddr Gautisson.

Dragon Rock

As he drank our precious water and Asbjørn told him all that had happened Dagfinn came to me, "Leif, not only have we run out of ale but with ten extra men we are running out of water. We need to either enjoy some rain or find some land where there is water."

I nodded. He was right but it would involve danger. I waved over Christof and Joseph, "We need to land in the next two or three days."

Dagfinn said, "Two would be better."

"We need water. I do not want to land in Al-Andalus. That means Frankia."

Christof shook his head, "The Franks will be like wild wasps at Bordèu."

Joseph said, "Then let us make it Nervouster. We know the island and that there is water there."

I clutched my Hammer of Thor, "And Gandalfr is there too. That will be closer to three days, Dagfinn, but it will be a safer place to visit."

I consulted with Joseph and involved Lars in the discussion. We studied the maps and the compass. We all agreed that we were almost level with the village and the lagoon where we had found Maria. "If we can keep this wind then that will be just over three days and nights." I looked at Lars. "Can you do this?"

He grinned, "Aye, Captain."

"Then I leave the steerboard to you while I speak with Oddr."

Joseph gave the slightest inclination of his head. He would watch over Lars for me.

Oddr was sitting with his back to the mastfish. Asbjørn was with him. I knew the bond that shield brothers enjoyed. Oddr looked up and smiled, "I have heard that, once more you saved the ship and uncovered the mystery of Lord Arne."

"It has been a most interesting time." I sat next to him, "Tell me, if you can, what was it like?"

"Like?"

"Did you not come close to Valhalla? We left the sword in your hand in case you were taken."

He said, "I dreamed. There was a long black tunnel and I heard the sounds of fighting and then silence but I saw nothing. The silences were almost painful. I thought I was dead and I would have to endure this forever. When I woke and opened my eyes I was relieved beyond words." I just nodded. I knew that the noises he had heard were our battles and the silences were when the crew were asleep. "You have a plan, now?"

"Yes, but as you are with us once more I am happy to change it."

"No, let us stay with whatever you and Joseph have devised." He touched the shaved part of his head. Joseph had told me that wounds healed better left in the open. The stitches and the raw wound stood out. "He has saved my life and I am pleased that you made him free."

"It was *wyrd*." I touched my hammer. "I plan to sail back to Nervouster." Oddr's eyes widened, "I know the danger but we cannot risk the coast around Bordèu and we need to land somewhere that we know. The enemy will be watching. We know that we can approach the island from the west and also where there is water to be found. There is also food there." I saw he was not convinced, "Oddr, we will run out of water in the next two or three days."

"Then we make for Nervouster and afterwards?"

"Snorri warned us of the dangers of the waters close to Frisia. I intend to sail along the coast of Dumnonia. The king there does not regard us as enemies. We would then pass the land of the Wēalas and while they are fierce warriors they are not sailors. Mann has Norse living there as does Dyflin and I hope that we will not be treated as enemies."

"But then we have the wild waters of the northern lands and islands. There are fierce people there too."

"If Snorri were here what would he advise, Oddr?"

"You are right. We are in your hands until we reach home."

I laughed, "And that day is when I can put the hourglass and compass away and enjoy the fjord, my family and peace."

The winds did not cooperate as they should have. After a day sailing north they changed to blow from the west. We were still able to sail north but the current and the wind threatened to send us towards the coast. I knew that soon we would be passing the land of Vasconia. I did not think that Duke Felix would have forgotten us. We had hanged one of his men and we had destroyed his ships. We had killed his cousin and we had taken

Dragon Rock

his silver. He would remember the Norsemen. It was still the kind of sailing weather that would suit the fair weather Vasconian ships. They could sail close to the coast and watch for our sail. That there would be just one sail was immaterial. They would now know what a dragon ship looked like.

Lars was a much better helmsman now than he had been but he was still learning and I did not want to risk him standing a night watch. It meant I felt like a creature of the night. I stood the night watches with either Nils or Harland. I slept during the day and my times awake and in daylight were limited. I was growing used to it. I made sure that I spent at least one turn of the hourglass at the start of the day and one at the end with Lars. What I could not teach him and he would need to learn for himself was how to detect changes in the wind and the current. I had not really learned to do so until after Gandalfr's death and I had been aided by following the jarl and Lord Arne. Lars was alone.

"The wind is changing again, Lars, remember to keep us well away from the coast. I do not want us to be seen." The truth was that if we had not been short of water we could have stood well out to sea. The one rain shower we had was welcome but it filled just eight pails to top up the barrels and bought us one day. If we were further out to sea there might be more rain but that was a gamble. There was water in Frankia.

"I will do so, Captain, but it is a hard thing to judge."

I went to sleep, wrapped in my wolf skin with a mind that was wrestling with more problems than I liked. I had a disturbed sleep. The motion of the ship was not as smooth as it was normally. When I woke I saw that the sky was darker. That boded well. It meant there might be rain. As I stood I glanced to steerboard. There was a bank of cloud there but I detected something else. It was Anders who was on the masthead and I shouted, "Anders, what lies to steerboard? Look carefully."

Anders had taken the odd watch and he was reliable. He shouted, "There is a cloud, Captain…and I see land."

Once more my sleep might have cost us. Lars looked at me in horror, "I am sorry, Captain, I…"

I smiled and went to the steering board, "It was an easy mistake to make. The cloud might have confused anyone. I will take over." I was not telling the truth but I did not want to wreck Lars' confidence. I would need to sleep less and to watch more. I moved the board more to larboard. "Trim the sails." Every time we moved the board we had to trim the sails. We needed to make as much progress as we could.

Anders had continued to watch the coast and he said, even before we were on our new course, "Sail to steerboard."

We could not see it but that didn't mean it was not there. Lars was still close to me and his face showed his feelings. "I am sorry."

"It is coming on to night and he may not report seeing us. Let us not worry until we have to." I waved him away, "Go and rest. I have the watch."

Christof said, "I am sorry, Leif, I missed it too."

"None of us are perfect, Christof. Get some rest. Night comes to our aid and in the morning, well, we shall see."

Oddr has seen the discussion and was aware of our change of course. He came over. He was still a little unsteady on his feet. Joseph had said that this was normal with head wounds. "Trouble, Leif?"

I waved for him to sit on the dragon chest, "There might be. We are closer to the land than I would like and we have seen too many sails for my liking. If we saw them then they saw us. The Vasconians will know that there is a drekar in their waters."

"It is coming on to night. There is little chance that we will be seen."

"And if these were not the waters controlled by the Duke of Vasconia then I would not worry. When we have filled our barrels and we can head into the deeper seas then I will have an easier mind. For now I will worry."

"Can I do anything? Stand a watch?"

"You can heal and become Oddr the leader once more. We will need your sword and your bravery before we reach our fjord."

"Aye, you know when the jarl mentioned this idea and coming on the back of Brokkr becoming hersir I thought our luck had changed. I truly believed that a year away, raiding and bringing back silver was good. Now I am not so sure."

Dragon Rock

"One thing about the long watches alone at night is that it helps a man to think and I have been thinking about home. As far as they are concerned, it does not matter if we are away for half a year, a year or as this is now, almost two years. Their lives go on. My father and uncle will still fish. Lars Greybeard will raise sheep. Anya Hróolfrsdotter will make cheese. Falco's father, Galmr, will have made chairs and tables. He might even have decorated the hersir's hall while we have been away. If they knew what happened to us they would be worried but Snorri will be home and the silver we took will make them smile. He will tell them of the success that the Clan of the Otter enjoyed and that we were just going to the Blue Sea and then returning. We are the ones who are in fear of our lives. I take comfort from the knowledge that my mother will not grow a grey hair because of the Arabs or the Vasconians."

"You are right. Let us find water and then fly home as fast as we can." He looked to the west where the sun was setting. "How long do you think to get home?"

I made sure I was holding my Hammer of Thor when I answered, "As you know, Oddr, the winds are normally from the west at this time of year. The journey we take might be longer in terms of the miles we travel but it will be faster than the normal route past Denmark. Once we have the water then twenty days should see us home."

He smiled and looked, not west but northeast. He was seeing his home. He had been visited by death and survived. His return would be all the sweeter for that. "Do you mind if I sit here and watch with you? I will not disturb you."

"Company, even silent company, is always welcome on a night watch."

He did not stay awake for long and when he fell asleep I covered him in my wolf skin. He needed it more than I did.

Chapter 17

I was relieved when dawn brought an empty horizon. I sent Nils to rouse the watch and watched the sun climb higher in the sky. Lars took over at the steering board and his arrival woke Oddr. He stretched. He saw the wolf skin. "I dreamed of wolves. Now I know why. Thank you, Leif Wolf Killer. Joseph is a fine healer but you have skills too. I feel better this morning."

The next two days were hard. It was not the weather, which was as benign as I could ever remember, and it was not our ship, for *'Ægir'* behaved perfectly, it was the long nights I endured at the steerboard. I had just Anders and Benni for company. My ship's boys slept so that they could be alert during the day. It was also the diminishing water in the barrel. I took less than I really needed and I know that Joseph did too. We had to have water for the goat and Maria. We had fish to eat but the threat of no water hung over us. We saw sails. That too caused a problem for it was normally when I slept and I was woken to make a decision. The sails never stayed visible for long but we had to make a course correction each time we saw them. We usually headed out to the west and the wide ocean. We needed to keep our destination as secret as we could. Any ship we saw was more likely to be an enemy rather than a friend. All the changes made the journey longer. These waters might be the most dangerous of all. We had fought and defeated the people and we had sunk their ships. Had we not needed water then we would have kept well out to sea and continued sailing north.

We used the Franks we had rescued this time. It was in their interests to keep us safe. I consulted with them, using Joseph and Christof as the interpreters. I wanted no misunderstandings. One of them, Guiscard, proved to be invaluable. I knew he was using us to help him and the others to get home but it suited us. He said that there was a patch of water, he called it a *petit lac* not far from Nervouster but on the mainland. He confirmed what we already knew, that there were few people on that coast. There was a safe beach, he told us, where we could land and, most importantly, as we had not raided that particular piece of coastline, I did not expect anyone to be looking for us. It meant that the Franks would be able to make their way to their homes which lay further north. He said that the water was just a couple of miles inland.

We lay off the coast until it was night and then slipped in with a reefed sail and under oars. There was no water left whatsoever and a small patch of water was needed to fill the barrels quickly. Even though it was nearer the process would still take some hours. For that reason I insisted that the Franks stay with us and help us. I feared that once they were back on their home soil they might see us not as rescuers but enemies. On the way to the landing we saw no sails. We smelled no woodsmoke. We crept onto the beach warily. While oars kept us in the surf, Dagfinn and Brynjar led eight warriors to scout out the land beyond the dunes and when they returned with the news that there were no people close by, we staked the ship to the beach.

Dagfinn looked happy, "The land is marshy, Leif, and crisscrossed with water courses. It is flat land that lies to the east of us but you can pick your way through them. We saw no hoofprints. If we were desperate we could use water that is there but…"

Oddr had been listening as Dagfinn reported to me. He shook his head, "We do not risk bad water. We have not come this far to die from pestilential water. If you say there are no enemies then we have time to get good water."

Asbjørn selected the men he would lead. Dagfinn and Brynjar went with him and the Franks. They carried the barrels that they would use to store the water. These were the same barrels we had taken in Bordèu. Strange that it was not the silver of Bordèu that might save us but their barrels. The Franks would go with our men and guide them to the water and return with the barrels. After that we would go our separate ways. The Norns had spun and we had spent time with men who, in other circumstances, might have been our enemies. We had survived a common enemy, the pirates of the Blue Sea. I knew that in other times we might have to battle them but for this brief moment in time we had been friends. I had my crew check the ropes and I went ashore to check the hull. I wanted to see if the repair had held. The scars had gone. The sea had scoured them. *'Ægir'* was sound. The ones not fetching water sought shellfish and greens.

Oddr risked a fire. We would be travelling in colder, more inhospitable waters from now on and hot food might make all the difference. The warm sun that had burnished our skin was a long way away.

The men were away for half a day. It was an interminable wait. We were vulnerable on the beach. If an enemy came then we would be taken. Armed sentries watched from the dunes that protected the marshland. The crew continued to collect shellfish while we waited. When the water gatherers returned, men rushed to help them to roll the now filled barrels to the beach to be loaded aboard the ship. Once they reached the dunes it was simple to let them tumble down to the waterline. Hoisting them aboard took time. We had to rig a crane to hoist them back onto the drekar. It was almost dark when it was finished. We might have spent the night ashore but a rising tide decided us. We bade farewell to the Franks. We gave them weapons taken from the guard ship and food. They shared a waterskin but they would not have to go far to find water. They had already disappeared northeast as I had the oars pull us from the shore.

With enough water to see us home I headed due west. The tide helped us but I had the men row until I deemed we were far enough out to sea to be safe. The men rowed for two turns of the glass. Once the oars were stacked I turned the steering board to take us north. When dawn came we would head a little more to the east to take advantage of the winds but, for now, this was a safer part of the ocean. Speed was not as important as secrecy. We had to remain hidden.

I now felt like a creature of the night. I slept during the day, admittedly in small dozes, but I was now attuned to the night. I had grown familiar to its noises and its movement. We never sailed with full sail at night but we had more sail than when Lars had taken a watch. It was a need to get home as quickly as possible that made us do so. The motion in this ocean was more exaggerated than the Blue Sea. Even with the slowest of winds there were still troughs and crests. These were not the mountains of the storm but we still rose and fell.

Nils was also now a better sailor. He shared the watch with me and kept me company. He would walk along the deck filled with sleeping men to the prow. Once there he could clamber

Dragon Rock

along the prow of *'Ægir'* and look ahead. As he came back down he would search the sides for danger. It was not long before he was due to turn the hourglass that he said, with a chuckle, "You know, Captain, I think I must be losing my mind."

"Why is that, Nils?"

"I thought I saw the flash of a sail to the east of us." He shook his head, "It is night time and we are the only ship that is here."

I nodded, "It could be a larger wave. Such rogues can look like a sail. There are few ships that would do as we do and sail with the wind at night. Even we sail with a reefed sail."

He nodded, "I think I am ready to go home, Captain. I think I have begun to grow into the man I will become and I see my future." He turned the glass.

"And what will that future be, Nils?"

"When I go with my father to fish I can help him more. I now know that I was a passenger before. I sat in the boat and let him do the work. I thought I was working but I was not. The work will make me stronger and when I am ashore I will practise with the sword I now have. We will be at home for long enough for me to make a good shield and join the others learning how to make a skjaldborg. I think that all of us will be stronger after this. Fritjof died and his death will not be in vain. I will live as though for him."

I felt the wind shift. It was now coming more from the west. "Good, now fetch me some water." Just then a few drops of rain began to fall. I laughed, "And now that we no longer need it we get rain. Take out my sealskin first." The wind had veered. There was a shower approaching from the ocean and such storms were not brief. The wind was not the wild one which had almost destroyed us close to the straits but it would drive us closer to the land.

Nils had a watch that kept him busy as he collected water and topped up the barrels. He would be soaked by morning for he had no sealskin. As we watched the first light in the east he said, "And I will hunt the seal. I would rather be dry than wet."

I nodded, "Wake Lars and Harland."

I was teaching Lars how to be a better navigator and that meant showing him how to determine the day from the dawn. After Harland had made water and Nils had brought me my water the four of us stood in the rain. "The day will be a wet one and that means the visibility will be poor." I smiled, "What is good about that, Lars, is that we are well out to sea and here there are no rocks." I pointed north and east, "There are islands there but before we reach them we will have turned north and west."

"Why do we not turn sooner, Captain? Snorri said that the rocks at Dumnonia were treacherous. Surely we should get sea room now?"

"The wind and this rain takes us faster than when we turn. We will have to choose our moment to turn carefully. Soon we will encounter the men of Wessex and they hate Norsemen."

Nils asked, "Then is the threat from the Vasconians and the Franks over?"

"Not yet but soon. Now full sail then, Nils, you can enjoy a bed and, Harland, you will have to endure the masthead."

He said, "At least this rain is warm."

"It is. The winds which bring it come from the southern oceans. They can be as warm as the Blue Sea."

When the sail tugged us at a faster pace men woke. The sun now showed a lighter part of the eastern sky but the low clouds to the south had spread to the east. This would be a damp and dismal day. Nils stripped off his wet clothes and rolled naked in the sleeping animal skin that was still warm from Lars' body. As his head disappeared beneath the fur Lars took the wet clothes and laid them in the lee of the gunwale. If the rain ceased we would be able to dry them.

Christof and Oddr came to join me at the steering board. I saw Oddr peer to the east, "We have done with Frankia then?"

"I hope so." I looked north, "I wonder what happened to the jarl."

Oddr nodded, "It has been on my mind too. His second son, if the jarl does not return, is too young to lead the men of the fjord and Lord Arne is dead."

"Has he an elder son?"

Lars said, "He was a ship's boy on *'Byglja'*." I knew then that if the jarl was dead his son would be too. "There might be a younger brother at home, I am not sure."

Oddr looked at me, "Then it looks as though your uncle will be the one to make decisions."

The thought disturbed me. My uncle wanted a quiet life. While he would be happy as headman of Bygstad he would not want to make decisions for others. I prayed that the jarl was alive.

"Sails to the north and east."

Harland's voice was like a knife sliding into my back. Oddr looked at me and clutched his Hammer of Thor. "Can this be Charlemagne's fleet? I thought Snorri said that they guarded the waters between Frankia and the land of the Angles."

Christof said, "Perhaps they are not a threat."

I shook my head, "Christof, one sail would not be a threat. Harland said sails. This is a threat." I knew then that Nils had not been dreaming when he saw a sail. They had been searching for us. If we saw them then they would have seen us. I handed the steering board to Lars. There was enough light for him to steer. I went to the backstay and used it to pull me up to stand on the gunwale. I did not want to climb the mast but I would have a better view of the potential danger from the slightly loftier position. "How many sails?"

There was a pause and Harland called down, "Three and they have changed course and are heading north and west."

The threat was confirmed. I peered east and I saw one sail. It was not a drekar. Over my shoulder I said, "Lars, ease us a little more to larboard."

Oddr shouted, "Awake! There is danger."

The calls and the noise had woken some of the crew but there were always a couple who had to be roused. A naked Nils stood. I heard Lars say, "Take dry clothes from my chest."

As I watched, the single sail became two and then, even as we turned a little to move into safer waters, they became three. That they were warships became clear as the light behind them improved. They were hunting us.

I climbed down. "They are Franks and they are chasing us."

Oddr asked, "Can we outrun them?"

"*'Ægir'* is faster than any Frank afloat but I would not risk the Norns. We will try to stay ahead of them. This will be a long stern chase."

Dragon Rock

I looked up. The rain clouds that were heading east were bringing more rain and keeping us from the course I wanted to take. The advantage we had was that the Franks had the same problem as we did. Eventually, they would tire of the chase and give up. I was surprised that they were so desperate to have their revenge. I would be at the steering board until they did so. Even as I resumed my place at the steering board my mind was busy working out how to outwit the Vasconians. They were not deep-water sailors. They kept to the coast; however, they knew the waters of the coast well. We would need to head further out to sea. I eased the steering board over a little to take us further west. The troughs and crests through which we ploughed made us rise and fall like a man on a wild horse. The crew were all awake now. They would know that soon they might have to row.

Harland's voice came from the masthead, "Captain, I can now see the ships to the east of us. There are four ships. Two large ones and two small vessels."

They outnumbered us but they were to the east of us. Our ship was faster than any vessel we had yet met. With the winds as they were and our positions we would escape. Harland's voice came back just a moment, it seemed, after his first call. The rain was still falling but it was not as heavy. With it came slightly better visibility. Harland was not the boy who had come aboard to learn how to be a sailor. He was seasoned and he had not just looked east. "Three sails to the north, Captain. They are not full sailed and look to be waiting."

They were waiting for us and just holding their position against the wind. Oddr heard the shout and he did as I had done and viewed the danger from the gunwale. Until I was closer to the waiting ships I need do nothing but I had to work out what to do. As soon as we neared the ships we would have to alter course and either go to the east or the west of them. If we went east then we could be caught in their pincers. If we went west then we would have to fight them for they would use the wind once we neared them. We could see them and they would have lookouts watching for us.

Oddr came to me, "Harland is right. They have set a trap and it looks like they have caught us."

Dragon Rock

I had been able to think a little and I said, "No matter which way we sail the ships ahead of us can catch us. At the moment they are into the wind. They can manoeuvre but until we tell them which way we will sail they have to wait." I nodded at the pennant. "The rain is stopping and the wind will change. See the clouds. Now that they are thinning we can see the way they move. It is more to the northeast than the south. I believe that they will change and when they do then we will struggle to evade the trap."

"But you have a plan."

"I do. Have the men eat and then take to the oars. I wish to outrun the ones behind and to the east of us. I want speed. We will try to pass through the blockade of ships for that is what it is. It is like the river once more but now they have only one ship to watch."

"You intend to risk the oars? If they are shattered then…"

"No, Oddr, the oars are to get us close enough for me to see their ships. They have to have a gap between them. I will order the oars in and then men can use their bows. Once we have passed these ships then I will run before the wind."

"You are taking a risk, Leif."

I shook my head, "We are being toyed with and this trap relies on us doing what they predict. There is a net around us and this time they can tighten it whenever they choose. If we do nothing we are caught. If we sail east we are trapped. The only way for us to escape is to use our speed and our oars. Don't forget we have the men we rescued. Haraldr One Eye and the others will row harder than anyone."

"We are in your hands." He smiled, "And I will take an oar. My head does not need to row and my back and arms are still hale." He left to give his orders.

My ship's boys had been at the steering board and listening. I said, without looking at them, "Lars, Nils, go and ensure the sheets and stays are tight. The Saxon, Edgar, can watch from the prow. Then return and prepare for war. I will have my helmet and wolf skin. Strap on my sword."

Lars said, "Your wolf skin, Captain?"

I smiled, "These Franks and Vasconians think we are barbarians. If they see a wolf at the helm then it might make some of them afraid. If nothing else it will draw their attention to me and the crew will be able to send our arrows before they do. We have the wind and they do not."

They nodded and left to do my bidding. It was only a slight advantage but once our men were in range we would be able to send arrows before the enemy could.

Oddr shouted, as my skin was fitted over my helmet and secured around my neck, "Oars ready, Leif Wolf Killer. Let us fly." The men, seeing the wolf skin, cheered. Joseph led Maria to join me. She would shelter in her nest and Joseph would be on hand to minister to any wounds.

I shouted as I stamped, "Row."

I began to mark the beat. As the oars bit I slowly increased the stamping. We began to speed up. Harland was still at the masthead and he shouted, "The ships from the east are closer, Captain."

I shouted, "Watch them and let me know if they change course." This was a planned ambush. One of those sails we had seen before we landed and collected water had to have reported seeing us. The Duke of Vasconia would not know where we landed for water or for food but he would know our route home. The time we had spent ashore had allowed them to get ahead and lay their net.

Joseph said, "One ship against," he peered around to count the sails, "seven. Those are not good odds."

"But these are not wolves, Joseph. Their plan is clever but we will not do what they expect. We are the cunning wolf and we have sharp teeth."

"And a sharp brain too, Leif Wolf Killer."

We were now racing and I knew that the ships to the east would not catch us unless we were stopped by the three ahead of us. I glanced at the pennant. The wind was shifting, albeit slowly. It was now from the south by southwest. I knew that eventually it would become the normal one in these waters and be from the southwest. That would be when we would lose them but only if I could break through their line.

"Lars, go to the prow. I need to know the size of gap. The ship to the east is ship one and the one to the west is ship three."

"Aye, Captain."

Dragon Rock

I could see the ships but not as well as someone at the prow. The mast, the sail and the prow itself all made the estimation of distance, difficult. Lars had good eyes.

When he returned he said, "Between one and two there are two ship's lengths and between two and three slightly less."

His words made my decision for me. I would go between the narrower of the two gaps. They would not expect that. I knew that we could make it and that course would allow us to head north and east once we were through. I could see the strain on the faces of the rowers. They were now at full speed. With the wind on our quarter we were going as fast as I had ever known. I eased the steering board to make it look as though I was heading for the wider gap.

Harland's voice came from above, "The ships ahead are taking the reefs from their sails."

That suited me. They were preparing to close their trap and loose their sails. I asked, "How far away are the three ships?"

"Twenty lengths."

At the speed we were travelling that was close enough. "Oars in."

Oddr's voice boomed, "Take bows and be ready to rain death upon our enemies."

"Joseph, take my shield and cover yourself and Maria."

"What about you?"

"I need to be able to see and the shield might impair me. I am content."

I could now see the enemy sails filling. The shifting wind meant that they would either have to turn into the wind or sail with it. The gap between the first two was closing as they sought to trap me.

"How far, Harland?"

"Ten lengths."

It was time. I said, "Lars, Nils, to the stays. I am going to turn to larboard and head for the gap. I want the sail to be full for the whole manoeuvre."

I waited until I saw them in position, by which time we were a length closer and then I shouted, "Prepare to come about."

As I put the board over I saw the men with bows take a wider stance and each nock an arrow. Oddr would give the order to release the missiles. My task was to thread the needle. Lars and Nils were good at what they did and the sail remained taut through the turn.

"They are turning, Captain!" Harland's voice screamed from above.

As soon as I had made my turn they had been forced to do the same. Had they stayed in their blockaded line they would have made the task harder but the gap became wider.

"Loose!"

I was watching the gap but I heard the arrows as they soared into the air. Each archer would continue to send arrows at the enemy. Not everyone who used a bow had the same skill. Some would fall harmlessly into the water. Some would hit the sails and hull but even one or two could hit someone and that could only help. The turns of the enemy ships were much slower because they were turning into the wind. The ships that were coming from the east would be closing but they could not reach us. All that might stop us would be if I miscalculated and hit one of the ships. This was where our escape from the Blue Sea would come to aid me. I had calculated well once and with that experience I should be able to do so a second time. I saw the bows of one ship just forty paces away. We would be within a length of her. She wallowed like a cow that needed to be milked as she turned for the wind was holding her. They had taken the reefs out too soon. They had a small bow castle and archers were inside. Their arrows began to fall. There were too few to be a shower and our men could avoid them. At the steering board I could not. The arrow which slammed into my shield, held above Joseph and Maria, told me how close I had come to being hit. However, it vindicated my decision for Maria and Joseph were both safe.

I heard a shout from the enemy ship and saw, as she slowly turned, a figure I recognised. It was the Duke of Vasconia. His words were lost as he shouted and waved an impotent sword at me. I knew he would neither understand nor make out clearly my words but I shouted, "We are the Clan of the Otter and you cannot catch *'Ægir'*." Even as I shouted, I glanced up and saw that the wind was now from the south and west. "Prepare to come about." I pushed the steering board over. We had been

Dragon Rock

sailing north and west and now we headed north and east. The wind was pushing us hard and we were soon past the three ships which were still turning. I saw the ones that had been to the east were closer now. We could not stay on this course for long. Charlemagne had ships searching for Danes and Norsemen closer to Frankia and Wessex but I needed to create as big a gap as I could. I wanted the Duke of Vasconia to waste time turning.

"Joseph, the danger from arrows is past."

He stood and plucked the arrow from the shield. He shook his head, "We might have died." He looked at me, "You might have died."

"But I did not. It is time to turn the glass and work out our position."

"Yes, Captain."

Maria emerged and she smiled. Birger had taught her many of our words and she said, "Thank you, Leif. I will bring water."

I smiled back and glanced astern. The enemy ships were still following. "Harland, keep a watch on the enemy. Tell me what they do."

By the time the glass had been turned and I had drunk the water the enemy had recovered from our sudden move. "Captain, they are spreading out into a long line and following us."

The Duke of Vasconia was keen to get us. It struck me that he might think we still had his silver or perhaps he just wanted revenge. Whatever the reason he was dogged. Joseph made his calculations. He pointed a thin finger at the chart. "I think we are here, Captain." I looked and saw that we were heading for the coast of Frankia which jutted out to the north and west. We had avoided it on our journey south for there were more rocks and places to rip out a ship's keel than open water. It was more than half a day away but soon we would need to make our turn. The Duke of Vasconia had to know about Charlemagne's ships. He was driving us to them. I had been at the steering board for too long but I would have to stay there even longer.

"Oddr, at noon I will turn to the north and west. If the enemy closes with us then we will need to take to the oars."

He nodded, "You need to be relieved."

"Once the sails are no longer on the horizon I will let Lars take over."

Dragon Rock

When the hourglass was turned I came about. This would be a test of ships. I trusted *'Ægir'*. Over the next hour Harland's reports were reassuring. The enemy ships were falling further and further behind. The wind was with us and we did not need to take to the oars. Once the horizon was clear and there were no sails, I said, "Christof, Birger, Lars, I will sleep."

The three of them came to the stern. Birger said, "Brother, you look awful. Your face is rimed with salt and your eyes look like hollow caves."

"Thank you, Birger. It is good that you told me for otherwise I might not have noticed. Hold this course. Joseph has the chart and he knows where we are. Wake me an hour before sunset. We have passed the dangers posed by Vasconia but I have never sailed the waters ahead and I know that they are dangerous. We shall have to creep around the coast like a thief in the night."

Before I rolled into my blanket and fur Joseph insisted that I eat and drink. He was like a second mother. I was asleep the moment my head touched the deck. The familiar motion of the drekar rocked me like a baby.

Chapter 18

As dawn broke it was Nils who saw the rocks that lay ahead. We had reefed the sail before dark and with the wind from our larboard quarter we were sedately sailing through these dangerous waters. I eased the board over and had Joseph bring me the chart that Snorri had marked when he had visited this land. The rocks were the beginning of the string of islands called Syllingar. Although they represented danger they were also reassuring for they marked our course for us. Once we were past them we could sail north and west along the coast of Dumnonia. We made the turn and headed more to the north.

When dawn fully broke we saw the coast of the mainland to the northwest of us. I waited until we had clear water ahead and the wind from the south and west before I ate and prepared to retire. Haraldr One Eye came to me with Edgar the Saxon. "Edgar wishes to know when he can be landed."

I looked at the coastline, "Is this his homeland?"

He shook his head, "No Leif, he is from Wessex."

"We cannot land in Wessex."

"He knows that, but to the north of Dumnonia is a more debatable land. It is close to the land of the Wēalas. There are beaches and no rocks. If we put in there for water he would take his chances."

I turned to Christof, "How is the water?"

"We are half full."

I did some calculations. We would not have enough to get home. We would need to land again. It might be dangerous to do so here but the coast of Wēalas was largely rocky and beyond that was the land of the Mercians. I said, "Oddr." He came over, "Edgar wishes to be landed. If we land and fill the water barrels then we need not stop again."

"Your decisions have proved wise. You decide."

The Norns had spun and put Edgar in our care. Once he was ashore then everyone else would be happy to sail home. I did not want the spirits to punish us and so I nodded, "We will land. Christof, I will sleep now as will Lars. Can you steer with Nils and Birger?"

"Aye, but Edgar might prove useful. He is the only one with knowledge of this coast."

I nodded, "Then have him watch with you. If he can add details to the map then so much the better." When the course was set, the sail trimmed and Edgar stood next to Christof, I slept but it was a fitful sleep. I wanted to be home but it seemed I was destined to sail on and on.

When I was roused it was four hours past noon. The coast to steerboard was made of cliffs and rocks. Clearly we could not land. When Lars and I were fed and watered we took over and a relieved Christof and Nils were able to enjoy food and water. Edgar stayed with me. He was eager to be home and desperate to be useful. Joseph had kept the hourglass turned and the map marked. If nothing else we had charts to use around these dangerous coasts.

Christof said, "I stood a watch for four hours and I feel exhausted. You have watched for half a day before now. I do not know how you can do so."

"Because I have to. I did not choose this. Gandalfr made me his heir and then he died. I am not sure that I will ever do this again. For one thing I want to be with my family and for another I think the crew have no further need to go a-Viking. If we reach home and if Snorri was there before us then we have silver enough. The men with families will want to see their families and those without them will want to begin them. The women of Bygstad will be looking for our return and their needs will be as ours are. First, we have to reach our home."

Christof nodded and said, "And is there a place for me, there?"

"You have done wandering?"

"I have spent many hours on watch with your brother, Birger. When Maria came into his life it changed him. I envy him and I would have what he has." I saw that he meant what he said. "And I still owe you a life. From what you told me your uncle has no sons. You might be the hersir one day and you will need hearthweru. I would be your hearthweru."

I laughed, "Even the Norns have not yet spun that web. There is a place for you in Bygstad and I will happily stand in a skjaldborg with you."

"Then I am content."

When the land began to become sandier and less threatening I sought a place to land. I consulted with Edgar. He said he needed a better view and went to stand on the gunwale and hold on to the backstay. It was getting on to dark and would be the perfect time to land our passenger and seek water. I had the men put water from one barrel into another so that we had six empty barrels to take ashore. When Harland spotted the river that spilled out into the sea I decided that this would be a good place to land for there were beaches on both sides. Edgar came back. "Do you recognise this land?"

He shook his head, "No, but when I watched with Christof I saw that we had passed most of Dumnonia. This river marks the start of Wessex. If you land on the north bank," he pointed, "there, I will take my chances."

"Good." Oddr came down and I told him what I intended, "The river looks wide enough for us to sail down. The water here will be too salty. I will sail until the water is drinkable and then land Edgar."

"I will have the men who are going ashore arm themselves. This is not a land to go without weapons."

I stopped where a river joined the one we were on. It flowed from the south and I knew that the water here would be drinkable. It meant we did not need to go ashore. We would not need to land as we could fill the barrels with buckets. Edgar had a waterskin and a sword. We had given him fish we had dried while we sailed. He was happy and I knew that I had not upset the Norns. He clasped arms with the other slaves first and then thanked me. We sculled closer to the beach and Edgar waded ashore. He slipped over the side. When he reached the beach he kissed the ground and then took off like a hare. He disappeared from view within moments.

It took some hours to fill the barrels but we neither saw nor heard anyone. What we did notice was a faint smell of woodsmoke coming from the south. There was a settlement there. We caught freshwater fish while we were anchored and that would enliven our diet. The tide was against us and so I slept for an hour. When it changed I was woken and we rowed back to the sea and then set a course to sail as far from the coast as we could. Once we reached Mann then we would have passed the dangerous waters of Wēalas.

We saw sails, or rather the watchkeepers saw them. Often I was asleep but they woke me when sails were spotted. They were traders and avoided dragon ships. Word might spread along the coast but our speed was such that we would be beyond danger when word reached those who might harm us. When we had passed the sacred island of the people of Wēalas I knew that we were getting close to Mann. There were Vikings on Mann but I did not know if they were friendly or not. I sailed us as close to Mercia as we could. Edgar had told us that northern Mercia had few people living there. They were raided by Norse, Hibernians and even men from Caledonia who came to steal cattle and slaves.

I thought we had passed danger until Nils, who was at the masthead, spotted the sail and, even more alarmingly, the distinctive shape of a drekar. We were in another's waters and we were the stranger. I summoned Oddr, "I think we should row."

He nodded, "We have enjoyed many days of rest. It is better to have a weary back than risk a battle."

We rowed and did so for four hours until the sail disappeared. It was at that moment that the wind which had helped us so far changed direction. We could no longer travel quickly and the men were beyond tired. I tacked and turned as we made our way to the constricted waters between Hibernia and Caledonia.

Once more the Norns spun. I was woken at dusk by Birger and saw, to the east of us, mountains rising high and stretching for some miles. Snorri's map helped us for he had marked the land with the picture of a wolf. It was Úlfarrberg that I could see, Wolf Mountain. Snorri had told me that there were Norsemen living there. From what he told me they valued their isolation and would not trouble us so long as we did not trouble them. I had no intention of landing there and we pushed on. Knowing our location helped me and I had the sail reefed so that we just kept steerage way. I wanted to sail the dangerous passage between Hibernia and Caledonia in daylight. It meant I would have a long shift ahead of me but my body now seemed used to it. As usual Joseph came to show me the chart and to make sure I was fed. He was no longer my slave but the bond between us still remained. I had just Harland with me and he stood at the prow. He would walk down the ship to turn the hourglass. If he was late I called him with a low whistle. In that way we knew the passage of time at night. It was seven hours into darkness and he had just turned the hourglass when we heard the collision. It could not be a rock for Harland would not have left his post or failed to warn me had there been such danger. We heard a scraping along the steerboard side and I glanced over the gunwale. I saw a huge piece of timber. From its shape it was part of a drekar, a keel. Some ship had been destroyed by the sea and the wood had sailed through the treacherous waters until it struck us.

"What do we do, Captain?"

"Until daylight we do nothing. The ship is still afloat but such was the noise that I am sure we suffered some damage."

As if to prove my point Dagfinn came towards us. "I was woken by a noise."

"Ship's wreckage has struck us."

"Are we hurt?"

"I do not know but to be on the safe side I will sail a little closer to the coast."

Harland said, "Snorri warned us, Captain, not to land there."

I said, patiently, "I know but if we are hurt we need to land somewhere. If we can find the river that flows from the northern edge of this land we might be safe. He said their land ended at the mountains." I saw the fear on his face. Snorri's tales had unsettled him. "The Norns have spun, Harland, and we deal with each problem as it comes. Back on watch. There may be more wreckage and I would, if I could, avoid it."

Dagfinn said, "I will watch with you, shield brother."

We watched the land grow closer in silence. It was useful having another pair of eyes. When I saw the land was free from mountains and I saw beaches, I was a little relieved. Even if we were holed we could still beach the ship and save it. I whistled for Harland. When he reached me I said, "I want the barest of sails. I wish to stay as close as I can to this shore. When dawn breaks I hope to see a river and then we can land and see what damage there is." Snorri's map had shown a wide estuary to the north of Úlfarrberg.

When the sail was reefed Harland went back to the prow and Dagfinn sat on Gandalfr's dragon chest, "I will be glad to get home, Leif. When Mikkel left us I thought he was a fool. Now I am not sure. You have a wife and so does Mikkel. I have yet to father a son. We have come close to death too many times on this voyage. A man needs to leave his mark behind."

"You want a tale to be told of your deeds?"

He laughed, "No, but we buried men and they have left nothing. We will talk about Fritjof for a while and he will be mourned when we reach Bygstad but soon that memory will fade. Birger's song will be sung but it will not bring back Fritjof. Even Gandalfr left nothing save this chest."

"But I will not forget him. Even if I never leave the fjord again each time I am afloat I will think of him." I tapped my head, "He is in here."

"You will be remembered. It is not just that you are Wolf Killer. You are chosen. The finding of the dragon rock was magical."

"And that was Gandalfr."

"It is the stuff of legends and men do not choose those paths. They are chosen for them. When Oddr returns and speaks to his children it will be about the flight from the wild men of the Blue Sea and how you found a passage over rocks."

"And you want to be remembered like that?"

He shook his head, "I just want Dagfinn to be spoken of when I am no longer here. It may be that the Sisters choose an adventure for me but I will no longer seek one. What I learned on this voyage was that people fight for their own lands. The men of Frankia and Vasconia fought for their land as did the wild men of the Blue Sea. I would fight for my home and the family I have yet to father."

"I will speak of you, when you are no longer here, as will Brynjar and Mikkel."

"That is a comfort," He sighed, "but when we reach Bygstad then Freya and your son will give you a fine welcome. I want that for me."

"Then let us see if I can get us home as soon as we can. But for this accident we would have been back in home waters in ten nights." He nodded, "Wake Oddr. I need to tell him what has happened."

Oddr and Christof joined me at the stern and I told them my plan. "We will keep close to the coast and land somewhere quiet. I think we have been damaged for the drekar feels more sluggish."

Oddr shrugged, "*Wyrd*."

When dawn broke I could see the river. It had a wide estuary. I also saw the signs of men. There was a stone building on the southern shore, it looked like one built by the Romans and there were men upon its walls. These were the Norsemen who protected their privacy and that alone made my mind up. I waved Oddr over, "Let us take to the oars and row to the northern bank. I can see no people there and there are trees."

Even with men pulling hard on the oars we did not slide through the water. For one thing we were damaged but we also had something of a tidal race that we had to fight. Eventually, we made the northern bank and the ship's boys leapt ashore to secure us to the trees that were at the edge of the beach. The ropes we had taken at Bordèu were still proving useful. Asbjørn led half of the men inland to ensure we were safe while the rest hauled on ropes to pull us higher up the beach.

I clambered down and saw that we were holed. It was not a large hole but the wreckage we had struck had done its best to sink us. Luckily we still had pine tar and we had the wood we had hewn in the Blue Sea. I had men lift the deck and begin to empty the water we had taken onboard. Joseph lit a fire for we would need to heat the tar and Falco and I began to shape the wood we would use to repair the ship. Gandalfr was still helping us. He had directed us, along with Verðandi to the cove close to dragon rock where we had been able to find wood. We still had that timber. We could save the ship.

Asbjørn came back and reported no sign of any enemies. Oddr said, "We will keep a good watch ashore. How long will you need, Leif?"

"The rest of the day. With luck we can try to sail on the evening tide."

"Do you need help?"

"No, Falco and I can manage but if you could hunt a squirrel its tail would be useful."

"Good, then when the boat is dried we will forage for food and water and," he added, "enemies."

It was left to Maria and Joseph to use the fire to cook food. We never missed an opportunity to have hot food even though it would alert those who lived close by that there were strangers in their land. The rest of the crew were also working. Falco and I were repairing the ship while the ship's boys were lifting the deck to empty the water we had shipped. I put the pine tar on the fire to melt and then we took the tools we would need to repair the ship.

When we examined the hull it was clear to me what had happened. The piece of ship's wreckage must have had a large nail protruding and the timber had driven into our bow. The distinctive marks left by the nail told their own story. The strake had been ripped and a hole made. While I used a small axe to cut away the damaged strake, Falco used the shaping tools to make a replacement. It was a short piece of wood that was needed. We both knew that the longer we stayed on this hostile shore the more danger we could expect. This would not need to be a polished repair. It had to be a makeshift one.

"Captain, the tar is melted."

Joseph was telling me so that he could use the fire for the food. I nodded and took a cloth to lift the pot to the side. We did not want it too hot and the side of the fire would keep it fluid. By noon the food was ready and our men had made their way back. Falco had finished the wood but we both knew that it would be a fiddly job to make a snug fit. It did not have to be a pretty repair but it had to be a watertight one. Anders threw the red squirrel tail to me. I nodded my thanks and while Falco trimmed a little more from the strake I tied the tail to a small branch I hacked from the nearest tree.

"It is ready, Leif." I handed him four nails and he banged them in. He held his hand out and I gave him two more.

I said, "Take some moss from the trees and pack it between the strakes. It will help to seal them."

Falco's father was a fine carver and aesthetics were important to him. His son had learned to appreciate a neat job. "It will be ugly."

"We have to sail as soon as we can, Falco, we cannot guarantee that the tar will be fully dry."

He nodded and did as I said. His father's training took over when he used sand to smooth the edges and make it a little neater. We used the last of our precious pine tar to coat the damage. We kept painting it until all the tar was gone.

Oddr came over. He had returned some time earlier but had not disturbed us. "When can we sail?"

"That depends upon the tide. It is now low tide and we need the sea to return to float us. The time will not be wasted for the tar will continue to dry."

"But there may be enemies. We saw no people but there are hunters' trails that come to this beach. The fire and the smoke are both necessary but they act as a beacon to any who live close by."

"You are right. I will fetch my weapons and check that the hold is dry."

I climbed aboard and saw a half-naked Lars and Nils replacing the deck. "It is dry now, Captain, and little was spoiled. The spars and yard we cut are soaked and will need to be dried before they can be used and the ropes that were there are also sodden." I opened my mouth to ask something and he smiled. "We brought them on deck to dry out."

"Good, you are becoming a navigator. Now dress and arm yourselves. Harland, take to the masthead and watch for danger."

I had been hot while I had worked but now I knew that I was in northern waters. I felt chilly. I donned my top and then fastened my wolf skin around my neck. I felt warmer straight away. I fastened my sword belt around my waist and donned my sealskin boots. I slipped a seax into my belt and a dagger into my boot.

"Food, Captain." Joseph's voice drifted up to me.

I clambered down and dropped to the sand. As I did I looked at the forest that stretched away to the north. This was not thinly forested like the cove. The trees were thick here and fought for light. As I wandered to the fire I reflected that it told me the people were not seafarers. The trees were straight with thick trunks. Such trees would have been valued by men such as we and used to make good ships. Before I had gone a-Viking I had not thought of such things but now I understood the value of good timber. The rest of the men were eating.

I kept glancing towards the trees and, smiling, Dagfinn said, "We have men on watch, Leif."

"Good."

I took the bowl of food from Joseph. I saw that he had put some of the squirrel meat in my bowl. As I ate I turned to look at the river. The tide was on the way in but it would be at least an hour before we could float the ship. In an ideal world we would have waited for at least three hours until the tar had dried a little more. I handed my bowl to Joseph and went to touch the repair. Not only was the tar not dry, but it was also still warm to the touch. We would need more than an hour.

I saw that the food had been eaten. "Joseph, take Maria and the cooking pots aboard."

Birger said, "Maria needs to make water."

"Then do so. This is not a safe place to be."

Oddr said, "We will put the shields back on the ship."

It was a good idea. Half the men did so and then relieved the watchers so that they could make water and replace their shields. Maria and Birger were away some time. When they returned I asked, "Is there a problem?"

Birger smiled, "No, Brother, but it is good to have privacy. We went into the forest. All is well."

Maria smiled at me, "Thank you, Leif."

I did not know what she was thanking me for but I smiled.

When the shields were all aboard the men returned to the beach. Dagfinn and Brynjar stood with me. "How long before we can sail?"

"Perhaps an hour, maybe less, Brynjar."

He nodded, "Like Dagfinn I am anxious to get home."

"We all are."

"Men are coming!"

The shout came not from the forest but the masthead. Harland was a good lookout.

"Arm yourselves." I drew my sword and seax. Oddr shook his head, "You are the captain. You should be aboard."

"We cannot sail yet. The tide is not right. You might need every warrior."

Birger returned. He had his spear with him. He said, "Harland saw movement in the distance. The trees were moving."

Oddr called, "Bygstad, back to the drekar." He then turned and said, "Two lines. We have no shields but we have spears. Leif, you will be next to me and when I order you to return to the ship then do so." I nodded and he said, "Where is your helmet?" Like the rest of the crew he had his helmet on his head.

"On the ship." I slipped the wolf's head over my skull, "This will have to do."

I shouted, "Lars, you and the boys use bows. Do not wait for a command. Kill whoever comes down the path."

Asbjørn stood on his other side and Christof placed himself between me and Dagfinn. I saw the angry look from Dagfinn. He and Brynjar were my shield brothers, I said, "This is good, Dagfinn. The centre of our line has strong warriors and we guard *'Ægir'*." The prow was just above our heads. The carved figure would also terrify whoever came.

Bjarni and Haraldr One Eye led the men who had been on watch. He shouted, as he led them to the second rank, "There are more than fifty wild men running through the forest."

Oddr said, "Any mail?"

"Two or three helmets that is all."

We could hear them now as they approached. They were screaming and shouting. Men who were trying to bolster their courage did that. We waited in silence. Even without shields we were confident in our skills and our togetherness. Whilst we had no shields before us many of us had two weapons. My seax was like a short sword and could be used like a shield. The warriors burst from the trees. Each had chosen their own path and they came at us not in a mass but piecemeal. Three arrows flew from the ship's boys and all found flesh. They might not have been mortal wounds but they would thin the enemy numbers. It was Oddr who drew first blood. He deflected the fire hardened spear that came at him with contemptuous ease and slashed the man across the middle. Spears darted out and as ours were tipped with iron they made terrible wounds. Ten or so of their warriors fell before a warrior with a helmet and a good sword shouted out an order. I did not understand a word he said. They formed a line and advanced. There were, perhaps, ten shields amongst them. Most of the men had either spears or long daggers. This would be a test of skill for we were outnumbered.

The chief did not go for Oddr. Instead he spied me and advanced towards me. He had a small round shield that was much smaller than ours. I think he thought a warrior with a wolf skin was a leader. I had drawn him to me by donning the skin. *Wyrd*. I had learned to fight my own battle. The men who looked at how others fought usually died. I would not underestimate this warrior who was as big as Lord Lupus. The difference was that this man wore no mail. He would be a brutal fighter who would fight until he could no longer raise his sword. He was fighting for his home and his family. He saw us as a threat and sought to remove us. I had to kill him and do so quickly.

His sword was longer than mine and he brought it down to strike at my unprotected head. I blocked the blow with my sword. He was strong and my sword came down towards me. I held him with my blade and he tried to punch me in the face with his small shield. I saw it coming and moved my head to the side. The shield caught my right shoulder. I slashed blindly at his side with my seax and when his mouth opened in a feral scream I knew that I had drawn first blood. As I expected the wound made him angry and he roared and tried to move closer to me. Birger's spear came over my shoulder and drove into his cheek, ripping a savage looking hole. The blow drew his eye behind me and it allowed me to strike with my own sword. I hit his helmet and dented it. He reeled a little and Birger's spear darted at his shield. He was forced back a little. He was wounded but the blood seemed to give him strength and he struck at my head again. This time I was ready and when his sword struck mine, his weapon bent. It was not as well made as mine. I had the advantage for his sword would now be unbalanced. I saw anger in his eyes. Blood was pouring down his face and I knew that my blade had hurt his side. I was aware that we were winning but so long as their leader lived then they would fight on. I used trickery. As I raised my sword I hooked my right leg around his and I pushed at him.

When he tried to step back he tumbled to the ground. This was no time to show mercy. I slashed my sword across his neck as he lay prostrate on the ground. Christof took his sword and completely severed the head. He held the severed skull in the air and then threw it towards the warriors. It broke their spirit and they ran.

Oddr shouted, "Kill their wounded and take our own wounded and dead aboard." He turned to me, "And you, Leif Wolf Killer, need to be aboard the ship." He nodded towards the river, "The tide has come to our aid."

I nodded and sheathed my sword, "Thank you, Birger. The chief's sword is yours. It is a poor one but Alfr can melt it down and recast it for you."

"Thank you, Brother."

I climbed aboard and put my sword and skin in the chest. "Lars, Nils, Harland, be ready to cast us loose when I give the command."

As the men came aboard so Maria and Joseph went to tend to their hurts. I also saw three bodies carried aboard. We had lost men. The last man to climb aboard was Oddr. I shouted, "Take to the oars."

As the crew did as I bid I glanced at the pennant. The wind came from the southwest. Once we cleared the estuary we would be able to use it but until then weary men would have to row.

"Cast off."

Lars and the boys untied the ropes and then pushed the prow of the drekar. The tide was rising and the ship was anxious to leave. The three would climb up the ropes. "Back water." The oars helped to pull us into the estuary, "Steerboard row. Larboard back water." By the time Lars and the other two were aboard, bedraggled and wet, we had turned. I began to stamp my foot as I shouted, "Row."

The oars were just single manned but all we needed was steerage. The river and the tide were doing the hard work and taking us to the sea. The sea led to our home and with water barrels that were full we could reach the fjord. Unless we had another disaster then I had no intention of landing again. We would sail home. Once we cleared the mouth of the river I had the oars stacked and the sail loosed. It was a good wind and soon we were in the open water between Hibernia and the islands that lay off the coast. It was there we buried Leif the Silent, Dargh and Frode. We had lost three men and added to Fritjof it was a heavy price we had paid. Dargh had survived the sinking of the *'Nidhogg'* and the galley but the Norns had spun and cut his thread.

The journey was not over and the Norns had not yet done with us. We had a hard voyage around the islands that guarded the coast of Caledonia. The repair that Falco and I had made was truly tested in the squally, stormy weather as we turned east to head through icy waters to our home. Here the seas broke over the prow and showered us all with bone chilling, wintery water. I stood longer watches than I ought to have done but each time we marked our position on the chart I was reassured for it marked a steady progress home. The weather was unpleasant but the winds were taking us home and each day saw us closer to familiar waters.

When we saw the coast that rose from the sea with sharp cliffs and few beaches I summoned Haraldr One Eye to the stern. "I know that you, Erik, Hrolfr and Sven wish to return home but I have a duty to this crew to take them to Bygstad."

"I understand, Leif Wolf Killer, and if we have to spend a month in your village while we wait for a passage then it will be no hardship. We have learned that this crew is a good one."

Something in his voice made me ask, "You did not think so before?"

He looked at the deck and shook his head, "Lord Arne said that you were an untried crew and as you did not even have a hersir to lead you then you were fodder for the Franks."

Suddenly many of the things that had happened to us made sense. When we had fled Bordèu it was we who had led to risk the wrath and traps of the Vasconians. Lord Arne had also used us to lead the way to the Blue Sea. He had paid the price for his arrogance.

"I am sure that Snorri will take you home."

Oddr had joined us and listened to the last part of the conversation. He said, ominously, "The way the Norns have been spinning, Leif, we cannot count on that. I hope that the three ships all made it home but if not then we have done all this for nothing. All the silver was sent ahead."

He was right and as I turned to head for the mouth of the fjord, I wondered if we would have to leave again to raid. How long would I have at home with my family?

Epilogue

When we spied **'Byglja'** anchored in Askvoll I was pleased. It meant that the jarl had survived. It was three hours past noon when we neared the quay at the jarl's home. Our ship had been seen and people flooded down to greet us. I headed for the empty berth. That disappointed me. We had sent three traders home and yet none of them were at Askvoll.

The jarl came towards us with Haldir at his side. I saw that the jarl had his arm in a sling. His son had also survived and was at his side. That was good. I saw some of the warriors who had sailed with the jarl as they came from their homes to meet us. I recognised Halfdan. He had been the helmsman who had saved the drekar in the fight with the Arabs. We put the gangplank down and Oddr led the crew from the ship. It had been twelve days since we had fought the wild men north of Úlfarrberg.

The jarl put his good arm around Oddr and hugged him, "We thought you were dead."

Oddr said, "We thought the same of you. Thanks to Leif Wolf Killer we survived. You know that Lord Arne and his crew perished?"

He shook his head and his hand went to his Hammer of Thor, "We guessed but we did not know."

Oddr pointed behind him, "Haraldr One Eye survived and he can tell you the tale. We will leave for home."

The jarl shook his head, "No, we would hear your tale. Surely you can give us this one night?"

Oddr sighed, "Jarl, we have been away longer than any others from this fjord."

Haldir nodded and said, "That is true but your ship has returned and," he nodded towards Joseph, "your healer can examine the jarl's arm. Our volvas have done their best but your slave…"

I said, "Joseph is a freed man. He is paid as one of the crew."

The jarl smiled, "Then I will pay. One night, Oddr, that is all we ask."

Oddr turned to me and I nodded, one night would be acceptable. It meant we could arrive home not long after dawn.

Dragon Rock

With the ship tied up and the goat tethered by the grass we entered the magnificently carved longhouse. We would sleep beneath a roof. It seemed like a lifetime since we had last done so. I did not count the houses in Bordèu; the house had not been a longhouse. The heat from the hall seemed, to me, to be as hot as the deck of the drekar when we had been in Africa. Joseph joined us at the table with the jarl. He had examined the broken arm while the food was being prepared and pronounced that, after he had applied his salve, it would heal. The jarl slipped him some silver. It was his first payment and I saw the smile on his face. As keen as we were to return home, the freshly brewed ale and mead were a joy. When we had eaten the jarl asked for the tale. All eyes looked at me. I was reluctant to be the centre of attention and it was my little brother who came to my rescue. Since he had sung the saga of Fritjof the crew had often asked him to sing. He had more confidence and he stood and told the tale for me.

He gave a half bow towards me and smiled, "I had the least to do in this adventure but I have spent the time since we left Bygstad watching my brother. I think that I have the tale and the words to speak it." I began to realise that Birger had all the skills to be a good skald. He chose words that were perfect and his voice carried the listeners with him. I had lived the tale but listening to Birger's words was like hearing the story of a hero from the past. He made me sound more heroic than I was and I found myself squirming under the smiling nods from, not only the jarl's crew but also ours. When he had finished everyone banged the table and there were such cheers and shouts that my head hurt.

The jarl stood, "Our tale will seem as nothing compared to the saga of Leif Wolf Killer and his dragon rock but I will do my best." He smiled at Birger, "Perhaps this young skald can turn our humble story into a story that will amuse." Birger nodded his head. His face was still flushed and excited from the applause. "When the storm struck, your two ships disappeared. We all thought that you were dead. We lost our sail and had to take to the oars to maintain our position. Thanks to Halfdan we stayed afloat and we let the wind take us south. We found calmer waters and a beach on an island. We repaired our sail and took on water.

Dragon Rock

We decided that the Sisters had spun and that our voyage was done. We headed home. It was not until we spied Úlfarrberg that we found danger. A drekar came from Mann to challenge us and we fought. Odin favoured us and when Beorn Bear Teeth hurled the anchor into their ship they took on water and sank. It cost us eight men but we survived. We reached our home and found Snorri here. That is our tale. It pales next to yours, Birger the Skald, but we were just happy to be home."

I said, "Jarl, the ship you sank tried to sink us. It was the reason we had to land in the land of the wild men."

Men clutched their hammers and silence fell on the hall. This was truly *wyrd*. The web that had been spun had many strands.

The silence lasted a little longer and then conversation began as men asked about those who had not returned and sought details missing in the telling. I was close to the jarl and Haldir as well as Oddr. We spoke.

"Snorri is well?"

"Yes, Leif. He brought the three ships home. He seems to prefer Bygstad to Askvoll and his ships are moored there."

Haldir said, "Jarl, remember that he arrived back more quickly than we did and he lived there for a month before we returned."

The jarl looked at us, "Haldir, you are a loyal hearthweru but we all know that Lord Arne used all of us for his own ends and he has paid the price. Snorri lives where he feels happiest and that is good. He will winter there and when he sails will return to the place he calls home. I am content for I am paid a tenth of his profits for doing nothing."

I said, "And *'Ægir'*, Jarl, when do you need her returned to Askvoll?"

He laughed, "She is not my ship. She never was. Gandalfr built her and his blood was in her keel. He is gone but the tale told me that she has chosen you, Leif Wolf Killer, as her captain. She belongs to Bygstad. Lord Arne thought little of you but he was wrong."

"And if we choose not to sail again?"

The jarl looked at us and Oddr, said, "When we were lost in the Blue Sea all we could think of was home. At the moment men do not wish to raid again."

Dragon Rock

The jarl nodded, "And that I can understand but, when the spring returns we have another voyage to make." We all looked at him and I was aware that silence had descended again as men listened to this conversation. "We have vengeance to visit on Erland Brynjarsson. We lost men thanks to his treachery. He has profited since he abandoned and betrayed us. The men of Askvoll would end his life and that of his son."

It was my shield brother, Brynjar, who answered for us. He stood, "And the men of Bygstad will sail our drekar and join you. I swore a blood oath and even if I have to go alone I shall. The Clan of the Otter will have revenge!"

Everyone banged on the table, me included. I might have the winter at home but once spring came I would sail away from the family I had yet to see and I would be the navigator for one more voyage. The Norns were spinning still.

The End

Glossary

Allionis - Châtelaillon
Bóndi - Freemen who were allowed to use weapons
Bordèu - Bordeaux
Blót - a Norse sacrifice
Bjórr - Beaver
Dumnonia or Curnow - Cornwall
Frilla - a concubine
Guedel - Belle Île
Hnefatafl - Viking board games. Skáktafl is chess
Herkumbl - a piece of metal fixed to a helmet to identify the allegiance of the warrior
Hlad - a ribbon or headband of leather tied around the hair
Leude - lord (*pl.* 'leudes')
Liger - River Loire
Nervouster - Île de Noirmoutier,
Østersjøen - The Baltic Sea
Sanctus Nazarius de Sinuario - St Nazaire
Sea fret - fog over the sea
Sequana - River Seine
Sild - Norse for herring
Skjaldborg - Shield wall
Skrei - Norwegian cod
Úlfarrberg - Helvellyn
Volva - a Norse witch, a spinner of spells (quite literally- they would use a hand spinner)
Wēalas - Wales/The Welsh. Saxon for foreigner

Norse Calendar

Gormánuður - October 14th – November 13th
Ýlir - November 14th – December 13th
Mörsugur - December 14th – January 12th
Þorri - January 13th – February 11th
Gói - February 12th – March 13th
Einmánuður - March 14th – April 13th
Harpa - April 14th – May 13th
Skerpla - May 14th – June 12th
Sólmánuður - June 13th – July 12th
Heyannir - July 13th – August 14th
Tvímánuður - August 15th – September 14th
Haustmánuður - September 15th - October 13th

Dragon Rock

Days of the week

Sunnudagr - Sunday
Mánadagr - Monday
Tysdagr - Tuesday
Óðinsdagr - Wednesday
Þórsdagr - Thursday
Frjádagr - Friday
Laugardagr - Saturday
Canonical Hours
Matins (nighttime)
Lauds (early morning)
Prime (first hour of daylight)
Terce (third hour)
Sext (noon)
Nones (ninth hour)
Vespers (sunset evening)
Compline (end of the day)

Historical Background

There is a school of thought that argues the attack on Lindisfarne and the other religious houses was not just prompted by the love of silver and gold but as retribution for Charlemagne destroying the pagan holy places in Pomerania, Saxony and Denmark. It makes sense for how would the Norsemen who raided Lindisfarne know how rich they were? It could have been that the land in Norway and Sweden did not support the number of people who wished to live there. Whatever the reason the fact remains that in the late eighth and early ninth century seafarers from Norway, Sweden, Denmark and Frisia began to raid the east coast of England. They took religious artefacts, gold and silver as well as slaves. Apart from the odd Romano-Saxon shore fort, there was nothing to stop them. Din Guardi or Bebbanburgh and then Bamburgh as it came to be known was just a rocky outcrop with a wooden wall, mead hall and harbour. It was not a castle with a rapid response force of horsemen to deter the raiders. The result was that the people we now refer to as Vikings had no reason to stop their plundering. It was highly profitable, and the greatest danger came not from the Saxons and their warriors but from the sea. For the Norsemen, it was a mighty undertaking.

The word *wyrd*, from which we get the English word weird, means, in the context of my Norse books, Fate. It translates as *'nothing that can be done'*, *'inevitable so don't fight it.'* Nidhogg (roughly translated to The Corpse Gnawer or Corpse Sucker) is the dragon said to live under the great tree, Yggdrasill. This tree nourishes all life in the Norse world, and the dark dragon, Nidhogg, munches on its roots in the meantime, feeding from both the tree and the corpses that make their way down there.

'Ægir' is the Norse name for sea and is also the name of a jötunn who is married to Rán. Although he is male all ships are normally called she.

Noirmoutier was the location of an early Viking raid when raiders attacked the monastery of Saint Philibert of Jumièges that same year. Noirmoutier was an island at this time. Nowadays a road connects it to the land and the island is bigger now than it once was. The Vikings established a permanent base on the island around 824, from which they could control southeast Brittany by the 840s. The island where they repair the drekar is Burhou north of Alderney. It was, from ancient times, a place of refuge for fishermen and somewhere they could hunt rabbits. The monasteries at this time were largely built of wood. The stone ones that remain to this day were begun after the time of the Normans and when the Franks became the French. The coastline of Gascony, Anjou and Aquitaine was not as populated then as now. The towers that I mention are still visible in Italy and Southern France but there were slave traders who attacked little isolated villages. Eventually they would be repopulated, but this was a dark time for any who lived close to a coast or a river. The Vikings were not the only ones who raided.

Vasconia was, at this time, an independent Duchy. Some of the names of their dukes were: Felix, Lupus, Odo the Great, Hunald and Waifer. They paid homage to Charlemagne and eventually would be subsumed into what became Aquitaine.

In the Völuspá, the three primary Norns Urðr (Wyrd), Verðandi, and Skuld draw water from Urðarbrunnr to nourish Yggdrasill, the tree at the centre of the cosmos, and prevent it from rot. They are said to be deities who can predict and shape future events. Some say that they are derived from the Parcae (Roman Fates) however as the Norse famously wrote little down and I doubt that they would have studied Latin texts, my view is that the belief in these deities gave the Norse a viable explanation of strange events. They gave structure to a world which might appear chaotic.

The rocks I describe lie to the southwest of the Balearic island of Mallorca. Few people lived on the island at the time. It has pine trees and the area where I have the Norsemen land is riven with gullies and water courses. I discovered, first the cove and then the rocks on a research trip to Mallorca. The cove is a few miles from Peguera, now a resort, but in the times of the Vikings was largely uninhabited. The rock is called Crocodile Rock. As soon as I saw it I thought of the Vikings and the idea of this story began to ferment. The three rocks looked, to me, like the Norns. When I returned to England I discovered that the Vikings raided the whole island in 840. The island and its major

Dragon Rock

city, Palma, was between Byzantine and Arab rule. My story takes place thirty years earlier. The pine forest there would be perfect for a Norseman repairing his ship. When they returned to Norway I daresay they would have described the island and that may have prompted the major raid by many ships. I have included the photographs I took. You have to imagine the island without buildings and more trees. The cove is forty yards wide and one hundred yards long. A drekar would easily fit there and be hidden by the use of camouflage.

Figure 1 Dragon Rock

Figure 2 The cove

Figure 3 The cove through the eye

Figure 2 The Three Sisters

Dragon Rock

The river where they land Edgar is the River Yeo in Devon. Barnstaple was not yet a town and the only settlements close to it were Appledore on the Torridge and Pilton on the Yeo.

For those who like a perfectly rounded story, the homecoming will be the prologue of my next book. It just seemed right to me when I finished this book. As with all my books I start the writing but then the characters and my dreams shape them…

Griff Hosker
February 2025

Books used
Charlemagne – Roger Collins
The Age of Charlemagne – Nicolle and McBride
Norse Myths and Legends – Schorn
Vikings Life and Legend – British Museum
Saxon, Viking and Norman – Wise and Embleton
The Vikings – Heath and McBride
Viking Hersir – Harrison and Embleton

Dragon Rock

Other books by Griff Hosker

If you enjoyed reading this book, then why not read another one by the author?

Ancient History

Roman Rebellion
(The Roman Republic 100 BC-60 BC)
Legionary

The Sword of Cartimandua Series
(Germania and Britannia 50 A.D. – 128 A.D.)
Ulpius Felix- Roman Warrior (prequel)
The Sword of Cartimandua
The Horse Warriors
Invasion Caledonia
Roman Retreat
Revolt of the Red Witch
Druid's Gold
Trajan's Hunters
The Last Frontier
Hero of Rome
Roman Hawk
Roman Treachery
Roman Wall
Roman Courage

The Wolf Brethren series
(Britain in the late 6th Century)
Saxon Dawn
Saxon Revenge
Saxon England
Saxon Blood

Dragon Rock

Saxon Slayer
Saxon Slaughter
Saxon Bane
Saxon Fall: Rise of the Warlord
Saxon Throne
Saxon Sword

Medieval History

The Dragon Heart Series
Viking Slave *
Viking Warrior *
Viking Jarl *
Viking Kingdom *
Viking Wolf *
Viking War*
Viking Sword
Viking Wrath
Viking Raid
Viking Legend
Viking Vengeance
Viking Dragon
Viking Treasure
Viking Enemy
Viking Witch
Viking Blood
Viking Weregeld
Viking Storm
Viking Warband
Viking Shadow
Viking Legacy
Viking Clan
Viking Bravery

Dragon Rock

Norseman
Norse Warrior*
Dragon Rock

The Norman Genesis Series
Hrolf the Viking *
Horseman *
The Battle for a Home *
Revenge of the Franks *
The Land of the Northmen
Ragnvald Hrolfsson
Brothers in Blood
Lord of Rouen
Drekar in the Seine
Duke of Normandy
The Duke and the King

New World Series
Blood on the Blade *
Across the Seas *
The Savage Wilderness *
The Bear and the Wolf *
Erik The Navigator *
Erik's Clan *
The Last Viking*

The Vengeance Trail *

Danelaw
(England and Denmark in the 11th Century)
Dragon Sword *
Oathsword *
Bloodsword *
Danish Sword*
The Sword of Cnut*

Dragon Rock

The Aelfraed Series
(Britain and Byzantium 1050 A.D. - 1085 A.D.)
Housecarl *
Outlaw *
Varangian *

The Conquest Series
(Normandy and England 1050-1100)
Hastings*
Conquest*
Rebellion

The Reconquista Chronicles
Castilian Knight *
El Campeador *
The Lord of Valencia *

The Anarchy Series England
1120-1180
English Knight *
Knight of the Empress *
Northern Knight *
Baron of the North *
Earl *
King Henry's Champion *
The King is Dead *
Warlord of the North*
Enemy at the Gate*
The Fallen Crown*
Warlord's War*
Kingmaker*
Henry II
Crusader
The Welsh Marches
Irish War
Poisonous Plots

Dragon Rock

The Princes' Revolt
Earl Marshal
The Perfect Knight

Border Knight
1182-1300
Sword for Hire *
Return of the Knight *
Baron's War *
Magna Carta *
Welsh Wars *
Henry III *
The Bloody Border *
Baron's Crusade*
Sentinel of the North*
War in the West*
Debt of Honour*
The Blood of the Warlord
The Fettered King
de Montfort's Crown
Ripples of Rebellion

Sir John Hawkwood Series
France and Italy 1339- 1394
Crécy: The Age of the Archer *
Man At Arms *
The White Company *
Leader of Men *
Tuscan Warlord *
Condottiere*
Legacy*

Lord Edward's Archer
Lord Edward's Archer *
King in Waiting *
An Archer's Crusade *

Dragon Rock

Targets of Treachery *
The Great Cause *
Wallace's War *
The Hunt*
The Prince and the Archer*
Warbow

Struggle for a Crown
1360- 1485
Blood on the Crown *
To Murder a King *
The Throne *
King Henry IV *
The Road to Agincourt *
St Crispin's Day *
The Battle for France *
The Last Knight *
Queen's Knight *
The Knight's Tale*

Tales from the Sword I
(Short stories from the Medieval period)

Tudor Warrior series
England and Scotland in the late 15th and early 16th century
Tudor Warrior *
Tudor Spy *
Flodden*

Conquistador
England and America in the 16th Century
Conquistador *
The English Adventurer *

English Mercenary
(The 30 Years War and the English Civil War)

Dragon Rock

Horse and Pistol*
Captain of Horse
Lion of the North

Modern History
East Indiaman Saga
(East India Company 1790-1856)
East Indiaman*
The Tiger and the Thief

The Napoleonic Horseman Series
(Europe 1790-1815)
Chasseur à Cheval
Napoleon's Guard
British Light Dragoon
Soldier Spy
1808: The Road to Coruña
Talavera
The Lines of Torres Vedras
Bloody Badajoz
The Road to France
Waterloo

The Lucky Jack American Civil War series
(Ireland and the USA 1850-1863)
Rebel Raiders
Confederate Rangers
The Road to Gettysburg

Soldier of the Queen series
(Africa 1870-1928)
Soldier of the Queen*
Redcoat's Rifle*
Omdurman*
Desert War*
An Officer and a Gentleman

The British Ace Series
(Britain, Europe and Persia 1914-1926)
1914
1915 Fokker Scourge
1916 Angels over the Somme
1917 Eagles Fall
1918 We will remember them
From Arctic Snow to Desert Sand
Wings over Persia

Combined Operations series
(1940-1951)
Commando *
Raider *
Behind Enemy Lines*
Dieppe
Toehold in Europe
Sword Beach
Breakout
The Battle for Antwerp
King Tiger
Beyond the Rhine
Korea
Korean Winter

Rifleman Series
(WW2 1940-45)
Conscript's Call*

Tales from the Sword II
(Short stories from the Modern period)

Books marked thus *, are also available in the audio format.

Dragon Rock

For more information on all of the books then please visit the author's website at www.griffhosker.com where there is a link to contact him or visit his Facebook page: GriffHosker at Sword Books or follow him on Twitter: @HoskerGriff or Sword (@swordbooksltd)
If you wish to be on the mailing list then contact the author through his website.

Made in United States
Orlando, FL
09 July 2025